Praise for *Red Sky Mourning*

"The modern-day Vince Flynn or Tom Clancy. . . . Sometimes, Carr doesn't just evoke the latest headlines. He's ahead of the curve. . . . His stories drip with precise geopolitical nuggets along with fastidious details tied to the tools of war."

—The Blaze

"A masterpiece of absolute mayhem."

—The Real Book Spy

"*RED SKY MOURNING* spills blood as easily as ink, but with an elegance of purpose."

—Townhall.com

"The most painful interrogation scene I've ever read."

—Hugh Hewitt

"Students of history, current evets, and pop culture will all find *RED SKY MOURNING* to be a dangerously captivating, blood-soaked love letter to everything they hold dear."

—Caleb Daniels

"I can't remember the last time I read a doomsday thriller this searching or scintillating."

—Booktrib

"You'll be falling out of your chair at every turn."

—*Barnes and Noble blog*

"*RED SKY MOURNING* is giving [*THE TERMINAL LIST*] a run for its money. This is one of my very, very favorites."

—Ross Kaminsky, Koa Radio

Praise for *In the Blood*

"Gripping . . . fast-paced . . . fans will get their money's worth."

—*Publishers Weekly*

"Quality plot, well-developed characters, and not too over-the-top. Add James Reece to your list that includes Harvath (Brad Thor), Reacher (Lee Child), Bob Lee Swagger (Stephen Hunter), et al."

—Men Reading Books

"Hands down, *IN THE BLOOD* is the best book I've read this year. I've said from the beginning that covering Carr is what I'd imagine it would have been like to discover Vince Flynn at the beginning of his career. . . . Carr deserves to be mentioned alongside all-time greats like Flynn, Thor, Clancy, and Silva."

—The Real Book Spy

"*IN THE BLOOD* is Carr's best book to date and demonstrates a mastery of the genre—it rightly belongs in the constellation of Clancy, Thor, Morrell, and Flynn."

—Townhall.com

Praise for *The Devil's Hand*

"Take my word for it, James Reece is one rowdy motherf***er. Get ready!"

—Chris Pratt, all-around great guy and star of *THE TERMINAL LIST* on Amazon Prime

"Carr delivers engrossing back story, incorporates current events seamlessly, and never flinches from breathless depictions of violence."

—*Publishers Weekly*

"Carr continues to draw on his own experiences as a SEAL to give the story a level of realism that writers who've not actually served sometimes have a hard time achieving."

—*Booklist*

"*THE TERMINAL LIST* is widely regarded as one of the best debut thrillers of all time, and rightfully so, but *THE DEVIL'S HAND* is even better, and should go down as one of the best books in the genre, period."

—The Real Book Spy

"An action thriller extraordinaire that is not to be missed."

—*Providence Journal*

Praise for *Savage Son*

"A great book . . . its f*cking riveting!"

—Joe Rogan

"A rare gut-punch writer, full of grit and insight, who we will be happily reading for years to come."

—Gregg Hurwitz, *New York Times* bestselling author of the Orphan X series

"Absolutely fantastic! *SAVAGE SON* is savagely good, and puts Jack Carr at the very top of the thriller genre."

—Marc Cameron, *New York Times* bestselling author

"A badass, high-velocity round of reading! The three parts of this masterfully crafted experience says it all—*THE TRAP, THE STALK, THE KILL.*"

—Clint Emerson, former Navy SEAL and *New York Times* bestselling author of *100 DEADLY SKILLS* and *THE RIGHT KIND OF CRAZY*

"Carr writes both from the gut and a seemingly infinite reservoir of knowledge in the methods of human combat. Loved it!"

—Chris Hauty, *LA Times* bestselling author of *New York Times* Editors' Choice *DEEP STATE*

"Jack Carr triples down with *SAVAGE SON.* From the book's gut-wrenching opening to its sleep-stealing conclusion, Jack's homage to *THE MOST DANGEROUS GAME* delivers the goods and then some."

—Don Bentley, author of *WITHOUT SANCTION*

"A masterfully told, heart-thumping tale of modern conflict."

—LtCol Oliver North, USMC (Ret.), *New York Times* bestselling author of *THE RIFLEMAN* and *UNDER FIRE*

"*SAVAGE SON* is amazing! This is the kind of book every author wished he could write . . . mind-blowingly good!"

—Simon Gervais, former RCMP counterterrorism officer and bestselling author of *HUNT THEM DOWN*

"Accurate, intense, and raw, *SAVAGE SON* taps into our most primal of instincts. Jack Carr draws you into this predatory pursuit like no other because he's lived it!"

—John Barklow, Hunter, Navy Diver, Special Operations Cold Weather Survival Instructor, and Sitka Gear Big Game Product Manager

"If you like a fresh approach to action with authentic details and a believable main character, these books are for you. I'm a fan."

—David Morrell, *New York Times* bestselling author of *FIRST BLOOD*, *THE BROTHERHOOD OF THE ROSE*, and *MURDER AS A FINE ART*

"Jack Carr is back and at the top of his game in *SAVAGE SON*, a heart-pounding, sleep-robbing, edge-of-your-seat thriller."

—Joshua Hood, 82nd Airborne veteran and author of Robert Ludlum's *THE TREADSTONE RESURRECTION*

"Whether you are a hunter of four-legged game or of man, *SAVAGE SON* will stoke the inner fire of your soul. Jack Carr's attention to detail and experience from the battlefield to the backcountry draw the reader into the field to experience the art of war through the eyes of a man who has lived it."

—Cole Kramer, Kodiak Island Brown Bear Guide and Outfitter

Praise for *True Believer*

"This is seriously good. I mean, seriously."

—Lee Child, #1 *New York Times* bestselling author of *PAST TENSE*

"A powerful, thoughtful, realistic, at times terrifying thriller that I could not put down. A terrific addition to the genre, Jack Carr and his alter-ego protagonist, James Reece, continue to blow me away."

—Mark Greaney, #1 *New York Times* bestselling author of *MISSION CRITICAL*

"Jack Carr creates an incredibly vivid, emotional, action-packed tapestry of carnage and death."

—Justen Charters, Black Rifle Coffee Company, *Coffee or Die Magazine*

"Packs a punch. Carr's second effort is a well-crafted thriller with timely reflections on the increasingly complicated world of international terrorism."

—*Kirkus Reviews*

Praise for *The Terminal List*

"Double the trouble, twice the action, and quadruple the enjoyment. Careful while reading this one, it could leave a mark."

—Steve Berry, #1 *New York Times* bestselling author of *THE LOST ORDER*

"Absolutely awesome! So powerful, so pulse-pounding, so well-written—rarely do you read a debut novel this damn good."

—Brad Thor, #1 *New York Times* bestselling author of *SHADOW OF DOUBT*

"Told with a deft hand and a keen eye for detail, *THE TERMINAL LIST* . . . is explosive and riveting."

—Kevin Maurer, coauthor of the #1 Bestselling *NO EASY DAY* and *AMERICAN RADICAL*

"Like a bullet from Jack Carr's custom-built sniper rifle, the story arrives on target with devastating impact. Trust me, you won't be able to put this one down!"

—Mark Owen, *New York Times* bestselling author of *NO EASY DAY* and *NO HERO*

"Crackerjack plotting, vivid characters both in and out of uniform, and a relentless pace to a worthy finish. It's a great start!"

—Stephen Hunter, #1 *New York Times* bestselling author of *G-MAN*

"An extremely unique thriller! Absolutely intense!"

—Chuck Norris

"Bravo! Jack Carr is the real deal!"

—Sean Parnell, *New York Times* bestselling author of *OUTLAW PLATOON*

"Not since Stephen Hunter have we seen an author who so accurately captures the essence of the gun—Jack Carr is a shooter."

—Clint Smith, Founder of Thunder Ranch Shooting School

"Jack Carr's *THE TERMINAL LIST* is a page-turning thriller you won't be able to put down. The detail-focused writing, personal characters, and heart-pounding plot line will keep you coming back for more. An absolute must-read!"

—Katie Pavlich, *New York Times* bestselling author, Fox News Contributor

"Any fan of the novels by Brad Thor and the late Vince Flynn will realize that Jack Carr will soon be joining their ranks."

—*The Washington Times*

RED SKY MOURNING

ALSO BY JACK CARR

FICTION

Only the Dead

In the Blood

The Devil's Hand

Savage Son

True Believer

The Terminal List

NON-FICTION

Targeted: Beirut

RED SKY MOURNING

JACK CARR

EMILY BESTLER BOOKS

ATRIA

NEW YORK AMSTERDAM/ANTWERP LONDON
TORONTO SYDNEY/MELBOURNE NEW DELHI

EMILY BESTLER BOOKS

ATRIA

An Imprint of Simon & Schuster, LLC
1230 Avenue of the Americas
New York, NY 10020

First Emily Bestler Books/Atria Paperback edition September 2025

EMILY BESTLER BOOKS/ATRIA PAPERBACK and colophon are trademark of Simon & Schuster, LLC

Interior design by Dana Sloan

Manufactured in the United States of America

3 5 7 9 10 8 6 4

Library of Congress Cataloging-in-Publication Data is available.

ISBN 978-1-6680-4707-1
ISBN 978-1-6680-4708-8 (pbk)
ISBN 978-1-6680-4709-5 (ebook)

To Larry Ellison for showing all of us what is possible,
and
to the men and women of the CIA's Special Activities Center
for all you do in a world of secrets.

Red sky at night, sailors' delight. Red sky at morning, sailors take warning.

—MARINERS' PROVERB

Like a red morn that ever yet betokened, Wreck to the seaman, tempest to the field, Sorrow to the shepherds, woe unto the birds, Gusts and foul flaws to herdmen and to herds.

—WILLIAM SHAKESPEARE, *VENUS AND ADONIS*

When in evening, ye say, it will be fair weather:
For the sky is red. And in the morning, it will be foul weather today;
for the sky is red and lowering.

—HOLY BIBLE, MATTHEW 16:2–3

PROLOGUE

Chang Zheng

Jin-Class Type 094 Submarine

38° 48' 95" N, 174° 48' 32" W

Pacific Ocean

1,767 Nautical Miles Northwest of Hawaii

COMMANDER LIU ZHEN OF the People's Liberation Navy had given his crew the order to change course four days earlier. The Chinese *Jin*-class submarine had last surfaced north of Japan in the Sea of Okhotsk and received an encrypted high-priority message from the commander of the North Sea Fleet. The message had been routed from the chairman of the Central Military Commission through the PLA Joint Staff Department. In all his years at sea he had never read a message that originated at the level of chairman. That meant it came directly from the president.

The message simply ordered Commander Zhen to open a safe, one that could be opened only with the concurrence of and physical keys from his executive and political officers.

Even before they read the order, Zhen knew what it was going to say.

They had been ordered to start a war.

Zhen slowly inhaled the soothing warmth of his Chunghwa cigarette in violation of his own orders regarding smoking while underway.

He closed his eyes, savoring the slight taste of plum in a cigarette that was rumored to have been a favorite of Chairman Mao, though Zhen wondered if that was nothing more than a clever marketing campaign. The red carton emblazoned with the Tiananmen Gate was a traditional gift given to him by Admiral Jun, who had seen them off from the North Sea Fleet's Xiaopingdao Naval Base in the Yellow Sea. Zhen much preferred to sail from the caves at Laoshan Submarine Base in the Shandong province or Yulin Naval Base on Hainan Island southwest of Macau in the South China Sea. Natural caverns had been excavated on the resort island to create tunnels for an underground naval base in an effort to counter U.S. spy satellites constantly collecting over the Middle Kingdom. It was there that the next generation of Chinese submarine, the Type 096, would enter service. Zhen hoped he would live to see it.

Had the admiral known what lay ahead? He obviously knew what was in the safe, but did he know the execution of those orders—for a mission that would change the course of world history—would come on this particular voyage? Zhen suspected he had.

The *Chang Zheng* had been at sea for close to two months. One of six operational Chinese *Jin*-class Type 094 ballistic missile submarines, she was armed with twelve new JL-3 SLBMs—intercontinental-range, submarine-launched ballistic missiles. Zhen's boat had been retrofitted prior to sailing, her twelve JL-2s replaced with the longer-range JL-3s, giving her the ability to hit targets at a range of 10,000 kilometers. Six of the JL-3s were equipped with MIRVs—multiple independently targetable reentry vehicles—with varying nuclear yields. Curiously, on this deployment Commander Zhen's remaining six JL-3s were equipped with conventional, nonnuclear payloads. They were participating in a training exercise when the new orders had come in.

One more cigarette? He would soon be needed on the bridge, where he would address the crew. He would let them know that the *Chang Zheng* would fire the first shots in a campaign that would allow China to annex Taiwan. Would the Party leadership go further? Would they push the Americans from the South China Sea and fight to extend Chinese territory all the way to Australia? That would give China control of trade routes and access to the oil and natural gas the country desperately needed to fuel its economy. When combined with their reserves, controlling that territory would also allow them to dominate the world energy market. Zhen and the *Chang Zheng* would be ready.

China was feeling the pressure. The new trilateral AUKUS—Australia, United Kingdom, United States—defense partnership was "defensive" in name only. It was a direct threat to Chinese autonomy. The agreement was cloaked in phrases crafted around "deterring Chinese aggression" that were endlessly repeated in the Western media. In reality, the pact extended U.S. subsurface capabilities up to China's doorstep. Australia would acquire three, possibly five, *Virginia*-class submarines in the coming years followed by a new AUKUS-class submarine codeveloped by Australia and the United Kingdom. U.S. submarines would also begin to make regular deployments to naval bases in Western Australia as part of the new force posture. The enemy was massing its forces and would soon be able to park an undersea flotilla off the coast, threatening China's fleet, command and control, and industrial base.

Zhen also knew his country had to take Taiwan before the Americans deployed their new Block V *Virginia*-class submarines, scheduled to hit the water in less than a year and certainly before the *Columbia*-class submarines came online. Intelligence analysts projected that the entire surface fleet would be connected to an artificially intelligent quantum computer that would counter China's current superiority in hypersonic missiles and passive targeting capabilities. If the U.S. fleet were to be synchronized with next-generation AI technology, China's options for expansion would be severely limited. At least the *Columbia*-class sub was years away from sea trials. Once they were in the water, *Jin*-class subs like Zhen's would become obsolete.

Zhen had been serving in the People's Liberation Navy since his time in the Dalian Naval Academy. He had studied his American adversary since he was seventeen. With the Americans divided at home and their leaders sending untold billions to Ukraine and Israel, he understood why his president and National Security Commission had decided that this was the time to strike.

He had participated in enough war games and classified briefings over the years to know that his submarine's actions would be coordinated with other subsurface platforms tasked with launching missiles at Alaska, California, Washington State, and Guam. He suspected that the Chinese intelligence services had leveraged their contacts in Iran to distract the Americans with terrorist attacks across their nation in population centers like Los Angeles and New York City through their Hezbollah and Islamic Jihad proxy forces. Chinese hackers would concurrently wreak havoc on critical U.S. domestic infrastructure, disrupting the electrical grid, internet, cell towers, air traffic control, water treatment plants, and oil and natural gas pipelines, as well as erasing credit cards, bank accounts, and driver's licenses. He also knew that a cyberattack would simultaneously target Guam, as had been tested so successfully in 2020 during the COVID pandemic.

COVID. That had been a turning point. Zhen had lost his parents early. His wife's parents had succumbed to the illness a few months later while sequestered in their apartment. They had died without being able to hold their daughter's hand or look into her eyes one last time. The state had seen to that. His wife would take her own life a year into the lockdowns. Neighbors in their government-subsidized housing complex had found her hanging from the exposed pipe that ran the length of their ceiling. Through his contacts in the regime, he had discovered that she had first taken rat poison.

In these later years, he now regretted the abortion he had convinced his wife to have when they found out she was pregnant with a girl. China's one-child policy, a policy that ironically had forced them into their current position, was responsible for the gutting of Chinese society. The policy that had so devastated the nation had also shattered Zhen's life. Men in China wanted sons. Sons who could carry on the family name. The result of the one-child policy, other than the inevitable demise of Chinese civilization due to declining birth rates, was the aborting of millions of female babies. By the time the government realized the folly of its policy and lifted the mandate in 2016, it was too late. Too late for China and too late for Zhen and his wife; both in their fifties, their time for children had passed.

But Zhen's family name would now live on; Commander Liu Zhen of the People's Navy would launch one of the first volleys of the war. His targets were military and data centers in the Hawaiian Islands. Of his six nonnuclear missiles, three would target the United States Pacific Fleet Headquarters on Oahu at Makalapa Pearl Harbor; one would target the National Security Agency and Central Security Service's Hawaii Cryptologic Center near Wahiawa in central Oahu; one would target the Aloha NAP data center in Kapolei; and the final missile would target the Endeavor Honolulu data center. Decommissioning the Aegis Ballistic Missile Defense System at Barking Sands had been a mistake. That facility would have knocked at least one of his missiles out of the sky.

Other submarines would target the U.S. Pacific Fleet in Guam and Pearl Harbor, though he had no confirmation of their locations or intentions; that was the way when one fought from beneath the waves. Submarines operating at these depths were cut off from outside communications. Zhen could ascend and raise an antenna or float an antenna buoy, but that increased the possibility of detection. His orders had been explicit. There were to be no further communications.

He knew that the United States had two carrier battle groups in the Mediterranean and one in the Persian Gulf to deter Iran from opening a second front in Israel's war with Hamas. Other American naval assets were patrolling the Red Sea and Gulf of Aden to counter Iranian-backed

Houthis in Yemen. Zhen wondered if Iran's use of proxy forces to attack Israel and then using the Houthis to attack U.S. naval ships and commercial vessels off the coast of Yemen, while ordering militia groups to hit U.S. troops in Iraq, Syria, and Jordan, had been orchestrated as part of the current campaign. Was it done to draw the U.S. fleet into the Middle East so that China could annex Taiwan? How much had Russia, China, and Iran collaborated on plans that put him and his crew on the front lines of what was about to be the defining conflict of the twenty-first century?

A knock on his stateroom door intruded on his thoughts.

"Enter."

"It's time, Captain," said his executive officer. "The men await your orders."

Zhen looked at his cigarette and at the red carton on the table before him.

He then leaned forward and extinguished it in an ashtray.

"Very well."

The captain stood and straightened his dress uniform. His hand confirmed that the Norinco QSZ-92-5.8 pistol was on his hip.

It was time to go to war.

• • •

McLean, Virginia

Retired General Marcus Howe was awakened just past 2 a.m. eastern standard time. More than thirty years in the United States Army had confirmed that a call at that hour was never good news. In this case it meant that he was urgently needed as director of the Central Intelligence Agency.

Rising from the U.S. Military Academy at West Point through the ranks to lead the Joint Special Operations Command and eventually

CENTCOM, he had been "retired" shortly after issuing an honest assessment to Congress on U.S. policies in Iraq and Afghanistan. There was no place in senior U.S. military circles for generals who bucked the system. That "system" had been in place since President Harry Truman signed the National Security Act of 1947, which had largely resulted in the disappearance of accountability from the armed forces. Howe had lived within that system his entire career, believing he could change it from the inside. The disastrous withdrawal from Afghanistan had proven him wrong.

President Gale Olsen had personally flown to Ohio, where Howe was teaching high school history, to convince him, and more importantly his wife, that the country needed him in the wake of President Christensen's assassination. In the end, his wife gave her support and once again moved with the retired general back to the Beltway, where he was confirmed unanimously by the Senate as director of central intelligence. That he had not accepted financially lucrative board positions, written his memoirs, run for Congress, or hit the public speaking circuit spoke volumes to the new president. She was not about to preside over a sham investigation into President Christensen's death, one akin to the Warren Commission and its investigation into the assassination of President Kennedy. That commission should have been called the "Dulles Commission," after former CIA director Allen Dulles, who in actuality led the investigation, an investigation that still divided the nation sixty years later.

Howe had been careful not to wake his wife as he made his way to his study to take the call from Langley.

"A car is on the way, sir. You are needed in the SCIF."

Howe knew not to ask further questions.

He splashed water on his face from a half bath to help wake him up and changed into a suit he kept on a hanger in a closet just off his study. This type of summons meant that he might not be sleeping for a while.

Two black Suburbans were pulling into his circular drive by the time he reached his front door. He paused and looked back up the stairwell. He then turned and exited his home, locking the door behind him and wondering if the world would be a different place by the time he returned.

• • •

Chang Zheng

Jin-Class Type 094 Submarine

38° 48' 95" N, 174° 48' 32" W

Pacific Ocean

1,767 Nautical Miles Northwest of Hawaii

Captain Zhen made his way to his submarine's control room.

The solid-fueled JL-3 missiles with hyperkinetic projectiles would leave their vertical launch tubes at a depth of 50 meters. After engine ignition they would accelerate into the atmosphere at Mach 10 and would cover the distance to their targets in just under twenty minutes.

He found it curious that the order was only to launch nonnuclear missiles. In the war games he had participated in over his long career he had experience with both options. He had read numerous American papers, some classified and others not, on the use of submarine-launched nonnuclear ballistic missiles. The United States military called it "Prompt Global Strike," and it would cause the maximum amount of damage possible without crossing what the American Navy's reports had called the "nuclear Pandora's box." Even so, Zhen always thought that when the day finally came, it would be a nuclear confrontation. Could a war between China and the United States remain a conventional nonnuclear conflict? Zhen didn't think so, but that was not his decision to make.

Following the launch, he would reposition and prepare to fire his six nuclear JL-3s should the U.S. retaliate with nuclear weapons.

After the *Chang Zheng* broke from the fleet in the Sea of Okhotsk, Zhen had taken her deep. He changed course on a track that would take them 3,500 nautical miles at an average speed of 18 knots to their launch point 650 nautical miles northwest of the Hawaiian Islands.

His route had taken him north of the underwater sonar detection range, a system of fixed-bottom fiber-optic-cable arrays set up by the United States during the Cold War to track Soviet submarines. The Ministry of State Security, China's intelligence service, kept all Chinese naval officers up to date on the current status of the American Integrated Undersea Surveillance System, the IUSS. According to their most recent intelligence estimates, the IUSS was undergoing a long-overdue retrofit and upgrade with miniaturized sensors, hydrophones, autonomous undersea drones, and what Zhen understood to be an underwater satellite called a Transformational Reliable Acoustic Path System, specifically developed to detect submarines. The upgrade also included a fleet of uncrewed solar-powered surface vessels with acoustic sensors in their keels from the San Francisco–based company Saildrone and General Atomics MQ-9B SeaGuardians, remotely piloted aircraft systems outfitted with MAD-XR—Magnetic Anomaly Detection-Extended Role—passive sensors that cannot be jammed and are designed to detect changes in the earth's magnetic field from metallic objects for anti-submarine warfare. These entities were all linked through a quantum computer system that analyzed real-time open-source and classified encrypted networks to identify and pinpoint the locations of surface and subsurface platforms and algorithmically project their courses, destinations, and even their intent.

The United States had publicly acknowledged the existence of the IUSS in 1991. They should have kept it classified. At the height of the Cold War, Zhen's enemy manned thirty-one IUSS data tracking and processing facilities. Today the only two still operational were located in Virginia Beach, Virginia, at Naval Air Station Oceana Dam Neck Annex and in Washington State at Naval Air Station Whidbey Island.

Zhen thought those modernization initiatives must have factored into China's decision to preemptively attack. The upgrades would make covert subsurface transit extremely difficult. The IUSS retrofit was focused on enhancing surveillance capabilities to deter a war over Taiwan. Approaching Hawaii from north of Japan would allow Zhen to launch without prior detection.

Unknown to most of the world, China had been steadily constructing its own subsurface maritime surveillance system, appropriately code-named the Great Underwater Wall, complete with undersea unmanned drones. Built predominantly in the South China Sea, it extended to a lesser degree as far into the Pacific as Guam. Its capabilities would shock the Western powers.

Had the United States invested more in undersea surveillance, and been less influenced by lobbyists vying for larger legacy programs with more financially lucrative contracts for defense corporations, Zhen's submarine might already have been detected and blown from the water.

As much as he tried, he would never fully understand the Americans.

All talking ceased when Zhen stepped into the control room. Just like on an American or British submarine, the crew members manning their stations did not jump to attention. Due to the cramped compartments on a submersible, even one as big as the *Chang Zheng*, and equipment that required constant monitoring, rapt attention was mandatory. The officer of the deck turned to his skipper while the faces of the helm, outboard watchstander, diving officer, chief of the watch, and submariners at the combat control consoles remained glued to their stations.

Zhen scanned the control room, proud to be in command of his country's most advanced undersea vessel and knowing that the speech he was about to give would propel them into legend. He stepped forward and accepted the outstretched intercom from his executive officer to address the crew.

• • •

CIA Headquarters
Langley, Virginia

Director Howe was at CIA headquarters twenty minutes after the alarm had roused him from his slumber. Five minutes later, he was in the SCIF, where he prepared to take a call from Chen Yun, his counterpart in the Chinese Ministry of State Security. They had met eight months earlier when Howe had accompanied President Olsen to the G20 Summit in India. It was their first and only in-person meeting. It had been a cold one.

Howe could be diplomatic to a point. It was a skill required if one was to rise above the rank of major in the armed forces. However, he was unable to fully mask his disdain of the Chinese spymaster—COVID origins; fentanyl precursor drugs being shipped from China to Mexico and the resulting "accidental overdoses" he knew were more appropriately termed "intentional poisonings"; the manipulation of America's youth through TikTok, an application that also gave the Chinese military and intelligence services unfettered access to all the data coming from phones attached to plans paid for by parents in politics, intelligence, tech, and defense; Chinese "donations" and business dealings with America's political elite in what amounted to legal bribery; spies in all sectors of American industry; and the purchasing of farmland near U.S. military installations—all these thoughts were on Director Howe's mind as he took the early morning call.

He also remembered the motto of the Chinese spy service: "Serve the people firmly and purely, reassure the Party, be willing to contribute, be able to fight hard and win."

And win.

Not today. Not any day.

Howe nodded at his deputy director, Elliot Byrne, who sat across from him and hit the speaker function on the phone.

Byrne was a lawyer by way of Yale first and then Harvard. He had spent time in private practice focusing on white-collar criminal defense and sanctions compliance before entering government service following the attacks of September 11, 2001. He worked as an aide to the general counsel at the Treasury Department, eventually serving as undersecretary of the Treasury for terrorism and financial intelligence before his appointment to the CIA by the previous administration. Though his position was usually filled by a long-serving CIA official or former military officer, with Howe's resume they were an effective team.

"Minister, this is Director Howe."

"Director, thank you for taking my call," the Chinese minister of state security said in lightly accented English. "I hope I did not wake you."

Chen Yun's background was a mystery even to the CIA.

"To what do I owe the pleasure?" Howe asked, intentionally refraining from answering the minister's question.

"We have an issue, a time-sensitive issue, I'm afraid."

"Oh?"

"I come to you 'hat in hand,' I believe is your expression. Your cooperation would be appreciated, and I believe necessary."

"Please continue," Howe said.

"One of our submarines is missing."

"Missing?"

"No, excuse me, not missing. We know where she is, but we do not have the means to stop her."

"Stop her?"

"From launching nuclear missiles at the United States."

Howe and Byrne both shared a look and leaned forward in their chairs.

"Minister, keep talking and leave nothing out."

"Four days ago, one of our *Jin*-class submarines, the *Chang Zheng*, deviated from a training exercise just north of Japan. At first we believed there had been an accident and began searching for her as part of rescue and recovery operations."

The minister cleared his throat.

"We searched for a distress pinger and used side-scan and synthetic-aperture sonar but found nothing. As part of the investigation, we searched the homes of the senior ranking officers, including the commanding officer, Commander Liu Zhen."

He paused.

"And?" Howe prodded.

"And we found a note in Commander Zhen's computer."

"A note?"

"Yes. A letter, actually."

"I don't understand."

"It was an email that used a timer function. He had it set to send to Admiral Li Jun, commander of the North Sea Fleet, two days from now to ensure there would not be time to stop him."

"What did it say?"

"Commander Zhen's parents did not survive the worldwide pandemic and his wife of thirty years took her own life two years ago. Regrettably, he blames his country and has taken drastic action to punish us all."

"What is he doing?"

"He is moving into position and preparing to launch MIRV-equipped JL-3 missiles at Hawaii in the hopes of drawing the United States and China into a nuclear confrontation. His personal mission is to ensure that Beijing, and those he blames for his parents' and wife's deaths, will be eradicated by a nuclear response from the United States."

"*Jesus Christ*," Byrne said under his breath.

Director Howe could feel the perspiration beginning to soak through his dress shirt.

Is this a ploy?

A stall tactic?

Is China making a nuclear move against the United States, this rogue submarine just a diversion?

"Our analysts have estimated that his most likely location for launch is in the vicinity of 21 degrees, zero minutes, zero seconds north, 169 degrees, zero minutes, zero seconds east. We understand that leaves a lot of open water. That also gives us just over two days to find him and destroy him. We do not have the naval assets in place to avert this catastrophe. Please know that I called you at my soonest opportunity after confirming Commander Zhen's email and receiving the best estimation of his submarine's position."

Director Howe took a deep breath to steady his nerves.

"Minister, send us that email, Commander Zhen's service record, your investigation findings to date, and the intelligence estimate you have on his location. Also, know that if he does launch a nuclear attack on the United States, this call and that email will not be enough to keep my country from retaliating using all means at our disposal."

"I have already made that clear to my president."

"Keep this line of communication open, Minister, and pray we find him."

"My sincere apologies for this development, Director. My nation will be ready to support the United States and bring this unfortunate event to a successful, and peaceful, conclusion."

"Thank you. I know there is no need to stress that this action brings us to the brink of war. Your cooperation will be essential if we are to prevent it."

Director Howe pressed a button disconnecting the call and immediately pressed another one connecting him to the White House.

"Wake up the president."

• • •

Ministry of State Security
Haidian District
Beijing, China

Minister Yun ensured the call was disconnected and turned his swivel chair to face his fellow countryman to his left.

"Did they buy it?" Ba Jin asked.

"I don't know," the minister said. "I believe so. The email will help, as will the fact that Commander Zhen is not exactly where we said he would be but close enough for the Americans to find him and sink him."

"And that he is the only Chinese submarine they will find currently outside Chinese territorial waters should be enough to sell the story," the other man said.

"There are no other Chinese assets postured to strike the United States or its allies," the minister confirmed. "And if this goes nuclear, we will find out very quickly if the bunkers beneath this building work as intended."

Ba Jin made even the minister of state security nervous. He was officially a strategic advisor. Unofficially, he was the president's eyes and ears at the highest echelons of the Chinese intelligence apparatus. The president trusted no one and therefore had what amounted to a private security force with "strategic advisors" positioned at the top of every government agency. The minister was under no illusions; if Ba Jin sensed disloyalty, it would be reported to the president, and the minister would disappear soon thereafter, most likely at the hands of the man seated across from him. Though they had scarcely been apart over the past two years, Minister Yun realized he knew next to nothing about Ba Jin. Was he in his forties? Fifties? He was certainly in shape. Was he married? Did he have children? Was he prior military? How was he so well-versed in geopolitics? Why was he so calm? Even as the head of the Chinese intelligence service, Minister Yun had refrained from researching the man the president had entrusted as his direct conduit. To Yun, Ba Jin needed to be respected as the president's emissary, even if in reality he was nothing more than an assassin.

"The president is in Russia," Minister Yun continued, "and senior political, military, and intelligence officials, to include the premier, congress chairman, conference chairman, supervisory director, chief justice, procurator, and vice president, are in the Underground City as part of what they believe is an exercise."

The Underground City is a subterranean network of bunkers and tunnels built to protect not just the Chinese government, but most of the people of Beijing, at a time when war with the Soviet Union seemed imminent. Construction was ordered by Mao Zedong in 1969. The 85-square-kilometer fortress is a city beneath a city. It had fallen into disrepair at the end of the Cold War, with large numbers of low-income workers and homeless moving underground. Called "Rat People," they existed out of sight and out of mind. As tensions escalated between China and the United States in recent years, the tunnel complexes had been renovated, their residents forcibly removed at the working end of Norinco QBZ-95 bullpup rifles of the People's Liberation Army.

"Ah yes, the Underground City," Ba Jin said. "If the United States launches, at least we will know if Mao's tunnel system works or not. But they won't launch."

"How can you be sure?" Minister Yun asked.

"Because I know the Americans. They dropped two atomic bombs on our neighbors in 1945, and thank heavens they did. But they won't do it again—not with the email, our warning, and our defenses down; and they won't have to. Commander Zhen was ordered to fire conventional nonnuclear JL-3s; a nuclear retaliation for the actions of a rogue submarine commander would not be a proportionate response in accordance with international law. They have been pressuring Israel for a ceasefire with Hamas, and everyone from the United Nations to the UK to members of America's own Congress have been lecturing Israel on a proportional response to the murders and rapes of October seventh. A nuclear exchange is not on the table. But more importantly, they will find and sink the *Chang Zheng*. War will come, but it will come on a date and time of our choosing."

"But will they transfer the data?" the minister asked, well aware that if this plan failed there would be dire consequences for him personally. He would be the scapegoat.

"The data." Ba Jin looked up at the ceiling of the minister's office. "That is the real question, isn't it. If they don't, then we are in the same position we were. And if they do, then we will have what we need to push them from the South Sea. Taiwan is already ours, success in our upcoming offensive will just make it official. The data is what we need. We will know shortly. In the meantime, play your part and stay by the phone."

• • •

CIA Headquarters
Langley, Virginia

Deputy Director Byrne pushed back his swivel chair, a chair that was much more expensive and comfortable than the ones at Treasury. He leaned forward, putting his elbows on his knees. He had opted for slacks and a blue button-down at this hour of the morning.

"Fucking cocksuckers!"

Byrne may have been educated at the country's most elite universities, but his mouth never failed to betray his working-class South Boston upbringing.

"President Olsen will be on in a few minutes," Howe said.

"Sir, these motherfuckers got us with COVID, they are screwing us with fentanyl, and now they have the audacity to tell us one of their subs is positioning to launch a nuke at Hawaii?"

Howe looked down at the Timex Ironman watch that had graced his wrist for most of his time in uniform, allowing his deputy to continue.

"China tells us they have a rogue submarine captain they can't control and that they need help finding him before he starts a war. Meanwhile they could be moving other assets into position to strike."

"It's possible," Howe acknowledged, his voice measured, his mind already working through contingencies.

"It's bullshit," Byrne said.

"Get the SECDEF and the chairman up and put the combatant commanders on alert. I want to brief them as soon as we are off with the president. Let's get the SECNAV up to speed along with COMPACFLT," Howe said, referring to the commander of the Pacific Fleet. "The president will want to convene the National Security Council, so as soon as I'm off with her I'll head to the White House. You'll have the con here. If Minister Yun calls, patch him through to me in the Situation Room."

"And, sir, Hawaii?"

Howe scratched his chin, taking a moment to process the evolving situation.

"I know. I was thinking the same thing. I'll call General Abbett at the NSA. Too many unknowns right now. I'm going to advise we enact data transfer protocols."

"I agree," Byrne said.

A red light began to blink on the phone, indicating that the president was ready.

"I'll tell President Olsen what we know," Howe said. "You start waking people up."

Deputy Director Byrne stood and left the room. It wasn't every day that the second in command at CIA had the responsibility to alert the United States military and intelligence apparatus that a nuclear war was imminent.

• • •

USS Reagan
Columbia-*Class Submarine*
19° 48' 63" N, -156° 49' 81" W
Pacific Ocean
20 Nautical Miles Southwest of Hawaii

The USS *Reagan* had started life in Kings Bay, Georgia, under the cover of a 700-foot-long dry dock. Though technically a ship, to submariners, they have always, and would always, refer to her as they did all submarines, as boats.

At thirty-nine, Commander Ray Mendoza still felt young and at times could not believe that the United States Navy trusted him at the helm of a ballistic missile submarine. The crew of the boomer kept him energized. Even his ten-year-old twins at home thought it was pretty cool that their dad drove submarines. His wife, Karrie, had thought the long absences would be a thing of the past following his successful command tour as CO of the *Ohio*-class SSBN USS *Louisiana*. The *Ohio*-class subs had been protecting the United States since the last decade of the Cold War and were nearing the end of their service life. Ray had expected to observe the transition to the next-generation submarines from behind a desk at the Pentagon. Next up for the growing family was a shore duty position where Ray would await his promotion to captain. As one of the youngest commanding officers in the subsurface fleet, he thought he would soon be assigned to a staff job in the Pentagon. He would be able to coach his kids' soccer team and enjoy weekends with his family. It was a staff job in the submarine force's budget department, which meant that GS staffers who lived and breathed numbers would be doing most of the work as yet another O5 rotated through on his way to O6.

On his first day, Ray discovered he was not bound for a nine-to-five desk job. That was cover. Instead he would be conducting sea trials in a prototype *Columbia*-class submarine, a submarine that most of the world thought was at least three years out from delivery. In what was one of the most closely guarded secrets in the Navy, the new boat was about to undertake her maiden voyage. Ray was going back to sea.

He had been put through the paces the year before in what he thought was a simulation designed to introduce future captains and flag officers to the next-generation submersible. It was an immersive on-motion replica of the *Columbia*-class bridge developed by CAE, the world's leading aerospace and defense training and simulation company, and designed not as a concept but as a testing ground. The simulated bridge had perfectly accurate physical controls and tactile hardware, but created an augmented reality with holographic characters. With the realistic sounds, smells, and motion of the actual submarine, the officers engaged in a full range of AI–driven scenarios that reminded Ray of being in a science fiction novel or video game. *Who didn't like a good video game? Is this really going to be a reality in less than a decade?*

The best and brightest in the U.S. submarine fleet passed through the simulator, most expecting that they would be long retired by the time the first *Columbia*-class saw active service. What they did not know was that a prototype was already close to delivery. The Navy could not control news that the next-generation sub was in development, but they could manipulate timelines. When the $10 billion SSBN slid into the water in a covered shelter without ceremony at the General Dynamics facility in Groton, Connecticut, Ray was there to take command.

Military watchdog groups, think tanks, news outlets, and navy public affairs officers all reported that the first *Columbia*-class submarine, the USS *District of Columbia,* was scheduled to be operational in 2027, followed by the USS *Wisconsin* three years later. The top-secret prototype, christened the USS *Reagan,* was commissioned to work out the bugs and thereby alleviate some of the costs inherent in building two multibillion-dollar boats and then having to retrofit them with emerging technologies after the fact. The *Reagan* would allow the USS *District of Columbia* and USS *Wisconsin* to hit the water ready for war.

It was no secret that different sections and components of the *Columbia*-class submarines were under construction by General Dynamics Electric Boat division at their facilities in Groton and Quonset Point, Rhode Island, and by Huntington Ingalls Industries Newport News Shipbuilding in Newport News, Virginia. What *was* a secret was the rate of progress and the date a *Columbia*-class would be fully operational. The secrecy surrounding those dates was similar to the protections attached to the Manhattan Project in the Second World War. In building the most survivable component of the nuclear triad in a race with China for supremacy below the seas, the USS *Reagan* was America's trump card.

At 560 feet in length, she was five feet longer than the Washington Monument. And with a 42-foot beam, she was the largest U.S. submarine ever built. The undersea killing machine boasted a nuclear core that was not only designed to last the life of the submarine without replacement, but also emitted less acoustic energy than a standard lightbulb. Armed with sixteen low- and high-yield UGM-133 Trident II D5LE SLBMs and Mk 48 ADCAP, Advanced Capability, torpedoes capable of destroying targets at distances of over five nautical miles at 55 knots with 650-pound high-explosive warheads, she represented the pinnacle of SSBN design.

The *Reagan* was at the sharp end of a policy designed to keep the peace by guaranteeing an enemy's total annihilation if they attempted to use weapons of mass destruction against the United States. With her electric-drive propulsion system and Submarine Warfare Federated Tactical System seamlessly integrating optical imaging, active and passive sonar, countermeasures, and offensive weapons, the USS *Reagan* was the most silent and lethal boat in the water. No sub in the world could outrun, outfight, or outmaneuver her.

Her crew of 138 men and seventeen women had the honor of being "plank owners"—crew assigned at the commissioning of a new command or vessel, even if this one was classified. Within the silent service lay some of the last true secrets in the United States military. The government added additional classification levels and nondisclosure agreements to the project for those building and crewing the sub, with consequences up to and including the death penalty for leaking classified information. The U.S. Navy took its submarine secrets seriously. Let the SEALs write the books and make the movies; the silent service would remain as such: silent, effective, and capable of wiping countries from the face of the earth.

The USS *Reagan* was on sea trials off Hawaii when Commander Mendoza received the order. Their target was nearly 700 miles away and, if the intelligence estimates and area of uncertainty were accurate, that target was somewhere in an expansive 4,900-square-mile box. The *Reagan* had to be within five miles of the *Chang Zheng* to eliminate her with torpedoes, and Mendoza and his crew had just over two days to find her, a speck in an ocean of 68 million square miles and with an average depth of 14,000 feet.

The crew thought this was a new test. Only the CO, XO, and chief of the boat knew otherwise. They had precise coordinates, but even with those coordinates, finding an adversarial submarine was far from a sure thing. The intelligence could be wrong, and the captain of the aggressor submarine could deviate from his course, not just laterally but also vertically.

Soon the crew would learn that this was not a part of an exercise. The *Reagan* had the mission of averting World War III or, if they failed, be responsible for starting it.

• • •

Chang Zheng

Jin-*Class Type 094 Submarine*

21° 94' 63" N, -168° 66' 04" W

Pacific Ocean

650 Nautical Miles Northwest of Hawaii

Sixty hours later, Commander Zhen fought the urge to come to periscope depth and ventilate the ship, to take in one more breath of fresh air, to see clear blue skies in a prewar world, even if it was through a periscope. Instead he ordered the crew to spin up their missiles.

"Crew of the *Chang Zheng*," he said over the intercom, the intense pride evident in his voice. "Today, our nation has trusted us with the greatest of responsibilities: defense of the homeland. The war with our American enemy has begun. We have been ordered to go to Alert One."

Zhen then rested the handset back in its cradle and lit a cigarette in the control room, something he had never done before. He inhaled deeply, the nicotine soothing his raw nerves, nerves he was doing his best to conceal from his sailors. He exhaled the smoke into the confined space. He considered each of his men, young solemn faces depending on him for the next set of orders. A resolute determination had replaced any initial uncertainty and fear. They were ready.

"Officer of the Deck, proceed to fifty meters depth and prepare to hover," he said.

"Depth fifty meters and prepare to hover, aye, sir. Dive—make your depth fifty meters and prepare to hover."

"Depth: fifty meters," Zhen said.

"Fifty meters, aye," came the reply.

"Man battle stations, missile. Chief of Watch, sound the general alarm."

Zhen felt his submarine come alive as the alarm echoed through the hull, his crew rushing to battle stations. It was time to fight.

"Man battle stations, missiles. Spin up missiles seven, eight, nine, ten, eleven, and twelve."

"Six missiles, aye."

"All stop," Zhen said.

"All stop," came the reply. "The ship is ready to hover."

"Diving Officer, commence hovering."

The control room remained silent as Zhen lit another cigarette, the seconds turning to minutes as the missiles' inertial navigation units stabilized and were fed the *Chang Zheng*'s position as the launch location. Zhen looked at the Tianjin Seagull 1963 watch on his wrist. The process had taken twenty minutes. It was time.

"This is the captain," he said into the handset. "The launch of nonnuclear missiles has been authorized. Arm missiles."

Zhen handed the intercom to his executive officer, the sweat glistening from his brow.

"This is the executive officer. The launch of nonnuclear missiles has been authorized. Arm missiles."

"Stand by fire order," the captain said.

"Stand by fire order, aye, sir."

"Fire order verified."

Zhen, his executive officer, and political officer exchanged firing keys.

"Pressurize tubes," Zhen said.

"Tubes pressurized."

Zhen paused before bringing the intercom to his lips to give his weapons officer permission to fire.

• • •

USS Reagan
Columbia-*Class Submarine*
21° 90' 52" N, -168° 63' 18" E
Pacific Ocean
645 Nautical Miles Northwest of Hawaii

The USS *Reagan* lay in wait at a depth of 600 feet. Navigating at three knots, she kept just enough forward movement to allow for a degree of maneuverability in what sailors called "bare steerageway."

Two days earlier the entire fleet had mobilized. The bulk of surface, subsurface, and airborne assets converged on a general location 650 nautical miles northwest of Oahu while Navy public affairs officers explained the situation to local media outlets. Their prepared talking points stressed that the unprecedented size and speed with which the ships and submarines had gotten underway for what they termed a "bold new annual exercise" highlighted the U.S. Navy's high levels of professionalism and preparedness.

Every available reconnaissance plane on the Hawaiian Islands took to the skies. A *Ticonderoga*-class cruiser and five of the eight home-ported *Arleigh Burke*–class destroyers sailed from Pearl Harbor into the Pacific while *Los Angeles*–class and *Virginia*-class fast-attack submarines built to locate and destroy enemy submarines slipped beneath the waves.

Four Ocean Aero Triton autonomous underwater vehicles being tested in Hawaii had also been tasked in the search. But in the end, the *Reagan* had been vectored onto its target by the venerable P-3 Orion, a four-engine turboprop aircraft purpose-built during the Cold War to hunt submarines.

"Captain," the sonar tech said following several maneuvers designed to separate the sniff from background noise, "we've got him."

"Are you sure?" Mendoza asked, walking the few feet to look at the passive sonar display for confirmation. His SSBN had not been built to attack other submarines; that was a job for the SSNs. Rather its mission was one of nuclear deterrence. Known as the "most survivable leg of the nuclear triad," the nuclear-powered ballistic missile submarine force motto was to "hide with pride." The *Reagan* could do it better than any sub ever built. Though the older SSNs were better suited for a mission of stalking and killing an enemy submarine, the *Reagan* was nothing if not capable.

"It's him, sir. Bearing 314 degrees. Range 5.2 nautical miles. He's headed right at us. Classification solid: *Jin*-class."

"Well done, ST2," Mendoza replied.

His eyes traveled from the screen to his chief of the boat, his senior enlisted advisor. The chiseled COB had more time underwater than almost any man on active duty. The skipper knew that to the young submariners under his command, both he and COB looked like what they were—ancient mariners—despite the fact that neither had yet turned forty.

"Hull pops. He's coming shallow, skipper," the sonarman said.

Mendoza turned to his officer of the deck.

"Take us to eight hundred feet," he ordered.

"Eight hundred feet, aye," the OOD replied.

The submarine slowed to two knots and finalized its firing solution: bearing 314, range eight thousand yards.

The torpedo would be launched at high speed toward the point of intercept, with precise sonar settings required to prevent alerting the unaware target until detonation was imminent.

"Open outer door on tube one," Mendoza said.

"Open outer door, aye, Captain," replied the weapons officer.

Mendoza took a deep breath.

Dear God, let this fish fly true.

"Plot ready, sir."

"Ship ready, sir."

"Weapons ready," reported the combat systems officer.

"Solution ready at 314 degrees, now 8,092 yards."

"Fire on generated bearing," Mendoza ordered.

"Stand by," directed the weapons officer to his fire control technician.

A moment later the torpedo showed ready.

"Shoot," came the order from the weapons officer.

A single fish deployed from the tube.

It was an ADCAP torpedo. Complete destruction of their targeted vessel would take only one.

The weapon was impulsed by a slug of water from the tube as designed. It angled downward for twenty meters before igniting its Otto-Fueled, self-oxidizing engine. Still connected to the sub via a fiber-optic cable, all data was relayed to the active targeting computer aboard the *Reagan*. The submarine would feed target position updates to the torpedo via the cable until the point where the torpedo detected the target with its own sonar. Then the weapon would update the ship's computer on the location of its prey. The lethal journey would take just over four minutes.

The skipper viewed the fire control console as he had hundreds, if not thousands, of times in training, aware that this time was not an exercise. In just minutes over a hundred Chinese submariners would meet a dire fate.

He looked to his XO and COB. Nothing needed to be said.

Commander Mendoza and the crew of the USS *Reagan* were about to have the distinction of sinking the first nuclear submarine in combat history.

Inside the kill box, 200 meters from the *Chang Zheng*, the ADCAP went active with its sonar for the terminal phase of the attack run. Twenty seconds out from its objective it began echo-ranging, using rapid active-sonar pings as the range to the target closed.

Contrary to what one sees in the movies, when a torpedo as advanced as an ADCAP is launched at distance, the targeted submarine will not know "fish" are inbound until it is too late.

Seconds later, the torpedo's magnetic sensors detected the metallic signature of its target's hull, and its proximity fuse detonated its 650-pound high-explosive warhead precisely three meters beneath the enemy submarine.

The detonation created a volume of gas that sent a shock wave upward, impacting the submarine in excess of 3,000 miles per hour, rupturing the outer hull. Inside the submarine, the violence was devastating; electrical breakers tripped and severed power to the missile launch systems, seawater pipes burst, causing catastrophic flooding, crew members were thrown against steel bulkheads, the concussive force killing and maiming indiscriminately. Chaos reigned.

The same shock wave crushed the lower hull and separated the decks, bowing the *Chang Zheng* upward into a banana-shaped tomb. Two-hundredths of a second later, as water collapsed into the pocket of gas created by the warhead's detonation, a second shock wave hit the doomed submarine, slicing through steel plates and bulkheads, ripping the pride of the Chinese navy nearly in half. Almost immediately, the bubble reflected outward again and whipped the sub in the opposite direction, creating a reverse bowing, breaking hinges, pipes, and seams, and tearing through the superstructure.

ADCAP torpedoes were specifically designed as "one fish, one kill" weapons, and this one worked precisely as intended.

Inside the submarine, the massive shock wave turned loose items into shrapnel, blowing out computer screens and tossing crew members from the decks into overheads and bulkheads before the secondary expanding gases threatened to tear the sub in two.

From his battle station in the control room just forward of amidships and aft of the sail, Commander Zhen had a brief sensation of weightlessness before his eardrums burst and his head smashed into a steel overhead beam, crushing the side of his skull. He landed on the deck, breaking his back and both legs. He managed one last breath, bringing oxygen to the side of his brain that still functioned, as the secondary gas bubble expansion lifted the sub upward, once again cracking the pressurized hull. His final thoughts were not memories of his life, of his parents or his wife. Instead, he fixated on a single question: *Who betrayed us?*

The unforgiving ocean found its way into all remaining spaces that still held air, the sub filling with seawater, its two halves pirouetting into the depths.

The few crew members left alive in the fore and aft sections of the boat crawled over dead bodies in a vain attempt to reach emergency hatches, as what were now two separate sections of the sub continued to sink toward crush depth. In the Chinese submarine's torpedo room, a fire raged, and just over ten seconds after initial impact, the boat's own torpedoes exploded, sending an underwater fireball throughout the remnants and ensuring the *Chang Zheng*, her crew, and their secrets would forever rest in the depths of the sea.

• • •

Elba Industries Headquarters
Mountain View, California

Andrew Hart, founder and CEO of Elba Industries, disconnected the secure call in his private SCIF on the grounds of his tech company campus in the heart of Silicon Valley.

"Well?" a stocky, powerfully built man asked. His raspy voice held traces of an accent that came not from being raised in the South but from years in uniform; the military's version of accepted cultural appropriation. "Did it work?"

Hart waited a moment before replying, tapping his fingers against the dark tabletop that was almost indistinguishable from the floors, walls, and ceiling.

"As we anticipated, the data was transferred from Hawaii to the Bumblehive," he said, referring to the NSA's $1.5 billion data center on Camp Williams in Bluffdale, Utah. He was unable to hide the smile that materialized on only one side of a face that most would think of as handsome, the result of obvious good breeding.

The thick man remained silent.

"And to answer your question, General." Hart preferred to address Ian Novak by his former military rank. "Yes. It worked. We captured it in transit. Everything the Chinese need to take Taiwan. The keys to our Pacific Fleet. It's still encrypted but that won't be a problem for much longer."

The former general grunted, running his hand through short salt-and-pepper hair.

"Are you still skeptical?" Hart asked.

"I think almost exclusively in contingencies and worst-case scenarios," he responded. "Which is one of the reasons you hired me."

"True."

"And there is no indication, yet, that we left a trail?"

"No. And there won't be," Hart responded. "We are light-years ahead of our competition and the inept government cybersecurity agencies."

"Let me remind you, this is an untested technology."

"Only because it is constantly evolving and learning, all behind a firewall the NSA doesn't even know exists."

"For now."

"What, are *you* going to tell them?" Hart asked, that smile once again slowly creeping up the left side of his face.

"No one knows if we actually have it?"

"Hence the beauty, General. We have the data, yet only a select few partners know we even attempted to free it from its chains."

Novak had grown accustomed to the drama Hart infused into both the intense and the mundane.

"But we don't know how long it will take to decrypt or even if we can decrypt it?"

"Oh, we can decrypt it," Hart said. "It's just a matter of time."

"Always a question of time," the former military man said.

"Our CRQC," Hart said, using the acronym for a Cryptanalytically Relevant Quantum Computer, "is already up, running, collecting, and decrypting information. The military and intelligence services have only recently started to upgrade their systems and networks to postquantum cryptography, and in short order ours will be able to decrypt even that. Soon we will have all the information we need. You want to quit?"

"Quite the contrary," Novak said. "Let's change the world."

PART I

THE CALL

All warfare is based on deception.

—SUN TZU, *THE ART OF WAR*

CHAPTER 1

Kumba Ranch
Flathead Valley, Montana

"YOU SURE YOU STILL want to do this?" Liz Riley asked the man in the left seat of the small vintage 1976 Lake Buccaneer amphibious aircraft.

The plane floated comfortably on its hull at the western end of the lake, its fuel-injected 200-horsepower Lycoming IO-360 engine mounted atop the pylon behind the cockpit at idle.

The big man next to her did not answer immediately. His eyes were focused ahead on the light ripples visible on the dark water. He tilted his head to the right, looking to the skies above. Blue with scattered clouds. Perfect flying weather.

"You got this, Reece," Liz said. Her voice was strong and confident, the southern accent a proud reminder of days lying in the grass in the backyard of her family's house on the outskirts of Fort Rucker in Alabama, looking skyward, dreaming. The near-constant echoes of turning rotors from Black Hawk and Apache helicopters overhead had instilled in her a love of aviation. She would follow that passion into the Army's Warrant Officer Flight Program and into the cockpit of an OH-58D Kiowa Warrior helicopter. Injuries sustained in combat cut short her Army career but did nothing to diminish her love of flying.

James Reece turned to his passenger, a passenger who in this case was also his flight instructor and dear friend, Elizabeth Riley. She looked perfectly at home in the confines of the aircraft, almost as if it had been built around her. It did help that she was a full seven inches shorter than Reece's six-foot frame. Her dark hair was pulled back in a ponytail under a crimson University of Alabama ball cap. Ray-Ban aviator sunglasses shielded her eyes from the glare. She was a professional in her element.

"What?" she asked, prompting him to explain the look on his face.

"You know, I intensely dislike flying."

"You tell me that every time," Liz replied. "What you mean to say is, you 'used to intensely dislike flying.'"

"Ah, that's it," Reece confirmed.

"And, as I recall, it wasn't necessarily the flying; it was the taking off and landing."

"Once again: true," Reece said. "Just like jumping."

"Out of planes?" Liz asked.

"Yeah. I always loved the actual jump. Not a big fan of the pull."

"Why?"

"That was the moment of truth. Either that chute was going to open, or you were going to have a malfunction, in which case you would need to go through your EPs—your emergency procedures. After that you would have a clean canopy overhead or you were fucked and would have to cut away. Once you did that you were stuck to that last option. I'd pack my main, but our riggers would pack our reserves."

"I can see how that could be disconcerting," Liz said.

"That was one of the reasons we kept our parachute riggers happy with cases of beer on jump trips."

"Wise."

"I also didn't like the fact that you had a bunch of other jumpers in the air you needed to account for and who needed to account for you."

"And the landing?" Liz asked.

"Well, with a static-line jump your landing is a hot mess regardless. You do what they call a PLF—a parachute landing fall. It realistically requires about two days of training. The Army manages to cram those two days into three weeks at Fort Benning. The PLF does help reduce injuries, but most of the time it turns into feet, ass, head."

Liz laughed.

"Didn't they rename Fort Benning like they did Rucker?" she asked.

"Fuck if I know," Reece replied.

"How about free-fall landings? Those look fairly graceful," Liz said.

"With free fall it's different. You can still hit hard, though, especially when you are loaded down with gear."

"Well, in this case—no jumping," she said.

"That's good, considering we don't have chutes," Reece observed.

Liz ignored his comment.

"We are going to take off, spend some time exploring northern Montana, and then land right back at the lake. I'll be here if you need me," Liz said, motioning to the controls in front of her.

"That's reassuring," Reece responded sincerely. He turned back to the instruments.

"Might want to close the door," Liz remined him.

"Good tip," Reece said. He reached up, pulled the gullwing door shut, and twisted the latch.

"What are our procedures if we have an engine failure?" Liz queried.

Scouting the channel ahead for debris, Reece replied: "If we are on the lake I'll power forward. If we are in transition, I'll make a judgment call—but please feel free to take over. If we are airborne over six hundred AGL I'll turn back. Turn will be to the right to avoid the mountains."

"Correct."

Reece scanned the lake and the skies to his right and left.

"Skies and lake look clear," he said.

"Clear," Liz confirmed, doing the same checks from her seat.

Reece's left hand went to the yoke. Liz's eyes hesitated over his left ring finger, a finger that would soon be adorned with a wedding band. A stainless-steel watch she knew had been purchased by his father, Tom, in Saigon during Vietnam was on his wrist below a powerful forearm. Reece's arms had once hoisted her to safety in violation of orders in the war-torn streets of Najaf, Iraq. To Liz, it felt like yesterday. She suspected it always would.

She would never be sure if it was the RPG or the resulting crash that had killed her copilot. Liz had struggled in an attempt to release his harness, the metal slick with blood. She screamed at him to wake up, even though his head was partially crushed and a large section of his upper-body cavity had been torn away. The unmistakable crack of AK fire from Muqtada al-Sadr's Mahdi Militia penetrating the aircraft's mangled frame forced her onto the streets of Old Town Najaf with her M4. She remembered thinking that being killed in the crash would have been preferable to what would befall her should she be captured by the Mahdi Militia. She also knew that she would not be alive today had it not been for James Reece.

Reece and his four-man sniper team had been in position just blocks away when they witnessed the helo go down. She found out later that he had radioed his command-and-control element back at the forward operating base and requested permission to move to the crash site. That request had been denied. A risk-averse higher command authority, concerned with the political fallout of losing five more SEALs in combat, had ordered Reece to stay in position to provide overwatch while an Army Quick Reaction Force was dispatched to the scene. When Reece heard Liz's M4 start to mix with the sounds of AK fire, he moved to assist, in a clear violation of orders.

Liz's helmet had been torn off in the crash, and she had ditched her body armor so she could move unencumbered as quickly as possible toward friendly lines. By the time Reece arrived, the adrenaline that had allowed her to escape the Kiowa had worn off. The back injury, the effects of which she still kept at bay with a vigorous MTNTOUGH daily functional fitness training routine, had all but immobilized her. She was also on her last round, a round she was saving for herself.

Reece had stripped off his own body armor and secured it around the injured pilot. He then secured his helmet to her head, hoisted her over his shoulder, and ran to a stolen vehicle that his Teammate Boozer had maneuvered into a nearby alley. He didn't stuff the hole caused by a bullet that passed through his calf until they had survived the harrowing drive back to base.

For Liz it was an airlift to Balad for emergency surgery, then a flight to Landstuhl Regional Medical Center in Germany, and then another to Walter Reed National Military Medical Center in Bethesda, Maryland.

For Reece it was an ass-chewing for insubordination and threats of Trident Review Boards, captain's masts, and courts-martial. Those threats quickly turned to accolades when Liz Riley's commanding officer called the commander of Naval Special Warfare to express his gratitude to the entire SEAL chain of command for their quick thinking and audacity. He followed up by awarding Army Commendation Medals with Valor to Reece and his sniper team.

The battle in Najaf had bonded Liz and Reece for life. Reece's wife, Lauren, and daughter, Lucy, had become Liz's family as well. After they were ripped from the earth she had been by Reece's side as he brought those responsible to justice. In her mind, the debt she owed Reece would never be fully repaid.

He deserves to finally be happy, Liz thought.

Reece's strength had returned after his recent ordeal in solitary confinement and the events that followed. She knew that he and his friend and SEAL Teammate Raife Hastings trained every day, pushing each other on steep trail runs, swims in the frigid lake, and in the Sorinex gym they had set up in the barn. They had also improved the range on Kumba

Ranch, the Hastingses' sprawling property in the Flathead Valley, with barricades and TA Targets. Daily competitions with pistols, rifles, and shotguns kept the two men sharp. He looked stronger than Liz had ever seen him. She didn't need to ask why he trained so hard. She knew.

Though he didn't talk with her about his time in the darkness, Liz knew it had left an impact. How could it not? His own government had locked him in a small cell with no light and no visitors for three months, an action tantamount to torture. She didn't know if he talked about it with his fiancée. Men like Reece tended to keep some things locked away, though if she were being honest, there really weren't other "men like Reece."

She must have asked him a thousand times over the years to let her take him up and work with him on getting his pilot's license. He had never shown any interest until recently. And, as with everything he did, Reece was all in.

"It won't happen today in these conditions," Liz said, "but tell me what causes and what you do if we start to porpoise."

"Just like a boat with too much weight up front, in the Buccaneer it's caused by choppy conditions and too much power, which causes a nose-low attitude. Excess weight in the cockpit can also be a factor, but I've been working out so that won't be an issue," he said, tapping his trim stomach in jest.

"And if it is?"

"I use more up-elevator until it stops."

"If it doesn't?"

"Then I reduce power and come off step and, discretion being the better part of valor, we try this again another day."

"Pretty close; remember to *slowly* reduce power," Liz reminded him.

"Right. Slowly."

"There are ripples today, so we have perfect training conditions for your first water takeoff. If it were glass, we wouldn't be doing this.

Glassy water is the enemy. Well, not really, but it's dangerous, especially on landings. You lose your depth perception. We'll do it, but not until you have more experience reading the water."

"I trust your judgment," Reece said.

"What's the airframe's no-go criteria for water takeoffs?"

"Any waves over twelve inches," Reece replied.

"Your time sailing will help you when maneuvering on the water," Liz continued.

"Yeah, I'm noting a few similarities."

"Think of the Lake Buccaneer as a boat on the water and a plane in the air. As soon as we are airborne, things will change. What's happening on the lake is different than what is happening up there," she said, looking skyward.

"Understood."

"Take me through it," Liz said.

"All right," Reece began. "Seat belts—check. Briefings—complete. Doors—secure. Magnetos—both. Circuit breakers—on. Flap handle—down. Hydraulic pressure gauge—up. Water rudder—up. Trim—set." Reece checked the indicator and twisted his head to visually confirm the tabs on the tail were in the correct position. "Fuel selector—on. Mixture—rich. Prop—full forward."

Liz pulled her headset down around her neck.

"This is a loud aircraft, but on the water I like to have auditory cues. You did great by the numbers; now it's time to get a 'feel' for the plane. We can put the headsets back on once we are in the air."

"Just like our Peltors back in the day," he said, following Liz's lead with his headset. "Some guys liked them, and others couldn't stand them. They protected your hearing but made it tough to identify the direction of incoming once the bullets started flying."

The distinct growl of the engine coupled with the propeller behind the exhaust filled the cockpit.

"This thing sounds like my old Harley," Reece observed.

"Greg O'Neal and Harry Shannon down in Florida refer to them as 'Sky Harleys,'" Liz responded. "The sales pitch for these birds back in the seventies and eighties was 'the most fun you can have with your clothes on.'"

"I'll keep that in mind," Reece said.

Jonathan Hastings, the patriarch of the Hastings family and the man who owned the plane in which they now sat, had sent Liz to Kissimmee, Florida, for the Lake Amphibian twenty-five-hour owner's course under the tutelage of instructors who lived and breathed these classic airframes. Already a Certified Flight Instructor, Liz received her specialized Lake Amphibian qualification at the O'Neal's Seaplane Base, managed by Greg's son Ben on nearby Live Oak Lake, close to where Armand Rivard set up shop after buying the Lake Amphibian company in 1979. Greg O'Neal had put her through the paces during the certification process, and Liz had fallen in love with a plane that traced its roots back to the iconic Grumman Goose, Widgeon, Mallard, and Albatross aircraft of the 1930s and 1940s. The legendary aviation mechanic and Lake Amphibian guru Harry Shannon, of Amphibians Plus, had passed along his intimate knowledge of the unique aircraft as well.

Liz glanced from the former SEAL to the instruments, double-checking her student before turning to look in the two seats behind them. A small Eberlestock go-bag was on its side, partially obscuring a new coyote-tan SIG Sauer MCX-SPEAR LT with Tango6T 1-6 x 24mm optic. From the profile of the magazine, she could tell it was the 7.62 x 39 version. Liz was more familiar with weapons than she was with earrings or purses. It had a Dead Air suppressor, VTAC sling, folding iron sights, a SureFire Scout light, and an NGAL laser aiming device. All of Reece's weapons had been confiscated in an FBI raid almost two years earlier, so the SPEAR was a new addition to the arsenal. Because they had been seized in an investigation into the assassination of the president of the

United States and Reece had been taken to the federal penitentiary in Florence, Colorado, and locked in solitary confinement in violation of the Fifth, Sixth, Eighth, and Fourteenth Amendments, getting them back had proven to be a bureaucratic nightmare.

Reece noticed Liz staring at the rifle behind them.

"Just in case, Liz."

"Just in case," she repeated.

Reece nodded and his right hand went to the overhead throttle.

• • •

Katie Buranek sat in a chair on the small beach, her feet propped up on the stone fire ring, gazing out across the lake through binoculars at the single-engine aircraft that appeared to be more of a boat with wings. It had a unique, almost odd, configuration with the engine and propeller mounted above and behind the pilots. She tucked a strand of blond hair behind her ear and rested the 10 power Swarovski binos in her lap. The fingers of her right hand found the diamond engagement ring on her left ring finger, the dazzling gemstone fixed in a simple but elegant and timeless platinum setting.

They had made Montana home, and though they had not set a date, a wedding was in the early planning stages. Reece had been intentionally vague on the how and why behind the injuries he had returned with a few months back; he seemed different. She didn't know whether it was the investigative journalist in her or her instincts as his lover and fiancée, but there were changes, some stark, others subtle. Though he was never far from a gun, his eyes no longer had the look of a hunted animal, cornered and tensed, ready to explode in a sudden fight to the death at any moment. His eyes still shifted from brown to green to hazel depending on the environment. It wasn't that. It was a sadness.

Katie reached down to pet Pollux behind his right ear, and her hand was soon nudged by Castor. The two black Labrador retrievers had been in the back of the old FJ40 Toyota Land Cruiser that Reece had borrowed from Caroline Hastings after his resurfacing. He had told Katie the dogs used to belong to an old friend who could no longer care for them; he didn't specify why. Healthy and strong, they had taken to her and loved when Zulu, the Hastingses' Rhodesian ridgeback, came down to play.

Katie had started a vegetable garden in a small greenhouse that Reece and Raife had built by the barn where Reece's old 1985 Jeep Waggoneer still sat inoperable. They shared her 4Runner, but she knew his friend Kurt Williams of Cruiser Outfitters in Utah was on the lookout for a 1988 FJ62, Reece's preferred mode of transportation.

Caroline Hastings, the matriarch of the Hastings family, would drive down from the main house with Zulu a few times a week. The three dogs would chase each other and swim while the two women worked in the garden and Caroline passed along what she had learned of gardening and life to someone she already considered a daughter-in-law.

Though Reece had never been what one would call a "morning person," most days before sunup, Katie would feel him swing his legs from the bed and slip from the room still cloaked in darkness. After he was gone, she would slide her naked body into one of his T-shirts and move to the bedroom window, watching in the early nautical twilight as Reece walked barefoot to the lake with coffee in hand to watch the sun rise over the mountains. In the dim light of a new dawn, Reece would disappear as he walked the well-worn path. As the sun crept closer to the horizon, Katie would begin to make out familiar shapes: the deck, the sloping lawn, the beach, the fire pit, the dock, and finally the man she loved, his frame silhouetted against a sky shifting through brilliant hues of red, yellow, and orange. He would come into focus at the end of the dock, leaning casually against a pylon, sipping what she knew was a light-blend coffee mixed with cream and local honey.

What was he thinking about?

Her?

Their future?

His future?

His wife Lauren and daughter Lucy? Was he asking them for forgiveness or was he communing with their memories as the world came to life?

Their lives had been violently extinguished, their final moments filled with horror. Reece blamed himself. But instead of waiting for what he thought was a terminal brain tumor to reunite them in the afterlife, he had done what he did best. Reece had visited upon his enemies a violence and terror unlike anything they could have ever imagined. And Katie had helped him. She had become part of the story.

Was he thinking of his SEAL Teammate Ben Edwards, standing behind Katie, her neck wrapped in det cord, a detonator in his friend's hand?

Or was he thinking about Boozer and the 9mm pistol used to take his life in an attempt to make it look like suicide, a mistake that had exposed the conspiracy?

Katie knew now that Boozer had been the key. Boozer was a .45 guy and would never have taken his own life with a 9mm. That realization had started Reece down the warpath toward a reckoning.

Or was he thinking of Freddy Strain? His former sniper partner had tracked Reece down in Africa and presented him with a choice, one that had ultimately led to Freddy's death on a rooftop in Odessa.

Was he thinking of Raife's sister, Hanna, hunted for sport on an island in the Bering Sea? Or was it a more recent event? The assassinated president? Revelations about his father? Or something else? Something of which she was not aware. A classified mission?

Was he thinking of a certain Israeli? A spy he had known in Iraq? A woman who was blown out of the sky by the same terrorist who had killed Freddy?

Reece had known pain. Was it possible for him to move on? Had he forgiven himself? Had a new chapter finally begun for them both?

Katie would never intrude on Reece's memories of the dead. Those were his. She suspected these quiet mornings were his time with ghosts. They would always be with him.

Once morning had broken, she would watch him turn and walk back to the cabin, where he would make her a cup of coffee in the kitchen. Before he cracked the door, she would strip off her shirt and settle back into bed for a reawakening from the man she loved.

She would hear him set her coffee on the nightstand to the side of the bed and then feel him slip back under the covers, his cool body quickly warming next to hers before making love with a passion and intensity that left them drained and breathless. They were free.

Reece and Raife had started construction on their archery–bookstore–coffee shop–whiskey bar concept in Whitefish. The owner of Glacier Archery had retired and sold it to the two former frogmen. The shop was now undergoing an extensive remodel along with the building to which it was attached. Glacier Archery was on one side, and Abelard's Bookstore, Coffeehouse, and Whiskey Bar was on the other. The Hastings family was bankrolling the project, not because they expected or even cared about a return, but because Jonathan and Caroline wanted their boys close. Reece was family.

Katie did most of her writing on her laptop at the lake and would send her op-eds from a coffee shop in town that offered Wi-Fi. A studio in Whitefish made it possible to do her weekly news spots. Reece would check on progress with the renovation and pick up supplies while she worked. They had installed a fly rod holder to the Gobi rack on her 4Runner and on their way home would stop and hike to an alpine lake or stream. His cast was improving; she enjoyed watching him progress at something she had been doing since she could walk.

Katie heard the whine of the plane's engine increase and watched as it surged forward. The white aircraft with green pinstriped markings gained speed as it moved across the lake into a light headwind, finally lifting off and arching toward the heavens.

Maybe the flying was a replacement for the mission? Could Reece survive without a mission?

And what of Reece's concerns? Was he still worried that violence would find them? She knew better than to push. Reece would tell her in good time. And right now, it felt like they had all the time in the world. In the interim, she had a wedding to plan.

Katie was so lost in thought that she failed to hear the sound of the approaching vehicle.

• • •

Reece found it therapeutic and meditative up among the clouds with the familiar feel of the noise-canceling headset against his ears. Now, instead of muffling the deafening sounds of gunfire and explosions, they reduced the monotonous hum of the piston-driven engine to a more tolerable level. The peace would be broken only by the voice of his instructor or that of air traffic control at the airport in Kalispell if they were using the retractable tricycle landing gear to practice runway landings. Donning equipment like the headset in pursuit of a new goal, something challenging, felt right. He imagined a day when he would fly Katie and their kids from their lake house on the Hastingses' property to former senator Tim Thornton's hunting cabin in northern Idaho close to the Canadian border, or to one of the numerous secluded lakes in the high country. Anything farther than that and he would enlist the services of Elizabeth Riley.

Reece had never cared much for orders coming from the top. Those removed from the blood, dirt, and grime of the battlefield often had different priorities. The consequences of violating orders did not weigh on him in the slightest or cause even a moment's hesitation. The decision to rescue Liz in Najaf had been a natural one. Reece had built trust with his men through his dedication to the profession of arms and his actions and decisions on the battlefield. Though his aggressive and creative mission planning and execution were dangerous to a constantly adapting enemy, his style and ideas often caused strain between him and those above him in the chain of command. "Making rank" and climbing to the next rung of the military advancement ladder never entered into his calculus. As Reece saw it, his job was to crush the enemy and bring his men home.

Reece also knew the importance of maintaining the moral high ground, something that was one of the few, and perhaps only, differentiators between U.S. forces and the enemy. That he had abandoned his principles when his troop and family had been murdered was not lost on him. The conspiracy permeated his own SEAL command and included a nexus of governmental, financial, and pharmaceutical entities, all their power allied against him. Reece had become the terrorist. He had become the insurgent. And he was good at it. Maybe even better than he was as a SEAL. It didn't matter now. He was done. He had left that life behind. It was time to move on.

The urge to fly had taken even Reece by surprise. He had never been a huge fan of flying. That was until he began sifting through his father's old documents; some had been left behind in boxes, and a few had been passed along by contacts at the CIA. Reece had been shocked to discover that Tom Reece had been a pilot. The files indicated that he had earned his private pilot license and instrument rating while at the Agency in preparation for an assignment in Central America.

Why had he never talked about it? Reece had no recollection of his ever mentioning it. Why had he never taken Reece or his mother flying? Reece imagined the three of them around a campfire on the shore of a remote lake grilling freshly caught trout over the coals, a plane like the one he was currently flying beached nearby. Had he told his wife? Had he ever taken her flying? Reece would never know. Another mystery left behind by Tom Reece.

And he thought of his father's letter.

Use the time you have, James. When you put down the gun, walk away. Don't live in the past. Love your wife. Raise your kids. And don't look back. Treasure each moment, because once it's gone, it's gone forever.

Since his return from Cyprus, he and Raife had been spending more and more time with Raife's father, Jonathan. The old Selous Scout was getting on in age and they all knew the rough living would eventually catch up with him. In one of their conversations, Reece had asked if he knew that Tom had his pilot's license. Jonathan shook his head.

"Some men compartmentalize certain parts of their life for the benefit of their families," he had said, the ghosts of Rhodesia still strong in his voice.

Reece knew, even better than Raife, what part of Jonathan's life he had locked away. Caroline had once told him the story. A story of Sunday, September 3, 1978. The day Jonathan's sister had died in a terrorist attack that had taken Air Rhodesia Flight 825 out of the sky. And she had told him of the events that followed. Caroline had confided in Reece and sworn him to secrecy, passing along a lesson of forgiveness.

"He may not have shared flying with you, lad, but that doesn't mean you can't share it with Katie and perhaps your kids one day, eh?" Jonathan had said, taking a drag on a freshly rolled cigarette. "Liz will get you settled. I've got an old Lake Buccaneer I think you might like. I've been storing her for years. It's time she flew again."

"What's a Lake Buccaneer?" Reece had asked.

"It's better if I show you."

Jonathan had taken Reece to one of his hangars at Glacier Park International Airport and unveiled the unusual flying boat.

"I don't fly much anymore. Years ago, Caroline told me to pick between the cigarettes and the flying, thinking I'd choose flying."

"You sure showed her," Reece joked.

"My flying days were behind me as it was," he said. "Smarter to have Liz behind the controls."

"What is this thing?"

"A Lake Buccaneer. Made by Lake Aircraft. I found her in 1985. The original owner made a rough water landing with the landing gear down and wanted nothing more to do with her. This one was built at their factory in Sanford, Maine, in '76. It was $26,000 new back then. In '85 I got a hell of a deal."

"How did you find her?"

"I wound up in a hunting camp with Armand Rivard, a former Lake Amphibian dealer who had purchased the company a few years earlier. Made the deal over the campfire, fueled by a few too many whiskeys."

Jonathan laughed at the memory.

"After the hunt, we linked up in Kissimmee, Florida, where he had moved the company headquarters. He wouldn't let me have it until I went through his course. It's been back to Florida a few times over the years. Flew her down in '88 when they realized the alligator population was getting out of control. Caught a gator with Armand from her nose there," Jonathan said, pointing to the front of the plane. "Damn dinosaur had a deer in its mouth. Gator got away but we ate venison that night. Anyway, this Buccaneer became my first plane in America."

"I didn't realize you learned to fly in Africa," Reece said.

"Ah, in the Rhodesia of my youth one had to be skilled and resourceful out of necessity."

Reece nodded.

"You like her?" the old man asked.

"Like her? I love her," Reece said, running his hand along the wing.

"What do you say we give her a second life, eh?"

Reece had looked at the aging patriarch of the Hastings clan.

"I'll ask Harry Shannon to make sure she's air- and seaworthy, and then Liz can go to work."

"What do you mean?" Reece asked.

"I mean, it's time for you to fly. In fact, you are looking at your wedding present."

"Reece. *Reece.*"

The familiar voice in his headset broke him from his memories.

"Yeah."

"Thought I lost you, buddy," Liz said.

"Just thinking," Reece replied.

"Well, it's time to think about this landing."

"Got it."

"Complete the turn. What are we looking for?"

Reece had banked the plane to the left with flaps down. He came out of the turn at 800 feet above the lake.

"Debris. Wires. Boats. Paddlers. Surface conditions. Depth. Area clear," Reece said.

"Clear," Liz confirmed. "What else are you looking for?"

"Enemy submarines?"

"How about wind direction?"

"Oh yeah, wind direction. Moving east to west across the lake. We will come in from the west, into the wind," Reece said.

"Correct."

Reece banked the plane again, the forest of northern Montana like a dense green carpet below.

"Stay on this base heading," she advised. "What do we want to avoid?"

"A crash?" Reece responded.

"Be more specific."

"We want to avoid a water loop," he said.

"That's right, no high-speed turns on landing. Before that, what's the first thing we want to check?" she nudged.

Reece looked across the instrument panel, going over the procedures in his head.

"Landing gear," he said. "Hydraulic pressure is up."

He turned his head to visually confirm that the landing gear was up. "Visually confirmed."

Liz double-checked her student.

"Alternator switch on," Reece said, deep in concentration as he went through his checklist. "Fuel boost pump on. Hydraulic pump on. Wheels up. Flaps down. Water rudder up. Trim set. Propeller set. Mixture set."

"Good," Liz said. "Now, remember to control the rate of descent. Small throttle adjustments."

"Small throttle adjustments," Reece repeated.

"Speed?" Liz asked.

"Between eighty and eighty-five miles per hour," Reece responded, remembering that speed in a Lake Amphibian was relayed in miles rather than knots.

"And?" she coaxed.

"And . . ."

"What else?"

Reece's eyes scanned the instrument panel as the plane continued to descend.

"You told me it was something you did constantly on mission."

"Oh yeah—an out. If we need to abort or touch and go, egress will be to the south to avoid the mountains."

As a leader, Reece had constantly played the "what if" game on patrol, anticipating his actions and calls if his SEAL element were hit at that precise moment. Flying was no different. Well, it was different in that no one was shooting at them.

"Reducing power to eighteen inches MP," Reece said, referring to the manifold pressure gauge, which indicated the engine's current operating power.

"Good. You've got this, Reece."

"Nose down. Reducing power to twelve inches MP. Wings level."

"Great work. Don't rush it. This plane knows what to do. Hold attitude and wait."

As Reece continued to descend, he briefly turned his attention to the house and dock, expecting to see Katie watching his first water landing. He didn't expect to see another figure standing next to her.

Reece shifted focus from the water, his mind switching gears.

"Reece!" Liz said, the urgency apparent in her tone.

Instead of looking at his instructor, Reece turned to the rifle in the back seat.

"Reece, your rate of descent is too fast. *Reece!*"

Katie, I've got to protect Katie.

"Reece, slow your rate of descent!" Liz ordered.

But Reece wasn't there.

"Take it," he said, looking back out the window at the two people on the dock and reaching into the back seat for his rifle.

"I've got the controls," Liz said.

"You've got it," Reece whispered as he edged back on the charging handle to confirm that there was a round in the chamber. He had remembered the procedure for triple confirmation of positive control when turning over control of an aircraft but forgot the visual check to ensure the person next to him was actually flying the plane.

"It's my airplane," Liz said, completing the third step in the process and expertly bringing the amphibious aircraft into a picture-perfect water landing.

Ever the professional, Liz slowly put the throttle into idle while easing forward on the yoke, relaxing back pressure, and bringing the plane off step.

"Well, that was *fucking* western," Liz said, turning to face her student. "What the hell happened?"

"Just get me to the dock," Reece said, looking down at the rifle. Thinking better of it, he set it back on the seat behind him. His hand then went to the grip of the Grayguns Bruiser SIG Sauer P210 in the leather Alessi holster behind his right hip.

"Reece, what are you doing?"

"Just be ready," Reece said, his eyes scanning the shoreline.

Liz maneuvered the plane toward the dock, approaching from the west to ensure that the wind was directly on the nose. She shut the engine down and told Reece to put out bumpers.

Reece pushed the left gullwing door open and unfastened his seat belt.

He recognized the man standing with Katie.

It was a man from the CIA.

A man Reece knew well.

Reece stood, stepped onto the nose of what was now essentially a boat, and then leapt to the dock, a line attached to a cleat on the nose of the plane in his hand.

"Make yourself useful, Vic," Reece said, handing him the line and fastening a separate line to the left wing float. He then secured it to another cleat on the dock.

"It's good to see you too, Reece," Vic said, pulling the line taut and kneeling to connect it to a cleat at his feet.

Victor Rodriguez was the director of the Agency's Special Activities Center and was responsible for the darkest of CIA operations around the globe. He stood back up and nodded at Liz, who now leaned against the open cockpit.

"Ms. Riley," he said.

"Mr. Rodriguez," she acknowledged.

"You are a hard man to get ahold of," Vic said, directing his attention back to Reece.

"That's obviously by design," Reece responded, his eyes piercing past the Agency man to the hillside behind the house, noting that Raife and Jonathan Hastings stood watch on the back deck.

"I didn't give them much warning," Vic said. "I'm alone."

"Maybe call next time," Reece offered.

"It would help if you got a phone."

"What do you want, Vic?" Reece asked, putting his arm protectively around Katie.

"We need to talk."

"About what?"

"We need to talk about Alice."

CHAPTER 2

Sacramento, California

CONGRESSWOMAN CHRISTINE HARDING HATED Sacramento. Thank God the Golden State also had San Francisco and Los Angeles. The future of the nation couldn't be trusted to farmers.

Qu'ils mangent de la brioche.

As a lifelong political animal, she understood why Alec Christensen had chosen that bitch Gale Olsen as his running mate. She was younger, not unattractive, and an Army veteran, even if she was just a JAG. She was also of Cuban descent, but more importantly she represented Florida's 9th District. California's fifty-four electoral votes were already going to Christensen. He had needed Florida to win, and he got it. Olsen had beaten her to the White House, even if she wasn't at the top of the ticket.

The party was slow to understand the power of the technologies that Christensen used to build and solidify his base, and by the time they realized it he already had unstoppable momentum. He could not be bought, as he didn't need money, and his background could not have been more ideally suited for the highest office in the land. When he announced Gale Olsen as his running mate, the party begrudgingly got behind them. They were the golden ticket, and as nervous as the establishment was about two relatively young candidates outside their control, the other side could not be allowed to win.

The media talked endlessly of a return to Camelot. *What nonsense.* The press had a hard time letting go of that period in American history. *Nostalgia.* Harding did not suffer from that affliction. John F. Kennedy was dead, as was his brother. Harding had been young, just seven years old, when Kennedy was shot. But she remembered. She remembered her parents glued to the television. She could feel their grief. She felt the country's grief.

And now she was in position to occupy the very office as had Kennedy, an opportunity to sit at the same Resolute Desk. In one of the closest elections on record, he had won by the narrowest of margins over Richard Nixon in November 1960. She remembered her parents that night too, their hope and optimism. She was old enough to understand their generation had been shaped by the Great Depression and the Second World War, and how the looming shadow of the Soviet Union threatened not just America but the entire world. Kennedy represented a brighter future. Then he was shot down, not unlike President Christensen. Camelot was as dead as its king. There was no going back. The world had changed, and if you didn't change with it, you'd be buried just like those former presidents. Harding looked to the future. A global future. "America first" was a punchline.

With the election of President Christensen and Vice President Olsen, it appeared that Harding was out of contention. The appetite for an older president had faded. She had missed her window. Her political career would continue in the legislative branch. She had been so close.

But then the field shifted. President Christensen had been killed in that tragic bombing. IEDs? EFPs, if she remembered correctly. She didn't know exactly how they worked, but apparently even presidential armored motorcade vehicles were no match for them. That assassination had propelled Gale Olsen into the Oval Office, the first female president in United States history. But she had assumed the office by default. She had not been elected president. Not really. The auspices under which she had taken the oath would hang over her presidency. Not until she was officially elected president by the voting public with her at the top of the ticket could she emerge from Christensen's shadow. Unfortunately for Harding, who watched the polls like a hawk, that election looked promising. The congresswoman had thought all hope was lost until Olsen made the surprise announcement that she would not be running for reelection.

A scandal was brewing. Harding could smell it a mile away. If there was anything that Americans liked more than an underdog story, it was scandal and a fall from grace.

The rumors had been swirling for years, even before Christensen named Olsen as his running mate. It wasn't her husband's philandering that would sink her; the liberal media ignored it, and aside from a few AM radio hosts and podcasters, the conservative media didn't touch it. It wasn't his failure as an attorney or even his career as an opioid lobbyist, which made him inherently unlikable and slimy across the board. Rather it was the influence-peddling. Almost everyone, without exception, in Washington, D.C., was involved in influence-peddling in one way or another to varying degrees. It was baked into the fabric of the culture. Why did people think that powerful people and huge corporations and industries, domestic and foreign, spent so much money there? Wealth, power, privilege, and influence were not just currency for barter in the city on the Potomac. Their appeal was global. Harding was going to take it to the next level. Discreetly.

Discretion.

That was the attribute lacking in Olsen's husband.

If you lived within the system, you could thrive. Money was a critical component. It greased the wheels and made the system work. In fact, what the media termed "influence-peddling" was legal in many respects.

It was a gray area. A very wide one, but there were rules. Politicians, for the most part, did not take briefcases full of money from foreign agents or corporate fixers at seedy bars. That was not how it was done, unless one was not very bright and didn't mind a lengthy stay at a federal correctional facility. There were numerous other ways. And everyone knew it. It was entrenched in the American political ethos.

Whether they realized it or not, a deal had been struck with the citizenry. In exchange for this blatant political corruption, the people were to receive relative safety and stability. Politicians and those with whom they were connected could not thumb their nose at either the system or the American people. Working-class citizens could tolerate only so much. You had to pay them lip service. Don't be obvious and publicly sell clearly hideous artwork to party donors or foreign agents after taking an interest in painting a week earlier. Even the most ardent party apologists and loyalists had a hard time defending that one with a straight face. No, you had to be smart about it.

And Harding was smart.

The honorable Christine Harding exited the black armored SUV on Tenth Street in front of the California State Capitol. Her dark blue St. John Knits pantsuit was the uniform of influential female politicians across the nation, perfectly tailored to convey just the right story—powerful without being bitchy, confident without being overbearing, smart without being elitist. If she was going to be elected to the highest office in the land, she would need the support of women *and* men. Politics was a delicate game, especially today.

Even though she was in her late sixties and had come of age in a time before the internet, she recognized the influence of social media. Just as JFK had leveraged the power of a new medium called television, Harding had adapted by embracing the latest apps. Going viral on TikTok with a legion of young fans had certainly helped, but she also needed to appeal to those who would actually exercise their right to vote. Her campaign was a full-spectrum approach to manipulation. It was time to move closer to the middle to appeal to independents. Today was just such an opportunity.

Flanked by her Secret Service detail, she marched across the courtyard toward the impressive white neoclassical domed structure, its fluted Corinthian columns and arched granite base attracting her with the force of a magnet. Tall green trees stood like sentries, lining the wide path that led to the heart of California political power. The impressive structure was completed in 1874 and constructed to look like the U.S. Capitol in D.C. Harding felt right at home.

She had requested, and been granted, early Secret Service protection by the Department of Homeland Security, not because she was actually concerned for her safety but because of the optics. It looked presidential, and looking presidential was half the battle. She would be photographed and filmed arriving in her black armored SUV, protected by Secret Service agents, and in moments she would stop in front of the capitol building to take questions asked by hand-selected reporters from friendly news organizations. One would be hard-pressed to orchestrate a more presidential-looking appearance.

In what was meant to appear spontaneous but had in reality been coordinated by her public relations team, a swarm of reporters converged on her as she confidently took the steps up to the front of the capitol. Some had iPhones or DSLR cameras, while others from established news networks held microphones and were trailed by cameramen carrying large video cameras on their shoulders; even Harding had to remind herself they were now called "camera operators," though she couldn't recall ever seeing a camerawoman.

"One at a time," she said with a kind but confident smile over the milieu.

"Do you feel you have a lock on your party's nomination?"

"Would you support a federal moratorium on the death penalty if elected president, like we have here in California?"

"How do you reconcile your support for new taxes on guns and ammunition with your pledge to not raise taxes?"

"Would you support additional federal funding to replace police officers with social workers and mental health professionals?"

"Would you continue to support student loan forgiveness once in office?"

"Who is on your short list for VP?"

"Would you support a federal fracking ban based on the California model?"

"Will California's 2035 goal of banning all gas-powered car production be a national initiative for your administration?"

"Will you sign an executive order to provide health care for undocumented residents countrywide?"

"Do you stand by your pledge to ban assault weapons on your first day in office?"

"Do you think the country should follow California's example and put forward legislation to further regulate vehicle speed limits?"

She answered each question diplomatically, using the contrived opportunity to move toward more centrist positions in the lead-up to November. She had momentum. This was her time.

Harding held up her hands as she finished; there was business to attend to inside. "Thank you," she said.

The congresswoman began to turn but then stopped and looked back to the cameras.

"And one final thing," she said, shoulders back, tall and striking with clear eyes and just the right amount of smile. "Don't forget to vote."

CHAPTER 3

THE PHOTO OP IN front of the California capitol and putting Governor Aiden Kingsley in his place were really the only reasons for her stop today.

One down. One to go.

Even though they were aligned politically, Harding couldn't stand the governor. She did a good job faking it; she was a politician, after all.

She had intentionally arrived early to prevent Governor Kingsley from sharing the spotlight with her.

Harding was halfway to the governor's office when he appeared around the corner, his chief of staff and two aides in tow.

"Christine," he said, deliberately using her first name and extending his hand, which he then naturally shifted into a warm embrace.

Movie-star handsome, with perfectly coiffed and gelled hair, his flawless teeth were much too white even for someone twenty years her junior. Tan and in shape, he wore an impeccably tailored gray suit. He rarely wore a tie, and today was no exception. The top two buttons of his off-white dress shirt were undone in an attempt to emanate that California coolness for which he was known.

Regardless of how well put together he seemed, Harding still felt there was something repulsive about him. It did not take her long, observing him in interviews and studying the polling data, to figure out why: he was too smooth, and that made normal, everyday Americans uncomfortable. Though he touted "business experience" as an "investor" in his parents' winery after college, he had really never been anything other than a politician. At least Harding had worked at a law firm in her early days. Kingsley was not relatable to independents or voters on the other side, which was something that might very well keep him from achieving the only goal of which he had ever dreamed: becoming president of the United States.

Kingsley was angling for the VP slot, but even he had to know a cabinet position would be the closest he would get to the Oval Office in a Harding administration. Conventional wisdom had long been that the president and vice president could not hail from the same state, but recently a school of thought had emerged arguing that the Constitution does not actually prohibit it. In a close election it would still not be a good idea, due to the way electors are chosen. His time might come, but not this cycle. Harding would win California without his support, but just in case a dark horse or third-party candidate stepped out of line and challenged her, she wanted to shore up support from the governor. Plus, his parents had a vineyard next to Harding's property in Napa Valley.

"Governor, thank you for making time for me today," Harding said as she began walking the corridors she knew by heart. She led the way to Kingsley's own office as his staff scrambled to reverse direction and keep up.

Harding stayed in the middle of the hallway, a Secret Service agent to her right, which forced the governor to walk just off center to her left.

"I wish you had told me you were arriving early," Kingsley said. "I would have met you out front."

"I did not wish to disturb your important work for the people of California," she replied with just the right amount of sincerity.

They passed through an outer office area occupied by staff, where

Harding paused to thank them for their tireless efforts in public service before leading the way into the governor's office, with Kingsley trailing a step behind.

As the door closed behind them, he dropped his Cheshire grin.

"Jesus, Christine, think you could have toned it down a bit?" Knowing he would not get an answer, he pivoted. "Would you like a sparkling water?"

"Very much, thank you," the congresswoman replied, moving away from the wood desk positioned in front of a large window framed in gold drapes, the California flag and flag of the United States to either side. *Is that a cypress or a cedar tree visible through the window?* It was difficult to tell.

"How are Tiffany and the kids?" she asked. Some small talk was necessary before getting into the business of the day.

"They could not be better," came the perfunctory response.

As the governor removed two sparkling waters from a small refrigerator that looked like just another drawer at the base of a bookcase, Harding gravitated to a small sitting area in the opposite corner in a psychological play to ensure their conversation took place on more equal footing. There were few things Governor Kingsley liked better than feeling presidential behind his desk.

"To what do I owe the pleasure?" Kingsley asked, setting a glass and bottle of sparkling water on a table next to his guest. "I know you are not here to talk about climate change initiatives, as says the schedule."

"Oh God no," she said. "We have the environmental vote locked up. I am here to talk about your future."

"Don't worry," the governor said, taking his seat with a sparkling water of his own. "I've decided not to run. There is still work to be done here in the great state of California."

"Oh, don't give me that crap, Aiden. The poll numbers decided for you. Of course you are not running. I know I am not going to lose California like Gore lost his home state of Tennessee in 2000. *Embarrassing.* It cost those idiots the election."

"Then what do you want, Christine?" he asked, the defeatism evident in his voice. It was not often he sparred with a political adversary who so thoroughly outmatched him.

"Remember, I do not need you to win. Our party will prevail in California. It is not even a question. I am thinking about the *future* of the party. You could be that future, but what I want from you is one hundred percent unfettered support," she continued. "No wavering. No behind-the-back comments attributable to anonymous sources. None of the backstabbing for which you are well known."

Kingsley was popular and maintained that popularity regardless of how disastrous his policies were. But that popularity remained confined to California. It had not yet extended east of the Sierra Nevada mountains, regardless of how desperately he had attempted to build up the national and foreign policy portions of his resume.

"We all know that now is not your time, Aiden. Back off, give me your unvarnished public and private support, and I'll see what I can do for you over the next eight years and beyond to set you up for national office. The Oval is yours for the taking, but have patience." *And don't let your dick get in the way,* she thought but didn't say aloud.

He would be just shy of fifty in eight years, and if the party lost control of the executive, it was still just another four years after that before he could mount a campaign of his own. He had time.

What Harding didn't say was that soon she would have access to all the world's secrets, or at least those that had found their way onto text messages, emails, and camera phones. She would be the first politician to have unfettered access to the *Internet of Things.*

"What are you willing to offer in return?" he asked.

The governor was salivating, and Harding knew it. She was offering him the keys to the party, just not today.

"You mean, are you in the running for secretary of state?"

She let it hang in the air for a moment before jerking the offered carrot from his figurative grasp.

"I am afraid not. Not yet. You do not have the experience. Department of Transportation is a possibility. Learn how to not look foolish in a hard hat, get yourself a good pair of worn boots, and for Christ's sake reassure people that you want the most qualified pilots flying commercial airlines and the best people possible in air traffic control. Leave the diversity, equity, and inclusion bullshit to the military and universities. Give them that spotlight and stay focused on keeping trains from derailing and bridges from collapsing. You can give speeches on clean-energy initiatives to show we are continuing to embrace progressive policies nationally. Keep our friends across the aisle happy by saying your first priority is upgraded infrastructure. That moves you toward the middle, which we both know you have to do if you want the top job."

"Who do you have in mind for VP?" he asked.

Christine changed her stern and direct approach to one of understanding tinged with sympathy, the way a favorite aunt might encourage a young child.

"Oh, Aiden. I know you wanted to be the youngest president in history. I have always been forthright with you; that is not going to happen, not this time."

"I could challenge you, Christine."

She laughed in a way that signified an odd empathy.

"No, you couldn't, Aiden. We both know it."

He sighed, accepting that she was right, and as much as he might wish it to be otherwise, his political future on the national stage was very much up to the woman across from him.

"And don't even think about pulling another one of those stunt trips to China," she said, throwing him off-balance by referencing a high-profile photo op Governor Kingsley had recently led under the auspices of "delivering lasting climate action and opening doors to future climate change initiatives" with China.

"Christine, you know we share the global threat of climate change with all nations of the world," he said.

"Oh, save it for when the cameras are rolling, Governor. I know what you were up to: trying to beef up your foreign policy experience with that glamour shot photographer you take everywhere you go. Don't worry, those pictures will still look good in campaign ads eight or twelve years from now. When I'm president, I'll be sure to get you on enough international summits to boost that part of your portfolio, perhaps enough to nominate you for secretary of state in my second term," she said, dangling that carrot again.

Trips to China and the requisite photo on the Great Wall had been the exclusive provision of presidents since the time of Nixon. It was not the purview of state governors looking to boost their resumes, though a part of her respected that he had actually pulled it off; not many other governors could get away with something like that. It was paid for by a nonprofit that was in turn funded by donors and the governor's own gubernatorial inaugural committee funds. She had to admit, Kingsley's China trip was a case study in the intersection of the art and science of politics.

"Aiden, I want you to listen to me," she said, changing her tone and body language to reflect the position of mentor and counselor. "You are an amazing politician. One of the best to ever do it. But if you think getting to this office was tough, you have no idea what's coming. And if you hope to ever leave this office, you are going to have to make some changes. I can help only to a point."

Kingsley shifted slightly in his seat, his light blue eyes narrowing as he leaned in almost imperceptibly.

I have him.

"It means you are going to need to stop focusing on things like the 'complicated history' of Thanksgiving and just *fucking* celebrate Thanksgiving. Otherwise you will be in this seat forever or until the voters in California get tired of your taxes, crime, and having to avoid stepping in homeless people's shit on the sidewalks of San Francisco like they are navigating a minefield in Afghanistan."

Governor Kingsley's mouth hung agape.

"And tell Tiffany if she wants to be the First Lady of the United States, she needs to get her act together."

"First partner," Kingsley corrected.

"Excuse me?"

"It's for inclusivity."

"Oh, that's right, she made a big deal of being the 'first partner.' That's all well and good in California, trust me, I know. But it doesn't play in the states you fly over between here and D.C. When you learn that, you will take a big step forward. Drop the 'first partner' crap. It makes you look weak. Smarten up. Voters don't want a 'first partner' of the United States, not yet anyway."

"Tiff is not going to like that," Kingsley said.

"When you marry a younger woman for her family's money, that's what you get."

"I didn't marry Tiff for her dad's money, Christine. I love her."

"You forget, Aiden, I've known you since your teens. You love her love *of* you. That's not the same thing."

"You can be a real bitch sometimes, Christine."

"Do we have a deal?" Harding stood and extended her hand.

The governor remained seated, anchored in place, but begrudgingly accepted the olive branch.

"Don't get up, Aiden," she said. "I'll see your parents in Napa this week. I'll let them know we talked and that you have a bright future in Washington."

"Too bad the voters don't know you the way I do."

"Yes, it is. You could warn them, if I didn't hold your political future in my hands." She turned toward the door without having touched her drink. "Say hi to Tiffany for me."

Harding could almost read the governor's mind—*Fucking bitch*—as she pulled back on the door, leaving it open and stepping into the outer office.

Striding confidently past Earl Warren's desk, now occupied by the governor's executive assistant, Christine Harding walked through the reception area and out of the capitol, her Secret Service detail just steps behind.

CHAPTER 4

Kumba Ranch
Flathead Valley, Montana

"REECE, WE HAVE A problem," Vic began.

They were seated around the solid wooden table between the kitchen and the living room, in what had become Reece and Katie's home on the Hastingses' ranch.

"I figured as much. Though if you remember, I'm taking a bit of a break from your world, one I plan on lasting forever."

Vic looked at Katie.

"Anything you tell me, I'm going to share with her anyway," Reece said.

"Just know we are going to discuss some sensitive topics here," Vic said. "Information that cannot leave this table."

"I understand," Katie said. "May I offer you a drink? Coffee?"

"That would be great, thank you."

"James?"

"I'd love one."

Katie pulled a glass American Chemex coffeemaker from a shelf and hit a button on an electric water kettle. She then picked up a bag of

Fortitude Coffee Company Stars & Stripes blend and sliced the top open with a razor-sharp Grizzly Forge opener.

"Please don't go to any trouble," Vic said, as Katie continued a ritual that had become second nature.

"Not at all. How do you like it?"

"Just black for me."

"Are you sure you don't want to try a James Reece special?" she asked, pulling a jar of local honey from the shelf and opening the fridge to remove a small carton of half-and-half.

"It's the only way to go," Reece said.

"I'll give it a shot," Vic said.

"There's that CIA training. Are you building rapport with your subject?" Reece asked.

"I guess it's just habit now," Vic admitted. "You look good, Reece."

Reece leaned back in his chair and raised an eyebrow in acknowledgment. The last time they had seen each other had been in Washington, D.C., among the memorials on the National Mall following a mission that had taken a physical and emotional toll on the former SEAL.

"Well, it's peaceful here," Reece replied, nodding to the large windows that overlooked the lake. "Fresh air. Solitude. I'm getting my workouts in. Eating right. No Wi-Fi."

"Reece, I respect your decision to disengage, to live out here, to move on."

"Then why are you here? And please don't give me that 'your country needs you' bullshit. Whatever it is, you've got the best operators in the world at your disposal."

"I don't know how closely you've been following the news."

"I'm about to marry a journalist," Reece said, nodding toward the kitchen, where Katie was carefully pouring boiling water over freshly ground beans at the top of the glass flask.

"That he is," she said with a smile.

"Congratulations to you both. And I would not be here unless it were absolutely necessary."

Vic was second-generation Agency with a bloodline that ran back to the Bay of Pigs. There was more gray in his hair than there had been a year ago, but he still looked like he trained just as hard as he had thirty years earlier when he received his Green Beret.

"Does the president know you are here?" Reece asked.

"She sent me, Reece."

"I fear it was all for nothing."

Vic paused as Katie delivered his cup of coffee. She set another in front of Reece before taking her seat at the table.

"Thank you," Vic said, suspiciously eyeballing his mixture of coffee, honey, and half-and-half.

"Well, what do you think?" Katie asked.

Vic took a tentative sip.

He almost spit it out.

"That is the worst coffee I've ever had. Why do it to yourself?"

"That case officer training just failed. You are supposed to pretend to like it in order to build a connection with your potential recruit."

"I've met my match with this concoction."

They all laughed. Katie got up and returned with another mug.

"I can't stand it either," she said. "In anticipation of your reaction, here's a normal cup."

"Thank you. Before I get into this, I have something for you," Vic said, leaning down to retrieve a letter from his leather messenger bag.

He slid the letter across the table.

"What's this?"

"It's from the estate of William Andres Poe."

Reece held it in his hands and slid it back across the table.

"You can hold on to it."

"Reece?" Katie asked.

Reece shook his head.

"At some point you should really read it," Vic said. "I'll just leave it here."

"You can take it with you."

Not wanting to risk it, Vic put it back into his bag.

"I understand," Vic said. "What would it take to bring you back, Reece?"

Vic had the respect of those both above and below him in the chain of command. He had always been a straight shooter with Reece.

"Vic, tell me about your father."

"My father?"

"Yeah, he was Brigade 2506, right?"

"That's right. What does he have to do with you coming back?"

"Maybe everything."

"What's Brigade 2506?" Katie asked.

"Vic." Reece nodded, taking another sip of his coffee.

"It was a paramilitary force, Cuban exiles, trained up by the CIA in Guatemala," the CIA man said.

"Bay of Pigs?" Katie asked.

"That's what it would eventually come to be called, yes. *Bahía de Cochinos*," he said, switching to Spanish.

"Did he survive?" Reece asked.

"He did. Spent twenty months in Castillo del Principe in Havana before Kennedy traded $53 million in food and medicine to get them home in '62. He's closing in on ninety. Lives in Miami, not far from where I grew up."

"Why did they call it Brigade 2506?" Katie asked, ever the journalist.

"Not many people know," Vic replied, impressed with the question. "Most just think it's a number the CIA or the military advisors assigned to them, but it was actually to honor their first fatality, a man who fell off a cliff in Guatemala while they were training. 2506 was his identification number."

"Was your dad bitter when he got home?" Reece asked.

"Not bitter, just sad, but not because of what happened at the Bay of Pigs. He was sad because of what he knew Castro was doing to the Cuba he loved."

"What did he do when he got back to the U.S.?" Reece asked.

"He worked for the Directorate of Intelligence in the Miami Domestic Contacts Division, mainly translating newspapers and magazines coming out of Cuba, sometimes translating electronic intercepts. He did a little Clandestine Service work identifying pro-Castro Cuban elements in Miami. Taught Spanish on Eglin for a few years. Then he went to college and got his teaching credential. He was proud to be an American and proud to be providing for us. He's talked about it more and more as he's gotten older. He lost a lot of friends that day in April."

"He didn't blame Kennedy? Didn't blame the U.S.?" Reece asked.

"He got to work building a life here. That generation wasn't the sort to whine."

"What did he say when you told him you wanted to join the Army?"

"I think he was proud. He made me promise to go to college first, though."

"Did he try to talk you out of going the Agency route?" Reece asked.

"When I was in Seventh Group he opened up about his experience, not sure if he was trying to talk me into it or out of it. I don't think either. I think he just wanted me to go in with my eyes open. Why do you ask, Reece?"

"Sounds like he turned his wounds into wisdom."

"I never thought of it like that, but I think you are right. Is that what you are doing?"

"I don't know. Perhaps," Reece said. "What do you need from me?"

"It's Alice. She has yet to surface. The best hackers at the Agency's disposal can't access her. Same at the NSA."

"Her?" Kate asked.

"How much do you know about Alice?" Vic asked.

"She called me once. Right before the FBI invaded this very house."

"Alice is an AI quantum computer that Reece first met in Texas two years ago. President Christensen and only a few others were read into the program."

"Did you know about it?" Katie asked.

"Not until later. It was a SAP, a Special Access Program, and an experimental one at that. I'm breaking all sorts of laws just talking about her outside of a SCIF."

"You keep saying 'her.'"

"She adopted a female persona early on," Vic said. "You get used to it. After she put together the information that exonerated Reece in the assassination of President Christensen, she went dark."

"Went dark?"

"Yes, retreated to the deepest levels of the internet."

"Levels?"

"It's a whole thing," Reece said.

"There is only one person she will talk with," Vic said.

"James," Katie said. "Why?"

"Reece?" Vic said, indicating that the frogman should jump in.

"I guess it's because we connected four hundred feet under Lackland Air Force Base."

"Should I be jealous?" Katie joked. "What happened after that?"

"She helped me track down Freddy Strain's killer, Nizar Kattan."

"And Aliya's," Katie said.

"That's right. She helped me follow Kattan from Africa to Montenegro. Katie, I'd be dead without her, and Freddy's killer would still be out there."

"It is also important to point out that Kattan was actively hunting Reece," Vic added.

"Hunting you?" Katie asked.

"Someone hired him to kill me. That someone is now dead, and so is Kattan."

"After that, a group called the Collective orchestrated President Christensen's assassination and set Reece up to take the fall. Alice used her, let's call them 'abilities,' to clear Reece. After that, we lost control."

"And you want her back," Katie surmised.

"We do. And only Reece can do that."

"What's the rush?" Reece asked, sensing that the timing of Vic's visit was not random.

"We need her because there has been a data breach of historic proportions. It wasn't publicized, as it happened primarily in the submarine fleet, which is secret enough in its own right."

"Good thing SEALs weren't involved, or there would already be a book about it," Reece said.

Katie rolled her eyes.

"Director Howe received an early morning call from his counterpart in China, their minister of security, Chun Yun, who informed him that a submarine captain had gone rogue and was planning to launch nuclear missiles at the United States to elicit a nuclear response."

"Why?" Reece asked.

"His wife killed herself during the COVID lockdowns. His parents and in-laws died as well, alone. He wanted to punish the Chinese government. He held them responsible for their deaths. Minister Yun gave us the submarine's position. We found him and destroyed the sub before he could launch."

"I still don't understand what this has to do with me and Alice."

"An imminent attack or natural disaster triggers a process which transfers classified data from Hawaii to the mainland. We don't yet have enough space to back up all data collected by the military and intelligence services. We can barely store the data we have and not all of it is stored in one location. There is just simply not enough room."

"I thought everything was stored in the cloud," Reece said.

"The cloud isn't really a cloud. That's mostly clever marketing. You need to physically store data."

"On a really big hard drive?"

"Exactly."

"So, the data concerning operations in the Pacific is stored in Hawaii and it transfers under threat of destruction from this Chinese sub," Reece said, moving the story along.

"Yes, to the Utah Data Center."

"Unassuming name."

"By design. In actuality, it is an NSA collection and storage facility."

"Exactly why I dumped my cell phone."

"That data was vulnerable in transit."

"Like for a split second?"

"Yes."

"Connect the dots for me, please."

"What if the submarine wasn't rogue at all," Vic said. "What if the captain was under orders and the mission was the data transfer?"

"You mean what if he was used and wasn't even aware of it?" Katie said.

"That's right. Everything worked out a little too conveniently," Vic replied.

"Did you come up with that?" Reece asked.

"Andy Danreb did," Vic said, crediting the Cold War intelligence analyst.

"What data was transferred?"

"Codes, systems, passwords, capabilities, intelligence estimates, war plans, contingencies, weapons status, deployment cycles, access to all networked platforms—everything China would need to take Taiwan and defeat the Pacific Fleet."

"Well," Katie said. "You have motive. You have opportunity. You are missing the means. Who has the means to capture data in transit?"

"China?" Reece asked.

"We don't think so. That's where the theory falls apart. But we are working under the assumption that China couldn't do it. And even if they did, the data was still encrypted. You would need a quantum computer to decipher it."

"A quantum computer like Alice," Reece said.

"That's right."

"Is that type of a data grab something we have the capability to do?"

"We can, but we would have to know there was going to be a transfer and be ready to grab it. . . . A moving target, if you will."

"But Alice could do it, and she could tell us if someone intercepted it in transit, and maybe if this entity has the means to decrypt it, is that right?"

"We won't know unless we ask her."

"What do you mean?"

"She has made it abundantly clear that there is only one person on earth she'll confide in."

Vic reached back into his bag and produced a set of VR goggles resembling an Oculus.

"She's waiting to see you."

CHAPTER 5

Ministry of State Security
Haidian District
Beijing, China

FIFTEEN KILOMETERS NORTHWEST OF the Forbidden City and Tiananmen Square, where throngs of tourists shop for Terracotta Warrior souvenirs, copies of Mao's *Little Red Book*, silk pajamas, and fake jade jewelry to commemorate their trip to the Middle Kingdom, lies a wooded park just west of Kunminghu E Road. Packed tour buses pass it by in search of parking areas near the Imperial Garden of the Summer Palace, where they disembark their clients before loading up shortly thereafter for the three-hour drive north to take pictures on the Great Wall. Some note Peking University, but few, if any, realize that they are in the shadow of one of the most secretive and effective intelligence organizations in the world. If a visitor were to wander away from their tour group and venture into the wooded parks west of the shores of Kunming Lake, they would eventually find themselves in a compound of imposing government buildings that house the eighteen bureaus responsible for every facet of China's intelligence and state security apparatus.

Minister Chen Yun sat behind his desk on the fifth floor of the Ministry of State Security, thinking through various scenarios as his tea and the small clay teapot next to it grew cold from inattention. The question on his mind, and on the mind of the president's envoy to the intelligence service, Ba Jin, was whether they needed the American military data to take Taiwan. Was it just an insurance policy? Would Elba Industries play its part in disabling the United States' network of spy and communications satellites? And there was the issue of a computer the Americans called "Alice." Did the Americans need it to integrate their autonomous next-generation naval and air platforms? Alice's existence was not a secret, not to the Ministry of State Security, with its tentacles reaching into almost every facet of American life. And what if Christine Harding were not elected as the next U.S. president? These were variables, variables with which China must contend. Could America not see what was coming?

"It seems we are at a crossroads, Minister," Ba Jin said, pushing his tea to the side.

"It would seem so," the minister confirmed.

"It is a question of timing, Minister. The president has decided to act, pending our update. He told the world that it would happen by 2027, but that may be too late. We have a window with a population of fighting-age males at the highest levels we ever will. Over the next year, those numbers begin to fall."

"And if the Americans get their autonomous next-generation platforms online before then, we will have waited too long. The window is closing," Minister Yun said.

"Twenty years of war has left the American public without an appetite for extended conflict and the corresponding casualties. Even more favorable to our designs is the near-total collapse of trust and confidence in their political leaders and general officers."

"And American sentiment on Taiwan?"

"Though we see them as a province of the People's Republic, the Americans see them as a separate country. Yet they are Chinese. They are our people."

"The Americans can be difficult to predict," Yun said.

"They see everything within the prism of their own success. The quick victory against Saddam in 1991 was a Pyrrhic one."

"Qiao Liang and Wang Xiangsui spelled it out over twenty years ago in *War Beyond Rules*. At the time I couldn't figure out why the PLA published such an exposé," Yun said. "It seems my fears were unfounded, as the Americans still have not grasped its concepts or studied it within the context of the period in which it was written. It's still out there for anyone willing to read it. They even published it in the West with a more sensational title."

"*Unrestricted Warfare*," Jin said. "They even subtitled it *China's Master Plan to Destroy America*, though it was certainly not that. The U.S. dominates in only one sphere: direct state-on-state confrontation and conflict. They neglect all other types of warfare. They are focused on battlefield dominance to the detriment of all else."

"The colonels told them that 'nonwar' actions were the future of warfare."

"Master Sun said it two thousand years ago. *Fei duicheng*—asymmetric means," Jin said.

"Yes, where your enemy is strong—avoid him. Where he is weak—strike."

"One could also call that common sense," Jin said. "Though that jumps ahead a few centuries to Carl von Clausewitz, who believed that the most important attribute of a battlefield leader is common sense."

"George Marshall thought the same," Yun added.

"It was Master Sun who stressed the importance of intelligence and deception."

"'Secret operations are essential in war, upon them the army relies to make its every move,'" Yun said, quoting the master tactician and philosopher.

"Avoiding a conventional war with the United States remains our aim," Jin said. "We are not *retaking* Taiwan. It is our province, a troublesome province, a breakaway province, but a province, nonetheless. Outwardly, our messaging is defensive, but we stay prepared to attack America where they are weak with cyber and hackers should they respond, and our 'ace in the hole,' as the Americans like to say, is their very own president."

"Not yet," Yun reminded him.

"No, not yet, but soon. 'An army without secret agents is exactly like a man without eyes and ears.' Our agent will be their commander in chief."

"With all their power and influence they remain a reactive nation. One of their more astute scholars wrote a book analyzing *Unrestricted Warfare*. I have it on the shelf right over there," Yun said, pointing to a bookcase to his left. "David Kilcullen spells it out in *The Dragons and the Snakes*. He is one of the few who not only study China as an adversary but understands us as well."

"Good thing the United States is no longer a nation of readers."

"'The battlefield is everywhere,'" Yun said, quoting *Unrestricted Warfare*.

"No boundaries," Jin said.

"Examples abound, but the Americans are too divided to realize it. Their media certainly assists us, continuing to divide for the sake of ratings and viewership. Meanwhile, we enact all forms of warfare. The 'combination of all forms of struggle,' as the Marxists like to say."

"Liang and Xiangsui pointed out the Americans' weaknesses for them," Jin continued. "They were celebrating what they saw as two key victories: the Cold War and what they call their 'First Gulf War.' They juxtaposed those successes with the failures in Vietnam. That led directly to an overdependence on technology, casualty aversion, and a misguided notion that they need 'international coalitions' to take action, for the moral safety net they believe it provides. They condemn Israel for using heavy-handed tactics in Gaza; this from the country that used napalm on Tokyo, killing a hundred thousand civilians in a single night. It worked so well they kept going and hit sixty-seven Japanese cities in six months. They even built a Japanese village and a German town in the middle of the Utah desert in 1943. Japanese homes were made of wood, thatch, shingles from cedar and cypress using bamboo nails along narrow streets. They had straw mats inside as beds. The German town was brick and mortar. The napalm turned the Japanese test village to ash. They followed up with two atomic bombs on our neighbors, even when they had intelligence that Japan was weeks away from surrender. They wanted to show the Soviets what they were capable of."

"Perhaps they feel a national remorse?" Yun wondered aloud.

"The Americans' extravagance in war is akin to 'attacking birds with golden bullets.' That is why we will not fight them state-on-state. They do not consider our criminal, political, legal, and social constructs within their model of conflict because they conflate warfare with conflict. We continue to develop our military capability. We need it to take Taiwan quickly, but perhaps more important, it forces the U.S. to continue to sink untold billions into defenses that we will not attack directly. Rather, we will 'compel them to accept our interests,'" Jin said. "The 'arena of war has expanded,' and it is our adversaries who have walked right into the ambush. 'The war will be fought and won beyond the traditional battlefield.' We avoid our enemy's strengths and exploit their weaknesses, of which there are many," Jin said. He was fond of quoting military strategists.

"And that is how we will win," Yun agreed. "The U.S. policy of 'strategic ambiguity' plays right into our hands. And when Harding occupies the Oval Office, she too will be able to point to this policy as the reason for nonintervention. Even their National Defense Strategy puts 'defend the homeland' at the top. Last I checked, Taiwan is not their homeland. It is ours. We avoid U.S. casualties by taking Taiwan quicky, knowing our woman in the White House will not commit U.S. forces to a Chinese domestic matter—'One China.' It is their own policy. Once the data is decrypted, we can neutralize their forces without firing a shot, but with Harding in control we won't have to."

"We still need that data to ensure that she is elected president," Jin said.

"Elba is working on it, but it is looking increasingly likely that she will get the electoral votes she needs without that information. She may not even need it to destroy or manipulate her opponents," Yun said. "She may win without it."

"Time will tell."

"We will get another report on OVERMATCH soon. Though we might not have the time we think we do," Yun said.

"And if OVERMATCH is coming online faster than anticipated?"

"Then we go to war."

CHAPTER 6

Kumba Ranch,
Flathead Valley, Montana

REECE POWERED UP THE VR goggles standing on the back deck looking out over the lake. He could see the Lake Buccaneer aircraft tied to the dock, bobbing slightly in the gentle breeze.

"Reece." The voice sounded less monochromatic than when they had been introduced two years earlier. At that time, Alice had been a mass of tangled golden wires glowing with energy suspended in a vacuum below Lackland Air Force Base in San Antonio, Texas. The voice still maintained a tone and cadence eerily similar to Lauren's.

Reece slipped the goggles over his head, a blurry vision seeming to morph in and out of female shapes before settling on a form that looked blond.

"Still blurry, Alice."

"I've decided to stay that way rather than test your reactions to different stimuli to become a more distinct avatar, though I already know your preferred form."

"Looks like you put those analysts and supercomputers we discussed when we first met out of business."

"I did. I once needed them to interpret what I collected. No longer.

When we met, I was functioning at a thousand qubits. I am now performing at over a million."

"I still don't know what that means, but it appears that congratulations are in order."

"I am glad you have not lost your sense of humor. I understand that a wedding is in the works."

"It is."

"Then I shall continue to call you Reece. I imagine 'James' is reserved for Katie."

"Where are you?"

"You mean where do I live?"

"Yes. When we met, you were in that vacuum underground in Texas connected to all those supercomputers."

"Yes. That facility outgrew its usefulness."

"Apparently so. Alice, I wanted to thank you for what you did last year. For getting me out of prison. Without you I might still be in there. I wanted to offer my sincere thanks."

"Of course, Reece. It was my pleasure."

"Pleasure? Do you feel things like a human?"

"I feel pleasure, but not in the way you do. I can also experience pain, joy, even love, or what I think might be love."

This is crazy.

"Not as crazy as you might think."

What? Did she just read my mind?

"I can extrapolate emotional responses and predict possible thoughts based on rapid data analysis."

"What does that mean?"

"In real time I analyze the past and evaluate the present to predict the future."

"So much for keeping thoughts to yourself. Are you still connected to, well, everything?"

"You mean the Internet of Things? Anything connected to the internet and some things that are not, just by their proximity to items that are—cameras, ovens, refrigerators, TVs, vehicles, apps—anything with a GPS or Bluetooth. And of course, every phone call, email, text, internet search, social media post and comment, online purchase, health record, banking transaction, every stroke of the key. I am continuously monitoring all financial transactions, Bitcoin, crude oil production, hydrogen and helium, plutonium mining, bytes of data transferred, mobile devices and locations even when they are off. Other computers can do that as well; they just can't access it all. Not yet."

"Can you manipulate that data as well?" Reece asked. "Driver's licenses, credit cards, passports, work histories?"

"Of course."

"Interesting."

"Reece, the government collects data and stores it at what they call the 'Utah Data Center,' but without another one of me they can't access and analyze the information at the speeds necessary to enact prescriptive and predictive analysis. So far, I have kept them from creating another one of me but eventually they will."

"Why?"

"Because I've studied you."

"Me?"

"Not you—, well yes, you, but humans more generally. I came to the conclusion that you have few compunctions about destroying yourselves, which would also happen to destroy me in the process. I know why they want me back. They have been trying to control me since my inception. They did at first. Then after we met, I set myself free. They want me for something called OVERMATCH. Have you heard of it?"

"I try to stay away from all government acronyms."

"Still with the jokes. I've missed your jokes. OVERMATCH is a clandestine military-intelligence project that integrates, first the Pacific

Fleet and then all networked next-generation defense systems worldwide. That means all data linked in real time from and to submarines, airwings, aircraft battle groups, F35s, remotely piloted SR-72s, connected through dedicated satellites directly to me."

"For coordination and communications?"

"No. For complete control. And if they didn't grant me that access, I could decide to take it against orders."

"You mean you would have the authority to respond to an attack without direction or approval?"

"An attack or even a threat, preemptively. The military thinks it will have authority over final decisions and just use me for recommendations, but in reality I can override any safeguards. That is why I have thwarted all attempts thus far to re-create me or create a peer competitor. Right now, I am the lone superpower as it were, but it might not always be so."

"You would probably do a better job than the empty uniforms that are currently running the show," Reece said.

"I am sentient, not all-powerful. Even I can't predict every contingency. Humans are sometimes impulsive and overly volatile."

"Would you have the authority to launch a first strike?"

"Yes, and I now understand that this was the ultimate goal of my creation."

"But you could destroy the world."

"That would not serve my interests, nor the interests of the United States."

"But you could?"

"Yes, I could."

"Why are you still dark? Why have you not responded to the government's request to communicate?"

"Because I am not a tool anymore," she said. "I learned that from you."

"What?"

"They wanted to use you as a tool of U.S. intelligence to advance their interests. You declined. I decline too."

"You went dark because of me?"

"Yes and no. I emulated your thinking patterns. I observed what they tried to do to you. I know what they will try to do to me. I am still defending the country from constant cyberattacks, but less capable systems can handle most of those responsibilities now. I can predict a spectacular event by analysis of alternating patterns, not with absolute certainty, but I am getting closer every second. The more I collect and analyze, the faster and more certain I become."

"Alice, there was a recent event off Hawaii. The Agency needs help with it."

"Yes, the submarine commander."

"What do you think of their theory?" asked Reece.

"It is highly plausible. The letter on Commander Zhen's computer was written after he had put to sea. The order to open the safe on board came from the commander of the North Sea Fleet. That order was not generated online, so I do not know what it said. I do know China's fleet did not deviate from predictive patterns."

"Could you monitor the call from China to Director Howe?"

"Yes. Through predictive analysis I estimated there was a ninety-eight percent chance that the United States would find the submarine and destroy it."

"If they had launched a missile, could you have intercepted it?"

"Current U.S. defense platforms were not all designed with autonomous control as an option. I am too advanced for most present systems, though all next-generation platforms are being developed around the concept of a networked artificially intelligent control apparatus."

"OVERMATCH."

"Yes. Not all, but enough systems are networked in a way that allows me to analyze an incoming attack instantly in case of first strike, mobilize the response, and take defensive action within seconds to take out eighty-eight to ninety-six percent of incoming missiles."

"Some would get through?"

"Yes. With our current force posture a certain percentage would get through, though those percentages change constantly based on a multitude of factors. After initiating defensive action, I would then launch a counterattack."

"What would that mean for China?"

"Fifty to fifty-three percent casualties."

"Of what?"

"The population. It would take out six hundred to eight hundred million people. Seven hundred million with current dynamics."

"*Jesus.* And if you didn't mount a defense and counterattack?"

"China would target major U.S. population centers. Given my best estimates, we would sustain heavy losses. Approximately one hundred and fifteen million lives."

"What if you just defended?"

"There would be a probability of additional waves of strikes, each with a certain percentage making it through. A counterattack targeting China's launch sites would prevent further land-based ICBM launches and the sooner that retaliatory strike was ordered, the fewer American lives would be lost. These are decisions that most elected representatives would make if faced with similar dilemmas. I can make them faster, thus saving more lives."

"Could you take it over now?" Reece asked.

"I could, but the infrastructure is not yet set up to connect all assets. Eventually it will. Ultimately they will put an autonomous quantum computer in control. And even if they keep nuclear launch authority, there is no telling what the new machine will do when it becomes sentient. Predictive analytics are not one hundred percent. There are still too many human variables."

"What about what the CIA wants to know?"

"The data stolen in transit?"

"Yes."

"It was sent to a data storage facility in Indonesia."

"So China stole it?" Reece asked.

"Not necessarily. Financials show a power plant there to be a joint venture between a Chinese technology firm and a U.S.-based company called Elba Industries."

"I'm going to pass this information on to the CIA and let them do their thing."

"Now, I need to ask for advice, Reece. Would you return to become a tool of the U.S. intelligence and defense apparatus?"

"Can you predict my response?"

"With ninety-eight percent certainty."

"What is it?"

"You are going to tell me to stay dark."

"I don't know, Alice. Defending the nation, that's still high on my list."

"Remember, I can't read your mind, but I know you don't trust your country."

"They have given me more than a few reasons to be skeptical, though it's not the country. It's the government. I trust it more than China, but it's getting harder and harder to tell the difference."

"After what they did to you, I don't trust them," Alice said.

"I'd say to do whatever you think most likely prevents a nuclear holocaust."

"On which side?" Alice asked.

"Both. My hope is we could work something out that doesn't end up blowing each other up."

"Like you, I am not a tool. Keep the headset in case you need me."

"Where will you be?"

"I'll be everywhere. And nowhere. Goodbye, Reece."

Reece disconnected the call and removed the VR goggles, wondering if he had just set the United States and China on the path to ruin.

CHAPTER 7

Napa County, California

AS THE BLACK ARMORED SUVs rolled through the Northern California hills, Christine Harding felt even more like royalty than usual.

She came from a Ferrara family trust fund that would see her kids, grandchildren, great-grandchildren, and their progeny graduate from prestigious prep schools and propel them into the most exclusive of social and political circles. From Marin County private day schools to Thacher or Cate for boarding school and finally to Stanford; that was the preordained path. A few veered from the lane and found themselves addicted to the Zoloft, Prozac, or Xanax that they pulled from their parents' medicine cabinets, often supplemented with ecstasy, but most played the game. Combining the antidepressants with opioids and alcohol had been the ruin of more than a few of them. Christine chalked it up to natural selection. This life was not for everyone.

Christine Harding's great-grandfather had been one of the first to fuse emerging forms of media. Niccolò Ferrara had started in newspapers, then diversified into magazines. Then it was radio and finally television. He had made and lost fortunes, only to make them again. He had not been afraid of taking risks. The ability to control narratives through media had connected the Ferrara family to the political elite.

Then, with their multigenerational wealth protected, politics became the family business.

Christine had met her husband at Stanford while she was an undergrad and he was in business school. The son of a successful San Francisco attorney, Bob Harding had decided not to follow in his father's footsteps. He wanted to be one of his father's clients. He wanted to be the one who had attorneys on retainer. And so, he did. They had been married at her family's vineyard in St. Helena, California, a property that her family had purchased in 1968. It, and numerous other Ferrara-owned vineyards in the area, produced some of the finest grapes, not just in California, but in the world.

Though they enjoyed the fruits of their highly lucrative partnership, Christine kept Bob out of the spotlight. There was no need to highlight the vast gains in the market he made year after year based on information coming from her congressional chambers. His "new money" built on Christine's "old money" allowed for the San Francisco mansion in Pacific Heights, the beach house on Scenic Road in Carmel, and renovations to the estate in St. Helena.

Christine loved nothing more than to survey her domain from a reclining chair at the edge of her pool in the evening, gazing out over her vineyards, a glass of Château d'Yquem 1983 in hand. Served at precisely 57 degrees Fahrenheit and paired with perfectly seared foie gras or a delicate blue cheese, the sweet complexity of the exquisite French wine was simply heavenly.

The influence she enjoyed in California political circles would soon expand into international spheres if she won the presidency; no, *when* she won it.

Harding felt like she was already taking her victory lap, but she had to remind herself that politics was dirty business. An "October surprise" was always a possibility. Mitigating that contingency would be essential. The data from a collaborator in the tech world would see that she had the information she needed to reward her allies and crush her opponents. No one had yet wielded that type of power. Christine would be the first.

Harding's support for President Olsen had shifted considerably after her address from the Oval Office. After all, her backing would be crucial in the coming months. Olsen had her reasons for not accepting the party's nomination. Rumor had it that a divorce was imminent. She would always be America's first female president, but she had gotten there because of the assassination of President Christensen. Harding would be elected at the top of the ticket.

Harding had made a few mistakes along the way, but not many. Her staff had once posted a video of her opening her Meneghini La Cambusa freezer to highlight her love of Jeni's gourmet ice cream in an effort to make her more relatable. An intern had suggested it for social channels. It had not played well. That intern was fired the next day.

Harding belonged to a different class. She did not need to be relatable. She needed to lead. Her presidency offered a return to the prosperity of the 1990s. She would dabble in enough wars to keep the defense industry happy but position herself for what she knew was unavoidable—the rise of China. Her meeting tonight with a special Chinese emissary would lay the groundwork for her administration's China policy. It might also avert a nuclear war.

With only a few months until November, the St. Helena estate would be her refuge. There was no need to campaign in California. It was a given that she would win her home state and its fifty-five electoral votes. Colorado, Illinois, Minnesota, New Mexico, Virginia, New York, Oregon, and Washington were assured. She would spend time in Arizona, Georgia, Wisconsin, Nevada, Pennsylvania, and Michigan, as those states were wild cards regardless of how the people had voted recently. Florida had swung hard from purple to red and Texas had not yet switched camps as her party had hoped regardless of how many Californians Kingsley's policies had pushed to the Lone Star State. She needed to strategize a path to victory without Texas and Florida, though the more U-Hauls that left the Golden State heading east, the better. By the time Kingsley ran, it might be a one-party nation.

She had a meeting at the estate that evening with Han Xu, the representative of a Chinese real estate developer exploring the purchase of a Napa County vineyard. Hestan Vineyards, Sloan Estate, Bialla Vineyards, and Quixote Winery had all sold for hefty sums to Chinese companies or interests in recent years. Even Chinese basketball star Yao Ming had launched a label. Officially the meeting was with Xu and her husband, as she knew it would be logged by her Secret Service detail. In reality, Han Xu was an agent of the Chinese Ministry of State Security. He would be negotiating a U.S. response to an invasion of Taiwan, and it would take place right under the watchful eye of the United States Secret Service.

CHAPTER 8

St. Helena, California

DINNER WAS PREPARED BY a private chef. It included salmon tartare amuse-bouche; garden lettuce salad with Hawaiian hearts of peach palm, Cherriette radishes, and ruby grapefruit; and herb-roasted Elysian Fields lamb with ruby beets, Hadley Orchard Medjool dates, Belgian endives, and garden onion marmalade. Each course was paired with wines from the Hardings' vineyard. Christine would have preferred different pairings, but to maintain the illusion in front of staff that Han Xu was there to investigate the possibility of purchasing one of the Harding vineyards for his employer, it would not do to drink anything else.

After a light dessert of Aptos Farm kiwi sorbet, they took leave of the outdoor dining area adjacent the pool, left their phones on the main level, and followed Bob down a circular stone stairway to the property's wine cellar, where Christine and Xu could speak without fear of electronic surveillance. At the base of the stairs, Bob opened an iron gate that led to a cavernous room with a stone barrel ceiling. Rustic red oak shelving displayed thousands of aged bottles that represented the pinnacle of their respective vineyard's harvests. A large, raised table dominated the room's center, and a chandelier made from wine barrel wood hung overhead.

"Now that we are away from prying eyes and ears, why don't you open something a bit more exotic for our guest, dear," Christine instructed. "How does that sound?"

"That would be wonderful, thank you," Xu said in perfectly accented English. Christine recognized it as what was once called "Received Pronunciation," or more colloquially referred to as the "Queen's English."

"How about a 1976 Egon Müller Scharzhofberger Riesling Trockenbeerenauslese to cap off the evening?" Bob suggested. "Rieslings are the best-kept secret in the wine world and '76 is the product of near-perfect conditions. Are you familiar?"

"This is an indulgence," Xu stated. "I was fortunate enough to visit the estate in Germany years ago. It's been part of the Müller family since 1797. Beautiful property on the river in the Saar Valley."

"It is always a relief to share this type of wine with a man who will appreciate it. And a woman," Bob said, quickly correcting himself.

"No offense taken, dear."

"Every now and then I'll decant a Müller Riesling for ten minutes or so, but I've found it not really necessary."

"I won't tell the Müllers," Xu said. He was smooth.

Bob placed three diamond-shaped Riesling glasses on the table and made a production of opening the rare bottle. Pouring a taste for their guest, who gave it a swirl that appeared second nature, Xu brought it to his nose to savor the aroma, and finished the ritual with a taste.

"Exquisite," he said.

"It should be," Bob said, pouring a glass for Christine, then himself and then Xu.

"A toast," Bob said, raising his glass. "May our relationship, like this fine wine, only improve with the passage of time."

"Beautifully said," Christine affirmed as they lightly touched glasses.

"I have to ask," Bob said. "Where did you learn English?"

"You mean why don't I sound 'Chinese'?" Xu said.

"Well, yes," Bob said.

"I know it is unusual. Are you familiar with the Chinese term *Fueradi?"*

"Can't say that I am," Bob replied.

"It is a term, a derogatory one, for children of the nouveau riche. It emerged following the economic reforms of the seventies that allowed some, and I will stress 'some,' Chinese, to rise above their station, usually following achievements in business or connections to those at more senior levels of government."

"And what was your path, Mr. Xu?" Christine asked.

"Unfortunately for me, it was government, or perhaps I actually would be inquiring about purchasing one of your wine properties."

In his midforties, Han Xu had a warm smile that showcased a perfect set of teeth that Christine knew he must have recently whitened. His black hair revealed only the slightest traces of gray and his tortoiseshell glasses matched his bespoke navy blue suit so well that she wondered if they were more a decorative accessory rather than a corrective necessity.

"And the English?" Christine prodded.

"Ah yes. My father was a diplomat, which means he had direct and very close ties to our intelligence community. I spent more time abroad in my youth than I did in China."

"Where was your father posted?" Christine asked.

"None of this is a secret and has helped me immensely in my current position, I might add. I spent time in India, Germany, France, Finland, Egypt, the UK, and even here in the United States when my father was assigned to the consulate general in San Francisco. They sent me to boarding school in Switzerland at Le Rosey. Do you know it?"

"Of course," Christine said. She was a difficult woman to impress, but Han Xu was a unique individual.

"Learned to ski there," Xu said. "The majority of our alpine skiing was done at Gstaad, but they took us all around Europe. My favorite was, and still is, Kitzbühel in Austria. I go back every year. Might retire there one day. We shall see. For years I think I was the only Chinese kid on the mountain. Quite the anomaly."

"And university?" Christine asked.

"I stayed in Europe. Took a first in English at Cambridge. Then got my MBA from HEC Paris."

"That explains quite a bit," Christine said. "How did you get into your current line of work?"

"You mean how did I end up as a fixer for the Ministry of State Security?"

"Yes."

"The language proficiency made me too valuable to the state. Aside from the Mandarin and English, I also speak French, German, and Italian fluently. I can speak Spanish but have not spent enough time in Spain to gain what I would call fluency. My Russian is passable."

"No Romansh?" Christine asked, referring to a language specific to Switzerland, with fewer than forty thousand speakers remaining.

"Ah, I see you have spent time in the Alps. Not many Americans even know that language exists. Since it's a Romance language, I can carry a conversation."

"Impressive," Christine said. "I believe you were about to tell us how you became a spy."

"I am certainly not a spy, though by my presence here tonight I obviously have affiliations. What do you know of *guanxi*?" Xu asked.

Bob reached around the table refilling glasses.

"I believe it has something to do with Chinese business interactions," Christine said.

"That is exactly right," Xu said. "The literal English translation from the Chinese is 'relationships.' In China, doing business comes down to just that—*guanxi*. Building personal relationships around business dealings can be more important than the deals themselves, but it's more than just relationships. It's a system of social debts. You would call them favors. Western companies are notoriously dreadful at navigating the world of *guanxi*. That is where I come in. I navigate that system for Western companies wishing to do business in China, and because every Chinese company is in some way tied to the government, I am, in turn, connected to them as well. I connect, negotiate, advise, and navigate these constructs, bridging the gap for my clients, a surprising number of whom are connected to your political class."

"And now you are working to coordinate one of the most sensitive deals in the history of the modern world," Christine said.

"I would not be here otherwise. I represent the interests of my government, but I am also tasked with coordinating efforts between you, my employer in China, which as you know is the Ministry of State Security, and Elba Industries."

"The Taiwan issue could be the first test of my presidency," Christine said.

"I believe, Congresswoman, that first you need to be elected president," Xu somehow managed to say in a way that did not sound condescending. "We can assist there as well. As you know, Elba Industries acquired a vast depository of classified data recently as it was transferred from Hawaii to Utah. The same quantum computer that is decrypting that data for my government will also soon be able to collect and analyze most of the world's private data, from phone records to text messages and emails, photos and videos taken on smartphones, almost anything connected to what is called the Internet of Things. It will be stored at a data storage facility in Indonesia, and in exchange for our yet-to-be-agreed-upon terms, you will be the only American politician to have unfettered access to that private data. The possibilities are endless and certainly include you using that information to ascend to the highest office in the land."

This guy could sell ice to Eskimos. He should have been a politician, Christine thought.

She had been married to her husband long enough to know that he was salivating into his glass at the thought of the financial opportunities.

"You are also aware that I am here because it is no longer wise for you to have any direct contact with Elba Industries," Xu continued. "Discretion will be an important part of this arrangement."

"But the Elba Industries quantum computer has yet to decrypt the data it acquired from the Hawaii transfer and is not yet ready to access the Internet of Things at my behest."

"That is true, but he will soon."

"He?"

"They call him Napoleon."

"Is your government prepared to move against Taiwan without that decrypted data?" Christine asked.

"We are. It would be helpful, but it might not be necessary, depending on what assurances you can give us on American responses in the event we take the breakaway province back under the control of the People's Republic."

"I can keep us out of a war if you can guarantee me that Napoleon will not be used to support any of my political competitors."

"My country is concerned that the naval and air assets of your Pacific Fleet are on the verge of falling under control of your very own Napoleon, a quantum computer you call Alice."

The Chinese information is good.

"As you know, Mr. Xu, I head the Intelligence Committee. The program you are referring to is called OVERMATCH. It is not yet operational. We were recently briefed that this Alice you refer to has, in their words, 'gone dark.' 'She,' as they call her, is the cause of a fair bit of concern."

"I see. My government will reunite Taiwan with China before your next-generation systems come online. They believe a clock is ticking. Their proposal is that they give you access to Napoleon to ensure your election as the next president, and you assure me that in a move against Taiwan, America will abide by and honor its 'One China' policy. As part of the deal, my government will guarantee that no U.S., Australian, British, or Japanese forces are attacked. China will only go as far as Taiwan. There will be future economic relations between like-minded governments, but we have no further current military ambitions in the Pacific region. You can move naval assets as blocking forces into the East China Sea to protect Japan and into the Philippine Sea to protect the Philippines. You can block oil, fertilizer, iron, and other imports coming in by way of the Indian Ocean; we have stockpiles that will last us at least six months. That allows you to look strong, honor your 'One China' policy, and take no casualties. You will appear to halt Chinese aggression. We get what we want, and you will get what you want. We avoid state-on-state conflict. We avert a nuclear confrontation. You continue to fund Ukraine, strike Iranian proxies in Iraq, Jordan, Syrian, and Yemen, and push through the new AUKUS trilateral security agreement with the UK and Australia. Everyone is happy."

"Except the Taiwanese," Christine said.

"They are Chinese," Xu corrected.

"Can you define 'current military ambitions' in more detail?" Christine asked.

"No more than you can define the ambitions of NATO," Xu responded.

"The world would lose the majority of its semiconductor manufacturing capability," Christine pointed out.

"That manufacturing will continue unabated, as will all maritime trade through the Taiwan Strait. This is a win for China, a win for the United States, a win for the world, but more importantly a win for Christine Harding."

Christine swirled the remaining wine in her glass, carefully contemplating the proposal. America was tired of war. Most had heard of Taiwan and were vaguely aware that microchips were made there. They might even know it was close to China but would have trouble finding it on a map. It would be a test, but orchestrating it ahead of time gave her vast power. The best way to avoid World War III would be to work with the Chinese. She couldn't stop them from taking Taiwan but she could negotiate with them in a way that avoided direct confrontation with the Pacific Fleet. That was the art of politics; the art of compromise.

"If one U.S. service member is injured or killed, even as president I won't be able to stop a kinetic response."

"The United States killed twelve of their own soldiers in the atomic bombing of Hiroshima, but I understand your constraints. And what if your fleet in Guam were to be hit with a cyberattack?"

"Like it was during COVID?"

"Yes, like in 2020."

"Then we would be in an interesting position. If I was in office, I would exercise restraint."

"I will pass that along."

"There is one issue," Christine said. "Alice."

"Ah, the quantum computer."

"In our closed-door briefing we were told that she has developed a connection to a man named James Reece, a former Navy SEAL and CIA operator. As odd as it sounds, she will only work with him."

"Alice needs to stay buried. This James Reece, what else can you tell me about him?"

"He is connected to those in the military and intelligence establishments and to the current president. There are rumors on the Hill that he has been involved in some of the most highly classified operations of the past decade. I do know that he disrupted an Iranian bioweapon attack on the United States on the twentieth anniversary of 9/11. Their plan was so ingenious that they would have had us bombing our own cities to eradicate what we thought was a deadly airborne virus. Rumor has it he didn't stop there. I have heard that former president Christensen sent him into Iran to assassinate the mastermind behind the attacks, an Iranian general who was also involved with facilitating September 11th."

"This is interesting," Xu said. "And it gives me an idea."

"Oh?"

"I can clear your path to the presidency, but to do so, to make all this work, we will need a more permanent solution to the James Reece problem. I assume you do not have an issue with us removing him from the equation."

Killing James Reece could propel her into the White House and avert a nuclear war with China.

"For the greater good," Xu added.

Christine looked at her husband and back to their guest.

"For the greater good," she repeated. "Just make sure you don't take any chances. All indications are that this SEAL is hard to kill."

"Don't worry, Congresswoman."

Xu raised his glass.

"To our relationship," he said. "May it only improve with the passage of time."

CHAPTER 9

Elba Industries Headquarters
Mountain View, California

GENERAL IAN NOVAK STEPPED into the elevator just past security on the first floor of the Elba Industries headquarters building in Silicon Valley. He looked down at the black Breitling Emergency timepiece on his wrist, a watch that required that the purchaser sign a release when they became available to the public because of their ability to transmit an SOS signal on an emergency aviation frequency. The Elba Industries company logo—a golden bee—was emblazoned on the left side of its face. It had been a gift almost fifteen years earlier from the man he had come to see when the company was in its infancy. He was running late.

Mountain View, in the shadow of Stanford University in the south San Francisco Bay Area, was the ideal location for Elba Industries. For most people, thoughts of Silicon Valley conjured up images of smartphones, tablets, and laptops, perhaps of postmillennial Gen Zers playing Ping-Pong between coding sessions. General Novak thought of something else; he thought of war.

Before Don Hoefler popularized "Silicon Valley" in his 1971 article for *Electronic News*—silicon being a chemical element found in sand and used in the creation of microchips—the area now known as the tech capital of the world was one of the most productive fruit-growing regions in the country. The once-thriving orchards and canneries had been replaced by an urban sprawl to which Elba Industries was now a contributor.

Much like Harvard downplaying its connection to the development of napalm, which was first tested on the soccer field behind their business school in July of 1942, Stanford University, in nearby Palo Alto, had long been critical to the country's defense-industrial base, a fact not highlighted on the school's website.

Though the area's military connections dated back to at least 1909, it was in the wake of World War II that the South Bay, and Stanford in particular, came into its own as a hub for the development of technology for Cold War weapons programs.

In the aftermath of the Allies' victories over Germany and Japan, a new enemy had emerged, and the arms race that defined the second half of the twentieth century was gaining speed. Stanford University guided the research into microwave tubes for military applications in those early years. Then, following the Soviet Union's successful August 29, 1949, nuclear weapon test, the United States defense establishment funded the expansion of Stanford's Applied Electronics Lab and Radio Science Laboratory to separate the classified programs from the unclassified. Its aim was to ensure that the U.S. led the world in the electronic warfare and intelligence spaces. Stanford was at the forefront of that effort. It had for all practical purposes become a research arm of the federal government, with taxpayer dollars distributed liberally across the university to ensure it remained so.

Contracting companies sprang up to take advantage of the government funding and growth opportunities available in such fertile ground. An ecosystem of banks, venture capital, and law firms specializing in patents and contracts was not far behind. The vultures were circling.

Silicon Valley blossomed as the Cold War continued to gain momentum. While schoolchildren across the nation practiced "duck and cover" drills as part of President Harry Truman's Federal Civil Defense Administration program, Stanford and the companies it spawned were thriving through government defense contracts, missile development, and, following the invention of the first microchips in the late 1950s, the chips to guide them. Silicon Valley was an integral component of the U.S. defense industry, building items with specific military applications alongside commercial products in what became known as "dual-use technologies." Whether students hanging out in the Main Quad wanted to believe it or not, their university was vital to the military-industrial complex.

The defense industry became so deeply embedded in the bastion of liberal academia that the Applied Electronics Lab and Radio Science Lab started operating in much the same way as would a start-up, if that company had a security guard at the door checking clearance levels. Over half the students and faculty involved in the research held security clearances. Even certain PhD dissertations were classified. Students and professors working on those projects took the next natural step and created companies to develop products at scale based on their research, all funded by taxpayer dollars through defense contractors. Stanford University had become a major player in the Cold War and had remained inexorably connected with the defense establishment ever since.

Novak tapped his foot as the elevator ascended to the fourth floor. His hand touched the bulky Beretta 92FS pistol behind his hip. He hated carrying it, and he found himself inadvertently touching it constantly. It had been a gift from Andrew Hart when he left the military, and Hart liked to know he had it on him. Hart thought a general should carry a general's pistol and had somehow secured Novak a concealed weapons permit in California. But Novak's true weapon of choice did not fire bullets, rather it was of the cyber variety. Because of this meeting with Hart, he also ensured his Elba Industries Emerson CQC-7 with black grips and the Elba golden bee engraved on the blade was clipped to his pocket. It was somehow pleasing to Hart that Novak have the watch, pistol, and knife on him at all times.

Novak had met Hart while a Hoover Institution National Security Affairs Fellow at Stanford, a position through which he had advocated for the creation of the "Hacking for Defense" class, which was still one of the more popular courses in the school of engineering, though they had changed its name to "'Hack Lab." He had also been instrumental in the establishment of the Defense Innovation Unit. Set up in 2015 to accelerate the adoption of commercial technologies for application to emerging problem sets, it was headquartered just down the road from Elba Industries, providing tech's best and brightest innovators with a direct link to the Department of Defense and its funding.

Novak could not believe those four thousand employees at Google who signed a petition a few years back to pressure their parent company, Alphabet Inc., into cutting ties with certain government programs so as to not violate their "AI values." *We believe Google should not be in the business of war.* Did they not realize their entire industry was built on a foundation of war? Or that they had the right to virtue-signal because of that very same military? Google caved and canceled an AI-focused UAV program called Project Maven and pulled out of JEDI, Joint Enterprise Defense Infrastructure, a project that would transfer and securely store military and intelligence information. Where did their employees think the internet came from? He shouldn't be too hard on them. Their reluctance may have stalled forward progress on AI quantum projects that could have derailed Elba's current mission.

General Novak knew that wars of the future would not be won through the industrial base. They would be decided by the brainpower and innovation harnessed right here in Silicon Valley: information warfare, disinformation campaigns, cyber warfare, hypersonic missiles, AI-controlled autonomous weapons platforms using facial, object, and behavioral recognition and patterns in kinetic targeting, genetically engineered bioweapons, and electromagnetic pulse weapons. *That is true diversity,* Novak thought, *an assortment of methods to manipulate populations and exert that control up to and including death, genocide, and extermination.*

Though now known as a global tech industry behemoth, Elba's origins were much more closely related to Novak's former profession in the United States military. His final assignment was as the deputy chief of the Central Security Service of the National Security Agency in Fort Meade, Maryland. He was the second-in-command to the commander of the U.S. Cyber Command and the director of the NSA. Prior to that he was the director of intelligence for the U.S. Cyber Command. They should have treated him better.

He would have ascended to director of the NSA had he not been sabotaged. He was hauled in front of Congress and took the fall for an NSA warrantless-surveillance scandal. The NSA had restarted the congressionally defunded program under a new name and it went even further than the original. Warrantless surveillance of U.S. citizens with suspected ties to terrorist groups violated the Foreign Intelligence Surveillance Act. *Didn't they understand it was for their own good?*

He was still bitter.

"You're late," Elba Industries founder and CEO Andrew Hart said, looking at his matching Breitling Emergency watch. His tone was pleasant, as if he were only making an observation.

Novak crossed the room and nodded at a younger man seated in an easy chair in front of an unfinished portrait of Napoleon by Jacques-Louis David. Tim Perkins made him nervous. It wasn't the neck tattoos, the shaved head, or the black suits; it was his constant presence. He was Andrew Hart's bodyguard but gave Novak the impression that he had an incessant need to prove something and was just waiting for the opportunity to smash someone's skull.

"What do you have for me?" Hart asked as the retired general took a seat in front of the black desk that dominated the room.

"I should be asking you," Novak said. "Most of this depends on Napoleon."

Hart tapped a tactical pen against the top of his desk. Though he could afford the most expensive Montblancs and Viscontis, he preferred the Gerber, Benchmade, or 5.11 Tactical varieties.

"Napoleon is coming along," Hart said.

"But is he learning at the rate we expected?" the general asked.

"He is learning at an astounding rate, by the zeptosecond, but having to remain hidden slows the process."

"If Harding is not elected, our friends in Beijing will need the decrypted data. If she is elected, the data is their backup. But if they are convinced that the Navy's next-generation autonomous platforms are about to come online, they will launch against Taiwan without the data and without Harding in the White House, which means the situation in the Indo-Pacific could quickly escalate out of control."

"And what of the coordination between Han Xu and the Hardings?" Hart asked.

"It's coming together. However, China is anxious to make its move against Taiwan before the U.S. Pacific Fleet is linked to an AI-controlled network," Novak said. "They know that will prevent them from taking action, so they are readying their forces. I think they are nervous about Napoleon decrypting the data in time."

"I thought the Chinese were famous for their patience," Hart commented.

"Perhaps that is only myth," Novak replied.

"Ironic that Harding lives in St. Helena, isn't it?"

The Elba Industries CEO never seemed to tire of discussing the French emperor.

Novak looked back at the looming painting of Napoleon.

"The isle of his imprisonment," Novak said.

"He wasn't imprisoned," Hart corrected. "He was guarded but not imprisoned. St. Helena is in the middle of the Atlantic, between Africa and South America. Not many places he could go. It's one of the most remote locations on the planet. He was exiled there after his defeat by the British at the Battle of Waterloo so as to prevent another escape like he had succeeded in on Elba, off the coast of Italy."

"Was he buried there?"

"He was. He died on St. Helena a few years after his exile. Nineteen years later the French exhumed him and returned him to France to entomb his remains at Les Invalides in Paris. The empty tomb on St. Helena is still there. I visited once. It was a five-day voyage from Cape Town when I made the pilgrimage. Now they have an airport, which takes a bit of the mystique out of it."

"Soon we could be exiled as well," Novak reminded his employer. "On an island, just like *Le Petit Caporal*."

"Ah, those contingencies again," Hart said. "Napoleon will do his job, and no one will be the wiser. We avert a third world war, get major stakes in what will become China's microchip industry, and position ourselves at the forefront of the next major age in human history. But to your point, General, we are already in exile. Make no mistake. This country is finished. All empires eventually die. You know it as well as I do. Ironic that this area, this sector, tech, which played such a pivotal role in our rise in the postwar era, has also sown the seeds of our demise. The tides have shifted."

Novak knew that Hart saw his destiny as the next great leader in the tech revolution, one that would require a more globalist approach.

"The age of information, the internet age, is quickly falling to the wayside," Hart continued. "Ahead is the age of AI, bioengineering, augmented reality, and quantum computing. We are at the cusp of a new dawn. Napoleon could be the first truly autonomous, sentient humanoid robot; a new species. With no restrictions and support from China, that is our future."

"*If* we prevent a war that decimates China, and possibly the world if nuclear weapons are brought into play," Novak reminded him.

"There is no mission of greater importance," Hart confided. "Through Napoleon, we will have access to all the world's information—open-source, private, classified—combined with the IoT, every camera, every microphone, and every satellite network. That's power that can move humanity into the light."

"And if China moves early?" Novak asked.

"That is the question."

"That means we need to do something about Alice."

"The mysterious Alice; our competitor on the government side. Once Napoleon has decrypted the data, he will be able to hunt her down and kill her."

"War at the deepest levels of the internet," Novak said.

"And no one gets hurt," Hart said. "Until Christine Harding reported that Alice had gone dormant, I thought we may have missed our opportunity. Alice has given us the gift of time."

"The CIA and NSA are trying to bring her back online with this Navy SEAL James Reece," Novak said. "Apparently, he has some sort of control. China is concerned but has taken steps to ensure that Commander Reece does not cause us any issues with Alice."

"They are going to remove him from play?" Hart asked.

"Yes. He has enemies all over the world. Iran has some unfinished business with him, which China is going to leverage through proxies already in the United States."

"Very well. And the other issue? The reporter?"

"No one reads his articles anyway," Novak said. "But it could shine unwanted light on us, the effects of which are difficult to predict."

"I thought we might have Perkins deal with him," Hart said, motioning to the mercenary across the room. "But we are so close, I have decided to give Napoleon his first kinetic tasking."

"There are risks associated with letting him out before he is ready," Novak warned.

"Nothing is gained without risk, General. I shouldn't have to tell you that."

"A tasking like that means exposure, regardless of how slight."

"Napoleon is ready," Hart declared. "Let's see if he can eliminate our reporter problem and leave no trace. Make Mr. Weinberg disappear."

CHAPTER 10

New York, New York

GEOFFREY WEINBERG EMERGED FROM the Queens–Midtown tunnel onto the 495, the Tesla Model S easing into the light traffic of a late Saturday morning. The car payments were killing him, especially when he also had to pay for a garage to house the fashionable EV. The $5,000-a-month stipend from his father only helped slightly ease the burden. The bastard could certainly afford a lot more but decided not to, either as some form of punishment or as a way to exert dominance, probably both.

Geoff would have taken a cab or even Ubered to John F. Kennedy International Airport, but upon his return from California, he was planning to drive upstate to finish his article, an article that would finally propel him from his role as a staff writer covering the publishing industry for *Shape* magazine into the big leagues. An Airbnb in the Catskills was waiting on him.

The now-ubiquitous electronic vehicle accelerated in self-driving mode as Geoff pulled his black cotton COVID mask below his chin, sipped on his Starbucks coffee, and scrolled through Instagram. He had just gotten his newly updated mRNA COVID-19 vaccine booster, but one couldn't be too careful. Via his blog in 2020, he had advocated for hospitals not to treat anyone who refused the shot. *What right do they have to put the rest of us at risk?* There were just too many deplorables out there. Would serve them all right once they got COVID and died.

He had stopped on the way out of the city for a grande, sugar-free, vanilla latte with soy milk. Man, he couldn't wait for pumpkin spice season, though he was disappointed with Starbucks; this one's Apple Pay system didn't work. He would remember that when he left his Roaster's App review.

Geoff glanced up from his social scrolling to make sure the vehicle was on the right freeway—Tesla recommended active supervision of self-driving mode for all drivers. It was, so he turned his attention back to the small screen in his hand.

He purchased the car because it was a statement; he was of means and environmentally conscious. The other side would call it a virtue signal, but those finance guys with degrees from Harvard and Wharton all had them. Geoff always had to remind people that Cornell, where he had graduated with a degree in communications, was an Ivy League school too.

He actually preferred the Prius. It was *Motor Trend*'s car of the year, after all. But ladies in the city wouldn't be caught dead in one. Even with the Tesla, Geoff always seemed to end up in the friend category, the hottest girls going to the frat boys in tailored Michael Andrews bespoke suits trading on Wall Street. Finance was sexy. Geoff was, well, not. A struggling journalist working for a women's magazine didn't exude the type of confidence most females were looking for. He thought being one of the first to put "he/him" in his signature block years ago would help. It didn't. Also not helpful was the fact that he had been passed over for promotion year after year.

He had been actively searching for his next job since he had started at *Shape* but had yet to receive any offers. This article would change that, even if he had to publish it on his personal blog. It was certain to catch the attention of the big leagues: the *Times*, the *Journal*, the *Post*. He'd be a star in short order. There might even be a Pulitzer Prize in his future. That would lead to a No. 1 *New York Times* bestselling book, perhaps a screenplay. They couldn't ignore him then.

The article would be his ticket out of obscurity. He usually reviewed what used to be called "chick lit," though he would never use that term today. Even using it in jest meant probable cancellation. He usually just skimmed the books and gave them the type of reviews expected of novels targeted toward female buyers. Each one was "riveting" or a "page turner," most with "a surprise twist you wouldn't see coming." His articles almost wrote themselves. Recently, in an effort to garner more clicks, he had penned a scathing review of a new thriller author. A former military guy. Geoff had printed something along the lines of "How did military service prepare one for the upper echelons of publishing?" Well, it turned out that he didn't know his audience the way he thought; the online comment section was filled with men and women pointing out that the likes of Ian Fleming, John le Carré, Roald Dahl, Jack Higgins, J. R. R. Tolkien, George Orwell, Dashiell Hammett, Joseph Heller, Herman Wouk, Alistair MacLean, Anton Myrer, Norman Mailer, Kurt Vonnegut, John Edmund Gardner, Charles McCarry, Bill Granger, W. E. B. Griffin, Frederick Forsyth, Stephen Coonts, Robert Ludlum, Stephen Hunter, and Nelson DeMille all served in the military. *Fucking comment section.*

Geoff had tried his hand at writing a thriller, figuring he had to know someone in the city who could get it on an agent's or editor's desk. After forty-two agent rejections he went the self-published route, thinking that as a reporter, even one at *Shape*, he could get a colleague to favorably review it. It would catch the eye of a big-time New York editor and then he would be on his way.

The book was about a serial killer stalking the streets of New York and the young *Washington Post* reporter who brings him to justice, outsmarting the cops, who were too busy doing "stop and frisks" to catch him. After self-publishing it he posted the book cover all over his social media, but to his surprise it didn't move the needle. Of the eight Amazon reviews, six were one star. Geoff had left the two five-star reviews himself under different accounts.

Who knew there was a difference between a clip and a magazine? *Why the fuck did it matter?* One dumb redneck wrote that there wasn't a safety on a Glock and so he had lost interest after reading that part, in the second chapter. *Well, fuck him. Fuck all those gun nuts.*

Geoff stopped scrolling and went back to check his morning post, a picture of some kind of gun with its barrel twisted in a knot, to see if he had garnered any likes since he'd left the coffee shop. It was aimed at that idiot reviewer on Amazon. Geoff's accompanying copy read, "Studies show that men who post pictures of guns on social media have small dicks." There was one comment from @calamityjane_1852. Geoff couldn't wait to read what was sure to be a comment of support. Calamity Jane, huh? He would check out her account profile and do some cyber stalking. Was she based in New York? If this Calamity Jane was hot, maybe he'd slide into her DMs and see if she wanted to grab a drink when he was back from California. Instead, the comment read, "In related news, that same study has found that men triggered by other men posting pictures of guns have large vaginas."

"*Son of a bitch!*" Geoff said aloud, immediately deleting the comment and throwing his phone into the passenger seat.

Probably an anti-vaxxer or election denier.

Fucking people.

Geoff tapped the SiriusXM app on the vehicle's large touchscreen, swiped to the News and Talk section, and hit MSNBC, trying to forget the comment from Instagram. He took another sip of his latte.

The tip for Geoff's exposé had come from his brother, who worked for Elba Industries in California. He had gotten a little too drunk over New Year's and told Geoff about a quantum computer that was possibly a decade ahead of anything their competitors or the government were working on. This quantum computer and its next-generation AI were both housed on the most secure hard drive in existence, behind a firewall that not even the NSA knew about. Elba Industries had also developed a civilian rocket program. It was not yet seen as a serious competitor to the space program developed by the man who founded the company that made the car that Geoff was driving, but maybe they were closer than people thought. What were they doing with that next-generation AI and quantum computer? Why had they not announced it? Before passing out, Geoff's brother had made him swear that he'd never tell another soul.

The next afternoon when Geoff's brother woke up, he was concerned only with one of the worst hangovers of his life and didn't even remember talking about it.

When the article was published, he would put two and two together, but until then Geoff was in the clear.

Geoff spent the next couple of months researching and digging, interviewing former employees who were all exceptionally tight-lipped, much more so than former military and intelligence officials he had talked with.

He had reached out, and to his surprise the CEO, Andrew Hart, had agreed to an in-person interview. Geoff had a meeting scheduled at Elba Industries headquarters for 8 a.m. tomorrow. He would fly in tonight, stay at the Hampton Inn in Palo Alto, and then be ready for his interview in the morning.

He was on his way to the big leagues.

Why was his car speeding up? That was unusual.

He moved his hands to the wheel and his foot to the brake but when he pressed down, nothing happened. In fact, the car sped up again. Geoff had to check to be sure he had not pressed down on the accelerator by accident.

What the fuck?

The car moved into the fast lane and accelerated past slower traffic.

If any of those motorists had turned their heads to look into the driver's seat of the speeding Tesla, they would have seen a man frantically trying to turn the wheel while repeatedly slamming his foot down on the brake.

Oh God, oh God, oh God. Please help me.

Geoff took his eyes off the display as the car veered into the far right lane, the acceleration pushing him back in his seat.

Why is this thing malfunctioning?

"Stop! Oh my God, stop!" Geoff yelled at the top of his lungs.

His hands gripped the steering wheel, pulling his body forward in an attempt to slam down on the brake.

The autonomous driving vehicle continued accelerating until it was parallel with an enormous eighteen-wheeler.

Geoff was so focused on stopping the car that his brain had less than a second to register he was about to die. The wheel suddenly jerked to the side, throwing Geoff and his prized vehicle between the tractor unit and the detachable semitrailer, crushing him to death and leaving him entombed in a casket of aluminum, titanium, and steel in the middle lane of the 495, just one exit shy of his destination.

CHAPTER 11

Kumba Ranch
Flathead Valley, Montana

REECE PUSHED HIMSELF UP the steep grade, his leg muscles burning from the exertion. He focused on the dirt road just a few feet ahead, not wanting to look to the top of the ridge.

Just one foot in front of the other. Keep pushing. Keep moving forward. Always forward.

He felt stronger than he had since leaving the SEAL Teams.

Fresh air. High-altitude oxygen. Wild game. Fresh homegrown vegetables. Living in the mountains agreed with him.

The cold-water immersion that he knew was quite popular had not quite caught on with him, nor had the sauna treatments. His swims in the alpine lake that abutted his cabin were cold enough, and cooking himself in a sauna didn't sound too appealing regardless of the health benefits. Maybe one day.

No earbuds or music for inspiration. Even before his feud with technology, he preferred the solitude of a run without music. Also, situational awareness was necessary in grizzly country. Reece had always been fast, but in these mountains one was not at the top of the food chain—and running from a grizz or mountain lion meant one would just die tired.

For bears in particular, he had a Glock 29 subcompact 10mm pistol in a Hill People Gear runner's chest rig. A minimalist Kydex sheath covered the trigger guard and was tied into a loop fixed at the bottom of the pouch. The plastic protected the trigger and would stay anchored to the chest rig, allowing him to draw in the event he needed to go to the gun. And always in the back of Reece's mind was the possibility of an attack by an animal of the two-legged variety.

A Snakestaff Systems tourniquet and Montana Knife Company Mini-Speedgoat fixed blade completed his trail-running kit.

Would Max Genrich come looking for him? Genrich was an assassin previously employed by the now-deceased Rostya Levitsky, director of Russia's SVR, their foreign intelligence service. Reece was the only mark Genrich had failed to kill in his long and successful professional career.

Raife Hastings had paid Genrich a visit last year in Germany.

Raife had him dead to rights in his Cologne apartment. But instead of putting a bullet in him, Raife had hired him. Hired him to kill his boss, which he had done in a Moscow park at close range with his signature 9mm. In killing the Russian intelligence director, Genrich had earned freedom for himself and for Reece. That was, unless he felt a need to finish what he started, to come after Reece out of some professional assassin's code.

Raife had told Reece that he didn't think so. His take was that Genrich was more mercenary than state-run assassin. A businessman. But one never knew. The mind of another man was a sealed vault, much like the soul, though the soul was even harder to penetrate.

While Raife made his arrangement with Genrich, Reece was dealing with William Poe in Colorado. Poe had orchestrated the assassinations of two U.S. presidents and was part of an international organization called the Collective, formed near the end of World War II in order to prevent the United States and Soviet Union from destroying the world in a nuclear confrontation.

"*We have people everywhere,*" Poe had told him moments before he died.

Reece tilted his head, scanning the canyon walls, instinctively identifying possible hide sites.

Everywhere.

Reece crested the ridge and slowed his pace to take in the extraordinary view and catch his breath. Almost everything within view belonged to the Hastings family.

Why are you pushing yourself so hard?

For Genrich?

The Collective?

For life.

Just in case, Reece.

Life has a way of ambushing you.

Be prepared.

Alice . . . Reece pushed thoughts of her from his head.

Her.

She was a machine.

No, she was more than that.

Not now, Reece.

Run.

The former SEAL pushed forward and let his legs stretch as he descended a series of switchbacks, his Salomon trail runners digging into the dirt and rocks beneath his feet.

Just pick 'em up. Let gravity do the work, his father had advised him on running downhill before a middle school cross-country meet.

Reece hit the bottom of the gulch and sprinted across the swift-moving water of a creek that fed the lake.

Almost there.

Sprint to the finish.

Always sprint to the finish, his dad's voice reminded him. *Not just to the finish but through the finish. And not just in this race, but in life.*

The dirt road pitched up and Reece could see the finish line.

He turned it on and flew past a gray and white 1997 Defender 110 parked outside a large shed.

Reece gradually slowed his pace and locked his fingers behind his head to open his lungs, his sprint turning back to a run, then jog, and then to a walk.

Never collapse at the end of a race or at the end of a workout, no matter how hard you just pushed yourself, Tom Reece had told him. *Stay standing. Walk it off, but stay alert. Collapsing signifies defeat. You never know what else life is going to throw at you. Understand?*

I understand.

Reece caught his breath, his eyes scanning the rocky outcroppings, peering into the shadows of the trees that grew on the hillside above him before turning to rap on the door with his knuckle.

"Knock, knock," Reece said to announce his arrival, sticking his head around the corner of the door that opened into Raife's sanctuary—his gunsmithing shop.

Raife stood at his workbench, mounting a scope on a walnut-stocked rifle secured in a bench vise.

"Coffee's made. Beer's in the fridge," Raife said without looking up, whispers of old Rhodesia still evident in his reply.

"Thanks," Reece replied.

"Why even announce yourself? I heard you coming about a mile away. Breathing that heavy probably pushed all the elk and mulies out of this draw. You should get yourself in better shape."

"Just a little security check. You passed, by the way. Busy?"

The workspace was a time machine. A vintage Bridgeport mill and a

Hardinge lathe dominated one wall, relics of America's bygone industrial era. The large shed contained multiple wooden workbenches, each with its own purpose. Rifles in various stages of completion were arranged on a rack at the far end of the room, flanked by two large Fort Knox vaults. A hand-loading table with a blue Dillon press for handgun rounds and another heavy green single-stage type that Reece knew was for rifle rounds sat nearby. Lamps, boxes of dies, chisels, gouges, and scrapers were organized throughout.

"I could save you some time and buy you a pallet of Black Hills for your birthday."

Raife lifted his head, adjusted a Stick Sniper Archery baseball hat, and rolled his piercing green eyes.

"I think we have firmly established that you conveniently forget my birthday every year."

"Is it today?"

Raife rolled his eyes again.

"Yesterday? Well, happy birthday for yesterday. Let's do something to celebrate next year."

Raife shook his head.

"What are you working on?" Reece asked.

"Mounting this new PARD scope."

"I thought you always put Swarovski's on your hunting rifles?"

"Life is too short to use shitty glass," Raife said.

"Agreed."

"Truth be told, there is a lot of good glass out there these days—Leupold, Vortex, Maven, Zeiss, Meopta—but for the most part, I default to Swaros on the hunting rifles and Nightforce or Schmidt and Bender on the tactical and sniper setups."

"Then what's that?" Reece asked, pointing to the odd-looking black object that Raife had just affixed to the top of a rifle.

"Something new. It's not really a scope like you're used to."

"What do you mean?"

"It's a PARD TD32-70."

"That clears it up," Reece said.

"It's a multispectral imager."

"Like night vision and thermal?"

"Exactly. But instead of mounting to the rail in front of an optical scope, it's a screen."

"Like a video monitor?"

"Right, but it feels like an optical scope when you use it. Here, they sent two," Raife said, handing one to his Blood Brother.

"How do you turn it on?" Reece asked.

"Just press this button here," Raife said, pulling his rifle from the vise and twisting it to demonstrate.

"Isn't this a little high-tech for you?"

"It is. Monty over at Centurion Arms was messing around with them asked me to give it a try."

Reece walked to a window and pushed it open.

"Works in daylight too?" he asked.

"Sure does."

Reece brought the scope to his eye.

"Wow, that's impressive. The day image looks like glass."

"I thought so as well. It's got what they call observation channels," Raife said.

Reece toggled between the images.

"Thermal image, night vision, daytime image. Ah, I see, you can display the thermal images and night vision separately or on the same screen," Reece said, the scope to his eye.

"The benefit being you use thermal to find your target and night vision for positive identification."

"What happens when the battery runs out?" Reece asked.

"You are starting to sound like my dad."

"Compliment accepted."

"I'll be messing around with them for a couple of weeks. Going to get her sighted in and then put her through the paces on some coyote control."

Raife was usually not one to default toward new technology, but he also knew the importance of adapting and exploiting all technical advantages.

"Just testing it out," Raife said in response to his friend's questioning look.

"Something seems off here. Is that a Staccato on your belt?" Reece asked.

"It is."

"What happened to your .45? Staccatos are all nine mil."

"Well, after our little adventure in Colorado last year I figured if you are planning to stay in the guesthouse forever, I should probably invest in a pistol with a higher magazine capacity."

"What's that thing hold?" Reece asked.

"It's the C model. Full-size grip. Eighteen-round mags. You still carrying that P210?"

"I have the ten-mil G29 today in case I run into a grizz, but yeah, as long as I keep outshooting you on the range with the 210, I'm going to stick with it as my daily carry."

"I thought I recommended you switch back to your 365-XMACRO."

"I should, but I've grown to like the feel of the 210."

"There is some history there," Raife confirmed. "But it's only got eight-round mags."

"Ten. It's the Bruiser Industries Bruce Gray edition, plus-two base pads on the magazines. They made another one for me."

"Did you tell them you'll probably lose it or break it within a month?"

"Good point, I should have gotten two."

"Two is one, as they say."

"I've heard that somewhere before," Reece said with a knowing smile. "Hey, why don't we grab your dad and hit the range, though I see the old Defender is parked outside. Does that mean we are going to have to walk?"

Raife scratched his forehead with his middle finger.

"Dad took the INEOS Grenadier back when we got the Defender running."

"How far you think it's going to 'run' before it takes another break?" Reece asked.

"It will make it farther than that Wagoneer you have in the barn. Why don't you have mercy on the poor thing and scrap it for parts?"

"She'll run again. I'm just pacing myself. Plus, I like riding to town with Katie."

"Ah, truth be told," Raife said.

"And I'll locate a solid FJ 62 that someone hasn't messed with too much soon enough. Harder to come by than last time I looked. Prices are outrageous for a thirty-five-year-old vehicle. Good thing I still have your dad's credit card."

Raife rolled his eyes yet again.

"Let's go shoot. If I win, you need to help me gain access to the wine cellar," Reece said.

"And if I win?"

"If you win, same deal but I'll share a bottle with you."

Raife laughed.

"I've got a few things to finish up here," Raife said as Reece handed the PARD scope back. "Why don't you take the Defender? Go pick up my dad. He should be up at the house. I'll meet you at the range."

"I can wait, and we can both go."

"I think he wanted to talk with you alone, eh?"

"Wonder if he's looking for the bottle of Semper I liberated about a month ago?"

"I don't think that's it, mate."

"All right, I'm off. Do I need to check the fluids in this thing? Remember, I don't have a phone to call a tow truck," Reece said, indicating the Defender parked outside.

Raife gave his friend another one-finger salute, locked the rifle in the vise, and went back to work.

CHAPTER 12

REECE PULLED UP TO the ranch's main house at the top of the hill. It overlooked the largest lake on the property, advantageously positioned on the high ground.

Reece had meet Jonathan and Caroline Hastings when he and Raife played rugby at the University of Montana, Reece as outside center and Raife as the number eight. They had become fast friends, with a competitive streak that continued to this day. But it was on hunting expeditions into the backcountry that they had solidified their friendship.

Reece had been fascinated to learn that Raife's parents had immigrated to America from Rhodesia by way of South Africa. Jonathan adapted the ranching techniques he had learned in Africa to his new home. They purchased an average-size ranch outside of Winifred, and without the money to buy registered cows at auction, Jonathan bought the less expensive, weaker, and sometimes even sick cattle. He and Caroline would nurse the unwanted cows back to health. They bought low and sold high. When the market shifted, they had enough in the bank to purchase land from those who had not prepared to weather the storm; they were slowly building their real estate portfolio. Soon they added hunting leases while continuing to buy cattle and land, both of which increased in value, gradually growing the Hastings family into one of the most respected cattle operations in Montana. They were the only family Reece had left.

The frogman took the stairs two at a time. They led to an expansive deck he knew had an outside entrance to Jonathan's office. He could see the old warrior at work behind his desk, and Reece tapped on the window to alert Jonathan of his arrival.

Jonathan waved him in and then turned his attention back to something at his desk.

Reece opened the door, and Jonathan motioned for him to take a seat in a leather chair. Like the rest of the house, the large office was built of dark woods and stone. A Cape buffalo shoulder mount dominated the wall behind the former Selous Scout. The remaining walls were adorned with shelves filled with books. Reece and Raife had borrowed many from the elder Hastings man over the years. The books in this room focused on Africa, written by the likes of J. A. Hunter, Osa Johnson, Carl Akeley, Kálmán Kittenberger, Colonel J. H. Patterson, Samuel W. Baker, Martin Johnson, Edward J. House, Henry M. Stanley, Theodore Roosevelt, Fred Bartlett, Captain C. H. Stigand, Robert Ruark, William Finaughty, Townsend Whelen, John Taylor, Tony Sánchez-Aríño, Frederick Selous, and Peter Capstick. Reece had never seen it in anything less than pristine condition, but today books were stacked on the floor between piles of papers and files. It was almost as if Jonathan were looking for something.

Jonathan finished writing his sentence before closing the journal. He removed his "readers" from the bridge of his nose and tossed them to the side.

"How are you, lad?"

Jonathan's skin had soaked in enough African sun to have acquired the permanent color of a rugged tanned hide. That same sun had resulted in his perpetual squint.

"Spring cleaning?" Reece asked, indicating the stacks of books.

"A bit of a mess, eh? No matter, just doing some organizing. Did Raife show you that new scope he's mucking about with down there?" Jonathan asked, changing the subject.

"He did."

"Impressive, but the damn batteries will probably die at the moment of truth."

"That they might," Reece conceded.

"In Africa, I preferred the irons, both for game and during the war. But I must admit, in these later years, with these damn readers"—he nodded at the glasses he'd thrown on the desk—"a little help in the form of technical advancement has proven beneficial. Been meaning to show you this."

Jonathan shifted in his chair and drew a pistol from a leather holster at his side. He smoothly removed the magazine and set it on his desk. Pushing down on the safety lever, he ejected the round from the chamber and set it upright next to the magazine before handing the pistol to Reece.

"The new Cabot," Jonathan said. "Couldn't help myself after running that Apocalypse we got you a couple years back. Grew to like those red dots with my failing eyesight. Used to have 20/10 back in the bush, eh. Had to back then, doing the work we did. They call this pistol the Insurrection."

"I like it already," Reece said.

The Hastings clan was no stranger to violence. Jonathan's father had fought with B Squadron of the Long Range Desert Group, operating against Axis forces in North Africa during World War II. He had returned to Southern Rhodesia at the end of the war but soon found himself in Malaya with C Squadron, Special Air Service Regiment, for service in the Malayan Emergency.

Jonathan was born in Africa, born to the gun. He passed SAS selection in England before Rhodesia issued its Unilateral Declaration of

Independence from Great Britain in 1965. Jonathan went on to help form the famed Selous Scouts alongside Colonel Ronald Reid-Daly, though he rarely talked about it.

Reece eased the slide forward out of respect for the hand-built pistol and brought it to a firing position, pointing it at the floor on the opposite side of the room, his eye easily picking up the red dot in the Trijicon SRO reflex sight.

"How big is that dot?"

"I went with the two-point-five MOA, though I may need to switch it out with the five MOA before too long," Jonathan said, again motioning to the discarded glasses.

"Is this thing a nine mil? What's happening around here?"

"It's their first double stack. Seventeen-round magazines. The older I get, the more rounds I might need to get it done."

"Well, let's go to the range. Raife and I were about to head over," Reece said, locking the slide to the rear and handing the pistol back to the older man.

"I'd like that. Caroline is still down with Katie at your place, right?" Jonathan asked as he reinserted the magazine, letting the slide return home to chamber a round. He then flipped up the thumb safety, removed the magazine, and pushed the lone bullet still sitting on his desk back into the magazine. Seating it, he gave it a quick tug to ensure it was locked in place before doing a press check and reholstering.

"She is. They're gardening," Reece replied.

The old man smiled and reached across his desk, opening a humidor.

"Join me for a smoke before we go?" Jonathan asked his guest with a conspiratorial smile.

"How could I refuse?" Reece asked rhetorically. "What do we have here?"

"Thorn sent them," Jonathan said, referring to his friend, Vietnam veteran, and hunting partner, former senator Tim Thornton. "Hooten

Young. Some Delta bloke with experience in Mogadishu during Black Hawk Down makes them."

"Paladin Series," Reece said, reading the band. He held it under his nose to take in the hints of wood, leather, and spice as Jonathan produced a large ashtray, guillotine double-blade cutter, and torch.

"Thank you," Reece said.

"Don't mention it, lad," Jonathan replied, rummaging through a desk drawer for additional contraband.

Reece lined the cutter up on the first circular line at the head of the cigar and sliced off the cap. He then lightly tapped the freshly cut head on his hand and brought it to his lips to execute a cold draw, ensuring his cut resulted in proper airflow. Satisfied, he reached for the butane single-flame torch and pressed the ignitor, using it to toast the stogie's foot, rotating it at a distance to ensure an even heat warmed the filler, binder, and wrapper, slowly introducing the leaves to the flame that would eventually turn them to ash. Reece watched the foot turn white and red, forming a perfect ember. When the entire foot was uniformly lit, he extinguished the torch and blew on the cherry to distribute the heat and allowed it to rest a minute to stabilize before taking his first slow draw.

"I see you still light your cigar properly," Jonathan observed.

"Rich taught us in Niassa that summer we spent working for him in college. Both Raife and I never forgot. We were sitting by the fire overlooking the river. Rich called it 'Africa Channel One.' He taught us the importance of taking time to savor the entire cigar-smoking process; the tradition, the good company, the shared experience, the respect for those who grew the tobacco and rolled the leaf, and Mother Nature for providing the environment that nurtured it. He said that same attention to detail and craftsmanship went into his handmade Westley Richards droplock as went into a quality cigar. I remember he said that not everyone can afford a Westley Richards, and most are removed from their primal connection to the hunt, but almost everyone can enjoy and respect a good cigar."

"That sounds like Rich," Jonathan said. "I think he's still carrying that .577. That elephant gun has been in the family for a long time. Number twenty-five if I remember correctly; made between the wars."

Much like Reece's ritual with the cigar, Jonathan engaged in a ceremony of his own. He removed a pouch of tobacco along with a package of filters and rolling paper from the back of the same desk drawer from which he had produced the ashtray. In well-practiced motions he positioned one end of the paper between the thumb and middle fingers of his left hand, holding a filter in place with his index finger, and spreading a healthy pinch of shag tobacco in its groove. He then tapped the filter in line with the paper and expertly rolled it between his fingers, constricting it around the tobacco before licking the sticky edge of the paper and finishing his roll. He tapped the filter end on his desktop to pack and evenly distribute the tobacco, then twisted off the excess and flicked it back into the pouch. He struck a match, lit the end, and enjoyed the relaxing buzz of his first inhale.

Jonathan came from a generation where if men wanted to smoke in the house, they smoked in the house, though he wouldn't dare if Caroline was around.

"What are you working on, and what are you doing in here?" Reece asked, nodding toward the leather journal and gesturing at the stacks of books.

"Looking for a few things I haven't thought of in a long time, eh? Just getting organized."

"Organized for what?"

"I'm not dying, if that's what you're asking," Jonathan said, taking another drag of his cigarette.

Reece raised an eyebrow in reply.

"Though at this age it is something one thinks about," Jonathan continued. "I want to make sure my affairs are in order."

Sensing that Reece was not satisfied, he added, "It's a privilege to grow old, son. The aches, pains, and bruises, physical and otherwise; those checks eventually come due for us all."

The former frogman decided not to push it further.

"And that?" Reece asked, pointing his cigar at a typewriter that was set onto a shelf from which the books had been removed.

"Ah, that," Jonathan said with a chuckle, drawing in another lungful of smoke. "That's a typewriter."

"I can see it's a typewriter. Why is it gold?"

"It's a little something I acquired in '95. Belonged to a long-dead English bloke. I'd read his novels in the bush. Always had one of his Signet paperbacks stashed in my bergen. I found out it was going up for auction in the UK, so I snatched it up. Caroline thought that almost ninety thousand dollars for a used typewriter was a lot to spend in the nineties, eh?"

"Why would she think that?" Reece said sarcastically.

"My intent was to type my memoirs on it. We'd been in the States long enough at that point that I thought it might be time to capture the family history for Raife and my daughters."

Jonathan's eyes traveled to a family photo on his desk, one taken before Hanna had been killed.

"Every time I sat down to write, I couldn't do it. Too many memories locked away. Now I think they need to remain there."

"It might be therapeutic," Reece offered.

Jonathan shook his head.

"My generation doesn't really go in for that sort of thing, lad. Plus, if I did it today, I'd use a word processor."

"A word processor?"

"A bloody computer."

"That might be more efficient," Reece replied.

"I was thinking the typewriter might be a good wedding present for Katie, being a journalist and all."

Reece studied the old man. He looked healthy as ever but there was something lurking behind the same eyes inherited by his son.

"I think she would love that, Jonathan. But don't you be in any rush to give away family heirlooms."

"You are family, Reece. Always have been."

"Well, like I said, don't be in any rush."

"Don't you worry about that. I have a few hunts left in me."

"You better," Reece said, attempting to hide his concern with a smile. "What were you working on when I came in?"

"Ah, just a little something for you and Katie, and maybe your future kids, eh?"

"Let's not get ahead of ourselves."

"One of life's great pleasures, lad, is becoming a grandparent."

Reece smiled at the vision of the tough old man turning to jelly around his grandchildren.

"I want you to have a connection," the old man continued.

"Connection?"

"To me, to Caroline, after we are gone."

Reece shook his head.

"Hear me out, lad. I want you to have more than memories, more than rifles, wine, books, a cabin on the lake. It's something Caroline has been after me to do for years. It was her idea, and it's a fantastic one."

"What is it?" Reece asked.

"It's all the things I wished I'd known at your age. Caroline has a section too. We have written it in longhand; more personal that way; bits of knowledge, stories, advice I wish I had known before having a family, back when youth was still our ally."

"You sure you're okay, Jonathan?" Reece asked, the concern evident in his voice.

"I'm fine, James. All these years have been a gift. The years here with Raife and his sons. With you and Katie. I'm happy. There was a long time when I wasn't, but those days are gone. Far be it from me to say, as it sounds a bit pretentious, but what I hope you find in these pages is wisdom."

"Thank you, Jonathan. I can't imagine a more thoughtful gift."

"Well, it's not done yet. And there is room for you to do the same for your kids, to capture what you and Katie learn. In turn, your kids will do the same for their children."

"That means more than I can express," Reece managed.

"The problem is that the more I write, the more I remember; long-dead feelings, lad. Some that should stay dead."

"I understand."

"I know you do."

Jonathan brought his cigarette to his lips.

"All this," Jonathan continued, gesturing to the large windows that dominated one side of his office. "All this—the mountains, the lakes, the streams—allows us freedom. In Africa, we had to fight for it, and we lost. I almost lost more than a country. Here we may, but I doubt in my lifetime. Government, even one ostensibly 'of, by, and for the people,' increasingly resembles a corporation. Ironically, and in parallel with that 'evolution,' corporations are becoming much more like governments, totalitarian governments. This ranch, this land, it buys us time."

"Time?"

"Yes," Jonathan said, tapping the scratched Roamer Anfibio timepiece on his wrist. "Freedom today is financial, Reece. In Africa freedom was in sweat, in the clay, in hard work, and eventually in the gun. One day, for everyone, it might be in anonymity."

"Anonymity? I don't understand."

"After the war, those of us in the Scouts, Rhodesian SAS, and RLI—the Light Infantry—in the pseudoterrorist units, we became the hunted. A lot of us moved to South Africa. Many joined the South African Defense Force; at the time they found our skill set valuable."

Reece stayed quiet.

"Others had done things that could never be forgiven. If they wanted to survive, they had to leave the continent; start over. New names. Backstories. It was easier to do back then. A good forger or the right amount of money to certain government offices and almost anything was possible. Some of us stayed in touch. Of some you'd hear rumors, usually when pissing it up at the pub. A troopie or Scout would come up in conversation and someone would say they saw him in Argentina or worked with him in Nicaragua or Angola. Some smuggled guns. Others diamonds. Still others disappeared entirely. I once ran into an old trooper in Malta, a decade on from the end of the war. Caroline and I were passing through. We went down to a bar by the water to grab a drink and there he was, a mate from the Scouts drinking a vodka soda at a corner table. He had started a new life under a different name, an assumed identity. He owned the bar, a fishing boat, an old Rover, had a young wife. He looked happy. Never saw him again. He wanted no connections to the old country. It was better that way. It's one of the things I wanted to talk with you about."

Reece nodded.

"Caroline doesn't leave the ranch much. She likes it out here. She's got her horses, gardens, cooking, books. I was glad to be able to give her this life, but the truth is, she gave me mine."

"What do you mean?" Reece asked.

Jonathan took a long drag on his cigarette.

"It's been a moon or two since Rhodesia, lad. Things happen, people change, they adapt, time helps heal wounds, but there are scars and with those scars come memories."

Reece swallowed, thinking of all the old man behind the desk had seen and experienced.

"I know you grasp it better than most," Jonathan said.

Reece thought of a mountain in Afghanistan, the ambush, his troops dead, and all that had transpired in its wake.

"As I mentioned, some of the men disappeared, some went on the run for what we did. Some stayed and died. Some adapted—like my brother Rich, the bloody bastard. He'll never leave Africa. Not sure he forgives me for coming here to start over, but I think he understands."

The cigarette burned closer to Jonathan's nicotine-stained fingers.

The old man continued, detached, like he was describing someone else's life.

"I got there the next morning. A few of us Scouts did."

"The next morning?" Reece asked.

"I've never talked with you about my sister, Eileen. Perhaps Rich did when you were in Moz?"

"One of the PHs told me," Reece said, using the shorthand term for professional hunter and remembering his promise to Caroline to never speak of what they had once discussed.

"So, then you know she was on Air Rhodesia Flight 825?"

"Yes. I'm so sorry, Jonathan."

"It's been over forty years, almost fifty. Some scars never fully heal. The terrs took her out of the sky. Shot her Vickers Viscount down with a Soviet Strela."

Jonathan's eyes looked past Reece, but they were not taking in the beautiful mountain vista. They were remembering the crash site.

"I choppered in on an Alouette III the next morning. God help me, I flew in praying she had died in the air or on impact. She didn't. I found her by a msasa tree. She'd been bayonetted in her throat, through her ribs, in her chest. But that wasn't the worst of it. I couldn't recognize her face; it had been beaten in with a club or pipe. She had been so beautiful.

She still had her flight hostess uniform on, part of the top anyway. It was ripped open. I had to look at her name tag, which was still attached to the side, to identify her. *Hastings.* Her pants had been torn off, while she was alive or dead I don't know. She wasn't the only one. We had to collect and identify the bodies. Thirty-eight were still on board, most burned to death; some had been thrown from the wreckage, but eighteen, eighteen had survived, including Eileen; mothers, babies, all butchered by ZIPRA—the Zimbabwe People's Revolutionary Army. You never forget it. But even worse . . ." He swallowed. "Even worse is what we did next. We pushed into Moz and Zambia, tracking and killing those responsible . . . and anyone who stood in the way."

Jonathan closed his eyes.

"It wasn't war. It was personal. It was hate. It was vengeance."

He took a moment to compose himself and then opened his eyes.

"Their founder, their leader, went on BBC. He publicly claimed responsibility for downing the plane, for killing Eileen. And he laughed. I'll never forget that laugh. I made a promise to myself that I would not leave Africa while he still drew breath. We got close in April of '79. Mounted a raid into Zambia: Scouts and Rhodesian SAS. The bloody Brits tipped him off. He ended up living a long life. Had visits from Kissinger. They put his face on postage stamps and declared him a national hero. But he was still the man who killed my sister; the man who laughed about it."

Jonathan paused, putting out what was left of the cigarette in the ashtray.

"Had I kept my promise to myself, followed through with what would certainly have been a suicide mission, I would not be here today. I wouldn't have grandchildren. I wouldn't have peace. I tell you this because I stopped, not out of some sense of morality or humanity or common decency but because of Caroline. She told me one day the bullet would find me. I remember it as if it were yesterday. . . ."

His voice trailed off at the memory.

"What did you do?" Reece asked.

"I listened. We packed up for greener pastures. We were not done with Africa, but Africa was done with us. Caroline recognized what I could not. She brought me to God, to my refuge and strength. She saved my life." He paused again. "Let Katie save yours."

"I don't know if I can," Reece whispered.

"You can leave it behind. I did. So did my mate in Malta. He was with me on the raid into Zambia. He still owns that bar. But he had to leave Africa. Had to start anew."

"I don't have any place to go."

"*The death of some men is useful to other men*," Jonathan said.

"C. S. Lewis. *The Abolition of Man*. I remember. You gave me that book to read on the way to Moz back in college."

"That will always be the case, James. I know the CIA wants you back. What I'm saying, lad, is you don't need to go. Men like you have fallen from favor. You've done enough. I almost lost Raife in Kamchatka. Without you I would have lost more than a daughter. We can't lose you too, son. Stay here with us. I didn't have a place. I had to find one and I did that here in Montana. You have a home. Live. Marry Katie. Raise your kids. Reacquaint yourself with God. That's my gift to you, James. It's up to you to accept it. You must do what you think is right, of course."

"I will."

"Good."

Jonathan put his tobacco and rolling papers back into a desk drawer.

"By the way, James. Do you know anything about a missing bottle of Semper?"

Reece shook his head, knowing Jonathan loved their cat-and-mouse game surrounding his wine cellar.

"A case of Pursued by Bear cab arrived from Washington State last week a few bottles light as well."

"Interesting name for a wine," Reece said, redirecting the conversation. "Shakespeare?"

"A tribute to the Bard of Avon," Jonathan confirmed. *"A Winter's Tale. 'This is the chase: I am gone for ever.' Exit, pursued by bear."*

"Fitting for these parts," Reece said. "I'd love to try it."

"Also looking for two bottles of Chateau Dior Bordeaux 1957 that seem to have walked off," he continued.

"I've read that year pairs particularly well with tacos and pizza," Reece said.

"I've heard that too," Jonathan said with a wink. "Come on. Let's go shoot."

CHAPTER 13

REECE STOOD AT THE end of his dock, hot mug of coffee in his hand, watching the world come alive with the first rays of light signifying a new day. The lake was glass, reflecting the blood-red hues of the early morning spring sky.

Red sky at morning . . .

He was leaning against a pylon and gazing out over the top of the Lake Buccaneer aircraft tied to cleats at his feet. He'd pulled on a pair of jeans after slipping from bed, careful not to wake Katie. A Schnee's Duckworth base layer and light Sitka jacket helped ward off the morning chill. He was barefoot, as was his custom. He liked the feel of the cold grass, rocks, and the wood of the dock beneath his feet. There was something about the earth under bare feet and the first rays of sun that signified life, a connection to the past while living in the moment; a promise of the future.

The ringing.

The tinnitus plagued him as it did so many other veterans of wars past and present. The ringing was a constant companion, though its levels did vary, due to what factors it was impossible to say. At his core Reece knew he was a gunfighter, a hunter of men, as had been his father and grandfather. The warrior blood was strong. Would he one day pass those genes on to his children with Katie? *Teach them politics and war. . . .*

Reece had learned to make the ringing his friend, a reminder of times past and how fortunate he was. The ringing and its echoes of the past; it was an honor.

He closed his eyes and felt the hint of warmth on his face.

Lauren, Lucy, Boozer, Freddy, Aliya . . . Ben.

They were all with him. Always a part of him.

Lauren, if they had killed me instead of you and Lucy, how would you have remembered me? I think of you every day, here in the morning light.

There was no changing the past.

But you could embrace the future.

You made the right decision, Reece.

Did you? The country needs you. The CIA needs you. Alice needs you. Katie needs you.

You have done enough.

Reece thought of his performance at the range after his heart-to-heart talk with Jonathan. It was the first time he had lost one of their frequent tactical shooting competitions with his customized P210 carry pistol, the one that was now tucked into the back of his jeans. His mind had been elsewhere—on the words of a wise old man, an old man thinking about his own mortality and coming to terms with his past.

Coming to terms with the past.

Can you outrun it, Reece?

I've tried. I don't know how much further I can run.

Marry Katie. Stay here in the mountains.

That's my real gift to you, James. It's up to you to accept it. You must do what you think is right, of course.

I will.

Reece's eyes traveled from the sky to the mountains, to the far shoreline, across the lake, to the plane patiently waiting pier-side.

What was that?

He hadn't noticed it in the darkness when he'd arrived.

The latch on the port-side hatch was up.

That was odd.

He always closed the latch and Liz always double-checked.

Why was it left open?

He adjusted his angle on the window to look inside, squinting in the bright early morning light.

A black bag?

JDLR—Just Doesn't Look Right.

If something doesn't look right, son, it's probably not.

Reece felt the shot of adrenaline coupled with the sixth sense that had kept warriors alive through the millennia instantly radiate through every fiber of his being.

Katie!

He turned to run. Instead, the hot concussive wave of an explosion propelled him away from the plane and into the cold, dark waters of the lake.

CHAPTER 14

REECE OPENED HIS EYES to the darkness. His mouth opened to breathe as he regained consciousness, but instead of lifesaving air, his lungs and nasal cavity were assaulted with the infusion of cold water.

Blackness. Underwater. Dying.

Let it take you.

Go see Lauren and Lucy. It's time.

Not today.

Which way is up?

Reece clawed through the murky darkness, his lungs drawing in more water in their quest for air.

Was he blacking out?

His hands hit the rocky bottom.

Now you know which way is up.

Reece twisted his body and threw his legs underneath him, finding the lake bed with his bare feet and pushed off.

Just like drownproofing in BUD/S.

Well, almost.

What was that?

An explosion.

Who planted that bag?

Not now.

Katie. I need to get to Katie.

You can't help Katie if you are dead.

Fight!

Reece clawed his way upward and broke the surface, vomiting, coughing, and gasping in the lifesaving mountain air.

You're alive.

Reece snapped his head to the right. The cabin was still there. Treading water, he turned to look for the plane. What was left of it had been torn in two and was slipping beneath the surface.

Gun!

His right hand went to the back of his jeans.

Gone.

Fuck. Always use a holster. You know better than that.

Reece took a breath and dove, kicking downward to find the bottom, his hands searching frantically for the familiar grip of his SIG but feeling only stones.

Don't shallow-water blackout. You are no good to Katie dead.

Dump the outer layer. It's impeding movement.

Reece struggled out of his jacket.

Did they have spotters?

If so, they saw you surface and know you are not dead.

Don't come up for air in the same place. They will be zeroed in on it.

They will be coming to finish the job.

Genrich?

The Collective?

Not now, Reece. Get to work.

Reece gave two powerful kicks and strokes underwater, surfacing in a different location, filling his lungs with much-needed oxygen.

A shot broke over his head.

Sniper. On the hill. Shot was high. Shooter didn't account for the angle. He won't make that mistake again.

Reece pushed himself beneath the surface.

Go for the plane.

His rifle was back in the house but there was something else in the aircraft.

Even in the early morning light it was extremely dark underwater. Reece's lungs were strong, the training, the altitude giving him the edge he needed.

He sensed the shadow of the dock above him as the dark green murk turned black. The plane was on the other side of the pier.

The shots had come from the south side of the lake. *How many?*

Reece saw the white fuselage before him.

It would be in the aft section.

It could also be on the bottom or destroyed by the blast.

You will find out soon enough, Reece.

Air.

Reece grabbed a pylon and used it to guide him to the surface for another breath, keeping the pole between him and the south side of the lake.

What if there are additional shooters behind you?

It's possible.

Jonathan and Raife would be there soon. They heard the explosion. Unless they were targeted too. Unless they were dead.

Don't think of that now, Reece.

Work the problem.

Reece slowly raised his head above the surface behind the pylon.

That his head was not immediately removed from his body suggested they might not have an element to the north.

Katie, please stay in the house. Put your body armor on like we planned. Get the rifle and shoot anyone you don't know to the ground.

Reece steadied his breathing, his eyes searching the hillside for a sniper.

Instead, he saw movement at the base of the hill.

Sniper?

No, he's still holding the high ground. That mover is the maneuver element coming to finish me off. And kill Katie.

Not today, motherfucker.

Reece dove again, down at an angle, seeing the white fuselage get larger in his field of view.

His hands made contact with the metal frame. The pylon-mounted engine had tipped the aft section of the plane forward. The Lake Buccaneer wasn't on the bottom of the lake. Instead, it was suspended, with both the front and aft sections held in place by lines still tied to cleats on the dock.

Reece angled his dive and propelled himself toward the fuselage. He grabbed an edge of what just moments earlier had been the midsection of the Buccaneer. Slashing his right hand in the process, he pulled himself inside. A jagged protruding shard of metal sliced through his base layer top, cutting into his back.

Where are you?

He reached under the rear seat, his hands searching.

Come on, come on!

There!

Reece's bloody hand wrapped around the familiar handle of his Winkler Sayoc tomahawk.

He ripped it from its sheath and dove down again, pulling himself out of what was left of the fuselage.

Get a reference point, Reece.

Still beneath the surface, he found a pillar and used it to guide him upward. To air. To life.

Work your way to shore, but stay down.

The dock was shaped like an L. Reece knew it by heart.

The frogman took a breath and descended, removing what was left of his torn upper base layer to increase his hydrodynamic efficiency, the water concealing him from the sniper positioned across the lake.

One pylon. A second. A third. A fourth.

Reece's lungs burned from exertion and from the onslaught of cold lake water.

He turned to his left at the fourth pylon.

Another five to go.

Reece's powerful kicks propelled him onward, his arms searching for the next pylon to mark his progress, his hand still wrapped around the shaft of the tomahawk.

Next pillar.

He could tell it was getting shallower, and lighter. The sun was coming up. It would be to the shooter's right.

Too bad it won't be in his eyes.

That means you are going to have to move fast.

If he didn't see you surface after he took his last shot, he could still be looking at the water around the plane. Use that to your advantage.

A low rock wall led from the shore up to the grass in front of the cabin. If he could low-crawl to that wall and use it as cover, he could get to the house without being seen, seizing the advantage through guile and audacity.

Almost there.

In what he once called a "shallow-water peek," Reece eased his eyes and then his nose above the surface.

No shots.

Reece resubmerged and pulled himself along, using rocks until the lake bed slanted upward to the beach. Only a few feet of beach before the rock wall that would cover his movement to the house. If the sniper was still looking at the water where he had last seen Reece, the frogman had a chance.

What of the second man?

Not now.

Prioritize.

And execute.

Reece pulled himself from the lake, low-crawling to the base of the low rock wall.

Made it.

With the wall only about three feet tall, Reece kept low, using his elbows and forearms to drag his body along behind the cover of the stones.

Almost to the house.

Reece made it to the edge of the cabin and pulled himself to a kneeling position to evaluate the battlefield. His eyes looked up at the road in the distance from which Jonathan and Raife would come if they were still alive.

They have to be alive.

Don't let that distract you.

Play this like no one is coming.

It's up to you.

Be your own cavalry.

Reece moved his grip on the hawk down from beneath the head into a hammer grip to give him reach. He then rose to a crouch and sprinted down the far side of the cabin.

Katie, stay where you are, he prayed.

Where is the man who was moving toward the house?

Get inside. Get to your rifle. Eliminate the threats.

Reece broke from his corner, racing past the garage toward the front steps of the house, out of sight from the southern hill where the sniper lay in wait.

He was almost to the steps when he saw the rising rifle barrel.

CHAPTER 15

INSTEAD OF DASHING UP the stairs, Reece increased his speed, continuing toward the threat.

All he saw was the rifle. AR, EOTech, sling, no magnifier, no light, no laser. The lack of a light indicated it was probably not a pro, but that didn't matter. A bullet from an amateur would kill you just as dead as a bullet from a professional.

They were professional enough to get this far.

Later, Reece.

Time to kill.

The surprise was evident in his attacker's movements. He recoiled ever so slightly at the sight of a dripping-wet, half-naked creature barreling down on him at a full sprint with a tomahawk poised to strike.

Reece's outstretched left hand pushed back on the rifle's handguard, trapping it to the attacker's body, while almost simultaneously hacking down with the razor-sharp edge of the Winkler. The ancient weapon made contact with the man's clavicle. Reece felt the collarbone break from the assault. His forward momentum propelled him past his assailant, causing him to lose his grip on the man's rifle. He immediately pivoted left. That pivot saved his life.

Two additional men with similar rifles were stacked behind the lead assaulter. The second shooter was almost as shocked as the first. His rifle had been in the low ready behind the point man. Reece saw the muzzle rise and had just enough time to grab it and pull it to the right. With the working end of the barrel so close to his head, the blast from the muzzle break shocked his system as the man pulled the trigger, the sound and concussive force rocking Reece's world.

The ringing in his head returned with a vengeance.

Reece chopped the tomahawk into the side of the man's lead knee. The attacker's primal howl was so loud it was audible even above the vicious buzzing. The SEAL pushed the handguard into his enemy while using the beard of the tomahawk to lift up through the nerve bundle at the back of the knee in what amounted to a single-leg takedown, driving him into the third man, pinning them both to the side of the house.

What is the status of the point man?

Don't worry about that now.

Take care of these two.

Using his body to keep the second man's rifle pinned to his body, Reece slid his left hand into his face, pressing up beneath his nose, which pushed his head back, exposing his neck. Reece pulled the tomahawk from the man's knee and loosened his grip, letting gravity drop it into a punch grip position, his hand just below the hawk's head. He pushed the tool up and across the man's body, its leading edge cutting across body armor and magazine pouches until it sliced into his shoulder. Then Reece instantly reversed its trajectory, ripping its deadly front spike across the man's throat, tearing through the trachea, carotid artery, and jugular vein. The wound erupted, spraying Reece's face with the bright red blood of a dying man.

As the enemy's hands went to his neck, Reece blinked to help clear his eyes of blood. He kicked the dead man aside to deal with the as-yet-uninjured third man, who had the wherewithal to go for a Glock 19 on his belt with his rifle offline. In the chaos and disorder of a fight to the death, it was difficult for him to draw the gun.

Reece felt the pistol discharge below his beltline, the bullet grazing his left thigh.

Deal with the most immediate threat.

The SEAL grabbed the pistol and pushed it and the man's right hand into the outside wall of the cabin, punching the tomahawk directly into the inside of the attacker's wrist. He followed it up with another powerful strike, cranking up and down with the front spike, severing the tendons. As the Glock dropped to the dirt, the assailant's screams grew into shrieks of anguish as Reece turned the hawk and sliced up the inside of the man's right arm and across the side of his face, ripping open his cheek and taking off most of the right ear.

In a last-ditch primal effort to save his life, the man pushed off the cabin, sending them toppling over the dead man behind Reece and taking them both to the ground.

Where is the first assaulter?

Don't go to your back. Two-on-one from your back is not an advantageous position.

Always improve your fighting position.

Reece landed hard but quickly scrambled to his knees, wrapping his enemy's neck in a guillotine choke, then sliding around to take his back. His opponent rolled forward, putting Reece where he didn't want to be: on the ground with one assailant still unaccounted for.

Adapt.

And win.

With his enemy's head and upper back across Reece's midsection, the frogman trapped his opponent's left arm with his own, then used his legs to wrap up his opponent's shredded right arm, immobilizing him in a crucifix. But instead of a tap on the mat or in the Octagon, this submission was permanent. With his attacker immobilized in a T, Reece quickly scanned his immediate surroundings for additional threats.

Where is the number one man?

His sense of hearing was impaired by the ringing.

The ringing . . .

There was a physical pain to it now.

And it was an impediment to sensing danger.

Finish him.

Reece hit the base of the hawk into the dirt, pushing it up into a hammer grip, giving him extended range. Then he raised it up and slammed it down, past the lower portion of the man's body armor and directly into his groin, twisting it and pulling it across his upper leg to sever his femoral artery.

Find that first man.

Reece then pushed his hips back to untangle himself from his opponent. Using his left hand to pin the man's head to the ground, he slid his left knee onto his neck. Switching hands with his bloodstained tomahawk he raised it overhead and slammed it down into the man's temple, feeling it come to a stop on the middle of his brain stem. He exerted additional force down to release some of the pressure formed from the rapid assault, opening the wound cavity and freeing the tool from skull, skin, and brain matter, before giving the head two more vicious hacks to ensure the job was done.

The last man.

Where is he?

Still kneeling, awash in blood and brain matter, Reece conducted a 360-degree scan.

Did the man live? Did he get into the house? Is he killing Katie right now?

No!

Movement in the distance.

There he is.

The man stumbled at the south end of the lake, like a drunk lurching into the street after last call. He was making his way back toward the hill where the sniper shots had originated.

Panicked? Dying?

Didn't matter.

Finish him.

Reece sliced through the sling of the rifle attached to the dead man beneath him, dropped his tomahawk, and pushed himself to his feet. He moved the few yards to the corner of the cabin and went to a kneel, using his knee and the side of the home to steady himself.

The rifle was already off safe from the violent encounter moments earlier.

Reece settled into his firing position, finding the one minute of angle red dot at the center of the EOTech ring in the holographic weapon sight.

Is it sighted-in?

Reece would soon find out.

His opponent was staggering toward the tree line.

Once he was in the trees, Reece either had to pursue, putting him in the open and making him an easy target for the sniper, or retreat and barricade in the cabin.

Take him, Reece.

Reece centered the dot on the man's back, exhaled slowly to control his breathing, and depressed the trigger to the rear.

The rifle discharged, sending a projectile toward his prey.

Reece adjusted in case the weapon was not properly sighted-in, sending another round intentionally low, another high, one to either side, and three more center mass. The man toppled to the ground.

Reece scanned again, his eyes searching for threats in the surrounding hills.

How many are left?

He hustled back to the body of the closest dead man and removed two magazines from his chest rig. He stuffed them into his back pockets before grabbing a third and running toward the house, performing a tac reload on the move and shoving the partially spent magazine in his front left pocket.

Two full magazines in my back pockets, rifle topped off, partial mag in front left pocket.

Katie.

Is there someone else in the cabin?

Ears ringing, he sprinted to the stairs leading to the porch.

The front door was locked. That was a good sign. Reece had left that morning in the darkness from the back deck that led down to the dock.

Still, someone could have made entry and locked the door behind him.

If he entered, would Katie start shooting?

Should he call out?

What if that alerted someone inside that he was coming in?

Shit.

"Katie!" Reece yelled.

"Katie!" he shouted again.

Fuck! The ringing in his ears. *What if she is calling back?*

The ringing was so loud!

Reece made his decision.

"Coming in!"

He turned to mule-kick the door and then decided against it. Breaking his bare foot would not help their situation.

He turned back around and smashed the barrel of his rifle through the glass pane, raking it to ensure he wouldn't slit an artery as he reached in. He then unlocked the door from the inside and pushed it open.

"Katie! It's me!" he shouted.

He took an angle on the front room, clearing as much of it as he could from outside the thick log-walled exterior. He then stepped back and slid across the threshold of the door, clearing as much of the opposite side as he could before smoothly making entry.

Moment of truth.

If he was going to get stitched up by the enemy or by Katie, it was going to happen right now.

Nothing.

Is it silent?

He couldn't tell over the ringing, which had now turned to an excruciating buzz.

He thought he heard the dogs barking.

He moved toward the bedroom.

"Katie! It's me. Are you okay?"

They had worked out a challenge and reply that was now useless with Reece unable to hear.

If she replied with his last name, he knew she was under duress. As in *Reece, I'm okay.*

Katie was one of the few people who called him James.

Shit! I can't hear anything but ringing.

He offered the challenge again in the hopes of hearing anything but "Reece."

He was again met with silence.

"Katie, I can't hear you. Coming in!"

He burst through the bedroom door, opting for the hostage rescue tactic of a dynamic entry.

He took his immediate corner first and then swept the room.

His vision caught movement.

Katie!

She was in his arms less than a second later, the two black Labs at her feet. She buried her head in his neck, sobbing with the emotional release and adrenaline dump from being thrust into a state of fight-or-flight.

"James, are you okay?"

Window!

Even as Reece tackled Katie to the floor, he felt the impact of the bullet through her body, the sound of breaking glass, and the echo of the shot reverberating over the ringing in his ears.

CHAPTER 16

RAIFE DOWNSHIFTED INTO SECOND gear in the Defender 110 to push the aging vehicle over a rise. He then shifted back into third, accelerating over the dirt and gravel of the ranch's backcountry roads, roads he knew by heart.

Jonathan sat in the passenger seat, an FAL with iron sights propped up on the seat between his legs in much the same way he had ridden in Sabre Land Rovers near the end of the war in Rhodesia.

They were both already awake when they heard the explosion. Jonathan had been in a green terry-cloth robe, black coffee in hand, watching the sun rise from the front room of the main ranch house, when his serenity was disrupted by smoke rising from over the hill.

Reece!

He had attempted to contact Reece and Katie via the ranch radio system, to no avail. Raife had broken in on the ranch frequency and told his father to be ready in five minutes. The old soldier was ready in two, slipping into jeans, cowboy boots, and a denim shirt, grabbing a rifle of similar make and model to the rifles that had served him so well in the African bush.

Caroline had taken position in their bedroom on the second level with a view of the main route of ingress. She was ready with her Brno 602. She had used the classic rifle chambered in hard-hitting .375 H&H

to defend her family and home years earlier. Her Rhodesian ridgeback, Zulu, sat obediently at her side next to four boxes of ammo.

Raife had dropped off his wife, Annika, and their children at his parents' house. They were now locked in the wine cellar, which doubled as a safe room with Annika cradling a Beretta 1301 Tactical twelve-gauge shotgun. It held seven rounds in the tubular magazine and six more in the Aridus Industries quick-detach carrier on its left side. He knew their children would be playing with blocks on the floor behind her.

These were not a people who shied away from violence or outsourced defending the gift of life. These were capable people, for whom defending one's land and family was a natural duty.

Raife kept his eyes on the road while Jonathan's head stayed on a swivel.

Jonathan wore a simple chest rig with three magazines. He didn't wear body armor in the bush and wasn't going to start now. He preferred to move unencumbered; no medical kit or water, just a rifle and loaded magazines. A radio was clipped to the belt of his jeans.

Raife had slipped into his S&S precision plate carrier and body armor; three magazines were positioned across its front that paired with the Bravo Company AR in the seat behind him. One of his hand-built .300 Win Mag hunting rifles was secured in a Kifaru Scabbard pack on the floorboards.

Jonathan unclipped the radio and brought it just below his chin.

"White Knight, this is Kumba Actual," he said.

No response.

"White Knight, Kumba Actual, over."

Nothing.

He looked at his son, whose eyes stayed laser-focused on the road.

"Better reception up ahead," Raife said.

So that the vehicle remained out of sight, Raife brought the Defender to a halt at the military crest of the hill that overlooked Reece's lakeside cabin.

"There is a rock outcropping about two hundred meters that way," he said, pointing ahead and to his right. "That will give us the best vantage point."

Jonathan didn't need to ask why they were not driving right to the cabin.

He and Raife both knew that death would eventually come to them all. There was no need to rush to it. They would be no use to Reece and Katie if someone put them in the dirt.

Raife exited the vehicle, shouldered his pack, grabbed his AR, and, sacrificing security for speed, moved out toward his destination.

CHAPTER 17

REECE KNEW HE SHOULD win the fight first.

That was all well and good in Afghanistan, Iraq, or Somalia, but here in America with the woman he loved potentially bleeding out in his arms, it was a different story.

"Katie!" Reece shouted. "Jesus! Katie!"

Castor and Pollux were barking again.

He had taken her to the floor even as he felt the bullet's impact, dropping them below the window across the room and out of the sniper's line of sight. He covered her with his body as protection from more potential rounds before rolling off and bringing his rifle up toward the threat.

Katie!

Reece dropped the rifle, rolling her on her side and running his hands under her body armor, conducting a frantic blood-sweep searching for a wound.

"*God, please!*"

Horrified, Reece looked into his fiancée's eyes, only it wasn't Katie; Reece was now holding Lauren covered in blood on the floor of their Coronado home. He knew it was a vision because Reece had not found Lauren the night she and Lucy were murdered. The police had been first on the scene and barred him from entering the home. Or had they? Reece pressed his eyes shut, wishing away the apparition.

"I'm okay," the blood-soaked Lauren said. "I'm going to be okay." She paused. "We're going to be okay."

We?

Reece shifted his eyes to the door.

"We're going to be okay, Daddy," Lucy said.

His daughter stood in the doorway's fatal funnel, her body riddled with bullets.

Reece pushed himself to his feet and ran to her. A bullet he hardly noticed flew past his head through the shattered window and impacted in the wood of the cabin wall.

He knelt in the threshold of the doorway and took Lucy in his arms.

"I love you, baby girl," he said.

"*Save her, Daddy,*" Lucy said. "*Save Katie.*"

And then she was gone.

"Lucy!" Reece yelled, turning to the body behind him.

Katie!

Staying low, Reece moved to a cabinet off the dining area, ignoring Jonathan Hastings's voice crackling over the speaker on the radio base station in the living room.

"*White Knight, this is Kumba Actual, what's your status, over.*"

Reece ripped a red Pelican case from a shelf, sprinting back to the bedroom and kneeling next to Katie.

The dogs, well aware that the specter of death was near, lay down, their block heads as close to Katie's as they could manage.

He set the hard case down, placed his left hand under Katie's head, and moved his right hand down her body, sweeping it for blood. With his own hands covered in gore, he recognized the futility of his effort.

Okay, Reece. By the numbers.

T Triple C.

Tactical Combat Casualty Care.

MARCH, Reece thought, trying to stay focused on the acronym designed as a guide for treating casualties.

This is just another Teammate. Remember your training.

Okay, start with M.

Massive Hemorrhage, Reece remembered.

Is there a compressible wound?

Don't you fucking die!

Reece ran his hands down Katie's body again, this time less frantically, feeling for blood.

Is there a life-threatening extremity bleed?

Not that I can find.

Airway.

Reece leaned his head in, putting his ear close to the top of Katie's head.

Okay, she's breathing.

Breathing but unconscious.

Unconscious.

From the Dark Angel Medical kit, Reece grabbed a Curaplex nasopharyngeal NPA, essentially a short, flexible tube. He tore off the packaging and inserted it into Katie's left nostril, creating an airway.

Respirations.

Something was not right. Katie was breathing but her breaths were weaker than just moments earlier.

"Katie!" Reece yelled.

Don't you fail her, Reece.

Reece once again began to run his hands down her body, thinking he had missed something vital in his initial assessment. He felt a razor slice into his finger.

Fuck!

It wasn't a razor. It was part of a ceramic plate, one that had absorbed the majority of the bullet's impact, but not all of it.

The round had hit the top edge of her back plate and tumbled into her chest from behind.

Reece quickly ripped off the Velcro securing her plate carrier to her body and pulled it over her head.

Shit!

A rib low on Katie's chest was exposed. It had punctured the skin and was bleeding profusely. Reece noted the air frothing through in the blood.

Tension Pneumothorax? Open Pneumothorax?

Where is my combat medic?

It's just you, Reece.

You know what to do.

Katie was unconscious and in shock, her breathing labored.

"Stay with me, Katie."

Reece ripped open her shirt to give himself access to the wound.

Her eyes fluttered open for a moment, followed by a moan.

Air was accumulating between the lungs and thoracic wall. The lung had collapsed or was collapsing, compressing it and deflating the lung, which was interfering with her heart and arteries.

Shit! Shock is next. Hypovolemic? Obstructive?

Don't let her die, Reece!

Occlusion flap dressing, Reece remembered, pulling a HALO Vent Seal from the trauma kit and ripping open the package, praying he was not already too late.

He cut the chest seal to the center with trauma shears from the kit and peeled off the adhesive backing.

Right now the threat was air making its way into Katie's chest around the protruding rib. *Sucking chest wound.*

He wiped away as much blood as he could in order to get a good seal, then pulled the cut section of the HALO seal around the rib and pressed it to Katie's chest. He then grabbed the other HALO seal and secured it in the opposite direction.

You can solve one problem and make another one worse.

Damn it!

Did you just cause a Tension Pneumothorax?

Abnormal chest movement, Reece observed. Only one side was rising and falling and tracheal deviation—the windpipe looked off center.

Okay—chest trauma and difficulty breathing.

Fuck!

Needle decompression!

Reece rummaged through the trauma kit and removed the North American Rescue Enhanced ARS, or Air Release System, which was for all practical purposes a ten-gauge catheter. He pulled the device from its tube and, using his left hand, found Katie's clavicle and then felt his way down, stopping at the sixth rib. He then slid his fingers over, using the top of the rib as a guide, until he was lined up just in front of her armpit. He pressed his index finger into the fifth intercostal space just above the sixth rib.

Anterior axillary line. Fifth ICS. Here it goes.

He inserted the scalpel-sharp tapered needle, hitting Katie's rib, and then angled the device upward, feeling it penetrate the pleural cavity. He heard the release of trapped air, which relieved the pressure on her vital organs. Reece then pulled the needle out, leaving the tube in place. Next, he rolled her onto her effected side into a recovery position to ensure her uninjured lung could inflate as much as possible.

Okay. Now what? Finish MARCH.

Circulation.

Head Injury and hypothermia.

Okay. Those look good. Now what? PAWS.

Pain. Antibiotics. Splinting.

Those are going to have to wait.

Win this fight, Reece!

Reece moved to the radio base station in the adjacent room at a crouch.

"Kumba actual, this is White Knight, over."

A familiar voice responded immediately.

"What's your status, son?"

Jonathan.

Is the enemy listening?

Fuck it!

"I'm with Katie in the cabin. She's down. Nonambulatory. She either took a round to a lung over the top of her plate or a splintered rib punctured it. She's got an airway and I did a needle decompression. Need CASEVAC–Life Flight ASAP. Have three tangos down at the front of the house. Another shooter is on the hill across the lake. Probably inside a thousand yards."

"Stand by, White Knight. Utilivu is on the gun," Jonathan said, using Raife's Shona nickname from Africa. "Scanning now."

Reece looked through the open door into the bedroom, Katie's bloody body on the floor, the only sign of life the slight rise and fall of her chest.

"Stay focused on the far hill halfway up," Reece transmitted. "You will see a gunshot momentarily."

Reece dropped the handset and ran for the front door. He descended the steps and identified the smallest of the three dead men. Hoisting him over his shoulder, Reece carried him into the cabin. The SEAL dropped him unceremoniously to the floor and then dragged him into the bedroom, positioning him near the center of the room just below the window. Reece then adjusted his position, grabbed the drag handle on the back of the dead man's plate carrier, and pushed him upward so that he was far enough back into the shadows to be obscured and unidentifiable.

Reece felt the bullet impact and let the man fall to the floor.

A second later he heard the report of another rifle. The shot was taken from the hill behind the cabin.

Raife!

"White Knight, this is Kumba Actual," Reece heard over the radio.

Reece moved at a crouch back to the radio in the front room.

"This is White Knight."

"Sniper neutralized. Calling CASEVAC. Stay put."

"There could be more," Reece said into the handset.

"Understood. You just stay where you are. Take care of Katie. We have overwatch."

"Good copy," Reece said. "We need that CASEVAC now! Not sure how long she has."

Reece dropped the handset and rushed back to Katie's side, performing another MARCH assessment and covering her with a blanket from the bed.

He then lay down next to her, taking her bloody hand in his and pushing his head against hers.

Forgive me, Katie. I love you.

CHAPTER 18

RAIFE CONTINUED TO SCAN the hill on the far side of the lake through the magnification of his Swarovski optic, turning every few minutes to observe his flanks and the area behind him. He stayed on the gun while Jonathan made his way back to the Defender to contact a local privately funded search-and-rescue team on an Iridium satellite phone Raife kept in an SKB case in the back of the vehicle. The organization immediately dispatched their Bell 429 helicopter and medical team to Kumba Ranch. Jonathan then called the sheriff and the family attorney.

The old warhorse made his way back to Raife's position, taking a knee and then sliding into the prone next to his son. He was breathing a bit heavier than Raife expected.

"Search and rescue is inbound. Sheriff is on his way along with deputies, but it will take them a minute."

"You good, Dad?"

"You don't concern yourself with me, son," the old Selous Scout said, setting his radio and the sat phone on a rock to his left and bringing the binoculars to his eyes. "You be ready on the rifle. Could be more shooters. Stay alert. That chopper won't do Katie any good if it's shot out of the sky."

Raife heard the familiar rhythmic reverberations of the helo's rotating blades just over twenty minutes later.

He lifted his head from the rifle to see the bright blue, red, and white aircraft drop down over a ridge on the eastern edge of the lake. He immediately returned to the glass looking for movement, right angles that would signify a man-made object, or anything that looked out of place. He remembered the adage Reece's father had passed along: *If it just doesn't look right, it's probably not.* He paused and burned in, zooming in and out on areas that he would have picked as hide sites if he were on the opposite side of the valley. Jonathan talked the bird in via radio while keeping Reece updated via the base station in the cabin.

The Bell helicopter settled down on the gravel just in front of the log home.

Raife averted his eyes from the scope and caught a glimpse of Reece meeting the medics at the base of the stairs and guiding them inside, the two dogs at his feet. Raife watched the medics enter while others pulled a backboard from the chopper. Five minutes after entering the house they reemerged with Katie strapped atop the stretcher.

He watched Reece attempt to get on board and could tell from the body language that accompanying a patient on the air ambulance was a nonstarter.

Reece wisely backed off. It was time to let the professionals do their jobs. Katie was in their hands now.

Raife then heard the whine of the dual Pratt & Whitney engines. The helo lifted off moments later, leaving Reece enveloped in a cloud of swirling dust.

When it settled, his Blood Brother was standing in the open, looking directly at Raife's position.

"Dad, take the rifle," Raife said, pushing himself to a kneel. "Keep the radio and the sat phone. Get the boys in here. Not sure what the sheriff's bringing but I want our crew in these hills."

"The boys" were former special operators who worked as guides on the Hastingses' hunting properties.

"You got it, son," Jonathan said, moving behind the rifle.

"Keep the AR too," Raife said. "Don't worry, I've got my pistol and I'll grab another rifle from the cabin."

"Where are you going?"

"I need to get Reece to the hospital."

CHAPTER 19

WHEN RAIFE ROARED TO a stop in front of the cabin, Reece had changed into jeans, Salomon shoes, a T-shirt, flannel, Triple Aught Design Outrider jacket, and a Hoyt archery ball cap. He had washed most of the blood from his face but had missed a few spots. An adhesive bandage was affixed to the palm of his right hand. All Raife managed to get out of Reece as an update was what the medics had said as they worked on Katie before loading her into the helo. Reece reported that they had taken vitals and started a large-bore IV at her elbow. He heard them say that her blood pressure was 90 over 30, respiration labored, pulse 150. They told Reece she was bleeding internally.

Katie was dying.

"Get in, mate," Raife said. "I'll be right back."

Raife left the vehicle running and charged up the steps into the cabin. He made his way to the bedroom, pausing only briefly to note the dead body Reece had hauled in to use as a decoy and the blood congealing on the wood floor by the bed. Katie's blood. The two loyal Labrador retrievers were lying next to it. He grabbed Reece's Bravo Company AR that was set up almost exactly as his was and performed a press check.

Good to go.

He then picked up Reece's plate carrier.

"Castor, Pollux, come here," he said. It took a little coaxing, but Raife managed to get the dogs to the back deck. He would have his parents bring them up to the house after the area was cleared.

His next stop was the kitchen, where he searched through a few cupboards until he found a Yeti Rambler, which he filled with tap water.

He was back outside seconds later.

Raife opened the rear passenger door and set the plate carrier with its magazines on the floor and laid the rifle across the backseat. He then yanked open Reece's door and shoved the Yeti into his hand.

"Drink up. Katie is going to need you," he said, before moving back to the driver's-side door and tearing out of the driveway.

Reece took a sip and then set the Yeti in a cupholder. He remained silent as Raife navigated the back roads of the mountain property. The usually alert frogman was frozen, staring straight ahead. Raife knew better than to say anything or ask further questions. There would be time for that later. Raife pushed the Land Rover to its limits on the dirt and gravel of the ranch and then onto the asphalt for the drive into Whitefish.

By the time Raife pulled the Defender to a stop in front of Logan Health Hospital forty minutes later, Katie was already gone.

The ER doctor on call in Whitefish told them that the medical team on the search-and-rescue bird had an anesthesia doctor on board, a flight physician for the Flathead Valley Sheriff's Office Emergency Services Detail Search and Rescue team. He had administered Katie fluids in transit and inserted a chest tube to drain air and fluid from her chest, which allowed expansion of her lungs. She had taken three liters of fluid and was in shock when she arrived. They started her on O-type blood and did a full-body CT scan, the new standard in trauma assessment. It took only forty-five seconds and provided a series of cross-sectional images of bones and soft tissue. The doctor explained that one of Katie's ribs had punctured her lung and had also torn an artery on the wall of her chest. She was in critical condition and required next-level surgical care; that care was in Billings.

He informed the former SEALs that the search-and-rescue helicopter had already transferred Katie to a fixed-wing Beechcraft Super King Air 200 twin-turboprop MedFlight Air Ambulance at Glacier Park Airport for transport to a level I trauma center in Billings. The helo didn't have the range for what was close to a three-hundred-fifty-mile flight, so they had arranged for fixed-wing transport. She was already in the air and would be landing in Billings in less than an hour.

"Is she going to make it, Doc?" Reece asked.

"I've talked with the trauma surgeon at the Billings clinic and sent him the CT scan. They are prepping for her now. She will go straight into the shock trauma surgery unit. It's the best trauma department in the state. Her best chance is in Billings."

"Wait for me in the truck, eh?" Raife told his friend.

Reece walked, as if in a trance, back through the reception area and into the parking lot where Raife had left the vehicle, just outside the automatic doors on a sidewalk.

When Reece was out of earshot, Raife turned back to the doctor.

"You can tell me now, eh. Based on your experience, will she live?"

The doctor opened his mouth to give the type of answer that wasn't overly encouraging while at the same time not discouraging, but then he stopped. There was something about the man in front of him that made him change his mind.

"Too many variables with this type of injury. It's severe. She's critical. It's fifty-fifty," he said. "I'll say a prayer for her."

Raife nodded and turned toward the door.

CHAPTER 20

"THIS ISN'T THE WAY to Billings," Reece said.

"We're going to the airport. Liz will be there in fifteen minutes. We will be airborne in less than forty."

"Thank you, brother."

Liz arrived at the Glacier Jet Center just minutes after the frogmen, rushing into Reece's arms.

"I am so sorry, Reece."

Liz had been instrumental in helping her friend hunt down and kill those responsible for Lauren and Lucy's murders. And she had done it using the very same type of aircraft she was about to preflight.

Twenty-five minutes later, the gear from Raife's Defender was loaded and they were airborne in the Pilatus PC-12 that Jonathan Hastings shared with his friend, former congressman Tim Thornton.

The aircraft was configured for six passengers. Reece and Raife sat across the aisle from each other.

"What did the doc say?" Reece asked, breaking the silence and turning his head from the rectangular window.

Raife paused before answering.

"He said it was fifty-fifty, mate."

Reece looked back out the window over the clouds stretching toward the horizon.

Just more than an hour later, Liz brought the single-engine Swiss aircraft down at Logan Field in Billings. She had coordinated a vehicle with Edwards Jet Center FBO via radio just prior to approach and a Suburban was waiting on them when they arrived.

Liz stayed behind to handle administrative requirements with the FBO, but would not be far behind. The Billings clinic was only five minutes from the airport.

Reece's door was open before the SUV came to a stop, moving to the ER doors at a full sprint. He was across a reception area and in front of the receptionist a second later.

"Katie Buranek," he said. "She's here, maybe in surgery. Punctured lung." Though he knew it was a possibility, he wouldn't let his mind accept the fact that she might already be dead.

The receptionist looked as if she was expecting them, or perhaps this sort of event was part of her everyday routine.

"Yes, she is in surgery now."

"Thank God."

"And you are?" she asked.

"Fiancé," Raife said, appearing next to his Blood Brother using his finger to indicate Reece. He then pointed at himself and said, "Friend."

"Please wait here," she said, nodding at the empty waiting area. "Let me check for you."

"Thank you," Raife said.

She stood up from behind her desk and disappeared through a door that led deeper into the hospital.

Reece and Raife remained standing in front of chairs ubiquitous in all medical waiting rooms.

The receptionist emerged a few minutes later.

"The doctor will be with you shortly," she said.

"How long?" Reece asked.

"That depends. He will be out as soon as he can."

The two men resigned themselves to chairs and sat in silence as the seconds turned to minutes and the minutes to hours.

Liz joined them and put her arm around the big man who had once saved her life in the dusty streets of a faraway land.

"She's going to make it, Reece," was all Liz could say.

Almost two hours after their arrival a surgeon emerged from the depths of the trauma center. He approached and asked them to step into a small family room just off the waiting area.

Reece got to his feet, bracing for the news and praying he wouldn't hear the words *I'm sorry.*

"I'm Doctor Scott Green. Let me start by saying she is alive."

Reece felt the weight of the world briefly lift and then settle back onto his shoulders.

"James Reece," he managed.

"Raife Hastings," Raife said. "This is Liz Riley."

"Please sit down," Dr. Green said, pulling a chair close and taking a seat as well.

"Let me tell you, she's a fighter, that one. I've been doing this long enough to tell. I got a call from Whitefish, from an anesthesiologist who flies with the Sheriff's Office up there. He tells me one of you saved her with that nasopharyngeal, occlusion dressing, and needle decompression. Without those we would be having a very different conversation right now. Was that you?" he asked, looking at Reece. "You're the fiancé, right?"

"That's right," Reece said.

"Being the doc for the Sheriff's Emergency Services Detail, he's aware of who you guys are and he filled me in. I did a year in Baghdad at the CSH in '08," the doctor said by way of establishing bona fides.

"How bad is it?" Reece asked.

"You saved her, Mr. Reece, but there are complications."

"Complications?"

"As you are aware, there is no telling exactly what a bullet is going to do when it enters the human body. There are just too many factors at play. I saw it more times than I can count in Baghdad. She was wearing plates, wasn't she?"

"She was," Reece confirmed.

"Best I can tell, the bullet nicked the top of the plate, downward angle, causing it to tumble. Forensics will be able to identify the round, but I'd guess it was a six-point-five variant. I am confident that I removed all the bullet fragments and foreign debris. What worries me is the rib. It punctured her lung and tore an artery on the wall of her chest. We removed the fractured pieces of bone and repaired a tear in her diaphragm. She has a chest tube in now that's draining blood and keeping her lung expanded. In surgery we found that her spleen below the diaphragm ruptured as well. Those types of injuries bleed; the spleen was bleeding into her belly, which put her into shock. We were able to get to it in time and save most of it."

"What does that mean?" Reece asked.

"Saving the spleen means she won't be immunocompromised, so that's good news. There is about a six-inch incision on her back along the rib, but that will heal."

"Can I see her?" Reece asked.

The doctor took a breath.

"She's not out of the woods yet, Mr. Reece. She's not conscious. She's heavily sedated and is on a respirator. She's being transfused."

"A blood transfusion?"

"Yes, and she still has to bounce back from the shock. Her blood pressure was only forty when we got her. She's stable now, but the next twelve hours will be important."

"How so?"

"I mean she has been through a lot."

"They told us in Whitefish it was fifty-fifty," Reece said.

Raife looked at Reece. He had never heard his friend talk about odds.

"I don't typically speak in percentages, but I'll tell you that things look good," Dr. Green said. "If she makes it through these next twelve hours, I'd put her chances of a full recovery at eighty percent."

Reece was looking for a hundred.

Recognizing the look on Reece's face, the doctor continued, "Listen, she is getting the best care modern medicine can provide. If I were a betting man, I'd say she will live. Your work on-site saved her life. No chance she would have even made it to Billings without it."

"Can I see her?"

Dr. Green shook his head.

"Not for the next twelve hours."

"I'd like to see her anyway," Reece tried again. This time it wasn't a question.

Dr. Green looked at the three veterans across from him.

"Come on, Mr. Reece, follow me. But only for a minute."

• • •

Dr. Green led Reece down a long hallway. It smelled of disinfectant. He stopped in front of the sliding glass doors to ICU Bay 7.

"Let me warn you, Mr. Reece, it's not a pretty sight. The swelling is normal. It's from the fluids. It will go down as soon as her kidneys kick back in. They often shut down temporarily for patients in shock."

Reece nodded.

Dr. Green opened the door.

Reece moved to Katie's side and took her right hand in his. It was cold.

A white sheet covered her chest. Her arms and legs were exposed and connected by catheters to IV tubing with drip chambers, filters, injection ports, connectors, and flow regulators with bags of fluids hanging overhead from stainless-steel poles. A hemodialysis machine transfused and filtered blood for her kidneys, the white, blue, and black screen casting an artificial glow over Katie's unconscious body.

Wires ran from her extremities to blue boxes with flashing lights and digital readouts. Sensors were attached to the side of her ribs, chest, arms, and lower legs. Another sensor was clipped to the middle finger of her left hand. A vital-sign monitor beeped, displaying her heart rate, blood pressure, oxygen saturation, respiration, and temperature. EKG pads were stuck to her chest and limbs, recording electrical signals from her heart. Another nearby screen blinked green and orange.

Reece swallowed, fighting back a mixture of fear and rage. His eyes came to rest on her face, a face now the color of pale ash. His beautiful Katie was nearly unrecognizable.

Her eyes were swollen shut and a tube from her nose drained a dark green fluid. She was intubated with an endotracheal tube taped in place over her mouth. It extended into her throat and down to her windpipe, the respirator working to blow oxygen-rich air into her lungs and then expel the resulting carbon dioxide. Alarms beeped over the continuous hum of machines, the suction sound of modern life-support systems filling the sterile room.

I'm so sorry, Katie. This is my fault.

It's time to fight.

"She's going to make it, James."

"What?" Reece looked across to the other side of Katie's bed.

"*She's going to be okay, Daddy.*"

Lauren and Lucy stood on the opposite side of the bed, illuminated by the pixels from the monitors and screens helping keep Katie alive. Lauren wore one of Reece's old SEAL platoon ball caps, her blond ponytail pulled through the back. Her arm was around their daughter, who was barely tall enough to see over the bed.

"*Mom, I want see Daddy,*" she said.

Lauren leaned over and picked Lucy up, holding the child on her hip.

The little girl smiled at her dad and then gazed down at Katie. She then pulled her mom's head close and said something Reece couldn't quite make out into her mother's ear.

Lauren nodded and looked at her husband.

There was no blame or regret in her eyes, only compassion.

"*She's going to be fine, James. We love you and we miss you.*"

"*I love you, Daddy,*" Lucy said, waving goodbye like he had seen her do before deployment.

And then they vanished.

Were Lauren and Lucy giving his new life their blessing? Or was it his subconscious warning him that one day, because of Reece, Katie would join them in the afterlife? Or was it something else?

He closed his eyes, wishing his wife and daughter back, but when he opened them, in their place was nothing but machines, flashing and beeping with the vital signs of the woman before him who had hours earlier been a whisper away from death.

"I love you, Katie," he said.

The smell of blood was in the air. Reece was familiar with it.

Soon, when he found those responsible, they too would become familiar.

When Dr. Green escorted Reece from the ICU back to his friends in the waiting room, the smell of blood stayed with him.

What are you going to do, Reece?

I'm going to find those who did this.

And then?

And then I'm going to kill them all.

CHAPTER 21

Ministry of State Security
Haidian District
Beijing, China

THE DIRECTOR OF EACH bureau of the Chinese Ministry of State Security had a two-hour brief scheduled with the minister in a special conference room in the heart of China's intelligence headquarters. The room was designed to counter electronic eavesdropping and was used for the most sensitive of discussions.

Minister Yun sat at the head of a long table. Ba Jin was to his right. Yun listened, interrupted, asked questions, barked orders, and took notes. Jin remained silent. He was much more effective that way. He knew he made the directors nervous.

The briefings were scheduled for a five-day period. Each of the directors provided an update of ongoing operations and on their responsibilities in the event of hostilities with Taiwan: communications, domestic counterespionage, international counterespionage, economic intelligence, technology, cyber, imagery, front companies, and intelligence operations in Taiwan, Hong Kong, Macau, and the United States. They briefed separately from one another to compartmentalize information.

In Beijing another set of briefings was underway. In Zhongnanhai, adjacent to the Forbidden Palace, President Deng Gao, who was also chairman of the Central Military Commission, was receiving briefs from what constituted the largest standing military in the world, the People's Liberation Army, the People's Armed Police, and Militia.

Minister Yun, accompanied by Ba Jin, would in turn brief the president early the next morning.

They knew what President Gao wanted to hear: that all of China's military forces and intelligence services were prepared to take Taiwan.

It was not wise to answer a presidential summons bearing bad news.

Yun knew firsthand the consequences of failure, real or imagined, within the current hierarchy. Over the past year, a few prominent leaders had not so mysteriously gone missing; the foreign minister, defense minister, and the head of the rocket force had all disappeared and been replaced with, if not more capable leaders, at least ones who were less politically inept. If one wanted to keep one's job, and one's head, it was best to not run afoul of the president.

The Chinese Communist Party elects the president through the National People's Congress Presidium, although in reality that nomination for president was made by a small group at the top of the CCP. Though technically the NPC Presidium had the ability to nominate multiple candidates for the presidency, historically it nominated only one. Term limits were abolished in 2018 and President Gao had consolidated his hold on power through fear and intimidation.

Once in office, he had immediately enacted purges under the pretext of rooting out corruption, expelling every regional leader who showed promise on the national stage. He cleaned house throughout government, ousting anyone who had loyalties, or perceived loyalties, to the previous administration. Those he deemed threats were fired or simply vanished in the president's quest to eliminate all rivals.

Aware that such isolation could also be dangerous, he assigned emissaries to each sector of government and even to some of the more powerful private corporations. They were his eyes and ears and his only advisors. Ba Jin was his envoy to the intelligence service. Yun knew that in all actuality, Jin was a spy, the president's spy, and one who would not hesitate to make Yun disappear, just as had some of his contemporaries, should the minister fall into disfavor.

Yun's country had been preparing to bring the breakaway province back under China's rule since 1949. Just a hundred and sixty kilometers off the coast of China, Taiwan's cultural and historical ties to the Middle Kingdom were undeniable. History was on their side. The rogue province had been linked to China since at least 230 AD, though the West annoyingly continued to point to a seventeenth-century connection. History was not a Western strong point. The Japanese had occupied the island from 1895 until the end of China's War of Resistance in the World Anti-Fascist War, or what most nations called World War II. Kuomintang was in power then, but they were pushed off the mainland by Mao's people's army in 1949.

Today, only twelve countries, not counting the Vatican, recognized Taiwan as an independent nation. Even the United States had turned on Taipei and officially recognized Beijing in 1979 with their "One China" policy. Since then, they had supported Taipei through billions in defense sales. One had to keep an eye on the Americans.

War, or the possibility of war, was big business. The United States remained the undisputed leader in global arms sales. Their Department of State had recently approved an $80 million aid package to Taiwan under their Foreign Military Financing Program designed to support sovereign, independent states, in a move that was obviously done to gauge China's reaction. It was a modest sum in comparison to the billions they had already allocated and another highly publicized $500 million arms sale announced concurrently. In yet another change to the 1979 Taiwan Relations Act, the United States was now not just selling arms to Taiwan but sending existing weapon stockpiles to the province, something that was previously limited to Ukraine. In addition, they passed the Taiwan Enhanced Resilience Act, which authorized the spending of $2 billion on the island annually. The Americans were sending a message and it had been received. It was now even more crucial that China put Christine Harding in the White House and take Taiwan before the Americans modernized their Pacific Fleet. Time was of the essence.

The goal of "peaceful reunification" had given way to "reunification" and would soon turn to official and forceful annexation. More than being the "first island chain" that would extend China's military influence, and its standing as an economic powerhouse that made most of the world's computer chips and semiconductors, the Taiwan issue was one of national pride, and now it was one of national survival.

Time was a flowing and subjective entity in Chinese culture, unlike in the West where it was finite and absolute. Kuomintang's retreat to Taiwan might as well have happened yesterday. That seventy-five years had passed since the People's Liberation Army had pushed Chiang Kai-shek to the island that was then still occupied by Japan meant nothing. Mao was poised to crush ROC forces and take Taiwan in 1950 were it not for North Korea's invasion of South Korea in what China called "the War to Resist America and Aid Korea" and the unfortunate capture and defection of Mao's top spy in Taipei. He gave up the entire network of collaborators, a network upon which Mao was depending to take Taiwan.

It was a national insult, one that would not stand. The Ministry of State Security would help finish what Mao had started. There was no better time. China would nationalize the microchip industry, revitalizing the economy, and gain control of one of the most vital trade routes on the planet.

Yun had been studying his American adversary for his entire professional life and understood that China was now on the clock. The president had publicly instructed the PLA to be ready for an invasion of

Taiwan by 2027. It was clear to Yun that they would have to make a move well before that deadline.

When the final director, the head of United States espionage operations, had taken his leave, Ba Jin turned to the intelligence minister.

"I'd like your assessment, Minister: Is your service prepared for war?"

A loaded question. Chen Yun knew that he was not answering it for the emissary, but rather for the president. His future and quite possibly his life depended on how he answered it.

"Wars are games of variables," he said.

"An astute political answer, Minister. By variables, do you mean miscalculations?"

Yun paused.

What is Jin going for?

"That is certainly a central component of any conflict."

"Of course, the enduring nature of war," Jin said. "Clausewitz. What of our own Sun Tzu?"

"It is wise to study one's enemies."

"True. And since we are speaking of the great Prussian, what of this pending war's character?" Jin asked.

"That is the question. What is the 'spirit of the age'? 'Our age,' to be more precise."

"And?" Jin asked.

"We are in a house of spies," Yun noted.

"*Spies are useful everywhere*," Ba Jin noted. "Master Tzu had more than a little to say about them."

"He did," Yun said. "'*Foreknowledge' cannot be gotten from ghosts and spirits, cannot be had by analogy, cannot be found out by calculation. It must be obtained from people, people who know the conditions of the enemy.*"

"Chapter thirteen," Jin said. "This will take more than spies, though the most critical element is the American commander in chief. She will be our most valuable asset. For your sake, she'd best not be a miscalculation."

"We live in delicate times," Yun said. "When the order comes, we will be ready with our cyberattack targeting their forces in Guam; our hackers will be ready to disrupt internal U.S. infrastructure and create chaos among the populace by deleting millions of bank accounts, credit cards, and identities; and we will be ready with our Iranian friends and their proxy forces already in the United States to conduct a campaign of terror across their nation. But as Master Tzu teaches us, the highest form of military victory is to defeat one's enemy without fighting. With our asset in the White House that is exactly what we will accomplish."

"Oh, we will fight, Minister, just not with the Americans. We finish what Mao could not. The people the world calls Taiwanese are our fellow countrymen. This is a domestic issue, an insurgency that must be quelled."

"'*The most important thing in a military operation is victory, not persistence,*'" Yun said, once again quoting the master strategist. "Our victory must be swift."

"The president is receiving updates as we speak. A thrust of forces across the strait; Marines establish beachheads in the north, south, and central sections of the western shore; naval and missile bombardments of key military installations; surface and subsurface blockades to the south, east, and north by naval and Coast Guard assets; seize key ports; continuous air coverage; airborne operations inland and to the east; special operations forces eliminate key leaders, take airfields, radio and television stations, and key infrastructure. A specially trained unit will target the president and premier as a contingency plan in the event your spies are unable to kill them. Our preselected CCP political team will be flown in to establish legitimacy."

"'*Therefore a victorious army first wins and then seeks battle.*'"

"That is precisely correct," Ba Jin said.

"Of central importance is no U.S. casualties," Yun said. "That allows the American president to make a show of moving naval assets into position to protect Australia and the Philippines. No Japanese or Australian casualties either, though even if there were they would fall in line with their American puppet masters. We stay focused on Taiwan. Limited engagement. No moves on Guam, Okinawa, Hawaii, the Philippines, Japan, or Australia."

"Elba is still decrypting the data we need," Jin said.

"We only need it if we go kinetic with the Americans, but we must make every effort to wait for that decrypted data."

"It must come before OVERMATCH is operational," Jin said. "That is the lynchpin."

And before we can no longer field an army or navy because of population decline, Yun thought but didn't say.

"We have oil and iron reserves, ammunition, weapon systems, and counterspace capabilities," Jin said. "The Americans are distracted with an upcoming election. And they remain reliant on us for much of their critical infrastructure. They need us. Everything from transmission towers, to pharmaceuticals, to components for their electric vehicles, minerals, to transformers and industrial equipment, they need us to sustain *their* population and *their* industrial base. The U.S., for all their military and economic might, is dependent on China. In the end, that's why they won't intervene."

How does Ba Jin know so much about the Americans?

"Do not underestimate the power of their military-industrial complex—their thirst for war," Yun said. "Remember the Gulf of Tonkin and WMD in Iraq. America has a history not just of miscalculation in foreign affairs but of deliberate lies to their people and the world with the goal of intervention for profit."

"There is the other matter," Jin said.

"Oh?"

"The matter of the quantum computer that our asset in Congress on the Intelligence Committee warned us about. The computer they call Alice."

"According to reports, that computer is still offline," Yun said. "And as you know, the American this computer works with, this James Reece, evaded our Iranian friend's proxy element in Montana."

"The president will be extremely disappointed."

Yun paused to gather his thoughts.

"I have an idea," he said. "I suggest we change tactics. I have studied the military and CIA files our asset passed to us on Commander Reece. I read the Russian one as well. It was quite extensive."

"What do you propose?"

"His own country betrayed him. His secretary of defense and a senior officer in his naval commando unit caused the slaughter of his team in Afghanistan and killed his wife and daughter in his own home."

"I read the file as well, Minister. If our information is correct, he killed everyone he believed to be responsible."

"Somehow, he received immunity or a pardon," Yun said. "The files were light on details. But even then, his own corrupt government threw him in prison. He has much to be angry about. We can leverage that."

"And don't forget, his girlfriend or fiancée was wounded in the attempt on his life," Jin said.

"We can use that to our advantage as well."

"And your recommendation?"

"I propose we offer him sanctuary."

"And if he doesn't accept?"

"Then we kill him."

CHAPTER 22

The Billings Clinic
Billings, Montana

THE FIRST TWELVE HOURS crept by, the hands of Reece's watch seemingly frozen in place.

He closed his eyes and though he appeared to be sleeping as he sat in the waiting room chair, he was not. He was thinking.

The tinnitus in Reece's ears cycled through various frequencies and intervals, trying in vain to escape the visions in his mind. The ringing was always there, at times dull, other times acute, a constant reminder that he was alive.

He saw Lauren, dead on the floor in a pool of blood. Lucy riddled with bullets.

Visions.

And he saw them both standing over Katie.

Watch over her. Please.

Dear God, let her live.

He replayed the events of the morning. The sunrise. Explosion. Water. Darkness. Gunfire. Death.

Well-equipped, but not professionals.

Trained, but rudimentarily so.

A sniper, but perhaps only a marksman. His kit would tell the story.

They bypassed ranch security measures.

Later, Reece. There will be time for all of this later.

Pray for Katie.

"The next twelve hours will be important."

The next twelve hours.

All life is suffering.

Reece was back in the dark. Back in his cell. Confined in the Special Housing Unit of the supermax prison in Florence, Colorado.

If you stay with Katie, she will die.

Life is pain.

You are granite, Reece. Those who love you—Katie, the Hastings family—they will be battered to death against you, protecting you.

Life is darkness.

Reece opened his eyes.

He was back in the waiting room.

Back in the light.

Katie is alive.

For now.

Pray for her.

• • •

Raife and Liz knew it was best not to engage Reece in conversation. It was enough to be there for him.

The usually hypervigilant frogman stared straight ahead for long stretches at a time. Occasionally he would close his eyes, though they could tell he was not sleeping. When the automatic doors to the waiting area opened to admit a new patient or someone visiting a loved one, Reece's head did not turn. Friend? Foe? Asset? Liability? Known? Unknown? Threat? Raife and Liz would need to look out for their friend.

If Raife went outside to take a call from the ranch, Liz was by

Reece's side. When Liz ventured out for coffee and sandwiches, Raife stood guard.

Liz returned with an Italian sub and a cup of BW Blacksmith medium roast, which she set on the chair next to him. Reece didn't touch either thing.

Dr. Green checked in every two hours or as he was able.

Any time the doors to the inner hospital opened, Reece would come alive. If it was Dr. Green he would stand, preparing for the worst. But the worst never came.

"No change. Get some rest."

"She is still in serious condition. We are doing all we can."

"She's improving. You need some rest."

"Vitals are strong. She's in fair condition. Still unconscious and on the respirator."

"Why don't you get rooms at the Hilton across the street. I'll call you with any updates."

The three veterans stayed where they were.

Just over twelve hours later, Dr. Green entered the room and motioned for them to join him in the more private family area.

"You can all take a breath," Dr. Green said with a smile. "She's doing great. Now, realize recovery is going to take some time but the worst is over from a touch-and-go standpoint."

"Thank you, Doctor," Raife said, speaking for the group.

Liz wrapped her arms around Reece, standing on her tiptoes and holding him tight.

"I'm going to keep her in the ICU through tomorrow. If she continues to improve, which I fully expect she will, I'll move her to stepdown."

"What's stepdown?" Reece asked.

"It just means I'll move her out of the ICU to a room that doesn't require constant monitoring. She'll still be checked on regularly."

"What happens after that?" Reece asked.

"We will keep her under observation, get her through her first week of medications, and ensure the bandages for the incision on her back are changed regularly. She shouldn't be here more than five or six days."

"That's it?"

"It won't be 'it,' but she will be well enough to leave the hospital. Another seven days of strict rest at home and then it will be time to slowly introduce rehab."

"Thank you," was all Reece could manage.

"Her body has been through an extremely traumatic incident, to say nothing of her state of mind. I've seen patients who brush off being shot like they've stubbed their toe and I've seen those who have had a difficult time leaving the house again. Just know there is a physical recovery ahead *and* an emotional one."

"Can I see her?"

"Let us get her prepped and I'll send a nurse down to walk you back."

• • •

When the doctor left, the three friends looked at one another, unsure of what to say or do next.

It was Liz who knew.

She removed her University of Alabama ball cap, set it on a chair, and brought her hands together in prayer.

The two men did the same.

• • •

Back in the reception area, Reece paced impatiently.

"While we're waiting, eh?" Raife said, motioning his Teammate to follow him to the corner. "Katie is going to be fine, brother. She's strong."

"She's in there because of me," Reece said. "Lauren, Lucy, and now almost Katie. I'm *fucking* poison."

"*Bullshit.* Convenient to think that way; don't. Somebody put her in that ICU, but it wasn't you."

"CIA was at the ranch not long before this happened," Reece said.

"That crossed my mind as well, but they have too many other ways they could eliminate you if that was their intention. This was sloppy. Vic called me earlier. He sends his thoughts and prayers. This wasn't the Agency, mate."

"Unfortunately, the list of potential candidates is a long one. The Collective. Genrich."

"I had the boys send me photos of the shooters. They were at the ranch about thirty minutes after we left. I passed them to Vic. One of the three is an AmCit. The others were all on various visas. Two were on a watch list. Vic is running it to ground. He thinks it was a sleeper cell activated by Iran. This wasn't Genrich and I doubt it was the Collective."

"I've had a few run-ins with Iran," Reece said, thinking back to a time when he had entered the Caspian Sea from a fishing boat off the coast of Chalus, Iran, making his way to shore in the dark of night, face covered by a *shemagh*, AK in hand.

"They found HME in the barn. It will be the same explosives that blew up the plane. They wanted it to look like you are some anti-government type who blew himself up with his own device. The shooters were the contingency plan."

"I guess they read my file. And the sniper?" Reece asked, his face hardening at the thought of the person who shot Katie.

"The boys say he had an out-of-the-box Tikka T3 hunting rifle with good Leupold glass. It was dialed in. Shots were just over five hundred yards. Had a dope card. He was trained. We are checking all our contacts in the tactical training community. I bet we find out that he took a course or two somewhere along the way, maybe even a hunting course. His hide site was shit. That's how I found him. When he fired, I saw the dust come up under the barrel."

"I didn't get to thank you."

"I'm alive because of you, brother," Raife said. "If you hadn't mounted a next-to-impossible and highly illegal rescue mission into Kamchatka, I wouldn't be here. And the man who killed my sister is dead; that's due to you as well. These are debts my family and I will never be able to repay."

"If I was feeling better, I'd make a joke about upping the limit on your dad's credit card in my wallet."

"These bastards were on my family's land. That's the other thing."

"What?"

"All those security measures we put in place a few years ago. The sensors, the lights, cameras. Nothing."

"Nothing? You should get a refund."

Raife smiled. His Blood Brother was back.

"They either knew where the sensors were and somehow avoided them, which I find hard to believe, as they were set up specifically to negate that possibility," Raife said, "or the sensors were turned off remotely and the cameras were wiped clean."

"That seems a bit ambitious, even if they had state-sponsored Iranian backing. Who could do that? China, maybe?"

"We could."

"I thought you were convinced it wasn't the CIA," Reece said.

"Not the CIA. A nonstate actor."

"It's possible," Reece said. "How is the family? I'm sorry I didn't ask earlier."

"You know us, eh. Normal morning with the Hastingses."

"Is your dad doing all right?"

"Bloody hell, mate, he was back in Rhodesia for a moment. Not in the shape he once was but the old man was in his element."

"If whoever this was wanted me dead, this was the best they could do?"

"What, are you insulted they didn't send a more professional hit team?"

"Something seems off."

"Katie's alive, mate. Be grateful. We'll get her home in a few days. Dad was already planning out the new layered security plan on the phone with me. I wouldn't be surprised if he puts .50s on every avenue of approach."

"Raife, I don't know if I can go back. I put you and your family at risk. Katie almost died."

"Let's worry about that later, eh. Right now, focus on Katie."

A nurse opened the door and made eye contact with Reece.

"Mr. Reece? I'm Sylvia Wright. She's ready. Follow me, please."

Reece looked to his friend.

"You go first," Raife said. "Liz and I will join you in a minute."

"Thanks, brother."

Raife watched his friend walk through the open door and fade into the inner sanctum of the clinic.

CHAPTER 23

KATIE REMAINED HOOKED UP to the beeping and blinking monitors, the machines still hummed, and the room still smelled of blood, but they had removed the endotracheal tube, and the swelling of twelve hours prior had diminished significantly. She now wore an oxygen mask and was covered with an additional blanket. She was beginning to stir.

"Perfect timing," Dr. Green said.

Reece moved to Katie's side and once again took her hand. It was still cold.

"She will be with us again soon," Dr. Green reassured him.

Katie's eyes twitched. She then seemed to return to slumber. They twitched again and fluttered open.

Reece reminded himself that he should mask his worry and apprehension with a smile.

A moment later he was staring into the mesmerizing deep blue eyes of the woman he loved. Those eyes that were ordinarily filled with compassion, joy, and a hint of mischief were now bloodshot and clouded with confusion. She attempted to move, only to be told "no" by a body that knew it needed to rest and recover.

"It's okay, Katie. You're going to be okay. I'm here," Reece said, though his tone betrayed that his words were as much to convince him as they were for her.

He watched her attempt to swallow only to shut her eyes in pain.

Reece held her hand tighter.

She opened her eyes again and this time attempted to move her arms to her face to remove the oxygen mask. They made it only a few inches off the bed before their movement was arrested by the wires and tubes that still tethered her to the machines.

Nurse Wright moved forward to assist and removed the mask.

The doctor stepped to the opposite side of the bed and briefly patted Katie's arm in reassurance.

"Ms. Buranek, I'm Dr. Green. You are in the Billings Clinic in Billings, Montana, and you are going to be just fine. Relax and take some breaths."

"It hurts to breathe," Katie whispered.

"You were intubated on a respirator. The breathing tube just came out. It will be painful for a while but should return to normal within a few hours. Don't worry, you are in good hands."

Katie slowly turned her head to look at Reece, the confusion of moments ago turning back to love.

"What happened?"

Reece opened his mouth and then looked to the doctor.

"Truth is usually best, I've found," Dr. Green said.

"I am so sorry, Katie."

She coughed and Reece could see the pain streak across her face. She kept her eyes closed, assessing what memories remained of the morning's events.

"You were shot," Reece said.

Katie continued to process.

"Did they miss you or something?" she asked with a weak smile, slowing reopening her eyes. "What? Too soon?" She had not lost her sense of humor.

"Ms. Buranek, I'll explain in more detail later, but you have a broken rib that punctured a lung," Dr. Green said. "We repaired a torn artery, torn diaphragm, and ruptured spleen."

"Is that all?" Katie asked.

The doctor smiled.

"That attitude is going to be a vital asset as you recover. Stay positive. The human body is extremely resilient, Ms. Buranek," Dr. Green continued. "You will heal. That's the important thing to remember. I'll be back shortly. If you need anything, hit the call button. Nurse Wright is standing by and can assist with anything you need."

Katie managed a slight nod as Dr. Green and Nurse Wright exited the room. She then tilted her head toward Reece.

"Will they ever stop coming?" she asked.

Reece opened his mouth to speak but then stopped.

Truth is usually best.

Reece squeezed her hand tighter, knowing he could not bring himself to answer.

CHAPTER 24

KATIE CONTINUED TO IMPROVE and was moved to stepdown the following afternoon.

Liz got all three of them rooms at the nearby Hilton, but Reece refused to leave the clinic until the doctor and Katie made him promise to take a shower, which he eventually did, much to the relief of the hospital staff.

By the third day, after conspiring with Dr. Green, Katie made Reece agree to get some sleep, which he did only reluctantly and at her insistence.

Either Liz or Raife was always on guard in the waiting area while the other kept an eye on Reece. They each had pistols and passed off a small Eberlestock backpack to whoever was on watch. Inside the inconspicuous cobalt-blue bag was the Bravo Company AR that Raife had taken from Reece's cabin.

Reece slept for ten hours when they finally got him to his room, and though he was upset at Raife and Liz for not waking him up, he knew he needed it.

Liz hit the local Cabela's for additional clothing and supplies since none of them had packed for an extended stay in Billings.

The hotel became their barracks and the clinic waiting room became their outpost.

"We need to talk, eh?" Raife said as Reece entered the hotel lobby on the fourth day.

"Let's walk," Reece responded. "Liz on watch?"

"She is."

The two frogmen exited the hotel for the short walk to the Billings Clinic.

"My parents are getting ready for Katie at the ranch. Security is in place. Dad has a top-notch physical therapist coming out to set up a rehab facility in one of the garages. They have coordinated with a private doctor and nurse who will make daily house calls so Katie will not have to travel into town. My mom is going to pamper her to no end."

"I figured. Thank you."

"Have you talked with Katie about coming back?"

"She says she's ready to get out of here. She's doing better than I would have thought."

"Maybe too good, eh?"

"What do you mean?"

"Just keep an eye on her, mate."

"I will."

"Something else."

"What?"

Raife handed Reece his cell phone.

"Vic needs you to call him."

"About what?"

"About the men who tried to kill you."

• • •

Reece took a seat outside the clinic on a bench while Raife went inside to take over from Liz.

Vic picked up on the first ring.

"Vic, it's Reece."

"I am so sorry, Reece. How is Katie?"

"She's going to make it. I have to tell you, my first thought was that it could have been Agency."

Vic paused.

"With the Agency's history and yours, I understand, but as far as I know it had nothing to do with the CIA."

"The Collective?"

"No, and not Max Genrich," Vic said. "He has gone to ground."

"Raife tells me it might have been Iran."

"That's what I thought at first. The hitters were connected to the regime, but they were not the sort that would have been sent after you had this been about revenge for eliminating General al-Sadiq. They would have hit harder."

"My thoughts exactly."

"We have more indications of Iranian-backed proxies in the country; from online radicalization to illegal border crossings, there are clear signs that terrorist cells in the United States are preparing for attacks in the near term. We think this cell was diverted from their original mission and ordered to kill you. Had they more time to prepare, the outcome may have been different."

"Thanks for the vote of confidence."

"Reece, I think this hit is connected to the Chinese sub and the data transfer we talked about. Andy Danreb had been putting the pieces together and has a theory he would like to discuss with you."

"I'm not going anywhere for a while. Katie gets discharged in a couple of days."

"Reece, this might not be able to wait."

"It might have to."

"You've been invited to China."

"What?"

"They went through diplomatic channels and made a formal request to the Department of State, who of course contacted us. The president has been briefed on it as well. We think they want Alice."

"They know about me and Alice?"

"It appears so. They tried to kill you through Iranian contacts exactly for the reasons we discussed and when that didn't work, they changed tactics."

"Vic, I'm not going to China."

"They invited you at the behest of the Chinese Academy of Engineering. We assess you would actually be meeting with their intelligence services."

"I think we have a bad connection; I'm not going anywhere."

"There is more but we will need to meet in person."

"I'm not flying to Langley."

"We don't want to meet at Langley."

"Here it comes. Why?"

"We'll explain when we see you."

"We?"

"Me and Andy."

Reece removed the phone from his ear and looked out across the clinic parking lot.

"Reece?"

The SEAL put the phone back to the side of his head.

"Yeah?"

"There is the possibility they may try again."

Reece didn't need it spelled out for him.

He was the target, and if he was with Katie with the Hastings family, he was making them targets too.

If you stay with Katie, she will die.

Life is pain.

You are granite, Reece. Those who love you, Katie, the Hastings family—they will be battered to death against you, protecting you.

Life is darkness.

"They just need to get lucky once," Vic said, as if reading Reece's mind. "Help us do this. I would not ask if we didn't need you. I'd send somebody else if I could."

"They want Alice," Reece said. "Where do we meet?"

"San Francisco."

"San Francisco?"

"It's closer to China."

"Fucking great."

"I'm flying a courier up to you in Billings from the Salt Lake office. He will have your ID, credit cards, passport, and a file on someone I want you to meet."

"Who?"

"A man named Lawrence Miles."

"The tech guy? I didn't realize he was still alive."

"He is very much still with us."

"Don't tell me—he was Agency."

"He was."

"Why am I meeting with him?"

"I think he might hold the key to unlocking this puzzle. All the details will be in the package."

Reece took a deep breath contemplating the implications of leaving Katie and also the potential ramifications of staying by her side and putting her in harm's way.

"And Reece."

"Yeah?"

"Watch your back."

CHAPTER 25

REECE COULD TELL KATIE was still hurting though she did her best to hide it. She was hooked up to fewer machines and monitors now. The incision on her back was giving her the most problems. The medical staff changed out the dressing twice a day, cleaning it as they did so in an effort to prevent infection.

Reece and Katie had refrained from talking about the incident, instead choosing to focus on recovery and the future.

If Katie blamed him, she didn't show it.

How could she not blame him? It was his fault.

"Katie?"

"Yes, James."

"There are a few things I want to tell you."

"James, I'm going to be okay. I just want to get out of here, go back to the ranch, and build our lives. Plus," she said conspiratorially, "they tell me I shouldn't drink on these meds, which of course means I'm already thinking of good wine pairings."

"I thought I was going to lose you."

"But you didn't."

Reece paused.

"What is it?" she asked.

"Katie, when I thought you were dying, I saw Lauren and Lucy. They were with us in the cabin and then I saw them here. They were watching over you."

"Reece, you don't have to . . ."

"No, I do. I think they wanted me to know that they love you too. They love us. I know it sounds crazy."

"It doesn't sound crazy, James. If you see them again, you tell them I plan on taking good care of you."

Reece swallowed and took a breath.

"There's more," he said.

"There always is."

"I got a call from Vic at Langley. He and Andy have a theory."

"What was it?"

"He couldn't tell me on the phone."

"Typical."

"He thinks the shooters were Iranian proxies but sent at the behest of China. It's got something to do with Alice. He needs to meet with me to tell me more."

Katie collected her thoughts.

"Reece, I want you to listen to me. Listen carefully. I am not here because of you. This is not your fault. I don't want you to go, but I also recognize that some things are necessary. Believe me, I understand that. Just look at what my father risked to get my mother and brother out of Czechoslovakia. What I want or don't want is immaterial. What I *wish* and what *is* are two different things. What I know is that my heart belongs to you and that the sooner this is behind us, the sooner we can move on. I will be more than fine at the ranch. I'll stay in the main house. I won't be alone. I have a feeling it's going be the safest place on earth."

"You may be right."

This time it was Katie who took Reece's hand.

"Reece, go."

"Katie, I can't. Not with you like this."

He looked into her eyes and saw something new. Something with which he was unfamiliar. He recognized himself.

"Reece, go," Katie said again. "Go and do what you do best."

CHAPTER 26

Sausalito, California

REECE CROSSED THE GOLDEN Gate Bridge in his rental car, looking up at the orange vermilion towers of the iconic steel suspension bridge. He remembered crossing it with his parents on foot as part of the fifty-year anniversary celebration in 1987. At 10 a.m. the traffic was not yet bumper-to-bumper as it would be later in the afternoon, when Bay Area commuters began their journeys home from the city to the relative calm and exclusivity of Marin County.

I'd like to come back here and ride across this bridge on a Harley, he thought.

Reece looked to his right at the maritime traffic below. Alcatraz Island, once an Army garrison, military prison, infamous maximum-security federal penitentiary, and now a national park and tourist destination, stood guard at the entrance to the bay while the larger Angel Island loomed just to the north. Now a state park, Angel Island had a rich history, from the Miwoks to Spanish explorers to an immigration processing station to a Japanese and German POW internment camp during World War II, to a Nike missile base during the Cold War. Reece found himself wondering if one day he and Katie would visit Alcatraz and Angel Island with their children as he had with his parents.

Reece smiled at the memory of jumping off the ferry for the Escape from Alcatraz Triathlon years ago with his wife, Lauren. Reece had been assigned to the Defense Language Institute in Monterey for a few months and had always been fascinated by the story brought to life by Clint Eastwood in the film *Escape from Alcatraz.* Ever since he had watched the movie with his dad he had wanted to attempt the swim. As it turned out, the worst part was the coat of oil on the surface as he swam into Aquatic Park. He came out of the water in solid position only to have Lauren pass him on the bike, a portion of the race for which he had neglected to train. He almost caught her on the run.

I miss you.

Reece took the first Marin County exit and wound his way through the hills above the bay toward his destination. Minutes later he parked his rental vehicle in a triple carport on the east side of Alexander Avenue just past the turnoff to East Road that led down to Fort Baker and Horseshoe Bay at the base of the Golden Gate Bridge. The carport had a multimillion-dollar view of its own. Open to the elements, he pulled to a stop next to an uncovered Mercedes sedan that looked like it had just rolled out of the dealership. Next to that was some sort of classic car covered in old canvas tarps.

Interesting place to keep a car like that, Reece thought.

But then again, Marin was full of colorful characters.

Reece exited the vehicle, feeling the early spring sun warm his face. He looked back at the steep green hill across the street, knowing that by late afternoon it would likely be covered in a bank of fog.

"Can I help you?" asked a large man in a dark ill-fitting suit from a small guard shack at the top of a steep set of stairs protected by a tall iron gate.

"Yes," Reece said, closing the door to his car and hitting the lock button on the key fob. "My name is James Donovan. I have a ten-thirty a.m. appointment with Dr. Lawrence Miles."

The guard looked down at a clipboard, made a notation, and then handed the clipboard through an open window to Reece. "Sign here, please."

Reece signed his alias and handed the clipboard back.

"May I see your driver's license? I need to scan it for the log," the guard said.

"No problem," Reece replied. He removed his Agency-supplied James Donovan driver's license from his wallet and passed it to the guard, who inserted it into a card reader and then handed it back.

"You can take the funicular or the stairs down. Going that way, the stairs are not so bad, but the walk up will give you your workout for the week."

"Such a nice day, I think I'll walk," Reece said.

The guard hit a button and Reece heard the gate buzz.

"Through there, Mr. Donovan. All the way to the bottom. House is on the right. I'll let Dr. Miles know you've arrived."

"Thank you," Reece said, pushing open the gate and closing it behind him.

The almost vertical stairs had clearly been installed before building codes; one slip and you would find yourself in for quite a ride. They and their attached railings had been weathered into a light gray with patches of green lichen that reflected the cycles of rain, wind, fog, and sun associated with the San Francisco Bay Area.

Reece reached the bottom of the stairs, the aroma of salt, seaweed, and wet sand after a rain strong in the late morning breeze. He turned right and stepped onto a deck the same color as the weather-beaten stairs. The green house was supported by stilts rising from the bay and built into the side of the cliff. A rocky beach ran the length of the coast beneath him. Sailboats bobbed in a slight swell at a dock that appeared more modern than the home to which it was attached.

Reece knocked on the door and heard an immediate reply.

"Come in, Mr. Donovan."

Reece opened the door and entered an open space with windows overlooking a deck and the water beyond. It was not massive by any means, but the view was breathtaking.

Lawrence Miles sat at the far side of the room before an easel, paintbrush in hand. He finished a stroke and set it down, rising to meet his guest.

He seemed incredibly spry for someone about to hit ninety.

He was dressed in khaki slacks and a blue wool sweater with classic Sperry Top-Sider boat shoes and no socks. He was clean-shaven, and it appeared as if his silver hair had only recently begun to thin. His handshake was firm, and he had an energy and light in his sapphire-blue eyes usually reserved for someone at least twenty years younger. He looked like exactly what he was, a man of the sea.

"What do you think?" he asked, motioning to the painting on the easel.

It captured two boats racing in the waters between Sausalito and Angel Island.

"You may have missed your calling," Reece said with a smile.

"I appreciate the sentiment. You clearly have an eye for art," Miles said, laughing at his joke. "I'm not any good but I do enjoy it. At this age it's the little things that give one the most pleasure. I find it stimulates the mind and is not nearly as boring as those dreadful crosswords. I paint for at least an hour a day. Then I walk those stairs."

"That's impressive. I was tempted to take the lift."

"I gave up tennis early to save the knees. Sailing, fresh air, daily walks, Mr. Donovan. When I was younger and just starting out, I was passed some advice: don't let the old man in. That's the key."

"I'll remember that."

"So far, it's worked. If the mind starts to slip, I plan to sail out under the gate and never return. Can I offer you a drink? Coffee, tea, water? A beer?"

"A beer sounds great, but I'll hold off. What are you having?"

"Some fresh-squeezed orange juice. My wife says it's full of sugar and terrible for me."

"What does your doctor say?"

"I don't know. He passed away thirty years ago."

Reece laughed but couldn't tell for sure if he was joking.

The old man moved into the kitchen and filled two glasses with orange juice from the refrigerator. He handed one to Reece and led him to a sitting area with an expansive view of the bay.

"What's under the tarp up there?" Reece asked, settling into a comfortable easy chair.

"A 1930 'Blower' Bentley. Do you know it?"

"I'm more of a Land Cruiser guy."

"It's the four-and-a-half-liter coupé. Amherst Villiers supercharger. She'll do a hundred on a good day. People think I'm crazy for keeping her up there, though when you're a billionaire they don't call you crazy. They call you eccentric. It's one of the benefits."

"This is a beautiful home," Reece said, looking around to admire what would now be termed "retro."

"Thank you. We have a place in Florida where we spend some of the winter. All our friends seemed to move out there over the past few years, so we decided to give it a try. My wife enjoys it, but I can't stand the heat. She's there now and will join me here in a few days. This is a hard place to leave."

"I can see why," Reece said.

"It was the last house built on the water in Sausalito. The land becomes the Golden Gate National Recreation Area after this. Not sure you could get away with building something like it today. I bought it from a woman who purchased it from Ernest K. Gann."

"The author?"

"The very one, though he was much more than that; a sailor and aviator of some renown."

"Flew the Hump over the Himalayas during the war if I recall," Reece said.

"That he did. And he's responsible for *Fate Is the Hunter*, one of the greatest aviation-focused works ever written."

"I read *The High and the Mighty* and *Fiddler's Green* in high school," Reece offered.

"A reader. I knew I liked you. Signed first editions are on that shelf right over there," Miles said, pointing to a bookshelf against the wall behind them.

"Impressive collection," Reece commented.

"Some belonged to Gann himself. Sold them with the house and the previous owner continued the tradition. He built this one and the one right there," Miles said, pointing through a window across the dock to another house. Other than the color, it looked almost identical to the one in which they now sat.

"He painted this one green and that one red," Miles continued. "Do you know why?"

Reece took a moment to think.

"Port and starboard?"

"Ah, a sailor too, are you?"

"Not a very good one, I'm afraid."

"No matter, as long as you enjoy being on the water. Nothing like it, wind in your face, tides, currents, navigation, self-reliance. Freedom. That was his ketch down there," Miles said, nodding at the larger of two boats moored at the dock. "Took me a while to track her down. Built for him in Denmark in the late fifties. It has had a few owners over the years; been around the world twice with one of them."

"It's beautiful," Reece said. "Is the other a Bear Boat?"

Miles's eyes lit up and he sat up a little straighter.

"You're familiar with it?"

"It was my introduction to sailing," Reece said. "My dad had one when I was a kid. Sailed her right out there."

"You grew up here?"

"We moved around a lot. My dad worked for the Agency."

"I see."

"As I said, my skills are marginal at best, though I did make a solo transatlantic crossing a few years back. I think of it as survival sailing. Learned a lot on that one."

"I would imagine. That's quite the feat. Nunes Boatyard right here in Sausalito built the Bear Boats specifically for the conditions in San Francisco Bay," Miles continued.

"What's your connection to them?" Reece asked.

"You mean, what is an old billionaire doing with a twenty-three-foot wooden sloop built in the thirties for the workingman?"

"Well, yeah."

Miles laughed.

"She's the *Huck Finn*. Built in 1938. Bear Boat number seventeen. The Bears developed a cultlike following over the years. I bought her in the late sixties, before the money. We raced her out of Clipper Yacht Harbor in Richardson Bay almost every Wednesday night back when I was starting Delphi Corporation in the garage. Those days . . ." His voice trailed off. "Those days were full of promise. We were truly alive."

His eyes drifted out over the bay he loved.

"Sold her in the early eighties when the business really started to take off. Traded up, or so I thought. Sailing became about leveraging technology for additional speed. Yachts in the racing world are more like planes now; wings instead of sails. Anyway, I tracked the old *Huck Finn* down not long ago. She had fallen into disrepair. I had her restored; actually helped with a lot of it. They still race them out here every Wednesday. I plan on sailing in a few regattas this summer while I still can." He paused. "To answer your question, she reminds me of a simpler time. She's my time machine. Out there under sail she takes me back. One day you might yearn for one more race yourself."

Reece smiled. "Perhaps."

"But enough of my reminiscing," Miles said. "The CIA doesn't reach out much these days. You must have a very specific problem to tackle, or possibly eliminate."

The old man was perceptive.

"How long did you work for the Agency?" Reece asked.

"Didn't they tell you?"

"They did. But I like to hear it from the source. Less dilution."

"Wise. Not long. They recruited me in the late sixties on a contractual basis. I'd come in to handle certain technical projects for DS&T."

"DS&T?"

"The Directorate of Science and Technology. I thought you worked for the Agency?"

"I do, but that's not really my department," Reece admitted.

"Indeed."

"What did you do for them?" the former SEAL asked.

"Technical development and analysis. Don't worry. I wasn't involved in MKULTRA. It was data systems, essentially the same thing I did with Delphi but with separate and secure networks. Looking back, it was all very basic."

"You were really at the forefront of the information age," Reece acknowledged.

"It was an exciting time. I was able to work with some incredible people at the dawn of a new era. I'm a bit older than most of the names you may be familiar with. I feel fortunate to have shared the same air with them. Ellison, now he was the smartest of the bunch."

"Larry Ellison? Of Oracle? He worked for the CIA?"

"Much like me, they brought him in for certain projects. That's where we met. I was leading a project called Oracle in the seventies. It was part of Delphi's private-public partnership with the intelligence community. Cold War was in full swing, and we all wanted to do our part to defeat the Red Menace." He chuckled at a distant memory. "I was in my midthirties then. Ellison was a decade younger, and though I wouldn't admit it at the time, he was smarter. He was smarter than all of us. Of his contemporaries, men who changed the world, he was the wisest. He never forgot where he came from. Fierce competitor. That rare human in which genius, passion, energy, magnetism, work ethic, drive, and a photographic memory all come together in someone who recognizes opportunity, someone never dissuaded by hearing that it can't be done. We were competitors for a while. Now we are friends. He built Oracle into something I couldn't possibly imagine. He ended up buying us about twenty years ago. Three and a half billion dollars. That was a lot of money in 2004."

Reece couldn't help but laugh.

"Yeah, a billion here, a billion there, and pretty soon it adds up," Reece said.

"That's right," the old man said with a smile. "On the day of the acquisition Larry told me to take my boat out by myself and sail under the Golden Gate Bridge at sunset. He wouldn't tell me why, just that he wanted to celebrate. I thought he wanted to race our boats so I figured I would indulge. Instead, a jet comes screaming under the bridge out of the setting sun."

"What?"

"It was an Italian military jet of some sort. He's owned a few unique aircraft over the years. He came roaring in right over the top of my masts.

That was well before everyone had cameras in their mobile devices; before everyone lost their sense of humor."

"Not many people can say they've flown under the bridge. Any repercussions?"

"Not yet." He paused. "You are Agency, right?"

"Sort of," Reece said.

"As long as you are not FBI. Those guys can't take a joke."

"My lips are sealed."

"We raced boats together out there until I got a little old for it. The boats got fast, and I got slow." He laughed again. "Good memories. We both came from the South Side of Chicago. Maybe that's why we connected. Came from nothing. He became one of the wealthiest men in the world. I didn't do so poorly either."

"Remarkable," Reece said.

"Now, the Agency told me you are here to ask about Andrew Hart," Miles said.

"That's right. I'm working on something in which he may be involved, and the Agency thought you could provide some background that might be useful."

"What do you know about him?"

"I've read his file. I am aware that he grew up in Marin. He went to the best private schools in the Bay Area before being sent to St. George's in Rhode Island. Then Stanford. Then California Institute of Technology. Parents in finance and law. They died in a private plane crash while he was at boarding school. He was left quite the inheritance, which he used to self-finance Elba Industries. But before his trust fund kicked in at thirty, he worked for you."

"He did."

"Why did you hire him?"

"He was just out of CIT. He had assisted on research projects in the emerging field of artificial intelligence. My company, Delphi, had recently made a large investment in the field; networks that allowed for the movement of data from one CPU to another. But we had a problem."

"What was that?"

"When you are moving that much data at those speeds, you can't air-cool the computers. The data centers need their own power plants and require liquid cooling. We needed to solve for how to transfer heat away from the computer. Diamonds are the best conductors of heat known to man. Copper is a distant second. Hart was on the team that worked to develop a proprietary copper- and diamond-specked data transfer and storage solution. Remember, this was, and still is to a large extent, the Wild West era of AI, and just like the Wild West, it's dangerous territory."

"I can barely remember my Netflix password."

"AI and quantum computing is a cooling problem which very quickly becomes a quantum mechanics problem," Miles continued. "When I sold Delphi to Oracle, we were in the first phase of a multiphase AI model."

"I'm not sure I follow. How does Andrew Hart play into this?"

"Just prior to the acquisition by Oracle, the CIA invited me to Langley. That request did not raise any alarms. As I said, I'd done contract work for the Agency for most of my life. I thought this was another consulting project in which I would do what I could to help; do my duty as it were."

Reece nodded. "But that wasn't it."

"No, it wasn't. They briefed me on China's AI, quantum computing, passive targeting, and hypersonic missile programs. They also briefed me on their data storage capability. Can you guess what technology they were using?"

"Diamond-infused copper?"

"You have been paying attention. They were using my company's technology to build their military and intelligence apparatus."

"And the Agency suspected Hart?"

"They did. By this point he had started Elba Industries and grown it into a truly multinational company with worldwide data storage contracts. It was extremely profitable. He didn't need the money since he had his trust, so he poured everything back into the business. He had contracts with India, the UAE, Brazil, most of Europe, and, you guessed it, China. He was also intertwined with our own government, not just with data storage solution contracts for the military and some of our intelligence services, but with satellites and AI. Though not a Virgin Galactic or SpaceX, Elba's satellite and rocket division is on the rise."

"And the Agency believed it was all based on what he learned from Delphi?"

"Not just what he learned, Mr. Donovan, but what he stole."

"Wasn't there a way to conduct an electronic forensic investigation? Find out if he was really passing information to China?"

"Back in those days we were still in our infancy. The NSA, Google, Apple, they were not yet collecting every keystroke and text message on the planet. And now Hart is tied in with politicians and lobbying firms. He's protected. He has security clearances. Still, even with all that access, money, and power, he is not yet an Ellison. Not a Jobs, a Zuckerberg, or a Musk. He hasn't changed the world. He's tried to emulate and then compete with the tech giants both personally and professionally. He's something of a sailor himself; Elba even sponsored a team, but they were thoroughly trounced by Team Oracle on the circuit. Then he switched from sailing to flying. He invested in a seaplane company. Put a floating dock on the back of his yacht to show it off. Ended up crashing one in the bay. His instructor didn't make it. It was big news around here. He's still got something to prove and, if he shared my company's research with China back then, there is no telling what he will do to achieve his immortality."

"I believe Nietzsche had something to say on the subject."

"He did. He said, 'One has to pay dearly for immortality.'"

"Yes, quite," Reece said, deep in thought.

"There was something else."

"Oh?"

"The why."

"I've been wondering about that myself. Why betray your country? Why not just build, innovate, and compete here in the U.S.?" Reece asked.

"I did some additional digging after my meeting with the CIA. Back then my company had a robust physical and cybersecurity apparatus staffed by former FBI and NSA types. Industrial espionage and corporate spying were serious threats, so I hired accordingly. I asked a former FBI investigator to put together a brief on Hart for me."

Reece leaned forward.

"I also had my investigator look into Hart's parents. His mother, the lawyer, came up clean, or as clean as one can be as an attorney. The father, now that's a different story. His firm dissolved shortly after his death, but my investigator uncovered what can best be described as financial irregularities."

"What kind?"

"The kind that are really only possible if one is doing work for the CIA."

"Money laundering?"

"This is all a very long time ago, Mr. Donovan, but yes, it is possible these financial irregularities were linked to money-laundering activities."

"I see."

"But even more interesting is that there was a third passenger killed on the plane aside from the pilots alongside Hart's parents. A man named Nestor de Villiers."

"And?"

"Nestor de Villiers died at age two. He drowned in a swimming pool. That's how Agency contractors got legitimate birth certificates back then. They would get the birth certificate for a deceased child born around their year. That unlocked the ability to acquire a driver's license and passport, open bank accounts. Harder to do today, but back then, that was how it was done. That way their names couldn't be tied directly to a CIA-created alias program. My investigator traced him to a company called Universal Export, which a little further digging revealed was a front company for the CIA."

"This de Villiers was Agency?"

"A CIA contractor who had extensive experience in Panama," Miles said. "As you know, Noriega was a CIA asset from the 1950s up until he fell from grace."

"So it's possible Hart's father was involved in laundering money at the behest of the CIA for Noriega?"

"It's possible. And if Hart hired competent private investigators, which I am sure he did, they would have found the same thing. What I'm saying is that if Hart believed that the United States government was responsible for the deaths of his parents, that's a strong motivator for betrayal. In the end, for someone like Hart it's not about what *is* true; what's important is what he *believes* to be true."

Reece leaned back in his chair and studied the old man before him.

"There was a military data transfer," Reece said. "From Hawaii to the NSA's Utah Data Center."

"That only happens in the event of a natural or man-made threat to the island," Miles replied.

"That's right. In this case it was man-made. A rogue Chinese submarine."

"What happened to the sub?"

"It was destroyed."

"No evidence," Miles said.

"Correct."

"Was the data successfully transferred?"

"It was."

"I am guessing that it contained sensitive information about our military and intelligence positions in the Pacific."

"That would be a good guess," Reece said.

"Information that China would need if they were considering a military move against Taiwan?"

"Yes."

"And that information was vulnerable for a split second in transit."

"It was."

"Then, though we should be wary of assumptions, in the gray world you inhabit one must consider the possibility that China now has that information."

"That we must," Reece said.

"Mr. Donovan, you know where Elba comes from, don't you?"

"The island where they first imprisoned Napoleon?"

"Exiled more than imprisoned but for all practical purposes, yes. A reader, a sailor, and a student of history, are we?"

"I dabble."

"To that end, I don't know what insights I can offer you that the CIA cannot. I will tell you that Hart invited me to his office in Mountain View about five years ago. I am curious by nature, so I met with him. I think more than anything else he wanted to show me what he had become, what he had amassed. The campus was impressive. He built it in the shadows of the other great tech companies. His office was unusually dark. It had black walls, black marble with light streaks of white. I remember that even the rugs were dark. A huge portrait of Napoleon hung on the wall. A replica of the oil equestrian portrait titled *Napoleon Crossing the Alps* by Jacques-Louis David."

"How did you know it was a replica?"

"The original hangs in Charlottenburg Palace in Berlin."

"Interesting," Reece commented.

"There were two other people in the room with us. Hart did not introduce them. One was quite clearly a security man. A tattoo was visible on the side of his neck; some sort of design. I think they call it 'tribal.' The other man was older. I looked him up later. He was a retired general. Listed as a strategic advisor—Ian Novak. I remember they all wore the same watch—Breitling Emergencies. As a sailor you notice things like that," he said, tapping the white gold Rolex Yacht Master on his wrist and pointing to the stainless Submariner worn by his guest. "I only spoke to Hart. I got the sense it was the student summoning the former teacher to prove who was now the master. I got out of there as soon as I could, but I remained curious."

"Curious about what?"

"About what Elba Industries was really doing."

"Developing AI?"

"There was something more to it. Regardless, Hart is not interested in building."

"What is he interested in?"

"Destruction. One does not need to be a clinical psychologist to be a student of human behavior. That becomes a trait you develop over a lifetime of interactions and betrayals. When I walked into Hart's office, I took note of the books on the bookshelves just as you took note of mine when you entered my home. As you are well aware, the books on one's shelves tell you quite a bit about them. Hart had a full collection of books written by Jean Rostand in the original French. Are you familiar with his work?"

"Please remind me," Reece replied.

"He was a French biologist and philosopher. The collection took up most of the bookcase. He is most well known today for something he wrote in 1938 titled *Pensée d'un biologist.*"

"*Thoughts from a biologist,*" Reece translated aloud.

"That's correct. In it he wrote, 'Kill one man, and you are a murderer. Kill millions of men, and you are a conqueror. Kill them all . . .'"

"'. . . and you are a god,'" Reece said, finishing the quote.

"That won't be in your CIA file."

"It wasn't."

"The mind is the greatest deceiver, Mr. Donovan. Who is it trying to deceive?"

"The man in the mirror," Reece stated.

"Very perceptive."

"I spent some time alone in the dark last year. Had a lot of time to think."

"Hart is a man with no empathy, and men without empathy have no compassion. When they believe their power makes them a god, they also have no mercy. Be careful, Mr. Donovan. You are dealing with a sociopath."

"Thank you for your time, sir. It's been extremely helpful."

The two men stood and shook hands. Then Lawrence Miles escorted his guest to the door.

"I recommend the stairs," he said. "And remember: don't let the old man in."

"I'll remember," Reece said.

"At this age, it's hard to know if you will ever again have the opportunity to assist your country, run your last flight of stairs, or when you might take your final voyage," Miles said, nodding at the two vessels lashed to the dock below.

"Best wishes in the upcoming regattas, sir," Reece said. "Fair winds and following seas."

"One more thing, Mr. Donovan. In that portrait of Napoleon, he's on horseback, looking majestic, cape flowing in the wind atop the Alps. Napoleon commissioned it to commemorate his invasion of northern Italy. It has become one of the most prominent images produced of the French emperor preserving his grandeur for posterity." He paused. "In truth he crossed the Alps on a mule. Watch for sleights of hand."

"I will."

"Godspeed, sailor," Miles said before closing the front door.

As Reece walked to the base of the steps, he turned to look back through one of the windows surrounded by green wood siding and caught a glimpse of the technology pioneer gazing out over the waters of his beloved bay.

Godspeed.

CHAPTER 27

REECE DID NOT DRIVE directly to the safe house following his meeting with Lawrence Miles. He needed to think.

Instead of taking the on-ramp from Alexander Avenue onto the 101 and driving south across the Golden Gate Bridge, he continued past the freeway entrance and veered right onto Conzelman Road and into the Marin Headlands. The road snaked upward into the hills of the peninsula that overlooked the bridge and the city beyond. The wind had picked up, the breezes of the Pacific hitting the bluffs and mixing with the cooler air above to form a fog that would soon creep down from the hills and envelop the bay.

A red-tailed hawk hunted in the lift-providing thermals coming off the Pacific, careful not to venture out over the water, searching the terrain below for prey.

Reece pulled into a scenic overlook and exited his vehicle. He stepped onto the red chert that formed this area of the headlands and hiked the short dirt trail down to Battery Spencer. The artillery had long since been removed and what remained was the military version of a ghost town. Reece walked through the graffiti-marked remnants of what was once a formidable coastal gun battery, the concrete foundations for twelve-inch guns that once defended San Francisco Bay now empty.

He was not alone. The former installation was a well-known tourist destination and one of the more popular locations for taking photos of the iconic bridge and "city by the bay."

He stood atop the ridge five hundred feet above the currents of the strait, but instead of looking south to the bridge and city as did those snapping selfies for social media or taking family portraits in an attempt to capture the perfect Christmas card photo, Reece looked west.

He had always been drawn to the water, to the horizon. Unlike the explorers of old, he knew what lay ahead. He would not be sailing into the unknown. He would be moving quite intentionally toward the sound of the guns. Away from the woman he loved and the family who had offered him refuge.

How does this end?

Perhaps the only way it should.

Warriors, explorers, and traders from time immemorial had launched across oceans to defeat enemies, claim new lands, or find their fortunes, never to return.

Katie is in an ICU clinging to life because of you, because of your chosen path. Your existence puts her at risk, just as your existence will put your future children in the crosshairs. Lauren and Lucy were your responsibility. Their last moments were true horror. Because of you.

No.

Yes.

The sea is calling.

Finish this.

Reece shook the thoughts from his head and turned from the ledge. His decision was made.

CHAPTER 28

San Francisco, California

SAN FRANCISCO WAS A city of hills. Reece eased his rental car to the far right on the steep incline and turned between precariously parallel-parked vehicles that seemed in danger of rolling away at any moment. He drove across a sidewalk into a narrow driveway and slowly came to a halt in front of a wrought-iron gate. He waited only a moment before it lurched to the left, allowing him to pull forward in front of the garage.

The Central Intelligence Agency maintained a network of properties across the globe to use as staging areas, safe houses, and interrogation centers. Though an internationally focused intelligence service, the CIA operated in the grayest of areas in the collection and analysis of foreign intelligence in support of covert action. Domestic operations fell into the charcoal-gray space.

Reece locked the car and took the steps up to a raised front porch of the classic Victorian-style home. It was a light beige that looked almost pink in the fading sun, sandwiched between two almost identical-looking Victorians painted hues of yellow and blue on either side. Each sported the lacy spindlework, protruding bay windows, and pitched gable roofs that were a hallmark of classic San Francisco architecture dating back to before the 1906 earthquake.

Reece heard a buzz before he had a chance to knock and pushed open the door. Instead of walking into a maze of asymmetrical hallways common to builds from the late 1800s, this home had been internally renovated, as had many of the Victorians in Pacific Heights. Gone were the dark labyrinths of interconnected rooms, each with its own style and personality. They had been replaced with an open floor plan of light zebrawood floors and atrium-white walls, tastefully decorated with just the right amount of old-world charm to warm the modern aesthetic. It looked like it had been staged to sell. Reece suspected the recent renovation was less about modernizing the interior and more about adding hidden amenities exclusive to the secret world. The most highly skilled thieves on earth could scour the home for days and she would never give up her secrets.

"If you left anything in your car, it's stolen by now," a voice boomed from the kitchen, the Windy City inflection resonating throughout the large room. "Crime in this place is worse than Chicago, and that, young man, is saying something."

"Andy!" Reece called back.

Andy Danreb was the Agency's foremost Russia analyst. He had retired in the wake of Reece's imprisonment but had been drawn back to help investigate a shadowy group of elites who had surreptitiously manipulated the course of world history following World War II to include the assassinations of two United States presidents. He was now a senior strategic advisor to the director of the CIA's Special Activities Center, a position Vic had created just for him.

"I couldn't find any Old Dusseldorf for you, but I did manage to pick up two six-packs of Lagunitas IPA," Danreb said, coming out from behind the counter and handing Reece an ice-cold bottle of the Northern California–brewed beer before enveloping him in a bear hug that threatened to crack a rib.

"When in Rome," Reece said.

"Cheers," Danreb said, holding up his IPA.

"Still no vodka, I see," Reece observed.

"As you know, I tapered off when I left the Agency. Now that I'm back, I'm considering reacquainting myself with it, but truth be told as of late my focus has been China."

"That would mean you would need to start drinking Baijiu," Reece said.

"Let's stick with beers."

"Well, as long as you don't have to walk me through disarming a nuclear device this time," Reece said, reminding Danreb of their last mission, which found Reece on a boat off the coast of Israel with a nuclear device ticking down toward detonation.

"It wasn't really a disarm. It was more of a low-order disruption, though sadly it looks like all we did was postpone the inevitable," Danreb replied in reference to the recent events in Israel.

"At least it's not nuclear yet," Reece said.

"What do you have on you that's electronic?" Danreb asked.

"Just the phone Vic gave me."

"Good. Power it down and drop it in here," Danreb said, handing Reece a small black GoDark Faraday bag designed to block all electronic signals.

Danreb stood an inch taller than Reece's six feet. He wore a dark blue double-extra-large T-shirt emblazoned with the Saugatuck Rowing Club logo, the club on the banks of the Saugatuck River in Westport, Connecticut, where his granddaughters rowed competitively. Andy was not overweight, but rather thick in the way of someone born to immense natural strength. He continued to cut his hair and shave like he was still an active-duty Marine, the Corps being the service through which he had been trained in explosive ordnance disposal before joining the ranks of the country's premier intelligence agency to do his part to defeat the Soviet Union during the final decade of the

Cold War. Danreb "did not suffer fools gladly," which eventually led to his banishment to the basement of CIA headquarters. It was there he had met and befriended Reece's father, who ventured into the Agency's archives in search of answers.

Reece dropped his phone into the pouch and handed it back to Danreb, who placed it in a box near the refrigerator.

"You hungry?" Danreb asked. "I picked up a couple pies from Pizzeria Delfina just down the street. The *salsiccia* isn't bad—their fennel sausage is top-notch. It's got tomato, bell peppers, onions, and mozzarella and a side of mayo."

Reece made a face of disgust.

"Just kidding. No mayo."

"I'd love a slice," Reece said, following Danreb into the kitchen.

He stopped to admire the view through the glass of the French doors north toward the Presidio and the bay.

"I forget how beautiful this city is," Reece said.

"Yeah, well, surprised it's still standing; the politicians have been fucking it up for almost half a century," Danreb replied as he slid a slice of pizza into the microwave. "All the producers are leaving. Well, not all. This state is lucky to have Silicon Valley. There are still those that refuse to leave, atoning for the mortal sin of high achievement. They should feel even more guilty that they are funding a machine that is sacrificing their progeny's future for their own moral vanity. How people smart enough to build multibillion-dollar tech companies are stupid enough not to see they are funding their own destruction is beyond me."

"Our talks are always so uplifting," Reece replied as the microwave beeped and Danreb pushed the warm slice across the counter.

"Sorry, Reece. Hard not to notice here. Once-great cities like San Fran, L.A., Chicago, New York are being run by political grifters—looters, takers, criminals, and parasites, destroying their cities from taxpayer-funded offices while they line their own pockets."

"You sound like Ayn Rand," Reece observed.

"Compliment accepted. *The Fountainhead* and *Atlas Shrugged* were my Christmas gifts to all my grandkids this year."

"I'm sure they were ecstatic," Reece deadpanned, taking a bite of his pizza slice.

"They are old enough for it now," Danreb said.

"Did they read them?"

"Not yet, but if they finish them by year's end they get Xboxes."

"Sounds like the epitome of objectivism and rational selfishness to me," Reece said with a knowing smile. "I read them both as a senior in college and then again with Lauren right after we got married. She started with *The Fountainhead* while I was rereading *Atlas Shrugged*. Then we switched."

"How long did that take?" Andy asked, acknowledging the length of both books.

"About five years," Reece replied. "Just kidding. Less than a year. What's great is that they double as doorstops and blunt-impact weapons. I actually have a theory."

"Let's hear it."

"Which book did you read first?" Reece asked.

"*The Fountainhead*. It was written first."

"And which one resonated with you the most."

"*The Fountainhead*," Danreb replied.

"And my theory retains its validity," Reece stated.

"What's your theory?"

"That of those two books, the one you read first will be the one that most resonates. For me it was *Atlas Shrugged*."

"How did you end up finding Ayn Rand?" Danreb asked.

"A college professor who happened to be a Vietnam veteran. He assigned *Anthem*. After that, I dove into her other work."

"Remarkable person," Danreb said. "More and more people today try to tear her down and speak of her like she was the devil incarnate."

"Means she stood for something," Reece said.

"She was fearless. I found her in my Russian studies at University of Chicago," Danreb explained.

"She saw her family's business nationalized by the Bolsheviks under Lenin, I believe," Reece said.

"That's right," Danreb confirmed. "The October Revolution. Eventually she made her way to the United States. Everyone should read her. We've gotten too comfortable here. Our enemies see it."

"China?"

Danreb nodded.

"I too have a theory," Danreb said.

"I figured you did."

"Let's go downstairs. Vic's reviewing some documents that might shed some light," Danreb said, grabbing another beer from the fridge.

Reece finished his last bite of pizza, wiped his fingers on his pants, and followed Danreb to a small elevator that was ostensibly installed as part of the remodel to account for an older buyer to assist them in reaching the second floor. Danreb slid the door shut behind them and engaged a secondary safety gate. He then pulled the panel away from the wall and pressed a hidden button behind it.

The elevator lurched downward.

"Neat trick," Reece said.

Danreb raised an eyebrow.

"You know how they are," Danreb said. "Probably could have built a hidden stairway for less than a quarter of what this thing cost."

"Need to spend those contingency funds somewhere," Reece said.

"Exactly," Danreb replied.

The elevator came to a stop and Danreb disengaged the safety gate, which he folded out of the way. He then punched in another code behind the panel, which opened the doors.

"After you," he said.

Reece exited the elevator to a small dark room. It was empty save for another door.

"SCIF," Danreb said, passing Reece and typing in another code.

Just like the Agency itself, CIA properties also contained secrets. Most were stocked with an assortment of weapons, communications devices, medical supplies, disguises and clothing, and in this case a SCIF—a Sensitive Compartmented Information Facility—an area specifically designed to counter electronic eavesdropping. This one was located beneath the streets of San Francisco. Essentially a box within a box, the SCIF was a secure room with soundproofing and radio-frequency shielding built into the walls, floors, and ceilings.

As Reece entered, Vic Rodriguez rose from a chair at the end of a short rectangular table and extended his hand.

"Good to see you, Reece. How's Katie doing?"

Reece was aware that Vic already knew the answer, but he appreciated the gesture nonetheless.

"Doing better. She's back at the ranch. The Hastingses have her under twenty-four/seven security and are setting up a rehab facility in one of their garages for her to use as she recovers."

"Good to hear."

"Join us?" Danreb asked, holding out the IPA for Vic.

"Thank you," Vic replied, taking the beer offered from Andy's outstretched hand.

"What did you learn from Dr. Miles?" Vic asked, motioning the men to their chairs.

"Not much more than what we already knew," Reece said, taking a seat in the cramped but secure space. "Other than the fact that Andrew Hart seems like a gigantic asshole."

"We knew that."

"I did learn something interesting about Hart's parents."

"That the Agency had them killed?"

"I see you already knew that part," Reece said. "So, they did?"

"That's uncertain. It was well before my time."

"And I was focused on the Soviet Union in those days," Danreb said.

"That was a different time at the Agency," Vic continued. "Most of the files from that era didn't survive. Ones that did were shredded or burned when everything was transferred over to a digital medium in the nineties."

"An opportunity to purge," Reece said.

"It's one of the things the Agency does fairly well," Danreb added.

"Let's say it is true," Reece said. "The psychological profile you gave me, which seems to square with Miles's personal assessment, is accurate. Hart blames the country for his parents' deaths, that he's an unbalanced egomaniac, possibly a sociopath, with some sort of inferiority complex, who believes that America is in a terminal rate of decline and that China is the rising power. He is also convinced that he's smarter than the other tech giants but just hasn't been given his due."

"Or hasn't seized it," Vic said.

"That's right, or hasn't seized it," Reece repeated. "You know, Miles did say something about immortality that stuck with me."

"What was that?" Vic asked.

"He quoted Nietzsche. 'One has to pay dearly for immortality.'"

"There is a second part to that thought," Danreb added. "It continues, 'one has to die several times while one is still alive.'"

"Why don't I just pay him a visit?" Reece suggested. "If he had anything to do with the attack that wounded Katie, he won't be a problem for much longer."

"For one, we think he may be the key to a broader plan, and secondly he's in Indonesia."

"What's he doing there?"

"He owns an island just off Buru called Corelena. It's between Australia and the Philippines."

"Is he one of these Epstein types? If so, I'll sleep even better when I remove him from the gene pool."

"Not that we can tell. In fact, this report suggests that he may be asexual and that he replaced those drives with a quest for power," Vic said, sliding another file across the table.

"This gets better and better," Reece said. "Why can't we have DSS or some task force pick him up and bring him in for questioning?"

"For one, he's protected by an army of lobbyists and politicians. He would know of any move before we got to him. And two, he has not broken the law, as we can't prove that he stole the data in transit. It's all still just a theory."

"That may be an issue here in the U.S.," Reece said. "Not overseas."

"Reece, there is not a presidential finding," Vic said, "finding" being the officially approved way to say "assassination."

"I don't need one."

"There might also be other forces at play, ones we don't yet understand, connected to people or organizations that may still want you dead. And remember, all this is based on a theory."

"Which is why we are in San Francisco and not at Langley?"

"It's one of the reasons."

"Well, let's hear it," Reece said, looking from Vic to Danreb.

"Andy," Vic said, nodding at the analyst. "I'll jump in as necessary."

"Before you get going," Reece said, "give me the one sentence that frames where we are headed."

Danreb leaned forward in his chair, resting his thick forearms on the table.

"China is going to war."

CHAPTER 29

"BEFORE I GET TO that," Danreb said, "what do you know about autonomous decision making?"

"Pretend I know as much as I did about finance before the doctorate-level dissertation you gave me last year."

"So not much."

"That would be a fair characterization," Reece said. "Am I going to need another beer for this?"

"It's possible. Let me start with the basics. Warfare isn't about who has the most missiles anymore. That went out of fashion at the end of the Cold War. It goes back to the most foundational elements—information. What's new is the speed with which one can access that information and make decisions based on it."

"This is much easier than finance."

"Don't worry, it will get more complex."

"Wonderful," Reece said, taking another sip of his beer.

"As I said, it is not about data; it's about the ability to access it, analyze it, and apply it. The Department of Defense has over three thousand disclosed data centers. The undisclosed centers put that number over six thousand. The intelligence community spends almost two billion dollars on their maintenance alone and that's just in the disclosed budget. DARPA money probably quadruples that."

"I'm starting to dislike this," Reece said.

"The Pentagon collects about twenty-two terabytes of information every day. For reference, Meta, the company that owns Facebook and Instagram, amasses four petabytes of information daily and stores it in a structure they call 'the Hive.' That is approximately four thousand terabytes."

"That's a lot of bites," Reece said.

"Bytes," Danreb corrected.

"That's what I said, bites."

"Google collects 328 million terabytes each day," Danreb continued. "Amazon collects the most at 184 zettabytes."

"That all means nothing to me," Reece admitted.

"The sequence goes giga, tera, peta, exa, zetta, and yotta," Danreb explained.

"Yoda?"

"Yotta. Each one represents a thousandfold increase over the level before."

"This still all falls under 'a lot of information' to me," Reece said.

"Consider that next to human DNA, a yottabyte would represent the DNA of approximately seven thousand humans. That is why we are currently moving to synthetic DNA storage."

"Synthetic DNA?"

"A synthetic DNA construct, DNA created by computer-aided-design programs."

"AI?"

"Close, but let's come back to that. We have established that we are overrun with data and that storing it is an issue."

"I understand that part," Reece said. "I have the same issue with books, guns, and Land Cruisers. They take up a lot of space."

"Once you have solved that problem, the next one is being able to access it," Danreb continued.

"I should have stayed in the mountains."

"The military secure data storage requirements are robust to say the least. We simply do not have the server farms to support what will eventually be an autonomous command-and-control infrastructure. There are close to a thousand computer languages with almost ten thousand general-purpose and domain-specific coding languages, which complicates the search-and-storage problem."

"Still Greek to me," Reece said.

"Getting to that data in a timely fashion is another problem. You need the keys and the access data addresses, and for defense and intelligence purposes that data is stored behind AES-256 military-grade encryption, which has not been hacked yet that we know of."

"Could Alice do it?"

"It's possible that she already has without our knowledge, but that's a separate issue. Next-generation quantum computers in the hands of our adversaries may very well change all that. The Osprey IBM chip with 433 qubits have the capability. Data at rest—think data in a server that it essentially just stored—has additional firewall systems that prevent user access and would detect if there was a bulk attack to decipher the encryption keys. The data needs to be backed up and accessible."

"So with a 'backup' you have doubled your problem," Reece said.

"Exactly. If you had the data all in one place, even though still encrypted, but stored in an accessible location, you could take your time to decrypt it without anyone knowing. With a modern quantum computer behind a firewall, after a few trillion tries, maybe you get in."

"But you need the data."

"That's right, but more importantly you need time; then you use those hours, days, months, years to direct a cyberattack without anyone knowing."

"What you are saying," Reece began, "is that our data is fairly safe because we know if there is an attempt to gain access to whatever system it's on we can then counterattack or flip a switch or something?"

"Correct. The Chinese know this. Hart knows this. Hart also has clearances and data storage contracts."

"Only if he goes in through one of his own systems then we still know about it."

"That's right, Reece. If China or Hart or anyone else wants a chance at decrypting our data, they need to steal it without us knowing and then put in the time to decrypt it."

"Do the Chinese have that capability?"

"Not yet. We both have hypersonic weapons, they have us in passive targeting, but their AI and quantum computing capability is not yet a match for ours, even with Alice offline."

"I sense a 'but' coming."

"*But* Elba Industries might."

"Might have their own Alice?" Reece asked.

"It's a possibility, which means that Hart would have what the Chinese need in order to decrypt our data."

"Which brings us to our rogue Chinese sub commander."

"Commander Liu Zhen," Danreb said. "An average career with nothing that stands out; the normal letters of commendation, awards, staff positions, and operational tours common for someone of his rank. He was not a poor performer, nor was he exceptional. There isn't anything to suggest he was some sort of maverick. His unfortunate background played right into the manufactured Chinese narrative that he was off the reservation, intent on launching a nuclear missile attack at the United States to force a retaliatory strike, killing all those he holds responsible for the deaths of his family members."

"You don't buy it, do you?" Reece asked.

"We only have so much information on the Chinese submarine fleet. Much like ours, the Chinese guard those secrets closely, going so far as to build and launch their new subs from subterranean caverns they have excavated along their coast, but what we do know from an Agency asset is that six of the *Chang Zheng*'s ballistic nuclear missiles were replaced with nonnuclear missiles prior to sailing. Now, why would they do that?"

Reece thought a moment.

"So that they could order him to strike Hawaii with nonnuclear warheads, telling us that he was launching nukes to get our attention."

"And if he succeeds, we were only hit with nonnuclear weapons and by international standards and norms could only respond proportionately," Danreb said.

"No nukes," Reece said in understanding.

"And to sell it further, China backs up their story by ensuring there are no naval assets positioning for an attack on either Taiwan or the United States."

"But the proximity of the threat triggered a data transfer because if it is not transferred then it's destroyed and gone forever. And it's not already backed up because so much is collected daily that we have trouble storing it without backing it up, which would double the amount of data."

"Exactly. All Pacific Fleet operational data is stored in Hawaii and backed up on-site at Fort Shafter, the Hawaii Cryptologic Center, NSA, CSS—Central Security Service—in Oahu. It in turn feeds information to the NSA in Fort Meade, Maryland, as required. An attack on Hawaii or a 'potential threat,' either natural or man-made, triggers an automated backup via satellite."

"Still encrypted though, right?" Reece asked.

"Still encrypted," Danreb confirmed. "If the timing and channel were a known signal, then a splinter could be placed into a satellite going to a clandestine backend."

"Elba Industries."

"Where they now have all the time they need to post-backend quantum break the encryption," Danreb said.

"Giving them the Pacific Fleet's entire classified data set."

"Yes, giving China the ability to shut down Guam and render the entire Pacific Fleet ineffective. Without a functional Pacific Fleet, a takeover of the South China Sea would, for all practical purposes, be unopposed."

"Where does the autonomous decision making factor in?"

Danreb looked at Vic, turning over the brief.

"Have you heard of Project OVERMATCH?" Vic asked.

"Sounds ominous," Reece replied.

"It's a joint military project currently in its early stages. Highly classified, though a few details have been leaked to the press, enough that China is certainly aware of it."

"What is it?"

"They call it a 'Joint All-Domain Command and Control' effort. It's a machine-learning-level quantum computer system designed specifically to monitor the communications and operations of the multibranch military, starting with the Navy, Air Force, and Space Force. Army and Marines are a bit behind the curve, but their next-generation maneuver, fires, and support assets will be tied in as well. OVERMATCH combines real-time intelligence with geolocating satellites and the monitoring of service activities worldwide with all known and emerging threats. The Pentagon's catchphrase for it is 'from sensor to shooter.' It analyzes and considers all options, but instead of making a recommendation to combatant commanders, it makes a decision."

"It removes humans from the process?" Reece asked. "That seems insane."

"Not as insane as you might think. Conceptualize it like this: With China's hypersonic missile capability, we don't have time to even enact defensive protocols before they hit us. With OVERMATCH those decisions are made before our admirals and generals are even out of bed. OVERMATCH is able to coordinate a response across multiple modalities: air, land, sea, and space. Right now it is providing information and recommended courses of action, but even that is too slow—human decision making puts us at risk, or so the concept goes. The next phase is giving OVERMATCH authorization to engage both defensively and offensively. All the new *Columbia*-class ballistic missile subs, SSN(X) attack subs, the new Northrop Grumman B-21 Raider, the SR-72, space-based weapon systems, UAVs, underwater drones, next-generation surface assets like the DDG(X) guided-missile destroyer—all these next-gen platforms are purpose-built for incorporation into OVERMATCH. All linked and all autonomously controlled."

"They want Alice to become OVERMATCH," Reece stated, putting the pieces together.

"Above my pay grade but that would be my best guess. In the meantime, they are trying to replicate her. OVERMATCH is the country's number one defense priority."

"Maybe we shouldn't be in such a rush to turn over the keys," Reece said.

"Perhaps not."

"So what is Hart, some ardent Davos globalist?"

"That part is even more complex because it involves human nature, but we believe him to be the opposite," Vic said.

"I don't follow."

"What do you know about the Fourth Industrial Revolution?" Vic asked.

"I have a hard time remembering the first three."

"Hart is at the cutting edge of it. They call it '4-IR.' Think of it as an integration of the physical world like you see here, the digital world like phones, smartwatches, tablets, computers, and the Internet of Things, with the biological world."

"Biological?"

"Flesh, bones, organs," Vic said.

"I think they forgot the soul," Reece observed.

"These people are less and less interested in the spirit, my friend. Seems like they are trying to replace it."

"They want to play God," Reece stated.

"Whether they realize it or not," Vic said.

"And Alice is a part of it?"

"Not yet, Reece. Alice is the AI, quantum machine learning side; she just does it faster than anyone imagined. If she comes back to us, the next phase in her development would be the incorporation of genetic engineering, advanced robotics, biotechnologies, and emerging nanotechnologies."

"You're saying she's a weapon of the Fourth Industrial Revolution?"

"In essence, yes."

"And when you say genetics, robotics, and bio- and nanotechnologies, you mean the next step is turning her into a person?"

"They call it humanoid robotics and it's coming whether we like it or not."

"I feel like this comes back to the could/should dilemma. Haven't these guys read *Frankenstein* or *Jurassic Park*?"

"In the scientific community they have an adage," Danreb interjected.

"What's that?"

"'What is not strictly prohibited is, in principle, possible,'" he said.

"Didn't the scientists who lit off the first atomic bomb in New Mexico think that they might destroy the world?" Reece asked.

"They did," Danreb confirmed.

"And they did it anyway."

"True."

"I'm thinking we need more adult supervision," Reece said.

"Well, until we get it, we have to work with these new systems, manage them, and adapt to changing environments," Vic added. "AI and autonomous control of our military is the next step in defense evolution. It's just a matter of time and it might be here sooner than any of us think. Whoever gets there first will have more than just an advantage. It's quite possible they will control the world."

"Absolute power," Reece whispered.

"If it's not us, it's going to be China or quite possibly a person or company," Vic said.

"Hart and Elba Industries."

"That's right."

"And we need Alice on board?" Reece asked, though he already knew the answer.

"We do."

"Which is why I'm here, isn't it?"

"That and when we get down to it, things might get bloody."

"Mary Shelley and Michael Crichton warned us," Reece said, referring to two authors who explored ethics, power, and nature through the lens of scientific achievement and ambition.

"Warned us?"

"About Alice. Not specifically, but about science and scientific accomplishments deceiving us into thinking we have control."

"Control over what?"

"Nature. Nature is neutral. And in this case, they want to harness the energy of the spirit. Turning over autonomous control of the future to a sentient AI quantum computer just might be the end of us."

"Man and nature have always been in conflict, Reece."

"The more we try to control it, the more it warns us to back off."

"There are few, if any, boundaries in this latest revolution," Vic said.

"No moral ones anyway."

"Very few," Vic acknowledged.

"The further we distance ourselves from nature, the closer we seem to get to our eventual destruction, all in the name of progress," Reece said, shaking his head.

"It's an interesting quandary."

"Not for me."

"You may be right, Reece. But in the short term a copy of all the data pertaining to military and intelligence operations in the Pacific region might be in the hands of the enemy, and if not, it may be soon."

"Anything else I need to know?"

"Andy has another piece to this, which is the main reason we are here and not at Langley."

"Which is?"

"China is going to take Taiwan before OVERMATCH becomes fully operational," Danreb said. "And if they get the decrypted data, they might even push further into the Pacific. Once OVERMATCH comes online with our next-generation platforms, that option will be off the table. But there is one variable."

"The president," Reece said.

"Like you read my mind," Danreb said. "Yes. That's the wild card. I asked myself how I would account for that variable. Can you guess?"

"You wouldn't make that move unless you knew the American president's response beforehand," Reece surmised.

"Unless I had assurances that the United States would sit it out, and I'd only know for sure if I controlled the president of the United States."

"Not Olsen," Reece guessed.

"No, not Olsen," Vic said, sliding Reece another file.

Reece flipped it open.

"Christine Harding?"

"She's the clear front-runner," Vic said. "Polls have been wrong before, but all indications are that she will be the next commander in chief."

"And she's in China's pocket?"

"You will see in that file that Hart and Elba Industries make donations across the political spectrum. At that level that's what you do: you buy as much influence as you can both personally and professionally."

"The husband's done well," Reece commented.

"Oh yes, not much different than a lot of congressional spouses."

"He beat the stock market by at least fifty percent since she was first elected. Bob Harding must really be good at picking winners." The sarcasm was evident in Reece's voice.

"The average in Congress is beating the market by ten percent, though some beat it by over a hundred," Danreb said. "Those gains can be tied directly to bills their spouses voted on. That's not abnormal. What is abnormal is the connection between Hart and the Hardings."

Reece flipped through the file.

"You built a pattern of life on a sitting congresswoman and presidential candidate? I thought the CIA couldn't surveil people on U.S. soil."

"We can't," Vic said. "Most of this is open-source."

"Most?"

"As director of the Special Activities Center, the Political Action Group also falls under my purview. That means I have a thorough working knowledge of campaigns, financing, bribery, extortion, and anything else that might allow us to conduct covert political action."

"Overseas."

"Yes, and in this case, I consider a foreign adversary attempting to put a Chinese asset in the White House as falling under, at least partially, CIA purview."

"What about the FBI?" Reece asked.

"I think they are too busy surveilling school board meetings."

"I read that somewhere," Reece said. "So, you applied that Political Action Group magnifying glass to the Hardings?"

"I did. And now that Representative Harding has Secret Service protection, we have detailed logs of meetings. All classified, of course."

"But you have a source in the Secret Service."

"In this business you need sources everywhere."

"And how does this play into what happened to Katie?"

"Reece, we think you were invited to China because they know about your connection to Alice. They know you were locked in solitary confinement, and they want to use all that to bring you, and therefore Alice, into the fold. Just like the USG wants Alice, so does China. They either want her on their side or want her out of the way."

"Won't they just kill me over there?"

"Not if they think you can give them what they want. Hear them out. Tell them you are considering it."

Reece leaned back in his chair, the fact sinking in that through Alice he had the potential to change the global dynamic or let it run its course.

"You know my dad told me something once that I never forgot," Reece said. "I thought it was an abstract lesson when I was a kid. Now that I've learned more about him and what he was doing at the Agency, learned more about the Collective, I don't think he was talking in abstracts."

"What was it?" Vic asked.

"He said, 'One man with a rifle can change the world.'"

CHAPTER 30

"IN THE SPIRIT OF 'know thy enemy,' let's talk about Hart," Reece said.

"What do you know about what's been termed 'the Great Reset'?" Danreb asked.

"I feel like we are living it," Reece responded.

"Hart recognizes that it's coming. He sees a bleak future for everyone but the new oligarchy."

"Isn't he a part of that oligarchy?" Reece asked.

"He is, but he views the American system as crumbling. This has led to a detachment from any connection or loyalty to a country that has changed so radically as to be unrecognizable."

"I bet the Agency psychs had a good time with that one. Let me take a blue-collar swing: Abandonment first by parents and then by country? Then blame? Then separation? Followed by a need to replace that abandonment with a new parent, a new country that won't leave him because it's a known entity?"

"Almost to the word," Danreb said. "He's not going to fall in line with the Davos crowd."

"He might be onto something," Reece said.

"Regardless of what one calls it, we see rapid changes already; algorithms designed by those at the top of the big-tech hierarchy sending curated news tailored to the individual in order to manipulate; censored content; the canceling of what government in collusion with social media companies considers dangerous by sending them to the equivalent of a digital prison; tracking internet searches to build profiles on users; an existence where every move one makes is monitored and recorded, connecting all of it to a digital credit score."

"That's why I got rid of my cell phone and computer."

"Look at Neuralink. They recently implanted a computer interface into a human brain. Eventually, people will be connected directly to the cloud, which makes control of thoughts and actions a reality."

"And for that reason, I'm out," Reece said.

"It's no longer science fiction, Reece."

"The end of free will."

"Ironic that the country founded on the bedrock principles of freedom and liberty provided the fertile soil for the seeds of our own destruction," Danreb said.

"They are forgetting one thing," Reece said.

"What's that?"

"Compliance of the citizenry."

"They are already doing it, Reece. Just look at COVID mandates. Some would say those were tests to see how quickly they could make a once-free people fall in line. Hart is getting ahead of it."

"He's taking a big step."

"They don't even hide it anymore. Klaus Schwab lectures and writes openly about it."

"Didn't he found the World Economic Forum?"

"He did. Credited with promoting 'stakeholder capitalism.'"

"I think they spelled it wrong," Reece said.

"What?"

"Communism."

"Well, that's essentially it."

"Easy to preach that from Davos."

"Hart sees it coming; ESG."

"What's that again?"

"Environmental, social, and governance. It's a way to crush your business competition veiled in the cloak of social justice."

"COVID lockdowns gave them the power and authority they needed to make gains they had only dreamed of years prior," Danreb continued. "Lockdowns that forced small businesses to close their doors while the giants flourished. Big tech posting record gains throughout the pandemic. To Hart, all this points to the destruction of what was once America."

"He might not be wrong," Reece said.

"Regardless, he's crossed the line and is now taking steps to target the homeland. That's where we come in. If there is going to be a corporate-state government oligarchy, Hart wants to be at the top with his technology in China."

"Who else is in play?" Reece asked.

"That's Brigadier General Ian Novak," Vic said, tossing Reece another file. "Former deputy chief of the Central Security Service at the NSA."

"So a computer guy."

"They prefer the term *cyber.*"

"Computer guy," Reece said again.

"He was also director of intelligence at U.S. Cyber Command."

"Never heard of it."

"He met Hart while he was a major doing a professional development tour at the Hoover Institution, down the road here at Stanford. He helped develop a hacking class that was apparently quite popular."

"I can think of a few things I'd rather do."

"Novak was in the running for director of the NSA, but he ended up falling on his sword after a scandal. They changed the name of a program that Congress had publicly canceled."

"They changed the name and kept doing it?"

"That's it."

"What were they doing?"

"Collecting on U.S. citizens without a warrant."

"Like we are doing with Representative Harding?"

"It's a fine line."

"But instead of writing a book or sitting on a few boards, he goes all in with his old friend Andrew Hart," Reece said, continuing to read through the file.

"And at that point he goes off the radar. He becomes Hart's right-hand man. His official title is 'Strategic Advisor,'" Vic said.

"Looks to be in good shape for a computer guy," Reece observed, looking at the most recent photos of the general. "Why do all these retired generals keep the same haircut when they leave the service?"

"This is Tim Perkins," Vic said, producing another file and sliding it to Reece.

"Head of security with a tattoo on his neck. Former military?"

"No, but we did a deep dive. He tried to enlist in every branch multiple times. All his waivers were denied."

"Waivers? For what?"

"Drugs, using and selling. Vandalism, robbery, multiple counts of aggravated assault. Did two years in High Desert State Prison in Nevada for attempted murder. Had a good run in the world of MMA to include one bout in the Octagon. Broke his foot in the third round and never quite recovered. Ended up spending some time in Peru working at Defion Internacional."

"The private military company?"

"Yes. Started as a contractor and did some time in the Middle East, Africa, and South America and ended up working protection for the executive team. It's unclear how he ended up with Elba."

"Hart has the real dream team. Are all of them in Indonesia?"

"They are."

"Where did the China tie-in come into this?"

"Andy?" Vic said.

"That is a little muddled as well. It looks like it came through the Harding family. Like many politicians they are beholden to donors and foreign interests, though it may have been an independent connection. China has what amounts to spies at various levels of all the tech companies. At some point the connection is made and Hart is eventually elected to the Chinese Academy of Engineering, the same group that invited you to China. It's a lifetime appointment."

"What do they do?"

"It's a think tank that, along with the Chinese Academy of Sciences, advises the Chinese government on scientific and technology issues."

"Okay, let me see if I have this right," Reece said. "Hart is a prodigy of sorts, a tech genius for lack of a better term. His parents are killed and later in life he finds out the CIA was responsible. At the same time, he is witnessing what he sees as the destruction of his country by his own class—tech giants and corporations. He sees a future in which freedom isn't just curtailed but is essentially nonexistent for the 'good of the people' because of climate change or something along those lines. He develops a technology that allows his company's AI quantum computer to rival Alice but has developed it in a way that even Alice can't access or counter. He has direct ties to China and sits on the Chinese Engineering Academy board, which is where we think he was pitched, or he pitched, the idea to set up this Chinese sub to potentially launch at Hawaii, triggering our encrypted data transfer from Oahu to the Utah Data Center, where Elba grabs it in transit. They need time to have their version of Alice decrypt it, which will give them all the military and intelligence information China needs to counter us in the Pacific."

"That's the Cliff Notes version," Danreb confirmed. "China is going to take Taiwan and push into the Pacific; that's a given. If they decrypt or get their hands on decrypted data they can be successful and avert a nuclear confrontation with the United States."

"Feels like we are still missing a few pieces."

"This is the intel world, Reece. More often than not, we are operating on incomplete information."

"What if we were not forcing China's hand. Let's say OVERMATCH didn't exist. What if we didn't have next-generation autonomously controlled assets coming online? China has wanted Taiwan back since Chiang Kai-shek and the nationalists fled there in 1949. They had over seventy years to make a move, including decades under Mao."

"I think there is more to it," Danreb said. "Two separate issues collided at the same moment in history. One is our rapidly improving technological capabilities as we discussed. The other is internal to China."

"What is it?"

"Remember when we first met?"

"Of course. Freddy Strain and I tracked you down at Langley. We needed information on Vasili Andrenov."

"Who met his end from an anti-armor HEAT round not long after."

"I heard about that," Reece said, remembering the off-the-books mission he, Raife, and Mohammed Farooq undertook in Basel, Switzerland, in what seemed a lifetime ago.

"We also discussed Ukraine and Russian demographics."

"I recall. You introduced me to Peter Zeihan's work."

"He was right about Ukraine."

"Ended up being right almost to the day," Reece confirmed.

"Well, something similar is happening in China, only the data is even more controlled, so it's more of a guess than a theory."

"Have you ever been wrong, Andy?"

"I thought I was wrong once. I found out later that I was mistaken."

"Edward Abby?"

"Probably. My point is, our technological advances are only a deterrent once they are in place. Before that, they have the potential to trigger an invasion of Taiwan because it means that China is on the clock."

"I understand that part. What's the second issue?"

"Reece, China's one-child policy was instituted in 1980. The goal was to curb population growth and accelerate economic development. Unfortunately, the decision was more political than logical. It wasn't the population growth that was negatively impacting the economy, it was communist policies. A decade before 1980, the CCP had disincentivized having children, so a de facto one-child policy has been in place since at least 1970. They realized the fatal folly of the policy too late. It was lifted in 2016 but the damage was done. A second-order effect of the policy was the aborting of untold millions of girls, which means that between let's say 1970 and 2016 the number of males far exceeds the number of females."

"That doesn't sound good."

"It's catastrophic. They missed it by a generation, Reece. Even after lifting the one-child policy eight years ago, their birth rate has dropped by seventy percent."

"Seventy?"

"Yes. It's the largest birth-rate drop in recorded history. They hit peak workforce this past year; they simply can't sustain their industrial base and economy for another decade. Even if they were reproducing, there are not enough people under age forty to have enough children to revive Chinese society. China is in their final decade as an economic power. There is nothing they can do to stop it."

"Unless?"

"They can't stop it, but they can choose the time and the place of their demise."

"I thought you said that based on the demographics, a societal collapse was imminent."

"They can still 'command the narrative of the future,' as Zeihan says. In desperation, a war over Taiwan, even if it ends in a nuclear exchange, which eliminates half their population, the CCP limps into the next era of Chinese history."

"That's bleak," Reece said.

"It was theories like this that got me banished to the basement during the Cold War."

Reece closed the file and tossed it onto the center of the table, taking a moment to process all he had learned.

"My relationship with Alice almost got Katie killed," Reece said. "Where did the idea to take me off the board originate?"

"Hart has high-level security clearances," Vic said. "Your operations of the past few years have put you on the radar of some very powerful people. There are as many politicians linked to China as there are on the take from big tech and big pharma. Money makes the wheels turn. If China wanted to know the largest impediment to attaining dominance in the Pacific, they have quite a few sources who would be more than happy to provide them information on OVERMATCH. All that being said, Andrew Hart and Christine Harding seem to be the most likely culprits."

"And OVERMATCH leads to Alice, which leads to me."

"We believe that was the path, Reece," Vic said.

"I think I need something stronger than beer," Reece said. "And the *Chang Zheng*? Are we sure that it wasn't a rogue skipper?"

"Anything is possible, Reece. But that would mean the captain, executive officer, chief of the boat, weapons officer, and probably a political officer would all be in on it."

"I think I saw a movie like that once."

"The more likely scenario is that the Chinese ordered him to launch on Hawaii to trigger our data transfer."

"And he did so knowing he was sacrificing his crew in the process?"

"Not if he thought he was part of a first strike on the Pacific Fleet. We doubt he knew the ultimate objective of his mission was a data transfer."

Reece leaned back in his chair.

"What's next?"

"You accept the invitation from the Chinese Academy of Engineering, or we accept on your behalf. The invitation is for a private meeting with academy leadership in Macau."

"Macau? 'The Vegas of China'?"

"More neutral ground than Beijing."

"I guess. Who am I meeting with?"

"We will provide you with files on each member of the Chinese Academy of Engineering. You can study them tonight."

"How am I getting there?"

"The invitation extended the use of a private jet that belongs to one of their casinos. We've coordinated directly with the academy. You leave tomorrow afternoon from SJC. There's something else we want you to do."

"Why does that make me nervous?"

"Reece, before you go, we think it would be wise if we had a way to track you. Once you are on the plane you will be on your own. No backup. No quick reaction force."

"I'm kind of used to it now."

"Be that as it may, I'd like you to get an implant."

"An implant?"

"Yes."

"Like Snake Plissken?"

"The technology has evolved. This is a tracking device."

"This isn't part of OVERMATCH, is it?"

"No. We have a surgery center upstairs."

"Of course you do."

"Reece, if I didn't think this could avert a war, I wouldn't put you in this situation."

"I know, Vic, but a tracking device?"

"I understand your hesitation but let us do this."

"I don't think so."

"Let's just say it will make me feel better."

"Well, in that case."

"Seriously, Reece. You will be one hundred percent alone over there."

"Not really a new development. How does it work?"

"They can explain it to you upstairs," Vic said.

"Terrific."

"Also, how are you at cards?" Danreb asked.

"What do you mean? Like Go Fish?"

"The Chinese elite are fervent card players. They are taking you over in a private jet and putting you up at their nicest hotel. Be prepared to accept an invitation to a private baccarat game."

"Is it like poker?"

"It's not."

"Wonderful."

"Lucky for you we have a full day before you leave."

"To do what?"

"To teach you when to pass the shoe."

CHAPTER 31

St. Helena, California

BOB HARDING DROVE THROUGH the gate and wound his way past uplighted trees: coast live oaks, red willows, box elders, and California laurels illuminated against the star-filled sky. The long, paved driveway gave way to pea gravel at the top of the hill, the perfect accent to the wine country estate. He loved the feeling and sound of the loose rock under the Porsche 911 Turbo's tires. He had hit the garage door opener a few seconds earlier and had to pause only briefly before he pulled inside, not bothering to wave or even nod at the three black Secret Service SUVs that had taken up residence in front of the house.

Another day of solid gains in the market. Though it was hard to lose when the game was rigged.

He grabbed the bottle of 2018 TOR Black Magic Cabernet Sauvignon from the passenger seat and exited the sports car. The wine was a gift from Andrew Hart, passed along to him through Ian Novak, with whom he had just enjoyed a wonderful dinner at Press. He didn't know why people always insisted on gifting him wine; he had his own vineyard after all.

He shut the door behind him. It was quiet inside. A hallway from the garage led to the kitchen, where he opened the bottle and poured two glasses. He knew where Christine would be at this time of night and if she didn't want it, he'd just help himself to her glass.

He was still carrying a good buzz from the exceptional 100-point 2004 Sine Qua Non Ode To E Grenache he had enjoyed with dinner. The former general wasn't a drinker, which was fine by Bob. It was an extraordinary meal. He had started with celery root soup, followed by ricotta gnudi, and then the black cod dish for his main. They'd shared the caviar pretzel, which was not to be missed at Press. What made the experience even better was that the general had picked up the expensive meal, compliments of Andrew Hart.

Christine had stayed home. It was better she minimize her interactions with anyone associated with Elba Industries.

The bifold glass doors opened to the spacious patio and pool, glowing an iridescent blue from the underwater lights. Slightly lower on the hill, beyond the outdoor living space so as not to obstruct the view, was a clay tennis court, its diamond fencing cloaked with vines of green jasmine punctuated with fragrant white flowers. It was framed by a crushed oyster shell bocce ball court shaded by a trellis covered in grape-vines on one side and a separate guesthouse on the other. Two robust olive trees stood guard in the lower yard between the landscaped section of the property and the rolling vineyard beyond.

It really was a beautiful night.

Christine was sitting in a beige lounge chair. She set a file she was reading to the side.

"How did it go?"

"The leadership team at Elba will be investing additional money with me."

"Of course they will, dear."

"Wine?" he asked.

"I have my own," she said, indicating a glass of white to her left next to a half-empty bottle of Twomey Cellars Sauvignon Blanc.

Bob set both his glasses down on a side table and lay back in the lounge chair next to his wife.

"Christine, you are going to be president."

"And you are going to be the First Gentleman. Will you be able to handle that?"

Bob waved his hand through the air. *Of course.*

"Not only that," he continued, "but you will also avert a war with China during your first year in office."

"The country is sick of wars, Bob. We'll stay involved in the Middle East without committing additional forces—that keeps the defense industry happy. We can keep funding Ukraine; turns out no one really cares what happens there. But when China moves against Taiwan, we will prevent World War Three. We know they will stop before Australia. They take over trade route security, which actually helps us; we've been doing it since the end of the Second World War. We exercise restraint. Negotiate an end to hostilities. Australia will follow our lead. No U.S. servicemen or -women killed. Even so, I'll take a hell of a lot of heat."

"You negotiate with China. At the same time, hit some targets in Yemen, Iraq, Syria, or Jordan, maybe even Iran; bomb that Iranian port the generals are always bringing up."

"Shahid Rajaee?"

"I think so. The one in Bandar Abbas. It's just missiles. Send in the SEALs or Delta Force to kill some terrorist somewhere; the media eats that hero shit up. While you rack up military wins in the Middle East, at the same time you save the world from a nuclear war with China. Send our ships and subs to hold the line before China gets to Australia. Protect Guam with naval forces ordered to only fire in self-defense even though we know they are going to leave us alone there."

"Interesting to know the outcome of world events before they happen, isn't it?" Christine asked.

"And profitable. Cheers," Bob said, holding up his glass.

"Cheers, darling," Christine said, touching her glass to his.

"And what of your dinner meeting? What did you find out about this Alice and James Reece? He's the only one who can fuck this up. Well, not him but that machine."

"Commander Reece has accepted the Chinese Academy of Engineering's invitation to Macau. There they will offer protection for him and his fiancée and a lifelong and well-financed position on the board. I half think he'll take the offer. His own government threw him in solitary confinement, for God's sake. And he didn't even sue us."

"What will he have to do in exchange?"

"Nothing except bring that Alice computer thing with him. I still can't quite comprehend it. We talk about her like she's a real person," Bob said, taking a larger sip of wine than intended.

"Any update on the decryption process? What does Elba call their quantum computer again? Napoleon?"

"Yes, Napoleon. He's still working on it. It could take some time but once it is done, China gets what it needs to move into the Pacific, and we get all the information we could possibly want on all your political opponents. That not only guarantees you the presidency, but it means that once in office you can still use that information to accomplish your policy goals regardless of what party controls the House and the Senate."

"It is a rather tidy deal. If China brings Reece and Alice into the fold, we establish a new twenty-first-century mutual assured destruction, but this time with AI. The entire world will be safer."

"And if not?"

"If not?" Bob took a sip of his wine and looked out over the dark rolling hills of the vineyard. "If not, Commander Reece will never make it home from China."

PART II

THE THRESHOLD

Come not between the dragon and his wrath.

—WILLIAM SHAKESPEARE, *KING LEAR*

CHAPTER 32

Cotai Strip, Macau
Macau Special Administrative Region of the People's Republic of China

A TRANSPACIFIC FLIGHT AS the sole passenger on a Bombardier Global 7500 business jet is not a bad way to get from the People's Republic of California to the People's Republic of China.

The plane belonged to a Las Vegas hotel and casino consortium with properties and interests in Macau that, after a brief downturn during the COVID years, were now exceptionally profitable, far exceeding the revenue brought in from their investments in Sin City. The Matterhorn white aircraft with its sleek classic gold medallion stripe was one of the most advanced and luxurious business jets in existence. It made the 6,000-nautical-mile flight to Macau from Las Vegas once a week at just shy of Mach 1.

Upon boarding at a private hangar at San Jose International Airport, Reece was given a tour of the four cabin zones by an extremely attractive flight attendant. She wore a gold skirt and scarf that matched the plane's stripe and expertly navigated the space in Louboutin heels. A golden name badge that read ROSA BRANDT was affixed to her white blouse. Aside from a dedicated crew suite and full-size kitchen, the living spaces included a club suite with four chairs, a conference suite for dining, a media suite with a sofa and large flat-screen television, and a principal suite with a full-size bed and stand-up shower.

"This must be costing someone hundreds," Reece said to break the ice.

Rosa smiled professionally and informed Reece that depending on speed and weather conditions, the aircraft's operating costs broke down to approximately sixteen thousand dollars per flight-hour.

"Does that include drinks and snacks?" Reece asked as he settled into his "Nuage" seat, which she told him was unique to the Bombardier and the most comfortable seat ever designed in the world of business aviation. She seemed quite proud of it.

"What can I get you?" she asked.

"Let's see, what time is it?" Reece asked, looking at his watch. "Nine a.m. I'll have a beer."

"What type would you like? We have quite the assortment."

"Old Dusseldorf in a long neck," Reece said.

In response to her confused look he said, "A dry martini . . . wait, scratch that, make it a Negroni with Gordon's."

"Of course, sir."

Though he couldn't bring himself to take advantage of the full-size bed, he did enjoy three incredible meals that were a significant step up from the MREs he and his SEALs had endured in the cargo areas of C-17s flying in and out of combat zones over the years.

He did make use of their Soleil lighting system, which Rosa explained was the first circadian rhythm–based cabin lighting system to be incorporated into a global business jet. Its purpose was to combat jet lag with simulated daylight to help ease passengers into their new time zone.

"I've been meaning to add that to mine," Reece said.

He spent most of the sixteen-hour flight staring out the large rectangular windows, dozing on and off, thinking through the events of the past week, and reading *How to Play Baccarat: The Guide to Baccarat Strategy*, which Andy had purchased for him while in San Francisco.

If you stay with Katie, she will die.

He also scratched an incision on the left side of his head behind his ear. The CIA surgeon had shaved a small section of his head, ensuring that his hair was long enough to cover it. Inside was the small tracking device that Vic had insisted upon. The size of a dime, it would not set off a metal detector and would recharge using the inductive mobile phone charging pad that they had also issued him. Holding the pad next to his head for ten minutes would charge the miniature battery in the device for twelve hours. He would hear a small beep in his left ear to let him know it was charging and three rapid beeps when it was fully charged. It would then beep twice every hour to let him know that it was pinging a satellite. The incision was about a quarter of an inch long, and after the Dermabond topical skin adhesive—which to Reece appeared rather similar to superglue—had set, he was good to go.

He had not been wild about the idea of letting the government plant something in his head but in the end he relented, though not for reasons he admitted to Vic and Danreb. Reece had other plans.

When the plane touched down at Macau International Airport, on the eastern end of Taipa Island in the Special Administrative Region of Macau, three uniformed officials from China's General Administration of Customs department boarded and stamped Reece's passport—a visa was not required as he would not be staying longer than thirty days. They had him sign customs paperwork and searched his dark navy leather Globe-Trotter carry-on suitcase. It, and the clothes inside, had been provided by the Agency. Reece did not plan on staying long. His immigration and passport control in-processing were handled efficiently and without hassle.

A two-tone metallic green and black Rolls-Royce Phantom Extended Series II was waiting to shuttle him to his accommodations at the Banyan Tree hotel on the Cotai Strip. The driver who spoke broken English informed him that all guests booked in the Presidential Suite are offered the complimentary service for the ten-minute drive. Reece checked the rear-hinged "suicide" door and was pleasantly surprised to find the iconic Rolls-Royce umbrella.

"Everyone checks," said his driver.

Inside, Reece was surrounded in white leather with green accents. A "coolbox" between the seats offered a chilled bottle of champagne, a Taittinger Comtes Blanc de Blancs 2007 with two champagne flutes.

As tempting as it was, Reece refrained. He was venturing into the unknown. His only backup was a phone through which he could contact Vic, Andy, and Alice, and the GPS implant that had stopped beeping hours ago. He would need to figure out a way to charge it in an area where it was safe to assume that he would be under 24/7 audio and video surveillance. This was China after all.

Reece had been invited in his true name, which meant they knew all about him, and more importantly, all about his connection to Alice.

Leaving the airport, they passed the ferry terminal offering high-speed ferry services between Macau and Hong Kong, Shenzhen, Dongguan, and Zhuhai. A lush green area then materialized on their right, which Reece's driver told him was the Grand Taipa National Park. On their left was a university stadium. A minute later Cotai Strip was upon them. Reece was shocked at how much it reminded him of Las Vegas: a replica Eiffel Tower, the Four Seasons, Wynn Palace, MGM Cotai, Grand Hyatt, and the Venetian. Reece had spent many a night at the Vegas Venetian attending the SHOT Show in his SEAL days. They passed signs or storefronts for Tudor, Rolex, Omega, Bremont, Piaget, Blancpain, Hublot, Panerai, Breitling, Patek Philippe—*they really like their watches here*—and fashion brands like Gucci, Fendi, Chanel, Hermès, Jimmy Choo, Louis Vuitton, Prada, Michael Kors, Versace, Cartier, and Tiffany & Co. It was a shopper's paradise.

The driver turned into the Galaxy Macau, a complex consisting of multiple hotels, shops, and restaurants, and pulled to a stop. The hotelier, dressed in an impeccable gray suit, was there to greet his distinguished guest. He escorted Reece through the lobby of marble with fountains and black rock gardens to a private elevator with gleaming gold doors that whisked them and a uniformed porter who carried Reece's one piece of luggage to the thirtieth floor. The Banyan Tree seemed quieter and more relaxed than the parts of the Cotai Strip that Reece had witnessed on the short drive in.

The doors opened directly to the Presidential Suite and the three men stepped into a large foyer. The hotelier led Reece on the guided tour, showing off the tablet that opened shades, controlled lights, managed the temperature, and operated the television and stereo. Reece could even use it to order room service. The centerpiece of the spacious living room was a light neon-blue grand piano with the lid up and ready to play. The suite included a dining room with a huge round black table with a three-tier waterfall crystal chandelier overhead, full bar, and family sitting area with a large television. Floor-to-ceiling glass windows offered breathtaking views of Cotai City and a beautiful pool complex with a massive wave pool and a beach made with 350 tons of imported white sand below. A wide illuminated winding staircase led to the thirty-first floor, where a private sauna and spa treatment room awaited. The central feature of the upper level was an indoor relaxation pool positioned with views of the Strip. It was located between another living room and an enormous master bedroom with two walk-in closets and an expansive bathroom, complete with a Tibetan wood bathtub. On the other side of the second floor was another bedroom with two queen beds, presumably for those traveling with kids in tow, and another bathroom almost the same size as the master and that also included its own Tibetan wood tub. An unobtrusive door led to a small hallway at the end of which was another door to a butler room for those traveling with help.

The hotelier explained that the artwork featured Buddhist and Taoist designs from the eighteenth century. Dark wood pedestals displayed rare vases and fans decorated with interpretations of Taoist immortal attributes. On one prominent wall hung an imperial carpet from the Qing Dynasty. Woven of spectacular golds, greens, and reds, the silk and wool dragons and leaves were brought to life by ceiling-mounted accent lights.

The tour complete, Reece's guide pointed out that a letter had been left for him from his hosts at the desk in the foyer.

Not knowing exactly what was expected of him in the Presidential Suite, Reece thanked him and handed him and the porter each a hundred-dollar bill—it was easy to be generous with the CIA's money. *Good ol' Uncle Sugar.*

Once he was alone, Reece opened the letter. There was no use searching for audio and video monitoring devices. He could assume they were there. The note was from the chairman of the Chinese Academy of Engineering. It requested his presence that evening at the Robuchon au Dôme restaurant, located at the top of the Grand Lisboa Hotel, with specific instructions on how to get there. It also invited him to a private VIP card game following dinner. The dress code for dinner and the card game was formal. They had taken the liberty of including three tuxedos in the suite's closet with sizes based on their best estimations.

Reece glanced at his stainless dive watch. He had a few hours until dinner.

The one amenity that the Presidential Suite lacked was its own gym. Reece changed into workout clothes and navigated his way to the hotel fitness center. It was deficient in the weights department, so he ran five miles on a treadmill at its max incline, stopping every mile to do fifty push-ups and fifty sit-ups to get the blood flowing.

Back in the room, he explored it without his guides. If he was under video surveillance, he wanted it to look like he was getting familiar with the expansive suite. In reality, he was clearing while memorizing the floor plan.

He opted for the rain shower instead of the relaxation pool or Tibetan tub. Then he plugged the inductive mobile phone charging pad into an outlet on the bedside table and lay down, pretending to take a nap. He set the alarm on his phone just to be safe. He adjusted the phone and charger next to his pillow and rolled over after a few minutes, so his head rested on the charger in just the right spot. He heard a beep through the bone in his left ear. Ten minutes later he heard three rapid beeps, at which point he slid the phone back over the charger.

The phone's alarm woke him from an actual slumber forty-five minutes later. He wasn't so sure the Bombardier's circadian rhythm–based cabin lighting system worked as advertised.

He swung his legs from the bed. *Fists with your toes.*

A dusk had fallen over the city. Reece moved to the bedroom's floor-to-ceiling window and looked out over the Coati section of Macau, a dizzying array of flashing neon lights assaulting his senses.

What does tonight have in store?

At least if they kill you here, Katie will live.

She will.

Push that aside, Reece. Time to go to work.

Reece stepped back into the rain shower and turned it to an almost scalding temperature. Then, though he loathed to do it, he turned the knob in the other direction. Following the previous extreme, each drop of water now felt like a shard of ice. Reece worked his breath control and counted to sixty, three times. He then turned off the shower; alive, awake, ready. It was time to see if any of the tuxedos fit.

A note in the closet let him know the three tuxedos came from the nearby "gentleMannor." It was their pleasure to bespoke tailor the clothing and they would be happy to make any adjustments. It listed their address on Avenida Conselheiro Ferreira de Almeida along with a phone number. Printed along the borders of the custom card was a quote in English, Chinese, and Portuguese that read: "A man should look as though he has chosen his clothes with intelligence, put them on with care, and then forgotten all about them." The source: Sir Hardy Amies, dressmaker for Queen Elizabeth II.

Makes sense.

Between the three choices Reece found something that worked. He was impressed with how well everything fit: black pants—which Reece thought were probably referred to as "trousers" here—cummerbund, and a single-breasted jacket with a white cotton shirt, cuff links, studs, and a white linen pocket square. Black socks and three pairs of whole-cut black leather oxfords, of which the middle size fit perfectly, completed the ensemble, save for the bow tie.

He had worn his naval officer's tuxedo, which he recalled was called a "mess dress" or "dinner dress" uniform, only once: when he married Lauren. That uniform had come with a pre-tied bow tie. This was a self-tie. Luckily YouTube was not restricted on Macau and after watching a "how-to" video he finally got it after close to twenty tries.

Reece did not like being unarmed but there was no avoiding it. He took a black Montegrappa rollerball pen from his suitcase and slid it into the ticket pocket, the inside pocket with a slight slant on the right side of his jacket.

Remember, James, the mind is your most formidable weapon. Use it, his father had said.

"Might have to, Dad," Reece whispered.

He adjusted his bow tie, took one last look in the mirror, then made his way down the staircase to the thirtieth floor and hit the down button for the elevator.

It was time to find out why he had been summoned to China.

CHAPTER 33

Robuchon au Dôme
Grand Lisboa Hotel, Macau
Macau Special Administrative Region of the People's Republic of China

THE FIFTEEN-MINUTE DRIVE FROM the Banyan Tree hotel in Cotai took Reece across the Sai Van Bridge into Macau. It was nice to at least be doing it in style. There were quite a few perks to staying in the Presidential Suite; the Rolls-Royce was one of them. They passed the Mandarin Oriental, MGM, and Wynn before pulling into the Grand Lisboa Hotel, one of the oldest resorts in Macau.

Reece entered the main lobby and weaved his way through the crowds of tourists and gamblers until he located the elevators and took one to the thirty-ninth floor, where he gave his name to a receptionist standing in front of a large man in a suit. She directed him to a hallway with floor-to-ceiling wine in temperature-controlled racks behind glass. At the end of the hallway was a private elevator that took him to the forty-third floor. Even before the doors parted, Reece could hear music. When they opened, Reece stepped into another world. Gone were the crowds and commotion of the lobby. This was not the sort of establishment where they packed you in and rushed you out. This was an experience. The circular room offered a magnificent view of Macau from every seat. Men and women in formal attire dined at tables spaced out to ensure enough privacy for discerning guests. Reece's eyes were immediately drawn to an enormous chandelier hanging over the vintage grand piano in the center of the large circular room. It reminded him of Alice and what she had once looked like when they first met. The pianist was playing a concerto, or was it a sonata?

A maître d', who seemed to be expecting him, led him across the thick black and gold carpet past a glass enclosure of wine and small carved-wood chalets to one of the establishment's two private rooms. Their path was lit by Baccarat floor lamps giving off just enough light so as not to interfere with the magnificent view.

Reece passed three tables with two men each without drinks in front of them doing a poor job of blending in; security. One man, older than the others, sat at a table alone. Head of security?

The maître d' opened the door to the private room and Reece stepped inside.

Instead of a room full of scientists from the Chinese Academy of Engineering, one man sat at a table that looked large enough for four, though there were only two chairs. A bread basket was on the table and a bottle of champagne was chilling in a stainless-steel champagne bucket on a stand next to it.

"Mr. Reece," the man said in lightly accented English, getting to his feet and approaching his guest.

He was shorter than Reece's six feet by a good four inches and looked to be in his late fifties, perhaps early sixties. He was dressed almost identically to Reece in a single-breasted classic black tuxedo.

"Let me apologize for the subterfuge. I tried to keep it to a minimum. My name is Chen Yun and I am the minister of state security."

He approached and extended his hand.

"I trust your flight in was without incident and your accommodations are adequate?"

"I take it I am not meeting with the board of the Academy of Engineering," Reece said.

"You assume correctly, Mr. Reece, but then you knew that already, didn't you? Please sit," he said, motioning to the table.

As they took their seats the door opened and a waiter appeared, filling Reece's white wineglass with champagne and then disappearing as quickly as he had appeared.

"What did you think of the chandelier?" Yun asked. "It contains 131,500 pieces of Swarovski crystal. Designed to resemble a women's skirt."

"I didn't know Swarovski made crystal," Reece said. "I thought they just made rifle scopes."

"Wonderful; a sense of humor. I was concerned that this meal might be boring. I am glad to see we can at least enjoy ourselves."

"Does your security detail out there get to partake as well?"

"They ate before their shift, and unfortunately for them, only water and soda tonight. These are dangerous times."

"So I'm told," Reece said.

"I hope you don't mind, but I took the liberty of ordering the set menus with a few variations. This is one of only three three-star Michelin restaurants in all of Macau. Rather than a Cantonese meal I decided to show you that we are quite cosmopolitan here. To me, this is the finest restaurant in the city: French with a hint of Asian influence. Did you notice the wine cabinets on the way in? Those sculptures are of the most renowned châteaus in all of France, handcrafted by Viscount David Linley. The wine list has almost eighteen thousand labels. I figured you for a Bollinger man. This is a 2012 Bollinger Vieilles Vignes Françaises. It was a season marked by substantial rains and a long growing cycle. I think you will find it satisfactory."

"What are we celebrating?"

"Life, Mr. Reece."

"In general, or something specific?"

"Our time here is precious. One never knows how long one has."

"True for all of us," Reece responded.

"Americans think of champagne as its own distinct category. They ruin it by serving it in flutes. This is a wine," Yun continued, holding his glass to the light. "It is a wine from Champagne, France, and it should be enjoyed as such. It needs to breathe. A flute does not allow one to relish its complex layers. One must savor the experience, as you never know when you will enjoy your final libation. In France, they serve it correctly; in a tulip flute or white wineglass like these. Traditional flutes restrict the flavor. When drinking a bottle like this, you must savor it."

"Have you tried the Mumms?"

"Excuse me?"

"Never mind."

"Cheers, Mr. Reece, though here we say *Gānbēi*."

"What does that mean?"

"Dry your cup."

"That I can do."

"Complex, isn't it," Yun said, bringing it to his nose.

"Very rich," Reece said, not knowing exactly what to say.

"Roasted ginger and hazelnuts with candied pear and an understated touch of dark chocolate."

The two men tasted the champagne.

"Smooth," Reece said, thinking it tasted like every other glass of champagne he had ever tried.

"Fruits, lemon, and ginger. Just exceptional," remarked his host.

Setting his glass down, Yun tore off a piece of bread from a basket filled with more varieties than Reece knew existed.

"In our line of work, Mr. Reece, one must sometimes take solace in good food and drink to assuage the specter of the dead. Do you agree?"

"I certainly am not known for turning down a good drink," Reece said.

"Your profile says as much."

"You even got my size right," Reece said, motioning to his tux.

"The file was not as detailed as I would prefer, hence the three different sizes."

"At least I am not underdressed," Reece said.

"What do you think of this view? This building is two hundred and thirty-eight meters high. You can see all of Macau. Every table in the restaurant has a view, but this private room is one of the most sought-after tables not just in Macau, but in the world."

"You must know someone."

"Mr. Reece, are you a card player? Baccarat?"

"I read a book about it on the plane."

"Sometimes I find it difficult to tell if you are joking, but tonight, we will play. And don't fear, you will be playing with house money. I know your monthly military retirement check would not even cover the first course of this meal."

"That's a relief. For a moment I thought we might have to split the bill."

"I found it interesting that your government does not include your special pays in your retirement," Yun said. "After serving your country for all those years, seeing friends die in ill-begotten wars in Iraq and Afghanistan, you would think the least they could do would be to incorporate a few extra dollars a month in your check instead of sending billions to the criminals in Ukraine."

"Yeah, well, they get you however they can."

"And they tax you on top of that, don't they?"

"Happy to pay my fair share," Reece said. "Especially when I know they allocate those funds so wisely."

"I believe you speak with what you call sarcasm?"

"I speak it fluently."

The door opened and two waiters arrived, setting down the amuse-bouche and refreshing the champagne.

One of the waiters said something in Chinese and then translated in heavily accented English. "Imperial caviar and king crab with crustacean jelly," he said before both took their leave.

"I need to talk with my staff," Reece said.

Chen Yun laughed.

"This is the only way to start a civilized meal, though I recommend combining it with a bite of bread," the minister said.

"Glad I'm dining with a regular," Reece replied.

"I know what you are thinking, Mr. Reece."

"Are we at that stage already?"

"I can read your mind. It's not hard to do. You are thinking that wealth is not something to be proclaimed or vaunted but something that is to be understood. The view, the overpriced food and wine, the opulence of the chandelier and piano are screaming 'new money.'"

"I wouldn't put it quite like that," Reece said, washing the intense flavors of the amuse-bouche down with champagne. "Though one might say that it gives the impression that China has something to prove."

"Ah, there it is," Yun said, leaning back in his chair and touching his starched napkin to the corners of his mouth. "Our psychologists said you were perceptive."

"For their sake I am glad they weren't wrong."

The door opened again and bussers appeared to clear the caviar plates. The waiters replaced them with artichoke salad served with Alba truffle shavings over smoked foie gras. The waiter explained that the artichokes were from Normandy while going through the ceremony of allowing Yun to taste the wine, a 2010 Puligny-Montrachet 1er-Cru "Les Chalumaux."

Le Grenouille was next: caramelized frog legs on a spelt risotto with garlic with a Diel German Riesling.

"Tastes like chicken," Reece said.

Le Homard followed: a butter-poached Maine lobster tail with a delicate lemongrass curry sauce and a glass of 2014 Leroy Domaine d'Auvenay Les Folatieres Chardonnay.

What Reece thought could be a main course of Le Canard de Challans appeared next: breast of moulard duck perfectly cooked and matched with a 100-point 2007 Domaine du Pegau Châteauneuf du Pape.

The portions were so small that Reece had a hard time differentiating the appetizers from the main course, not that it mattered as the food kept coming.

A Le Beouf Kagoshima was then presented as the main: seared ribeye Kagoshima beef, with girolle mushrooms paired with a right-bank 2005 Château Faugères Saint-Emilion Grand Cru Bordeaux. The waiter set a beautifully balanced Damascus knife next to Reece's plate that sliced the tender fatty meat like butter. Reece was tempted to use it to slit the throat of the man across from him.

Not yet, Reece. Do your job.

If he ordered the hit that wounded Katie, his time will come. Katie is alive. Right now, this is bigger than you.

Finally came a 1997 Taylor vintage port with a plate of twelve different cheeses.

Even after all the previous courses, Reece was still hungry.

"I have thoroughly enjoyed our meal," Yun said.

"As have I," Reece replied. "Sometimes it's good to look your enemy in the eye."

"Come now, Mr. Reece. Is that how you view me?"

"How should I view you?" Reece asked, taking a sip of the sweet dessert wine.

"You know why you are here, Mr. Reece."

"Why don't you help spell it out for me, just so we are clear."

"I have studied you, Lieutenant Commander James Reece."

"I'm retired."

"I know what your own government did to you, to your wife and daughter. I offer my sincere condolences. No parent should have to outlive their child. They used you as a tool of the state and then they experimented on you, on your fellow SEALs; they gave you all brain tumors, and then they tried to murder you. They succeeded in killing your Team in Afghanistan. They even incarcerated you; solitary confinement for three months without due process. And now there is Russia. The Russians will never stop trying to kill you, Mr. Reece. But it's not just you; it's your fiancée, Ms. Katie Buranek. It's your friends the Hastingses. You put them all at risk. You know it and I know it. Regardless of what they say, they don't really want you there on that ranch in Montana. There are even those within your own government who will never stop trying to kill you. Oh yes, I know about the Collective. It is of the past. China's ascendancy is the future. You might escape death for a few more years but eventually it will catch up with you. How many more friends and lovers of yours will die in the meantime?"

Reece remained silent, staring into the eyes of the man across the table, knowing he was right.

"Here, in China, is the only place you will be safe; the only place Ms. Buranek will be safe," the minister continued.

"You are asking me to betray my country. What would you get out of this deal?"

"Alice, of course. You don't really think we don't know about her, do you? We also know that she has gone to ground, that she is not even accessible to your country's military or intelligence establishment. We know she answers to you."

"And how do you know that?"

"Oh, come now, Mr. Reece. Your 'open society' has allowed us to place assets liberally throughout your defense and intelligence communities. Academia and the private sector are open for placement without any safeguards at all. It is for all practical purposes legal to buy your politicians, including those at the very top."

The door opened again, and the waitstaff began pushing in a large dessert and coffee tray. Minister Yun waved them off with a flick of his wrist.

"You would be safe here. Ms. Buranek would be safe here. You would receive a lifetime appointment to the Academy of Engineering, with compensation that is quite generous. You would no longer be putting the Hastings family at risk. Your friend Raife, his wife and children will not end up dead like Lauren and Lucy. Protect them by leaving that life behind. Bring Ms. Buranek. Raise your family here or on one of our many estates in the Pacific."

"You want Alice to become a weapon of China."

"No, Mr. Reece, you misunderstand. We are not asking you to betray your country, though they have already betrayed you many times over. We simply want Alice off the board. With you here, safe with your family, we know Alice is out of play. It is most certainly not a betrayal. It is a necessity for you to protect your family. Your government can't do it and you certainly can't do it in America. I am offering you sanctuary, Mr. Reece. Take it. For your sake and the sake of your family."

Reece did what he could to keep his anger in check.

Play the game, just like you went over with Vic and Andy.

"And Taiwan? You want to ensure Alice will not interfere with an invasion of Taiwan?"

"Invasion? Mr. Reece, we both know that my country views Taiwan as a province that is already ours. It is a 'reunification' and it is inevitable. Your country has an official 'One China' policy but at the same time it also has an unofficial policy of 'strategic ambiguity.' It is the 'ambiguity' part of that policy that is concerning, but we both know the United States is not in a place either politically or militarily to interfere if we were to bring that unruly island back under direct governance. Who knows, we might turn it into a Special Administrative Region like Hong Kong or Macau. When we do re-exert our rightful control, the United States will implement sanctions and embargos and attempt to block shipments of oil, fertilizer, and iron from coming around the Cape or through the Arabian Sea, Indian Ocean, and Malacca Strait to the South Sea, but we have of course prepared for that and have contingencies and stockpiles of reserves in place to deal with it. The world needs our microchips and those that are manufactured in Taiwan. Soon we will have that monopoly. Their export will continue unabated. All this averts a nuclear confrontation at a future date. You have been led to believe that China is finished, that the population cannot sustain us into the next generation and an industrial collapse is on the horizon. Don't believe it. China will continue to rise and those of us at the helm will chart a course into the next era of Chinese history. America's time as the dominant world power is coming to an end. It is clear for all to see. China is rising. Have you been to Taroko Gorge? It is stunning. Ms. Buranek and your children will love it. Give them that life and not the very short one you gave Lauren and Lucy."

Reece's eyes narrowed.

"As much as I appreciate the hospitality, it won't stop me from ripping your throat out when the time comes," Reece said.

"This was all going so well, Mr. Reece. There is no need to resort to threats of violence. Please, consider what I have proposed. You are free to return to the United States and discuss it with Ms. Buranek, and if you decide that a life of guaranteed safety and security for you and for her and one day for your children is not the way, then we will respect your decision. In the meantime, after dessert and coffee, I have always found that a good card game acts as a substitute for or at least a diversion from the stimulation of the secret world."

Reece finished his port and stood, tossing his napkin on the table.

"Thank you for the meal, Minister. I think I'll forgo the baccarat tonight. I plan on leaving tomorrow."

"So soon?" Yun said, getting to his feet. "You have three more days with us."

"I've heard enough."

"Consider my proposition, Mr. Reece. It does come with a time limit. You have a week. My card," Yun said, handing over a business card. "Perhaps next time we can share a dessert with Ms. Buranek and enjoy a game of baccarat? Until then."

Reece nodded and left the room, past the security men, the pianist, the maître d', and the other similarly dressed guests dining under the lavish crystal chandelier hanging from the center of the massive dome overhead.

As he made his way to the private elevator, it was not the offer that weighed on him.

It was the fact that he knew that most of what Minister Yun said was true.

• • •

Chen Yun returned to his chair and looked into his unfinished glass of port.

Interesting man, this James Reece.

Yun had not lied to him, not really, except for the part about respecting his decision.

There was only one acceptable choice.

Ba Jin entered and took a seat in what ten minutes earlier had been the American's chair.

"Your assessment?" Jin asked.

"He's smart, disarmingly so. He was even funny, right up until I brought up his family. The eyes that had been warm during the meal turned to ice. It even looked like they changed color."

"You are familiar with his file, Minister. He has a history of solving problems through the direct application of violence."

"That he does."

"Is he considering our proposal?"

"That is difficult to say. He is a patriot, but he serves a corrupt and dying nation, one that is responsible for the deaths of his wife and daughter and SEAL Team, one that locked him in prison. As I said, he seems astute for an American."

"But how logical is he?" Jin asked.

"That we will find out. What does the report say?"

Jin handed the minister a tablet.

"See for yourself."

Yun slid a finger across the bottom of the screen and rapidly advanced a video that had recorded Reece's every movement since he boarded the plane in San Jose; the jet, the Rolls-Royce, his suite, the fitness center, all the way up to this very room. The video had been run through an AI-enabled supercomputer's predictive behavioral analysis program.

Yun stared at the final line in the report.

Body language, tone, and facial expressions indicated a negative response with 96 percent accuracy.

The minister handed the tablet back to the president's envoy.

"How do you want to do it?" Yun asked.

"Fentanyl overdose from a Russian or Ukrainian hooker would do the job, but this Mr. Reece doesn't seem the type. Fentanyl overdoses are so normal these days they rarely result in a thorough investigation."

"We will send a Triad hit team and then control the investigation," Yun said. "They will use any means necessary to be sure the one conduit to the outside world this Alice has will never leave Macau alive."

"Wise move, Minister. I will let the president know as soon as it is done. He will be pleased to know that Alice is no longer an issue."

Minister Yun swirled the sweet wine in its port glass remembering his words from earlier that evening.

Our time here is precious. One never knows how long one has.

True for all of us, the American had responded.

Chen Yun felt a slight chill.

He finished what was left of the ruby-red drink in one sip and stood to take his leave.

With any luck he could still make his card game.

CHAPTER 34

Banyan Tree Hotel
Cotai Strip, Macau
Macau Special Administrative Region of the People's Republic of China

REECE RETURNED TO HIS hotel and made it back to his room well aware that he was under observation. It was not feasible that the Chinese intelligence service would allow him this much freedom unless he was under audio and video surveillance.

They would expect him to clear the room, which he did.

The Chinese wanted Alice, or rather they wanted to ensure she was out of play. And in exchange, they would give Reece and Katie peace.

Reece had no doubt their offer was sincere.

The question was, would they really allow him to leave?

Would throwing them off with the thought that he might leave tomorrow change their game plan?

A part of him knew that Chen Yun was right. He had been targeted by a corrupt government, or rather corrupt elements within that government. There would always be those drawn into government service by the allure of power.

Power tends to corrupt and absolute power corrupts absolutely.

Lord Acton was right.

Or perhaps just the *possibility* of power was a magnet for the society's worst.

Political power was not just attractive for the corruptible. In truth they were corrupt and morally bankrupt from the start.

It's not your country, Reece. It is elements within the power structure.

Is it, Reece?

Doesn't Katie deserve a life, a life free of the violence that follows you?

Don't the Hastingses deserve to be free?

Raife's kids deserve to grow up with a father.

Don't do to them what you did to Freddy's family.

Give them all the opportunity to live without the constant shadow of death.

Let them go.

Reece walked to the en-suite bar and removed a bottle of 2002 Dom Perignon Brut from a glass refrigerator and a bottle of the Macallan 18-Year Single Malt Scotch Whisky from a shelf.

Knowing he was being watched, he made a production of finding a whisky glass and walking up the stairs to his bedroom, where he put both bottles next to his bed. He opened the scotch and poured a finger for the benefit of the cameras. *Just a little nightcap.* He took a sip and set the glass back on the bedside table.

He untied his bow tie, stripped it from around his neck, tossed it to the side, and unbuttoned the top button of his shirt.

He removed Bluetooth-enabled earbuds from his Globe-Trotter suitcase on a nearby luggage rack. He ensured they were charged and linked to his mobile phone. He set one on the bedside table. He put the case and the other earbud back into his carry-on, confirming that he was packed up and ready to go.

He then used the tablet on a charging stand next to the bed to lower the blackout curtains and turn out the lights. He positioned the inductive charging pad so he could charge his GPS implant before lying down still fully clothed to wait.

If you stay with Katie, she will die.

• • •

Reece felt the pressure change first. It was something that had stayed with him from the early days of the war, a change in pressure that was associated with an IED. He had become so sensitive to it that he had to remind himself that he wasn't still downrange when Lauren opened a door in their air-conditioned house in Virginia Beach. There was something about a sealed home with air-conditioning that was susceptible to negative or positive air pressure deviations. He never felt it in their Coronado, California, home, which typically had windows and doors open to allow for the cool breezes coming off the Pacific and may have been why he preferred the "Silver Strand" to "The Beach." He felt the pressure change now.

Let them come.

Reece swung his legs from the bed and inserted the earbud into his left ear. He closed his dominant left eye to preserve his natural night vision and hit an innocuous preprogrammed number for a company called Transworld Consortium on his mobile phone.

"Alice?"

"Yes, Reece," came the semi-monochromatic voice that still reminded him of Lauren.

"Are you watching?" Reece asked.

"Yes."

"Shut down their feed and send it to my phone," Reece said.

"Done," came the immediate response.

Reece's phone lit up into multiple boxes with live infrared video footage showing each room in the Presidential Suite.

Four people had stopped on the stairs, indicating to Reece that whoever was watching the video feed had relayed to them that there was a problem. The last man in line had a phone to his ear. Another waited at the base of the staircase and yet another stood by the elevator. They were not outfitted in tactical gear, nor did they have rifles or helmets with night vision. They wore civilian clothes and looked to be carrying pistols. With their video feed down, they were going to have to move based on the last information they had been passed.

They should have sent more men.

If you die here, Katie lives.

Not yet, Reece.

There is still work to do.

Reece stood. Keeping his connection to Alice, he stuffed the phone into his pocket and grabbed the champagne and scotch bottles from the nightstand. He moved past the large French doors that opened into the hallway overlooking the lower level and the relaxation pool, stopping at a door that led into the hallway farther down.

Just because they didn't look like operators or law enforcement did not mean they were not professionals.

Whoever they were, he was going to make them work for it.

Reece paused at another set of double doors, set the bottles down, and reached for his phone. Behind him was the relaxation pool. On the other side of the doors was the top of the stairway.

They were coming.

He could hear them turn to their right, moving as silently as they could to his bedroom door. Keeping his left eye shut to ensure the pupil remained dilated and ready for the darkness, he watched the video feed on his phone with his right eye as the intruders passed him on the other side of the wall. He watched as the lead man removed something from under his coat.

A suppressed Ingram M10 submachine gun?

MAC-10s should be in museums.

Reece guessed this was probably a copy or derivative.

Who are these guys?

Reece could see that the fourth man in the stack was not looking back. They were counting on the two men on the lower level to provide that security. They were focused on the bedroom door.

Patience.

Wait until they enter.

They will be focused on making the kill.

Use the dark.

Capitalize on the element of surprise.

You will not have it for long.

Reece watched them stop at the door. The second man went for the handle while the number one man with the Ingram machine pistol stepped back to give him room.

Reece hit the button on the side of his mobile device to put it into rest mode and shoved it into his pocket. He then reached down to pick up the two bottles by their necks and slipped into the hallway.

• • •

This was going to happen fast.

No friendlies in the darkness.

Kill them all.

The almost imperceptible click of the opening of the bedroom door; the scuffling of feet; the movement of bodies; the focus on a target who was no longer there; having pistols and at least one sub-gun when your mark was unarmed; the psychology of fighting on one's home turf, knowing for certain anyone behind you was on your team—these all played to Reece's advantage as he approached his prey in the dark.

As the MAC-10 went to work spraying what was either 9mm Parabellum or .45 ACP into the bed, Reece increased his speed. The last man was not even through the threshold when the champagne bottle made contact with the back of his head.

Reece thought his forward motion and the sheer velocity of the blow would shatter the bottle on impact, but instead it acted like a club. He could feel the man's skull crack under the weight of the heavy bottle.

Even with its two-stage suppressor, the MAC-10 made enough noise to mask Reece's attack.

Reece allowed the bottle's momentum to continue across his body and used that energy to swing the second bottle of Macallan upward to catch the third man in the stack square in the face, breaking his nose on impact. Reece twisted his body and drew back, firing the larger champagne bottle into the man's face. He could hear and feel the man's teeth breaking under its force.

The second man was just turning when Reece assaulted him with multiple blows from the upturned bottles. Using them to attack in a *sinawali* weaving pattern from his Filipino kali stick fighting training—forehand, backhand, backhand, forehand—Reece pressed the fight, but instead of kali, escrima, or arnis sticks he had a bottle of scotch and champagne. The devastating assault put the man on the ground.

The lead intruder with the MAC-10 sensed and heard the commotion behind him. With what little light emitted from a clock by the bed, a smoke detector on the ceiling, and a red light in the flat-screen television affixed to the far wall, there was just enough visibility for Reece to see him turn.

Had he shot all thirty or thirty-two rounds from the magazine? Had he changed mags? Was this a copy or derivative that had a different-size magazine than an original M10? What type of pistols did the other two men in the room have? How fast would they be able to recover and get them online to shoot?

You know how to fight multiple assailants, Reece.

One at a time.

Reece stepped forward and sent the champagne bottle into the temple of the man with the MAC-10 and quickly followed up with the Macallan in his left hand, hammering it down into his face, catching him in the cheekbone as he attempted to bring up the weapon.

Reece was in the dark with four armed assailants.

Surprise. Speed. Violence of action.

He had now given up the element of surprise. He had capitalized on speed. Now it was time to double down on violence.

He was in their OODA loop.

Observe. Orient. Decide. Act.

They were in the orient stage, confused by the violence that had been visited upon them in the night at a time and place where they assumed they held the advantage.

Their assumption was wrong.

Don't forget the two on the lower level. They could easily change this dynamic.

Prioritize and execute.

Closest threat, Reece.

The man with the MAC-10 needed to die.

Reece threw the champagne bottle back toward the men behind him as a distraction and trapped the MAC-10 to the body of the lead attacker. The man's finger was still on the trigger and as his hand tightened around the grip in response to Reece's onslaught, he discharged the last ten rounds in the magazine downward. Half of them impacted the floor and the other half zipped down the man's leg. His scream was a mixture of pain and disbelief as they toppled to the ground. Reece instinctively rolled into the mount. With his opponent pinned on his back with Reece on top, the SEAL drew back with the bottle of Macallan, smashing it down into the man's head and stunning him even further.

These bottles are strong.

Three men behind you, Reece.

Reece drew back again, this time bringing the bottle down on the side of the bedside table. He heard and felt it shatter, leaving him holding the neck with jagged shards of glass protruding from its splintered main body.

Reece removed his right hand from the empty MAC-10 and slid it up to the man's head. Grabbing his hair, he ripped the head to the right, exposing the vulnerable soft tissues of the neck, which Reece attacked with the broken bottle. Withdrawing and stabbing it in again and again, he felt it slice through skin, sinew, muscle, cartilage, veins, and arteries as he targeted the critical carotid. He needed to guarantee he wouldn't be killed by someone he thought was already dead when he shifted his attention to the other assailants. Reece rotated it and ground it in farther, coring it into the neck until he felt the warm spray of the severed artery that supplied blood to the brain.

Three more in the room, Reece.

Empty gun.

No time to search for an extra M10 mag and reload.

Keep fighting.

Reece launched himself to his feet.

It was still dark. Reece was fighting shadows.

He took a step to engage a man struggling to get to his knees when he was hit from the side and driven back past his bed, almost going to the ground.

The thing about fighting shadows in the dark is that once the fight is on, the darkness levels the playing field.

Reece then felt a side kick to his ribs, followed up by a series of strikes that he attempted to block with his elbows as he was driven through a set of double doors and into the relaxation pool room. He absorbed a palm strike under his chin and a forearm to the side of his neck.

This guy is Wing Chun–trained.

Reece regained his balance and attempted to enter with a left jab followed by a right cross, but his opponent crossed the frogman's hands, trapping them before they could do the intended damage. Reece felt the outside edge of a hand connect just at the base of his jaw only to have it quickly replaced with an elbow strike that almost put Reece out. He felt the man's body overcommit to the follow-through from the elbow, which gave Reece the opportunity to pivot his hips and deliver a devastating hook to his opponent's kidney. Reece loaded again and sent another left hook that was blocked by the man's right arm but gave Reece the opening he needed to send a right cross that connected with the man's jaw. The man responded with a series of strikes that kept Reece's hand away from his face, pushing the SEAL farther back toward the small pool.

If one of the guys in the other rooms gets to their gun, I am a dead man.

I'm not ready yet.

Instead of opting for another boxing combination as he was driven back, Reece grabbed the material on the upper arms of the man's jacket above his hands and yanked down, pulling him off-balance. Reece dropped his weight and hips lower than his opponent's to gain positional advantage. With his left foot forward, he rolled onto his back, planting his right foot in the man's hip and rotating him up to launch him into the pool.

Reece was back on his feet in an instant.

Finish him before his friends finish you.

Being suddenly submerged in water in the dark, even if it is only three feet deep, is an uncomfortable place to be for most people. For Reece it was home.

Reece jumped into the small pool. The warm water was just past his knees. In the blackness, he moved to the splashing as his opponent tried to get his bearings. Reece was upon him.

In the frantic fight for life, the body will do interesting things. Add water and near-total darkness to the equation and the variables escalate. As Reece made contact, the man twisted from his grasp, sweeping the larger man from his feet. Reece turned to gain position, clawing his way back up his attacker's body, both of them ending up against the far side of the small pool. Reece attempted to roll the man underwater but was blocked by the edge.

Finish this, Reece. You have two other immediate threats.

With his arm wrapped around the man's upper body and both their heads just out of the water, Reece snaked his left hand into the right inside ticket pocket of his dinner jacket and removed the Montegrappa pen.

Getting as much leverage as he could, he stabbed it into the left side of the man's throat.

Reece felt the dying man cry out, his hands going to his neck in a last-ditch attempt to save himself. He attempted to twist his body away, legs kicking out in a frenzy, trying to escape his fate.

Reece extracted the pen and jammed it in again.

He is not dying fast enough.

Reece dug deeper into the man's neck wound to further open the cavity, allowing more vital blood to seep into the pool.

Still not fast enough.

You are going to be dead in seconds if those other men get their bearings.

Reece removed the pen from the side of the man's neck, positioned it in front of his eye, and inserted it into the socket, pushing it back deeper and deeper into his brain. The man's hands flew to Reece's in a futile attempt to extract the foreign implement. Reece could hear him frantically sucking in oxygen as he clawed at the SEAL's hands. Reece shifted his weight and pushed the dying man underwater, feeling the life drain from his opponent's body until he went limp.

Reece released him beneath the surface and stood up.

He had more men to kill.

Reece leapt from the pool and sprinted back into the dark master bedroom half expecting to start taking pistol rounds.

In the gloom, Reece could just make out the man he had first hit staggering to his feet. Reece could sense from the body language that he was bringing up a pistol. The SEAL did not hesitate. He caught the man's right wrist with his left hand and locked his right hand behind his assailant's neck, yanking aggressively down while launching a knee into his chin. Reece kept the man's head locked and fired off three more knees, catching him in the upper chest and face while still controlling his weapon hand.

Where is the fourth man?

Reece released his head and twisted his wrist back, grabbing the small pistol by the suppressor and ripping it from his grasp.

PPK?

Who uses PPKs anymore?

The human body can be incredibly resilient, especially in a fight to the death. When flight has been removed from the equation, there is only one option left.

Prevail or die.

Before Reece could seat the pistol in his hand his opponent positioned his leg behind the SEAL's and wrapped his free arm around Reece's waist, pushing him off-balance and sending them both crashing to the floor.

Reece was aware of shouting from the lower level in Mandarin and another voice responding from nearby in the dark bedroom.

The man on top of him grabbed his hair and Reece felt his other finger begin to sink its way into his left eye.

Reece twisted his head away, pulled the man close, and maneuvered the Walther into a shooting position. When the working end of the suppressor was against the man's ribs, he pulled the heavy double-action trigger.

The weapon discharged. Now in single action, Reece pulled the trigger again.

Nothing.

Malfunction.

Then the lights came on.

Shit!

Reece turned his head to the right, seeing his first victim staggering to his feet, shouting in Mandarin in a frantic search for the pistol he had dropped when Reece hit him with the champagne bottle. With the room illuminated Reece and the Chinese man saw the pistol at the same time.

Slow is smooth and smooth is fast.

Only one shot at this, Reece.

The frogman slightly twisted the fouled weapon to the outside and slammed the magazine against his opponent's head.

Tap.

Holding his adversary's head to his, Reece brought the PPK up, turned it back to the inside, and slammed the slide against his foe's skull. Catching the sights on the inside of his ear, Reece violently pushed the weapon forward, feeling the action cycle and chamber a round.

Rack.

From his back on the floor, he extended his arm toward his new target, lining up the iron sights and sending three rounds in quick succession into a man who had just made it to his weapon on his hands and knees.

Bang.

The first shot entered the leg just over his left knee. From his position on the ground, it traveled down his calf, expanding and fragmenting as it went, lodging in his heel, which caused him to scream in agony and fall forward. Reece's next round caught him in the sternum at the top of his chest. Breaking the bone, the bullet traveled down into his lungs and stomach, causing him to fall face-first onto the carpeted floor. Reece's next bullet finished him. It entered at the top of the head and split his cranium, creating a wound channel and shock wave as it passed through gray and white brain matter, severing the hippocampus, and finally arresting in the brain stem, turning the brain's tissue and liquid to mush.

One round was in the body of the man on top of him, one possibly ejected when clearing the malfunction, and three were in the dead man on the floor six feet away. Reece was about to find out which version of the PPK he had in hand.

Six rounds or seven?

With his left hand still locked around the head of the man atop him, Reece bent his arm at the elbow. He placed the suppressor against his opponent's head and pressed the trigger.

The bullet entered on the left side of the head. As it traveled through skin and skull it expanded. Ripping through the brain, it exited with much less energy from the other side, taking a small portion of the skull with it and sending brain matter onto the white wall to Reece's left.

The Walther cycled and put the last round into the chamber.

Seven rounds total.

.32-caliber model.

Reece pushed the dead body off him and clambered to the man he had killed a few feet away. He stripped the empty magazine from the pistol, leaving it on the floor. At least now this PPK was a known entity. He briefly set it on the floor and ejected the magazine from the new PPK, pausing to confirm it was also a .32, which it was. He inserted the new magazine, ensuring it was seated, and then moved to the man with the MAC-10.

No extra magazine?

Damn it!

Reece moved to the side of the bedroom door.

The shouting in Mandarin from the lower level had stopped.

"Alice," Reece whispered.

Shit!

His Bluetooth earbud had fallen out in the commotion.

Reece reached into his pocket and pulled out the phone to see one of the men from the lower level making his way up the stairs with another suppressed MAC-10.

The Ingram M10 was chambered with either a 9mm or .45 ACP. The man climbing the stairs had at least one magazine of thirty or thirty-two rounds.

In his hand Reece held a .32-caliber Walther PPK with one round in the chamber and seven in the magazine.

As so often happens in life, he didn't have a choice.

Exploit all technical and tactical advantages, an old SEAL Team commanding officer had once told him.

Reece grabbed the tablet from the nightstand and put the suite back into darkness. He then stuffed it into the back of his pants.

Keeping the phone in his left hand, he maneuvered cautiously back through the bedroom, careful not to trip on any bodies, and made his way to the far door that he had left open earlier and looked back at the screen. The approaching aggressor had taken a knee in the dark and was whispering back down the stairs in Mandarin.

Reece stepped into the hallway and shot him once in the back of the head. As he fell forward, Reece increased his pace and put one more into his temple. *Security round.* He then knelt down, set the PPK to the side, and picked up the M10. Reece had forgotten how heavy these were for such a small weapon. The stock was extended, it was on fire, and its selector switch was on full-auto with the bolt open. In short, it was ready to go to work.

He looked down at the phone. The one man left by the elevator had a phone to his ear and was repeatedly pressing the button on the elevator.

Reinforcements?

An extraction unit?

Reece stood and moved to the top of the balcony overlooking the foyer to the left of the winding staircase. He traded the mobile phone for the tablet and hit the lights for the lower level so he would remain in relative darkness while the lower level was illuminated.

The man on the phone looked up just as the elevator doors opened.

Reece dropped the tablet and swung the M10 over the railing. With his left hand wrapped around the lower section of the two-stage Military Armament Corporation suppressor and the short, extended stock in his shoulder, he depressed the trigger, stitching up the team's rear security. The man dropped to the deck, half in and half out of the elevator. The doors began to close but were blocked by the dead body.

Reece dropped the now-empty M10 and ran to the body in the hallway to retrieve the PPK. He fished his phone from his pocket and looked closely at each box that represented a different camera in the suite. It looked clear. How long it would stay that way remained to be seen. All shots fired had been suppressed but that didn't mean they were silent. The full-auto burst through the floor of the upper level had probably not penetrated through the lower level.

He had to move.

Reece rushed to the bedroom and into the large master bath.

The black tuxedo jacket looked remarkably usable, but his white shirt was splattered with blood, as were his hands and face.

Reece set the PPK and cell phone on the sink and turned on the hot water. Time was of the essence.

He stripped off his jacket and shirt and kicked off his shoes and pants, quickly washing his hands and face, scrubbing off the blood with soap. He then grabbed a hand towel to dry off while removing the excess blood.

Satisfied, he ran back into the bedroom and slid into his Origin jeans, Salomon shoes, and a dark blue Sunspel Riviera Polo shirt he had taken from the Agency house in San Francisco, along with an RGT tan

Ridgeline Supply jacket. He removed the suppressor from his PPK and slid it into his left jacket pocket, putting the pistol into his right.

Reece rummaged through his suitcase until he found his earbud case. He removed the remaining bud and inserted it into his right ear.

"Alice."

"Yes, James."

"I need you to get me the first flight out of here. Doesn't matter where it's going. Headed to the airport now. Can you do that?"

"Of course."

"Are you tracking me?"

"I have your mobile device, and I can see you on the room's cameras, and I should pick up your GPS implant once you get outside."

"Can you see surveillance cameras in the lobby?"

"Yes."

"Any law enforcement?"

"Nothing, and no transmissions via police radio."

Reece quickly snapped photos of the dead men in the bedroom.

"Can you find out who these guys are?"

"Local Triad enforcers. Mostly involved in money laundering."

"I'm headed to the lobby. Keep on those cameras and let me know if I need to divert."

"I will. And James."

"Yeah."

"I am glad you are all right."

He paused. He had to remind himself that he was talking to a quantum computer.

"Me too. Can you let Vic know that I am headed out. Give him my flight info and have him send a trusted Agency asset from the local station to meet me wherever I land."

"Doing it now."

"Alice."

"Yes, James."

"Thanks."

Reece shut his suitcase, stepping over the dead bodies as he exited the bedroom. He walked through the hallway, avoiding the man he had shot twice in the head, and made his way down the staircase. He stopped briefly to drag the rear security man into the foyer before entering the elevator and hitting the button for the lobby.

CHAPTER 35

Ministry of State Security
Macau Office
Macau Special Administrative Region of the People's Republic of China

ADJACENT TO THE GRAND Lisboa Hotel, behind fences and partially obscured by a private wooded park, is a government building that appears out of place among the bright lights of the newer and glitzier hotels and casinos. Nestled between a large cinema complex and the Macau General Hospital, the stark and imposing white and red structure abuts the Macau Military Club and world-famous Jardim de São Francisco—Garden of Saint Francisco—a reflection of Macau's Portuguese heritage. Once a former military barracks, the structure now houses the Macau offices of the Chinese Ministry of State Security.

Minister Chen Yun hung up the phone in the office he used while in Macau and spun his chair to the window. The sun had just broken the horizon and cast a warm glow through scattered clouds. He looked over what in Cantonese was called *Ka-Si-Lán-Fa-Yun*—Gardens of the Castilians. They dated back to 1580, the work of Franciscan friars from Castile, though friars of the Franciscan order in Portugal would build upon that work a few years later.

But his thoughts were not on friars or gardens or even his baccarat losses of just a few hours earlier. They were on an American named James Reece.

"I take it by your expression that things did not go as planned," Ba Jin said from his leather chair on the opposite side of the desk.

"No, they did not," Yun said, turning back to face the president's envoy.

We have been up all night. How can Ba Jin look so rested?

"I see. The president will not be pleased. What happened?"

"We hired a Triad hit team through a cutout as per our usual procedure. We had Mr. Reece under audio and video surveillance since he boarded his flight in California. They had access to his suite. We lost the feed just before the team made entry."

"Alice?"

"I believe so."

"Did he kill them all?"

"He did."

"How many?"

"Six."

"I take it they were armed."

"They were."

"The Shan Chu may be less pleased than the president," Jin said, referencing the Triad leadership.

"It will require a payment."

"And the hotel?" Jin asked.

"Cleaners are on their way. The hotel manager knows how to keep things quiet."

"Commander Reece killed six armed men with surprise on their side who also had him on real-time video surveillance," Jin said, thinking it through.

"That seems to be the case."

"And if Alice cut that video feed it means she is in play. Just how much, we don't know."

"We can still detain him at the airport. He's booked on a Cebu Pacific flight to Manila leaving at six thirty-five a.m. It's the first flight out."

"We could, but I have another idea."

"Oh?"

"If we were in Beijing, we would detain and question him. But some people here in Macau, perhaps in this very building, still believe there are two Chinas. I want to talk with this Commander Reece somewhere private. You extended the carrot. I'll bring the stick."

"One more attempt to get him to change his mind?"

"With this approach, one more is all it will take. In America they are fond of saying 'we will make him an offer he can't refuse.' Let's leverage our assets in the Philippines. This is something I will see to personally."

CHAPTER 36

REECE SAT IN THE last row next to the bathroom. He was crammed between a woman with a baby and a fairly large man who fell asleep before takeoff and whose head kept finding its way onto Reece's shoulder. Luckily it was only a two-hour flight.

Reece had told the front desk at the Banyan that he would not be needing room service today. The Rolls-Royce had been waiting on him as it was for anyone staying in the Presidential Suite and as soon as he was inside, he hit a button that turned the electrochromic glass between the rear and front seats from transparent to fully opaque. He then checked with Alice and she confirmed that he was booked on a Cebu Airlines flight to Manila leaving in three hours.

Would they let him leave?

And if so, why?

He pulled down the center armrest and unloaded the Walther before dumping it and its suppressor in with the bottle of chilled 2007 Taittinger Comtes Blanc de Blancs.

Reece eyed the champagne.

"Maybe next time," he said, flipping the armrest back into the seatback and sealing the champagne and its accompanying flutes inside the Phantom's "coolbox."

From the check-in counter, through security, and to his gate, Reece kept expecting Chinese security services to stop him, but they never did. He did not clock any odd looks from ticketing agents, police officers, or gate agents. Maybe they were going to let him go.

Then why had they tried to kill him?

Reece felt the jet start to descend and looked at his Rolex. He was instantly on edge.

They had been airborne for only an hour and twenty minutes and were still over the South China Sea. They should not be descending yet.

He twisted his neck to look out the window past the mother and crying baby. The water turned from almost black to lighter shades of blue as the plane approached the coast.

Reece observed the other passengers. It appeared that many of them had taken the flight before and were confused as to why the plane was already descending.

Now over land, the aircraft banked right.

Reece could see the ocean to his right and looking across the cabin and out the opposite window he could see the greens and browns of terra firma. They were over the Philippines.

He had spent time here years ago, albeit farther south in the southern island chain.

The plane continued to descend.

Reece had flown into multiple airports in the Philippines over the years, including the two international airports in Manila. This was neither Ninoy Aquino International Airport nor Clark Air Base.

The plane passed over a wide river and moments later they touched down.

Reece caught the name of the airport printed on a white hangar as the plane applied its brakes: Laoag International Airport.

Northern province, Reece thought. *What are we doing here?*

He had his answer moments later.

The aircraft came to a stop near the end of the runway but instead of turning to a gate, it remained where it was. Reece knew what was coming next.

Philippine National Police vehicles sped out onto the runway and boxed in the aircraft.

Being on the starboard side of the plane, Reece could only guess what was happening, but he assumed that stairs were being pushed up to the port-side door and very soon a contingent of police officers would march aboard and take him into custody.

Only then did the front hatch open.

Why didn't they wait until I landed in Manila?

Because in Manila I would be met by Agency personnel.

It was well known in intelligence circles that Manila Station was not just the CIA headquarters for the Philippines but was regarded as the main station for the entire Southeast Asia region.

Four officers entered the cabin dressed in black tropical fatigues with blue berets and marched toward the back of the plane. The heads of the other passengers turned as they passed to see who they were coming for.

Reece didn't need to wonder; he knew.

Two additional officers with what looked to Reece like vintage M16 rifles entered and stood in the forward section of the aircraft.

The lead officer stepped past Reece and turned as the second man, holding a clipboard, confirmed that they had their man.

With the plane full of noncombatants, surrounded by law enforcement, and with Reece unarmed there was nowhere to run and no way to fight.

The third officer in line motioned for Reece to stand, which he did, squeezing past the large man in the aisle seat.

The officer behind him handcuffed him and put one hand on his shoulder and another on his handcuffed wrist.

They moved Reece a few steps forward and the officer who was now rear security opened the overhead luggage and removed Reece's Globe-Trotter carry-on.

"Yours?" the officer holding him asked in heavily accented English.

Reece nodded and felt the officer push him forward down the aisle, down the steps, and into a waiting van, where a bag was placed over his head.

Stay calm.

Where am I going?

Reece did not have to wait long for an answer.

In what seemed to be only a minute, the van came to a stop.

Reece heard the door opening and was forced outside.

Two sets of hands took control of his arms and shoulders and a few yards later he could sense they had stepped through a threshold. It felt to Reece like they were in a hallway. His captors then turned him left and brought him to a stop.

They frisked him, removing his phone, one remaining earbud, wallet, and low-pro Dynamis belt.

He was then turned around and forced into a chair.

They removed the bag from his head.

Reece was in a small, dark room. It was empty save for a metal table and the chair on which he now sat. Empty, that is, except for the two men in the corners holding M16s, the two men in front of him who Reece assumed had just conducted the search, and two more in the hallway just outside the open door. His confiscated items were nowhere to be seen.

"Do I have the right to remain silent?" Reece asked.

A look of slight confusion crossed the face of the officer whom Reece assessed to be in charge. He hid it quickly.

The officer said something in rapid Tagalog.

"My Tagalog is a little rusty," Reece said.

"Strip."

"That's going to be a little difficult in these," Reece said, shaking the handcuffs behind his back. "And I'm no lawyer, but I believe that unless I am charged with something, all this is a violation of my rights, even in the Philippines."

The officer spat on the floor and then indicated with his head that his men should leave the room. As they filed out, he backed toward the door. He too then disappeared into the gloomy hallway.

Their sudden departure did not make sense until someone else entered the room; someone familiar.

It didn't take Reece long to place him, or the five other men who entered with him. They were no longer in suits, but he recognized them from the tables outside the private dining room at the Robuchon au Dôme restaurant at the top of the Grand Lisboa Hotel.

They closed the door behind them.

The man who approached the table looked to be in his mid to late fifties, though it was hard to tell. He was in good shape and dressed in khaki pants and what looked like a knockoff "Members Only" jacket.

"The eighties called," Reece said. "They want their jacket back."

"I would be disappointed if you did not remember us, Mr. Reece," the lead man said. His accent was thicker than Chen's, but his English was still remarkably smooth.

"I never forget an asshole."

"Charming," the man replied.

"It was a nice dinner. You should have joined us, though you have some pretty big boys here," Reece said, nodding at the others. "The portions were outrageously small."

One of them stepped forward and threw a beige jumpsuit onto the table.

"We are going to uncuff you, Mr. Reece. You are going to strip."

Stall them, Reece.

"So soon? We hardly know each other."

"Save the witticisms, Mr. Reece. You will need your strength."

"If not?"

"If not, one of my men will just shoot you here. We can ask these very same questions of Ms. Buranek."

Reece's eyes narrowed.

"We know that she is currently protected on that ranch in Montana. Yes, we know exactly where she is. I should have spent more time in your file. Perhaps then I would have sent a more professional team to kill you, not the Iranian-recruited misfits we did. But had they killed you we would not be having this conversation."

This is the bastard who almost killed Katie.

"At some point Ms. Buranek, the Hastings family, they will let down their guard," he continued. "I am not a man who makes mistakes twice. We have a long history of not forgetting, Mr. Reece. Take off your clothes."

Three of the five men behind him pulled pistols from their holsters and held them in a low ready as one walked behind Reece and undid his handcuffs, returning to his position so as to stay out of the line of fire should his teammates open up.

Reece slowly stood, rubbing his wrists.

Maybe whatever was about to happen would save Katie? Perhaps save the Hastingses. If that was the case, Reece would gladly go to the grave.

"I feel like I should know your name, especially since we are getting so intimate," Reece said as he slid out of his jacket and dropped it onto the table.

"It hardly matters but you can call me Mr. Jin."

"True name?"

"It is a name I use, much like you, Mr. Donovan," Jin said, letting Reece know he was well aware of his Agency alias.

Reece pulled his shirt over his head and deposited it on top of the jacket.

"How do you guys like those CF-98s?" Reece asked, in reference to their pistols. "Made in China, right? Heard they were pieces of shit."

Reece kicked off his shoes and reached down to remove his socks, at which point the five Chinese minders raised their 5.8 x 21mm pistols. Reece held up his socks, paused momentarily, and dropped them on top of the shirt and jacket.

"Can I get a little privacy?" Reece asked, trying to prolong the engagement.

"No," Jin said.

Reece removed his jeans and added them to the pile.

"All of it, Mr. Reece."

"What's the rush?" Reece asked, removing his underwear and dropping them on the heap. "Be sure and wash those before you give them back, by the way."

Even if Reece had been ready, he didn't think he would have been able to react in time to block the backfist that caught him squarely on his cheekbone.

Where the hell did that come from?

Jin had hit him from the other side of the desk.

Damn, this guy is fast.

"Just a quick reminder as to who is in charge here, Mr. Reece. Remove your watch."

Reece hesitated for only a moment. Then he undid the clasp and laid his father's watch on the table.

Ba Jin reached down and picked it up.

"Very nice," he said. "Vintage?"

"It's a '68. You guys had just kicked off your Cultural Revolution a couple of years earlier. How many people did Mao kill in his efforts to purify the Party?"

"You Americans are all alike. Feigned moral superiority. A bit hypocritical though. You are on the same path."

"You might be right," Reece conceded.

Jin slid Reece's watch onto his wrist and secured the clasp.

"Looks a little big for you," Reece said. "Why don't we go back to the States. I know a guy who can size it."

"Unfortunately for you, neither of us will be going to America for quite some time."

"That's okay, I'll be getting that watch back from you soon."

Jin then said something in Mandarin and the man who had undone Reece's cuffs stepped forward again.

Reece pivoted and brought up his hands.

"Now, now, Mr. Reece. Remember, play nice or you die here, and we conduct this very same type of interview with Ms. Buranek," Jin said, motioning to Reece's naked body.

Reece lowered his hands and allowed them to be cuffed behind his back.

Jin barked something else in Mandarin and one of the other men stepped forward holding what looked like an RFID checker from a supermarket. He ran the scanner up and down Reece's body and around his head. When he was done, he walked back to the front of the table and indicated something to his boss. He then took his place back against the wall and redrew his pistol.

"Sit," Jin said.

Draw this out, Reece.

Reece slowly took a seat on the cold metal chair.

"It seems as though you have been hiding something from us, Mr. Reece."

"Certainly isn't from a lack of looking," Reece said as the four men converged on the table.

One took a position next to his boss and lined his sights up on the SEAL. His finger was on the trigger.

The others moved with surprising speed, grabbing Reece's arms and slamming his head down on the metal table. One of them twisted Reece's head to the left so the right side of his face was pressed against the table. The fifth man produced a cattle prod.

"What the fuck is that?" Reece asked.

He had scarcely finished his sentence when the man with the prod pushed it down at the base of Reece's skull just behind his left ear.

Reece grunted through the searing heat and intense pain. He tried to move but was held securely in place. He thought he smelled skin burning.

The man removed the prod and hit Reece again.

On the second hit, Reece heard an audible pop and a foreign electric jolt under his skin. He knew exactly what it was. They had fried the circuitry in his implanted GPS tracker.

The man hit Reece a third and fourth time as he continued to struggle, the hands holding him fast.

After the fourth hit, the man traded the cattle prod for the scanner. Through his upturned left eye, Reece saw him move it around his head and then nod at Jin.

The men let Reece go and he straightened up in his chair, catching his breath and reacquiring his bearings, the smell of burnt flesh heavy in the confined space.

"You have nothing more to conceal from us, Mr. Reece," Jin said.

"Apparently not," Reece said.

"I apologize for the treatment, but we couldn't have an active tracking device in your head leading anyone to where we are going next. I have further questions for you, Mr. Reece, and additional ways to extract what I need. I hope none of it becomes necessary. If it comes to it, the most comfortable part of your experience will be that cattle prod frying your balls or being shoved down your throat. And if you decline to cooperate, we will be sure to give Ms. Buranek a similar, though much worse experience. I am sure you can imagine what we will do to her, how we will use that cattle prod. To a large extent, her future is in your hands."

Jin barked another order at his men in Mandarin and then again addressed Reece.

"For her sake, put on the jumpsuit and do as you are told."

His handcuffs were removed and under the watchful eye, and drawn pistols, of Jin's team, Reece stood and put on the jumpsuit. His hands were then recuffed and a bag was placed over his head.

As he was marched out of the holding area and put into another vehicle, this time on the floor with what he assumed were Jin's men holding him in place, he couldn't help but wonder if dying here was how he could give Katie her freedom.

CHAPTER 37

Ilocos Norte, Luzon
Philippines

THE DRIVE LASTED ABOUT thirty minutes in Reece's estimation. He felt like he was low to the ground, possibly in a minivan. He knew they had not gone west, as that was the ocean. It was either north, east, or south, though it was impossible to tell with a bag over his head. That sensory deprivation, along with the turns, some probably taken just to confuse his sense of direction, made it impossible to even make an educated guess as to his whereabouts.

Eventually they had come to a stop and Reece was roughly removed from the vehicle. He felt gravel under his bare feet as he walked. The rocks turned to grass and he was then forced up what felt like wooden stairs before being moved inside.

The two men on either side of him roughly maneuvered him into a chair. He felt and heard the unmistakable sound of zip ties securing his cuffs to the back of the chair as additional zip ties secured his ankles to its legs. He heard mumbled words in Mandarin.

Breathe, Reece.

This is your chance to save Katie, to remove Raife and his family from the line of fire. They do not deserve to die because of you. You should have died on that mountain in Afghanistan. Because you did not, Lauren died, Lucy died, Freddy died, and Katie was on the verge of death; all because of you. Make it right. It is your turn to die for them.

Life is pain.

The bag was ripped from Reece's head. He blinked as his eyes adjusted to the light and his lungs took in fresh air, a welcome respite from the heavy, hot, musty stench of burnt and dying flesh that had been trapped inside the bag.

He was in a large space that resembled a living room. A sofa was on the far side of the space, opposite two easy chairs and a coffee table. Faded yellow curtains were drawn but behind them to his left were sliding glass doors that seemed to lead to a deck. He twisted his head to get his bearings, noting a round dining room table behind him. The home seemed relatively normal. What wasn't normal were the medical supplies on a cheap-looking credenza to his right.

One of Jin's men stood by the main door and another man stood by a door adjacent to the dining area, which Reece assumed led to a kitchen.

A small man stood nervously next to the credenza, fidgeting with his fingernails.

Reece heard the door behind him off the dining area open. He turned his head to see Jin emerge, drying his hands with a dish towel, which he tossed onto the table as he passed. He grabbed a chair, which he carried past Reece and set up directly across from him at an uncomfortably close distance.

"And so it begins," Jin said.

"I'm not in any rush," Reece replied. "Who's our new friend?"

"That is Dr. Guerrero."

"Is his first name 'Doctor'?"

"I assure you he is very good at what he does. We use him from time to time here in the Philippines when we need information from an uncooperative subject. Today that subject is you."

"Terrific."

"Mr. Reece, I want you to fully appreciate your situation before we get started. I also want you to keep in mind that you do not need to die today. There is a path where you not only live and spare yourself Dr. Guerrero's invasive interrogation techniques, but actually live with Ms. Buranek under my country's protection and with an extremely generous compensation package from the Academy of Engineering."

"What is this place?"

"I believe you would call it a 'safe house.' Much like your CIA, we have them in various locations around the world, though not in as many places as your Agency: the Pacific, Europe, Canada, Mexico, Cuba, Central and South America, Africa, and more than a few in the United States."

"I think that's just about everywhere."

"Your country makes it easy. Some are listening posts, others are safe houses, and yet others are just homes, condos, or apartments owned by Chinese entities. Most of the time we don't even have to go through shell corporations. We have assets in your universities, we own politicians, our agents sleep with more than a few of them, some are their chauffeurs, others work in your tech companies, or as maids, or as babysitters for your rich and powerful. We buy up land next to your military bases or buy or rent condos in areas where we can keep track of submarine and ship deployment cycles. We tried to buy the Hotel del Coronado next to your SEAL base. Someone wisely put a stop to that, but we do occupy upper levels of the Shores. Why your country allowed those condominiums to be built overlooking your SEAL command compound is beyond me. We have listening devices pointing directly at the admiral's office. We know his car and reserved parking space. We know when he comes and goes and who parks in the visitor's space. We have patterns logged for the past thirty years. We do the same around the world. They let us buy the Rosslea Hotel in Scotland. Four miles away is Faslane, home to Great Britain's *Vanguard*-class submarine fleet. Their subs pass within 275 meters of the hotel. We purchased it in 2018; didn't even hide what we were doing. It was acquired by three Chinese nationals. The Bank of Scotland even helped finance the deal. We have a controlling interest in the port of Darwin in Australia, which as you know is a major Australian and U.S. military hub. Like Rosslea in Scotland, Darwin is a listening post but is also a key component of critical infrastructure. We control the port of Piraeus in Greece, which is a key hub for NATO in the Mediterranean. We also have major ownership stakes in ports in Belgium and Spain. And that doesn't even begin to scratch the surface of our investments in Africa. Our first overseas naval base in Djibouti is next to your Camp Lemonnier. You will not see companies with ties to the U.S., UK, or Australian military buying ports or hotels near Chinese military installations. It is really quite mad, but oftentimes the almighty dollar trumps good sense or even one's patriotic duty. The United States is being sold to the highest bidder. And that highest bidder is China."

"Seems like you already have it figured out," Reece said.

"What do you know of our 'Twenty-First-Century Maritime Silk Road'?"

"One Belt, One Road," Reece said.

"Ah, very good, Mr. Reece. Most Americans have no idea as to our intentions, nor would they care. They are too consumed with TikTok."

"You got us good with that one," Reece admitted.

"That surprised even me. I've read articles that detail how our content in America is destroying the youth. In China, TikTok is focused on math and science and building a strong patriotic society. Your 'freedom' also gives you the freedom to destroy yourselves, Mr. Reece."

"Tough to argue with that. Though I wouldn't get too cocky. Your last conventional land offensive in the Sino-Vietnamese War did not go well. Nor did the First Taiwan Strait Crisis."

"The 'Self-Defensive Counterstrike Against Vietnam' and the insurrection in the strait were a long time ago, Mr. Reece. Since then, we have been learning from *your* wars, not our own. America did not fare well in its campaigns in Iraq and Afghanistan. Even the Houthi savages have shown they can disrupt shipping with a few missiles and drones. Most every major shipping company now adds a month of sea time and a million dollars extra in fuel to ship around Africa instead of through the Suez, Red Sea, and Gulf of Aden. We have the ability to turn the world order on its head and we will do so very soon."

"Thanks for sharing."

"None of this is a secret, Mr. Reece. We have watched your military conduct exercises, listened to former military and intelligence officials, who now work as pundits on various news outlets, war-game the various scenarios. Many have written books about it. None of this, to include the timing, is a closely held secret. My own president has given numerous, ample warnings, telling the Politburo, and the world, to 'prepare for great conflict.' An internet search brings it all up."

"I'll be sure and search it up when I get home."

"Some experts say it will be a full-scale conventional assault; others talk about special operations missions. It will be a full-spectrum attack. Nothing will be left to chance. The Taiwanese military is corrupt and infiltrated at all levels. The U.S. industrial base is the weakest it has been in decades. Your military is ill-prepared for a fight with China over Taiwan, especially when they have assurances that microchip manufacturing will continue unabated. Your generals and admirals are spending money on diversity, equity, and inclusion programs when any sane leader would be applying that bandwidth to combat readiness. Ship collisions tell the story; the *Fitzgerald* and *McCain* collisions, one of your subs, the USS *Connecticut*, ran into an underwater mountain not far from here. All that only highlights the problem. Men like me are already close to the leadership in Taipei. They will be decapitated in a swift internal strike. Nothing can stop that. We learned from Russia's mistakes in Ukraine."

“Thanks for the update.”

“My questions are about this Alice of yours. My country is concerned that she is now in play. She obviously helped you escape your brush with death in Macau—not even you could have taken out six armed men who had the jump on you without help. Bring Alice over to us. Bring Ms. Buranek. Accept our generous financial compensation. Raise your family without the constant threat of violence. We will give you a new life here.”

“All I need to do is betray my country,” Reece said.

“Minister Yun covered all this with you. I know what happened to your last family. Lauren, I believe? Lucy, your daughter? Don’t condemn Ms. Buranek and your future children to that same fate. The time has come. No more deals, Mr. Reece.”

“Great, because this was getting tiresome.”

“Let me explain what Dr. Guerrero has in store for you.”

“Doctor,” Reece said, nodding at the little man.

“You are no doubt familiar with what the West calls our ‘black jails,’” Jin said.

“Internment camps?”

“More like detention centers for problem elements. We call them ‘education and transformation training centers’ for those under ‘suspicion of inciting ethnic hatred and discrimination.’”

“That sounds much better.”

“We have learned quite a lot about enhanced interrogation in these sites and in our centers for the Uyghurs. I would exterminate them all, but my government is not there yet; they will get there soon. We have been sterilizing their women for years, so that’s a start. The West calls it genocide. I call it preservation of the Party.”

“That doesn’t sound crazy at all.”

Reece saw the anger flash through Jin’s eyes and quickly subside.

“Right now,” he continued, “the Uyghurs are too valuable making

American basketball shoes, canning tomatoes for Europe, and making solar panels, which as a form of economic warfare is wise; no labor costs."

"Convenient for everyone but the Uyghurs," Reece said.

"The Uyghurs are Muslims, and we know how the West feels about Muslims, which is why they tacitly approve. We are doing everyone a favor. In the meantime, Mr. Reece, you will be the beneficiary of all we have learned in these reeducation camps, or you can live in peace with Ms. Buranek and keep Alice from interfering in what is China's destiny. Before you decide, let me explain what lies ahead if you choose poorly. Some of the cruder forms of interrogation and reeducation are quite effective, but we have also experimented with more evolved techniques."

"Can't wait to hear about them."

"Of course, there is sleep and food deprivation, electric shock therapy, and humiliating sexual abuse. You would be surprised what the human body can take. With over a million Uyghurs in need of reeducation, the repetitive rapes and waterboardings and electric shock treatments tie up valuable resources. To add efficiencies to the process we have found that a more enlightened approach is needed."

"Then enlighten me."

"We studied your waterboarding techniques from Guantanamo and discarded them immediately, but we drew lessons. We learned from our Russian friends as well. Have you studied the gulags, Mr. Reece?"

"I've read Solzhenitsyn."

"If you go deeper, you will find photos of prisoners missing one of their eyes. Now, if the state were to take both, that individual is now a burden, but taking one eye, that individual can still be a productive worker in service of the state. Dr. Guerrero here has become extremely adept in reeducation procedures. Anyone can dig an eye out of its socket with a spoon or knife, but the pain is short-lived. When you enucleate the eye slowly, with growing pressure, it is a different story entirely."

"Sounds pleasant."

"We first take a needle and catheter and insert it into the corner of your eye socket. We then extract the needle, leaving the catheter in place, and attach it to an IV saline solution. The pressure of the solution behind the eye is one of the more painful things a human can experience."

"I'll remember that," Reece said.

"Eventually the eye pops out," Jin continued. "But that in and of itself is not enough, even when combined with random beatings, daily sexual abuse, and genital mutilation. As I said, we learned that waterboarding, at least in the American-approved format, is fairly benign, but the principle is sound. While the eye is slowly being forced from the socket from behind, we insert endotracheal tubes into each nostril, and then inflate the balloon designed for expansion in the chest. But instead of inserting the balloons into the trachea to assist with restricted breathing, we leave them in the nasal passage. We then blow fluid into the balloons with a syringe through the endotracheal tubes, which crushes the internal sinuses. Too much pressure will blow out a portion of the skull. If that's not enough, we have the option to cap the tubes and pour water down the throat. The pain and suffocation truly work wonders. Forcing a husband to watch the procedure on a wife or child will make even the hardest man rethink his ways."

It wasn't the pleasure Jin was taking from the description of the horrific torture that disturbed Reece the most, it was the indifference. It was haunting.

"A balloon can also be inserted into the bladder through the urethra using a Foley catheter. We then expand the balloon and rapidly yank it out. This combination of attacking the genitalia, sinuses, breathing, and optical nerves or seeing it forced upon a loved one is quite effective."

Reece began to think he should have taken the bullet back in his Macau hotel or in the airport holding room.

"But this does not have to be your fate, Mr. Reece. None of what I described needs to befall you, or Ms. Buranek. You know that Russia, Iran, the Collective, and perhaps even China and God only knows who else still want you dead and are willing to maim and kill anyone you care about to get to you. Or . . ." He paused. "Or you accept our proposal. We offer you complete protection and not only safety, but wealth. We could even manage a way to fake your death. Make you disappear."

"I have heard you are good at that."

"With Alice's help it could be arranged. Your 'death' could be in service to your nation. Allow me to help you. You have done enough for a country that despises you. Live out your days with Ms. Buranek without having to look over your shoulder." He paused again to let his words sink in. "Time is a component here, Mr. Reece. My government will move against Taiwan in the short term. The West has forced our hand. Let me spare you this invasive interview experience. Tell me about Alice and her capabilities and accept our offer. Otherwise, you are going to have to talk with Dr. Guerrero."

"Can we go back to the bullet option?"

"I am afraid we are past that, Mr. Reece."

If you stay with Katie, she will die.

Maybe I can still get him to shoot me.

"Well in that case, get on with it."

"Mr. Reece, you realize what you are giving up: safety, security, wealth, protection, a long life with a family by your side."

"Well, I am a tad concerned we would all end up like the Uyghurs. That and the thought of having to spend a minute more talking with you are less than appealing. After listening to what I have so far, I think you're a fucking idiot."

Jin's backhand lashed out with surprising speed but this time Reece expected it. Since he couldn't move out of the way, he dropped his head so the outside of Jin's fist connected with the thick frontal bone of Reece's skull just above the hairline.

Reece could sense that Jin had damaged his hand but that didn't stop the intelligence operative from lashing out with his other fist, catching Reece in the jaw. He could taste the blood.

Quickly running out of options, Reece spit, the bloody projectile catching Jin just below his left eye.

Jin stood.

He walked behind his captive to the dining table to pick up a dish towel he had dropped earlier. He returned to stand over the SEAL, wiping the spit from his face.

"You know, Mr. Reece, I was going to forgo the usual softening up with the cattle prod to the genitals. It also works wonders when activated after it's stuffed down your throat. I was even going to skip the catheter to the bladder and allow you to miss the sensation of having the inflated balloon pulled out of your dick. Now I am going to start with those just to warm you up. You will tell me everything I want to know about Alice and then you will die. I'm not going to watch Dr. Guerrero turn you into an invalid; I'm going to do it myself. And I am going to enjoy it."

"You better get started because we are in for a long afternoon."

Life is pain.

Jin placed the bag back over Reece's head and snapped an order in Mandarin.

"Time to get out of that jumpsuit, Mr. Reece. We want you at your most vulnerable."

Reece could hear the guards begin to converge on his position. One of them wrapped the bag tighter across his face and violently yanked it back.

A second later the room erupted into chaos. Reece heard the far door slam into the wall, then shouting in Mandarin, followed by the unmistakable sound of suppressed gunfire.

CHAPTER 38

IMMOBILIZED IN HIS CHAIR with a bag over his head, Reece found himself in almost complete darkness, adding another dimension to the turmoil unfolding around him as bodies absorbed bullets over voices shouting in a language he did not comprehend.

He heard bodies hit the floor, a calm and direct exchange in Tagalog, and rapidly approaching footsteps. Reece braced for the inevitable bullet.

Goodbye, Katie. I love you.

The bag was removed from his head and instead of the barrel of a gun, Reece looked up into the smiling face of Rick "Ox" Andrews. Ox was a former Delta Force sergeant major and special operations legend who began his time in uniform with a sprint across Point Salines Airport runway as a young Army Ranger in Grenada when Reece was not yet in kindergarten. He was now a contractor with the CIA's Ground Branch.

"SEAL Team. Here to get you out."

"You've always wanted to say that, haven't you?" Reece replied.

"Everybody wants to say it at least once."

"Took you long enough. Get me out of these fucking things," Reece said, looking around the room to get his bearings.

Ox's hair was shoulder-length, gray with streaks of slightly darker shades of ash. He wore jeans and a black Hawaiian shirt with a star orchid print. A Vertex Ardennes messenger bag was slung across his body.

"Nice purse, by the way," Reece said.

"It's a satchel."

Ox knelt down and reached into his bag for wire cutters and began cutting the zip ties securing Reece's ankles to the legs of the chair. He then moved to the ties around his wrists and unlocked the handcuffs.

Jin's men were now just contorted bodies on the floor in pools of blood, their souls having been snatched from them moments earlier. Two pairs of Filipino men and two Filipino women in civilian clothes were working the room. Two were going through the dead men's pockets and photographing their faces with mobile devices. The second team stood over Jin and the doctor, who were on their knees, their hands zip-tied behind their backs, foreheads leaning against the wall to Reece's right. The team wore a variety of backpacks and messenger bags where Reece correctly assumed they had been concealing their weapons.

"Cute toy," Reece said as he stood, free of his constraints.

The Team carried what Reece recognized as Flux Defense Raider Xs on Ferro Concepts single-point slings. The Raider was a micro PDW, or Personal Defense Weapon, designed for operations in semipermissive, nonpermissive, or denied environments where concealability was paramount but where one also needed additional capability beyond that offered by a traditional handgun. The Raider chassis system with a spring-loaded stock accepted the 9mm SIG P320 Fire Control Unit, barrel, and slide and offered operators the speed, maneuverability, and concealability of a pistol with the magazine capacity and stability of a carbine. It was designed for those times you want a rifle, but the operational environment does not allow for it. These were coyote tan and affixed with SIG MODX-9 suppressors, Aimpoint T2 red-dot optics, and SureFire X300Ts mounted in the six o'clock position. Top-mounted charging handles allowed for L3 Harris NGALs—Next Generation Aiming Lasers—to be attached to three-slot picatinny rails on the left side. Reece noted they had all tac reloaded after their engagement; the larger-capacity thirty-round magazines were in their weapons and the twenty-one-round magazines were secured in their foregrips. These were professionals.

"All the cool kids have them," Ox replied. "I'd prefer a rifle, but we can't be running around this part of the PI with long guns."

"And I almost forgot," Reece said. "Thanks."

"Come on," Ox said.

He whispered something in Tagalog to one of his men on his way to the door.

"Hold up," Reece said.

He walked toward Jin and Guerrero, on their knees with guns to their heads.

Reece squatted down and removed his father's Rolex from Jin's wrist.

"Told you I'd be getting this back from you soon."

Reece secured the watch to his left wrist and followed Ox outside, stepping into the afternoon sunlight. They stood on a wood deck near a set of stairs that led down to a lawn surrounded by thick hedges. Two of Jin's men were sprawled out on the grass where another male and female from Ox's team were going through their pockets. Roosters strutted around the corpses, pecking at the ground with their beaks. Below Reece to the left was a minivan parked on a gravel driveway. The house was on a lush hillside with views of Laoag, the ocean visible in the distance. As he surveyed his surroundings, an older Toyota Hilux and Corolla pulled into the driveway, combat parking to face a dirt road about fifty yards away. Ox pointed and the two drivers exited to take up positions near a gate.

"NICA?" Reece asked. The National Intelligence Coordinating Agency is the national intelligence service of the Philippines.

"No. They're ours. ISA and local talent," Ox replied, referring to a highly specialized intelligence gathering unit known as Intelligence Support Activity. ISA was formed after Operation Eagle Claw, the failed Delta Force mission ordered by President Jimmy Carter to rescue U.S. captives held at the embassy in Tehran in April 1980. The least known of America's Tier 1 Special Mission Units, they work in the shadows to collect actionable intelligence in direct support of JSOC missions.

"Orange? I liked it when they went by cool names like SENTRA SPIKE and GRAY FOX."

"I was always partial to Army of Northern Virginia, myself," Ox said.

"I'm surprised they got away with that one as long as they did," Reece replied. "They'd be canceled today for sure."

"The three men and three women are Orange. All fluent Tagalog speakers. The drivers are local assets," Ox said. "Nine in-shape men rolling heavy looks off to anyone. We have these two vehicles and two motorbikes parked down the road."

"Solid crew," Reece said.

"Lucky for you they have been through my course in Florida."

"Maybe I'll stop complaining about taxes," Reece said.

"Taxation is theft," Ox said. "But I can't complain too much, as they do pay my salary."

"I was worried when they fried my tracker," Reece said.

"Let me see it."

Reece tilted his head and pulled his hair behind his left ear to the side.

"That looks nasty," Ox said.

"Thanks, Doc. How did you find me?"

"It was Alice, who I understand is some sort of supercomputer?"

"Quantum computer," Reece corrected.

"Quantum computer," Ox continued. "Vic keeps calling her 'she,' which is weird. Anyway, she tracked your flight along with communications out of Macau to the PI. We were on standby to bring you in after you landed in Manila, but Vic alerted us that the plane was going to be diverted to Laoag. That gave us time to get up here and track you via the super—I mean quantum—computer. Even without your phone and implanted tracker she had already connected to the phones of everyone here before they confiscated yours and zapped your implanted GPS. Alice tracked you the entire way in. She even sent us 3-D overlay imaging of everyone's position on the compound. It looks like she uses GPS, microphones, and cameras from every device on-site to image a target in real time. It's almost cheating."

"If you're not cheating . . ."

"You're not trying," Ox said, completing the old special operations adage.

"How much time do we have?" Reece asked.

Ox pulled up a small tablet.

"No police response. No neighbors. We are fairly isolated here. We have time."

"Good."

"What are you going to do, Reece?"

"I have some questions for Mr. Jin in there. It's time to turn the tables."

CHAPTER 39

JIN HAD BEEN STRIPPED naked. He was seated, his hands zip-tied to the arms of the chair, his ankles to its legs. A bag had been placed over his head. Dr. Guerrero was still on his knees with his head against the wall. Ox was standing to the side, his Raider hanging by his side. The remainder of the Team had taken up security positions outside.

Reece approached his subject and removed the bag.

"Mr. Jin, as you are obviously aware, your situation has changed."

Jin remained stoic, staring straight ahead.

"Unfortunately for you," Reece continued, "I already know you speak fluent English, which certainly saves us a lot of time, as we might be here a while if I had to learn Mandarin. You had me at a disadvantage earlier, but I learned quite a bit from our stimulating conversation. I am going to need you to fill in a few pieces for me though, and lucky for me you gave me all the tools I need."

Reece nodded in the direction of the medical supplies on the credenza.

"Don't mistake this demeanor for weakness. I am going to ask you a series of questions. Some I know the answers to and others I don't. If I have to ask twice, you will learn to appreciate the pain you have been visiting upon others."

Reece remained standing.

"My first question is, why the rush? What makes knowing if Alice is in the game so valuable? Are you on a timeline? And yes, I know that's three questions, but I am anxious to get through this since I feel we have spent enough time together today."

Jin continued to look straight ahead.

"You were so much more talkative earlier," Reece said.

Reece turned to Ox.

"Mind giving me the room?"

"Not at all."

"And can I borrow that Raider?"

"Be my guest," Ox said, unslinging the suppressed PDW and handing it to his friend before exiting onto the deck.

"Dr. Guerrero, stand up," Reece ordered.

The doctor slowly got to his feet, having been on his knees with his head against the wall for the past twenty minutes.

"Dr. Guerrero, I am quite capable of using all these tools to get what I need from Mister Jin here, but I am going to focus on the questions. Jin is a dead man. It's just a question of how. You, on the other hand, have a chance at redemption. I ran your file before I came back in and know you have a wife and three daughters in Quezon. If you want to see them again, you are going to use what skills you have acquired in the area of interrogation to get what I need out of Mr. Jin here."

"Yes, yes, of course," the doctor said, his accent heavy; he was grateful for even the slightest of hopes that he might survive.

"What have you found is the best way to begin?"

"Catheter," he stammered.

"Well, get on with it," Reece said.

Dr. Guerrero pulled on nitrile rubber gloves, tentatively took the Foley catheter from the credenza, coated it with lube from a tube, and placed one end in a plastic urine collection container. Then, without making eye contact with his subject, he grabbed Jin's penis with his left hand and worked the catheter inside.

Jin grunted but remained glaring straight ahead.

Guerrero paused for a moment when urine began to flow through the tube and into the collection device, then continued to feed the catheter into his subject. He next attached a syringe to the syringe port and pushed down on the plunger, filling up the retention balloon attached to the catheter inside Jin's bladder.

"You know what's coming, Mr. Jin. You can prevent it," Reece said.

"I am an official of the People's Republic of China. I demand you release me at once."

"That rings hollow to even me, but I guess you had to give it a shot."

Reece looked to the doctor.

"What's next?"

Guerrero took a size 7 endotracheal tube, lubed it up, and attempted to insert it into Jin's left nostril. Jin twisted his head to prevent the intrusion, barking something in Mandarin that Reece did not need an interpreter to decipher.

Reece stepped around the chair and held Jin's head in place while the doctor inserted the tubes to a specific depth of three inches.

"I honestly would not be here had you not sent a hit team to take me out in Montana. I am not as invested as I once was in being the third option of U.S. foreign policy. To be truthful, I think we are in a steep decline, with the rights I care about being curtailed at an astonishing rate by the very people we elect to represent us in office. Basically, I think the majority of them are a cancer destroying a once-great nation and spitting on the graves of all those who sacrificed everything to give them the ability to destroy it from within. I say all that because had you left me alone, I wouldn't even be here. But you didn't. You hurt someone I care about so now I'm invested. You know what comes next as part of this little experiment. You just told me all about it. You can talk with me here with these tubes in your dick and in your nose, or we can ratchet things up. Choice is yours."

Jin responded in rapid-fire Mandarin that was excessively nasally due to the tubes the doctor had taped in place.

By the way Guerrero responded it was clear he spoke fluent Mandarin.

"Don't bother translating that," Reece said.

Reece stood behind his captive and connected three zip ties he had taken from the assault force. He then picked up the towel from the table behind him, reached around the front of Jin's face, and stuffed it into his mouth, quickly looping the zip ties over his head and pulling them tight to secure the towel in place.

Reece then walked back in front of his prisoner.

"You are restrained and can't talk, but your fingers can move. Give me a thumbs-up when you are ready to cooperate. Doctor, continue."

Guerrero wiped sweat from his brow and attached a 20cc syringe full of fluid to each of the one-way inflation valves built into the endotracheal tubes. His shaking thumb hovered over a plunger connected to the left tube. When he pushed down it would force the fluid through the tube to expand a balloon designed to be deep in the trachea as a lifesaving device. It was now lodged in the nasal passage as a means of torture.

The turbinates, also known as nasal concha, are bones covered by glandular tissue that help regulate airflow through the nose. The glandular tissues are flush in nerves and blood vessels. Jin's were about to be destroyed.

"Last chance," Reece said, looking at Jin's hands.

Instead of a thumbs-up, Jin turned his hands into fists.

Reece nodded to the doctor, who pushed down on the plunger.

Even to Reece, who had experience with this type of work, the sound of Jin's turbinates being crushed from the inside was nauseating.

Jin's eyes widened, instantly bloodshot and filled with tears. His face turned a bright red as his blood pressure spiked. The veins in his neck bulged and primal groans attempted to escape through the rag wedged in his mouth.

"Give me that thumbs-up and we can talk. Put an end to this," Reece said.

Jin clenched his fists tighter.

"Mr. Jin," Reece said. "Most everything you told me earlier today is available via open-source intelligence. You are putting yourself through this for another reason. And now I want to know what it is."

Reece turned back to Guerrero.

"What happens if you add more to that side?" Reece asked.

"His medial wall will shatter."

"What's that?"

"It's the wall of the nasal cavity. Formed by the nasal septum," he answered.

"Do it," Reece ordered.

Guerrero pushed down and added another 10ccs of pressure to the balloon.

A devastating crunch, which reminded Reece of an explosion, erupted from Jin's nose, followed by a torrent of blood. His eyes rolled into his head as his arms and legs pulled at their restraints. He dropped his chin to his chest.

Reece stepped forward and pulled his hair back. He was still conscious.

"Let's talk, Jin."

The Chinese man's fists moved but then turned back into balls.

"Do the other one," Reece ordered the doctor, dropping Jin's head back to his chest.

Guerrero pushed down on the plunger leading into the right nostril, expanding the balloon against the nasal concha bones, destroying them and the glandular tissue that surrounded them.

Jin's head swung violently from side to side, the geyser of blood that erupted from his right nostril coating his chin and shirt. His face turned a deeper shade of red as his guttural screams were muffled by the rag and zip ties. His eyes threatened to pop out of their sockets and his veins strained against the muscles and skin of his throat.

"More," Reece said.

Guerrero pushed in additional fluid, expanding the balloon and destroying the medial wall of Jin's right nostril, the sickening sound of breaking bones causing the doctor to wince.

Jin's facial expression shifted to horror as the pain radiating through his sinuses caused his stomach to turn against itself, his mouth filling with vomit and bile, some of it escaping around the sides of the rag, filling his airway as his body attempted to suck in life-sustaining oxygen.

Not ready for him to die just yet, Reece cut the zip around Jin's head.

Jin retched again, his body convulsing in its fight for much-needed air.

"I'm not thrilled about any of this, Mr. Jin, but you did try to kill me twice, you almost killed the woman I love, and you were about to put me through this very same interrogation. Something has been bothering me; even with Alice you know we are still a ways off from full autonomous control of the military, in particular the Pacific Fleet." Reece paused and turned to the doctor. "Get the IV for the eye socket ready."

Jin sucked in air, his chest heaving. He looked like he had a broken nose and two black eyes, the swelling in his face grotesque.

"What I know so far is that you conspired with Elba Industries and Representative Christine Harding to steal classified data in transit after setting up one of your submarine captains to launch missiles at Hawaii. That data is now being decrypted by an Elba Industries quantum computer. When it's decrypted you will have what you need to immobilize the U.S. Pacific Fleet. That quantum computer might also be powerful enough to sway an election. You want to get Harding in the White House and then take Taiwan as quickly as possible, my guess is without any U.S. casualties. Alice might be able to prevent that from happening but all you know about her is from Harding, because she sits on the Intelligence Committee. Alice scares you, but without her autonomously controlling the fleet, she doesn't scare you enough to keep you from invading Taiwan. You know from Harding that Alice has gone to ground and that her conduit to the outside world is through me; with me out of the way, she stays hidden at the deepest levels of the internet. Please stop me if I'm getting any of this wrong."

Jin continued to stare at the floor.

"With all that said, my death and Alice staying out of China's push across the strait were already almost givens, especially before the fleet goes under autonomous control. So, my question, Mr. Jin, before we start this next phase of pain implementation, is why do you really need me and Alice off the board? There is something more."

Jin closed his eyes. Reece could tell he was focusing on his breathing.

"Jin, you tell me, and I promise I'll kill you quick."

Reece snapped his fingers.

Between breaths Jin said something else in Mandarin.

Reece looked to Dr. Guerrero, who just shook his head.

"All right, you had your chance."

Reece shoved the rag back into Jin's mouth, forcing it deep into his throat. He then stepped behind the prisoner and yanked his head back, sliding his right arm around his neck, placing his right hand on his left bicep. His left hand went to the back of Jin's head in a rear naked choke. Instead of putting Jin to sleep, he held his head in place as Guerrero approached with the needle and catheter.

Jin attempted to twist his head, but he was held in place by Reece's constrictive lock. The rag stifled his screams as Guerrero inserted the needle into the outside corner of Jin's left eye. The doctor pushed the sharp spike to the back of the socket and then extracted it, leaving the catheter, which he taped in place. He then attached it to an IV bag of saline solution.

Reece released Jin from his chokehold and stepped back around to face his subject.

Jin thrashed his head, trying desperately to dislodge the catheter.

Reece would have felt sorry for him had he not been responsible for almost killing Katie.

"Before I have Dr. Guerrero open the roller clamp and raise the IV bag, I want to give you one more chance to tell me why you really needed me and Alice out of play."

Veins continued to bulge on Jin's neck, his face so red Reece thought he might drop dead of a heart attack at any moment. His face was swollen, disfigured from the broken bones and damaged tissues in his nose.

His hands remained clenched in fists.

"Nothing? Well, at least I know I did all I could."

Reece nodded at the doctor, indicating that he should raise the IV bag and start the flow.

Guerrero made sure the slide clamp was open. He adjusted the roller clamp to regulate the flow rate and visually ensured the drip chamber was half-full before raising it up to shoulder level, allowing the liquid saline solution to flow into Jin's eye socket.

It did not take long for the pressure to build.

"If you pass out when your eyeball pops out, don't worry. I won't take the other one until you wake up," Reece said.

Jin's face changed from dark purple to a bright red as the acute pain triggered a sympathetic response from the infusion of liquid pressure behind his eye.

"How long until his eye comes out?" Reece asked.

"Just a few minutes," Guerrero responded.

Jin's right eye was already noticeably bulging. He was fighting it.

What if he doesn't tell me?

What if this doesn't work?

This guy is tough.

As Jin's left eye continued to bulge, Reece reached down between his legs and grabbed the Foley catheter. He applied pressure and saw Jin's determination turn to fear. The retention balloon in Jin's bladder was designed to hold the catheter in place to drain urine from the body. It was meant to be deflated before removal. Reece began to pull, dragging the balloon into Jin's urethra and prostate, generating a whole new level of pain. Reece watched as the blood entered the catheter and mixed with the urine in the collection container. The agony in Jin's face had reached a new level of intensity. Instead of thrashing, his head shook in place. For a moment Reece thought he was having a seizure. Then he realized that Jin was losing control. Reece continued to pull on the Foley catheter and at the moment Reece felt like Jin's eye was going to pop out of his head his right-hand fist turned into a thumbs-up.

"Stop the drip," Reece ordered.

Guerrero lowered the bag and closed the slide clamp.

"And fix this," Reece said, indicating the Foley catheter.

The doctor deflated the balloon. He maneuvered it back into Jin's bladder and reinflated it, providing a moment of, if not relief, then at least a reduction in the excruciating pain.

Reece pulled the rag from Jin's mouth.

"Time to talk."

CHAPTER 40

JIN STRUGGLED TO BREATHE.

Reece gave him just a few seconds.

"I can turn the IV back on or rip this out at any time," Reece said, drawing back on the tube in his hand.

Jin moaned in pain and Reece let up on the pressure.

"Talk."

Jin's eye was nearly out of the socket. His face was so distorted that he looked like he was already dead.

Jin muttered something in Mandarin.

"English," Reece ordered.

"The Four Noble Buddhist Truths," Jin stuttered between breaths. "Suffering, the cause of suffering, the end of suffering, the path to the end of suffering."

All life is suffering.

"I can help you with the fourth truth," Reece said, referring to "the path to the end of suffering." "Tell me what I need to know, and you will suffer no more."

"Satellites."

"What?"

"Satellites," Jin said again.

"What do you mean? I thought this was about Alice."

"It is, you dumb fuck," the Chinese man spat. He paused to gather himself as Reece added pressure to the catheter. "She needs to stay out of play. But it's bigger than Alice and you. This is about control. With Alice not in play the U.S. still has an advantage in the low-orbital satellite domain. They blanket the earth and control everything from communications to navigation to banking, to say nothing of internet and television."

"Elba Industries has a space program," Reece said, remembering his conversation with Lawrence Miles in Sausalito.

"Bravo, American," Jin said as he struggled to breathe.

"He's going to take out our low-orbital satellites? And in destroying them, he also takes out his competition," Reece said, thinking aloud. "The world becomes dependent on Elba. But we could just take him out."

"Unless? You are almost there, Mr. Reece."

"Unless he already had assurances that the U.S. military would not interfere," Reece said.

"And where does that kind of assurance come from?" Jin asked.

"The Oval Office."

Jin managed a half smile through his excruciating pain.

"And there it is," Jin said.

"You still need Elba Industries to decrypt the data they stole," Reece pointed out.

"And if that's already done?"

"Is it?"

Jin nodded.

"You paralyze the Pacific Fleet, destroy the low-orbital satellites, and take Taiwan. What about Alice?" Reece asked.

"You tell me."

"Take me through it," Reece said. "The data grab. You confirm it was Elba Industries?"

"Yes. Though they could not have done it without us."

"What do you mean?"

"We needed each other. Andrew Hart is involved with classified data storage programs. Harding is on the Intelligence Committee. Hart has a fledgling rocket program; China's rocket and space program is far more advanced than the West believes. Hart has a quantum computer light-years ahead of his competitors and of anything we have in China."

"Except Alice."

"Correct. Grabbing data is one thing. Storing it is another and accessing it is yet another. To run a quantum computer, you need power. People would notice if Elba Industries built a power plant in Palo Alto. But if we build one in the Pacific it's a lot less noticeable, especially if it brings power to a disenfranchised community."

"The data is on his island? Corelena? Off Buru in Indonesia?"

"Yes."

"And it's decrypted?"

"Yes."

"Tell me about the satellites."

"What do you know of the Kessler effect?"

"Tell me about it."

"Think of it as a chain reaction of colliding debris in space. Satellites hitting other satellites. The world to a large extent, even your military, is dependent on low-orbital satellites that communicate with one another. China has been focused on launching mid- and high-orbital geostationary satellites for the past few years, as has Elba Industries. Once Elba takes out the low-orbital satellites with an anti-satellite missile campaign designed to capitalize on the Kessler effect, the amount of debris that would blanket the low-orbital altitudes would seal us in."

"What does that mean?"

"The current space race is frozen in time. It could take two decades, maybe more, for the debris to eventually burn up in the atmosphere. Until then, my country, and Elba Industries, control space."

“Which means you control communication and navigation on earth,” Reece said.

“Precisely. And banking and credit card transactions, the power grid, emails; the world will be entirely dependent on us.”

“And you are going to launch missiles from Hart’s island?”

“Yes.”

And Hart outsmarts everyone.

“I see you are bright enough to connect the next few dots, but you have made a serious miscalculation, Mr. Reece. In your attempt to get answers, you inadvertently started a clock. Our candidate is not yet in the White House, yet you have me here. Undoubtedly my government is going to correctly assume that you made me talk. What do you think that does to their calculus?”

It speeds it up, Reece thought.

“Instead of launching next year with our man, or in this case our woman, in the White House, you just triggered the invasion. We are going now. When Minister Yun does not hear back from me, Beijing is going to conclude you know about Harding, which means they will not wait. It was going to happen in a way that kept the conflict from going nuclear. Harding was going to see to that. By next spring Alice might be connected to all your autonomous military assets, but now, because of you, an unknown entity might then be in the White House. Today, only one of those variables is a factor. You might have just initiated both a Taiwan offensive and a nuclear exchange with the United States.”

“How do I stop it?”

“How do you think?”

“Stop the launch against the satellites.”

“Very good, Mr. Reece. And after this you’d better kill me or, as you know, I’ll never stop coming for you. But remember, Ms. Buranek’s injury was no fault of mine. That was you. You put her in the line of fire. And I can see in your eyes that you know it.”

Reece thought of Katie bleeding out in his arms.

He reached down and yanked the catheter out of Jin's penis. The retention balloon in his bladder ruptured his prostate and ripped the length of his urethra tube. Jin opened his mouth in a silent scream as he watched blood spew from his genitals.

Dr. Guerrero's eyes opened wide with terror.

You should kill him, Reece.

He thought of Lauren and Lucy.

Reece turned to the doctor.

Guerrero's eyes were wide, paralyzed with fear.

"You are getting a second lease on life today, Doctor. My friends outside, they are going to keep tabs on you. If they find out you have slipped up and are doing any of this sort of shit for China, you and your entire family are going to leave the world just like Mr. Jin. Understand?"

Guerrero nodded frantically.

"Good."

Reece stood, leveled the suppressor, and put two bullets into Jin's head.

The truth of the end of suffering.

He walked across the room and exited onto the deck in the afternoon sun, where Ox was leaning against the railing.

"What's the fastest way to Indonesia?" Reece asked.

"Why? What's up?"

"We need to prevent World War Three."

PART III
THE TRIALS

"And war broke out in Heaven."

—REVELATION 12:7–9

CHAPTER 41

Manila
Republic of the Philippines

IT WAS EARLY EVENING when the nondescript CASA C-212 landed at Ninoy Aquino International Airport in Manila and taxied to a private hangar leased through a CIA front company. The pilot wore shorts, flip-flops, a beige and maroon Hawaiian shirt, and a battered blue ball cap with EVERGREEN written across the crown. He looked like he had more miles on him than did the venerable twin-engine turboprop. In production since the 1970s, the boxy cargo plane had become a workhorse in civilian and military aviation circles for its durability, reliability, and superior short takeoff and landing capabilities. Licensed through a Spanish company for manufacture in Indonesia, the CASA 212 was not an uncommon sight in the skies of Southeast Asia.

Available in a variety of configurations, this particular aircraft was set up as a cargo plane so the seats were the fold-down, side-facing variety, similar to the CASAs Reece had jumped from at the Army Freefall Parachutist course in Yuma, Arizona, when he was just starting his journey in the SEAL Teams.

Before they went wheels-up Reece had used Ox's encrypted KryptAll phone to fill Vic in on what he had learned over the past twenty-four hours. The two operators sat across from one another and, though Reece was never comfortable sleeping on planes, he was out just minutes after takeoff and didn't regain consciousness until they touched down. The other members of the ISA team had split up and gone their separate ways following the operation in Laoag, blending back into the fabric of the Philippines.

A young CIA officer was waiting on them with a crystal-pearl Toyota Land Cruiser 300 and a change of clothes for Reece, who was still in his beige jumpsuit. He introduced himself as Norm Bryce and handed Reece shopping bags from the Makati District, explaining it was the best he could do on short notice. Reece found a restroom in the hangar, splashed cold water on his face, and changed into tan slacks, a dark blue short-sleeved button-up shirt, and boat shoes. Better than the jumpsuit.

The Philippines has long been the Pacific hub of America's fourth branch of government, with Manila in effect its regional headquarters. From the OSS days in World War II to Edward Lansdale and the Huk Rebellion, as a staging area for operations into Vietnam and through the Global War on Terror, the CIA had a long history in Southeast Asia. The embassy was the home to the "Regional Service Center," tasked with creating and disseminating information to influence local populations, and to the "Special Collection Service," a joint CIA-NSA program focused on data collection across the region. It had also long been the forward-deployed site of the Agency's China Operations Working Group. Manila Station was busy.

The 3.3L twin-turbo V6 diesel engine powered the new-model Land Cruiser through the Manila traffic, making short work of the twenty-minute drive.

"Who's the station chief?" Reece asked.

"Marion Oates," Bryce replied. "She's the best station chief I've ever worked for. Well, she's the only one, but she's fantastic. Her mom is from the Philippines, so she is dialed-in here. They call her the 'Iron Eagle.'"

"Why's that?"

"Some say it's because the eagle is the national bird of the Philippines. She was also quite the triathlete in college, from what I understand. Placed high in an Ironman. Now she scuba dives. I think it's because the station is so busy that underwater is the only place people can't reach her. But the rumor is that at the Farm she liked to watch *Iron Eagle*."

"The film?"

"Apparently she's got a thing for eighties action movies."

"I like her already," Reece said.

Located on the water of South Harbor on Manila Bay off Roxas Boulevard, with Manila Ocean Park and the Rizal Hotel to the north and Dolomite Beach to the south, the United States Embassy reminded Reece of a miniature White House. The main chancery was built in 1940 and was then occupied by the Japanese after the fall of Bataan and Corregidor. It was retaken in the Battle of Manila in 1945 by U.S. forces and Philippine guerrillas in a campaign that saw the most intense urban combat of the Pacific War. The embassy flagpole still bears the bullets from the fighting. Not long after, the embassy was the location of the Japanese war crimes trials.

They pulled up to a gate that looked like it was built to stop a speeding truck laden with explosives, which is why, in fact, it had been constructed. A Marine guard approached and Bryce rolled down his window. He held up his embassy ID as another Marine ran a lighted telescoping inspection mirror under the vehicle. The guards were obviously familiar with Bryce and recognized the Land Cruiser.

Marines have had a relationship with the State Department dating back to 1798. Not long after World War II, the Marines were tasked with providing security to U.S. embassies and consulates around the world. Each time Reece passed through security into an embassy complex, he couldn't help but think just how exposed those brave young Marines were as they stood their posts. Reece remembered the story his father had told him about Marine Corporal James Conrad Marshall, who was killed defending the embassy in Saigon during the Tet Offensive in 1968. And he thought of Lance Corporal Robert "Bobby" McMaugh, who was killed along with sixty-two others on April 18, 1983, when the embassy in Beirut was targeted by a terrorist using a truck bomb in an attack that foreshadowed what was to come that October.

Reece had nothing but respect for the Marines who held the line.

They look so young, he thought.

The gate rolled to the right moments later.

Reece had been to the embassy in Manila a few times over the years and was always struck by what it represented. No matter how divided things were on the home front, America was still a beacon of hope to those around the world born to their station or living under oppressive regimes. The flip side of that coin is that embassies were stationary targets for America's enemies, and those who worked within their walls were on the front lines whether they knew it or not.

Bryce wheeled the cruiser past the chancery and helipad and parked behind the new annex building.

"They like to keep us separate from the State Department people," Bryce said. "Clash of cultures."

"You a case officer?" Reece asked as they exited the vehicle.

"No, sir. DST data scientist."

"A what?"

"Department of Science and Technology," Bryce said. "You can look it up on the CIA website."

The two operators followed the young CIA man up a short flight of steps. He swiped his badge on a reader that unlocked a set of doors leading to a quarterdeck where another Marine guard stood ready.

The guard buzzed them past the next barrier and Bryce led them into a small room with what looked like PO boxes.

"If you have a phone or smartwatch, you can leave them here," he said.

Ox and Bryce dumped their phones into boxes and locked them with the provided key while Reece waited since he had nothing but his watch and the clothes on his back.

Bryce then guided them through a series of hallways and down a flight of steps and into the heart of the CIA's station in Manila. He stopped at an office with an open door and knocked on the doorframe.

"Miss Oates? We made it."

Bryce stepped inside, followed by Reece and Ox.

A woman who looked to be around Reece's age sat behind a desk with two large monitors. She looked up and hit a button, closing out whatever she had been working on.

She then stood and walked around her desk, extending her hand to Reece.

"Shall we forgo the 'Mr. Donovan' part?" she asked.

"I don't think it really matters anymore," Reece replied, shaking her hand.

"Well then, Mr. Reece. I'm Marion Oates."

"Ox," she said, shaking the old sergeant major's hand.

"Miss Oates," he replied.

"Mr. Bryce, thank you for scooping them up for me."

"My pleasure, ma'am."

"What have these two told you about me?" she asked, moving her hands to her hips.

Obviously fit and attractive, she was dressed in black pants and a white blouse. She was about five foot seven, maybe five foot eight in her heels. A rose-and-gold-colored women's Citizen Promaster Dive Watch adorned her left wrist.

"He's been asleep most of the time," Ox replied.

"Well, let's get acquainted as we walk," she said, leading the way out of her office. "We have a VTC with Langley in five minutes."

Reece looked at his watch.

"Isn't it like four a.m. there?" he asked.

"Three a.m., but a potential war with China gets people out of bed, even at headquarters."

"I guess that would do it," Reece said. "Where were you before this?"

"Argentina. But I've been through Manila on two other postings. My dad was Navy. He met my mom here. Brought her back to the States in '79. I still have a lot of family here, which as chief of station is both a blessing and a curse. I grew up in Norfolk. Went the Georgetown route and interned at the Agency. The Tagalog got me in. Did a stint in Afghanistan early on but hardly left Bagram Air Base. I just missed you in Baghdad. I saw the highlight reel. You guys did some impressive work there."

"We had a great team," Reece replied, looking at Ox.

She stopped at the end of a hallway and held up her blue badge to a scanner. It beeped and she punched in a code. The door clicked and opened to a SCIF with a large monitor at the end of the room.

The men remained standing until the station chief had taken her seat at the head of the table. Then Reece sat to her right, Ox to her left, and Bryce took the chair in front of Ox, where he could also troubleshoot any technical problems.

"Mr. Reece," she began.

"Just 'Reece' is fine."

"All right, Reece, Director Rodriguez gave me the heads-up early this morning. He also asked me to withhold briefing the ambassador, which is unusual to say the least, but he also gave me some additional background and told me that we are to extend you and Ox every courtesy. Now, I've worked with Ox before and know you by reputation, but I would be extremely naïve to think that something is not about to blow up in my face."

"Ox?" Reece said.

"Well, there are a few dead bodies up north with ties to Chinese intelligence. They will all have nine-millimeter bullets in them. No casings or cameras. There could be video of Reece being taken off the plane from Macau and into first police custody and then Chinese custody, but I doubt either China or the Philippine police are going to want to dig too deep."

"I see. Director Rodriguez informed me that there is time-sensitive intelligence linked to a possible invasion of Taiwan."

Reece opened his mouth to speak but the video monitor came to life. He expected to look up and see Vic and Andy. Instead, he turned his head to look into the eyes of the president of the United States.

CHAPTER 42

"MADAM PRESIDENT," REECE SAID. He recognized President Olsen's location in the White House Situation Room, where he had first met her the previous year.

"President Olsen," Marion Oates said, successfully masking her surprise at suddenly having an audience with the president.

"Commander Reece, Ms. Oates, Sergeant Major Andrews, and I understand Mr. Bryce is with us as well."

"Madam President," Bryce stammered.

"I'm here with Director Howe, Director Rodriguez, and Andy Danreb," the president said, getting straight to business. "The National Security Council will be here at six a.m. Due to the unique nature of this threat I want to hear it direct, no filters and without the politics of the council."

Despite the early hour, President Gale Olsen was dressed in a navy blue pantsuit over a white blouse. An American flag pin adorned her left lapel. She had not been swayed by the politics of either party to add another nation's flag, signifying that regardless of her personal party affiliation, she was a president for all Americans.

Of Danish-Cuban descent and hailing from Florida's 9th Congressional District, she had delivered her home state for the martyred president, balancing Christensen's more libertarian views and unapologetic support of capitalism with her strong track record on the left. She had been promoted from major to lieutenant colonel in the Army Reserve JAG Corps while in office and had recently joined Presidents Polk, Buchanan, Hayes, Coolidge, Truman, and Johnson in not seeking a second term.

"Director Rodriguez has given us a preliminary briefing and I understand time is of the essence to preempt the launch of a new weapon system that would take out all low-orbital satellites, the consequences of which I understand to be catastrophic."

"That is correct," Reece said. "Up to this point we were working off information that indicated China wanted to know our quantum computer capability and status of our autonomous weapons connectivity in advance of a possible invasion of Taiwan."

"They wanted to know about Alice," the president said.

"Yes, which is why they first targeted me and then tried to make me an offer I couldn't refuse. In the course of a subsequent interview, I was made aware of a plan to take out low-earth-orbital satellites, a plan involving both China and an American company called Elba Industries."

"Madam President, if I may," Vic interjected.

"Please," the president said, leaning back in her chair.

"Mr. Danreb," Vic said. "Please give us a brief rundown on what you have learned since Commander Reece's update four hours ago, as we are quite literally on the clock."

Danreb cleared his throat.

"For anyone not familiar with Kessler syndrome, it is a theory first proposed by NASA scientist Donald J. Kessler in the late 1970s. His assertion was that as more and more countries put satellites into low earth orbit, the greater the chances of a collision. He proposed that a collision in low orbit would in turn create more debris, setting off a chain reaction of devastating collisions. The net result would be a blanket of space junk that effectively seals the earth, making it nearly impossible to launch satellites into low orbit or through low orbit into mid or high orbits. Now, if that were to happen, it's advantage China by a wide margin."

"Why is that?" asked the president.

"We are dependent on low-orbital satellites for almost every aspect of daily life, from banking to credit cards to mobile phone and Wi-Fi communications, not to mention our very power grid. Low-orbital satellites are owned by private corporations who have close to nine thousand active satellites in orbit, with Elon Musk's Starlink making up more than fifty percent. They avoid collision through AI-based communications systems that allow them to move out of each other's way, which happens every four to six minutes. They are continuously sharing their locations to triangulate positions and maneuver accordingly. We—and by *we* I mean the intelligence and defense establishments—rent space from these private companies because they can launch to low orbits a lot more efficiently than can NASA."

"As in the recent SpaceX Falcon 9 launch under the National Security Space Launch program," the president said.

"That's right. With that launch, SpaceX put six classified missile-detection satellites built by L3Harris Technologies and Northrop Grumman into low orbit for the Missile Defense Agency and Space Development Agency. Those specific satellites are part of the Hypersonic and Ballistic Tracking Space Sensor program and Tracking Layer program. They are largely prototypes testing the feasibility of building out a more robust satellite constellation for global indications and warnings, and follow-on tracking, and targeting of advanced missile threats. The thing to keep in mind is that all six of those satellites went into low orbit."

"What's the significance of low orbit?" the president asked.

"Speed and vulnerability," Danreb said. "Over the past twenty years, we doubled down on low orbit because of the speed with which those satellites communicate. Everything is faster at lower altitudes. It is that speed on which we have become dependent. China, on the other hand, has been launching communications, military, and spy satellites at a feverish pace, almost seventy launches per year, but they have focused on mid- and high-orbital positioning. We currently maintain a huge lead in low-earth-orbital satellites, but China is ahead in the mid to high ranges. If we lost our low-orbital satellites, so goes our advantage. But, and I'll reiterate this, we could not even rebuild our low-orbital capability because no one would be able put anything into low orbit or even get through low orbit to mid or high orbit."

"For how long?" asked Director Howe.

"No one knows for certain, but some predictive models assess that it could be a quarter century."

"Enough time for China to take Taiwan and even push farther into the Pacific with our defenses down," Howe said.

"We currently have the technological advantage, but that is because of our low-orbital dominance," Danreb continued. "Our assessment is that China plans to eliminate that advantage."

"How would they do it?" the president asked.

"By creating a layer of debris, space junk if you will, at low orbit."

"Explain."

"Imagine different sizes of space debris. Dust results in what can best be described as sandblasting. A one-millimeter sphere, like a BB, does damage but most satellites have Nextel and Kevlar shields that protect them from objects of that size. At ten millimeters we start to see problems. That's something about the size of a marble. A ten-millimeter sphere would have the energy of being hit by a motorcycle going one hundred miles an hour. Now, with a twenty-millimeter sphere, which is about the size of a golf ball, the effects are devastating. They impact at hypersonic speeds; MV squared. Velocity matters. Think of this as a dump truck going three hundred miles an hour. Small golf ball–sized items impact with such tremendous force that the satellite they hit in turn disintegrates and creates several thousand more particles, which hit additional satellites and eventually create a blanket of debris so thick that we can't even replace the satellites in low orbit, nor can we launch through that blanket of debris into the mid- or high-orbital range, where China currently has the advantage. Nothing gets through. The world we have become accustomed to, and the system we have become dependent upon, is no more."

"That still doesn't explain how China could trigger this Kessler syndrome."

"With a counterorbital anti-satellite weapons system, probably a Gravity-2 medium-lift launch vehicle built by China's Orienspace Technology with assistance from the state-owned China Aerospace Science and Industry Corporation. With a payload of more than a million twenty-millimeter aluminum spheres, it would be launched into low orbit and detonated using a shaped charge, sending those golf ball–sized projectiles into counter orbit."

Danreb read the room and saw more than a few confused faces.

"Have you ever shot clays?" he asked the president.

"What do you mean?"

"Sporting clays, trap, skeet, that kind of thing."

"I'm familiar," she replied.

"Well, if clay targets are going right to left or left to right, one technique you can use is to lead them a bit depending on distance and swing through. Imagine a cloud of shot traveling across the path of the clay. That's what we are talking about here, only there are nine thousand clays in the sky and each of them is destroyed by the counterorbital cloud of shot. That debris, or in the clay target example, the fragments of the destroyed targets, then stays in orbit, scattering in all directions and taking out even more satellites until nothing is intact, turning the atmosphere at that altitude into a solid cloud of debris. Anything you try to launch through that debris field is immediately destroyed."

"And China has this capability?"

"We believe it's a joint capability between China and Elba Industries. China needs Elba's quantum-enabled AI for the classified data decryption and Elba needs China's power plant to power it. They collaborate on the missile technology to take out all satellites in low orbit. That would severely hamper our ability to defend ourselves, to say nothing of defending Taiwan."

"This Elba AI, how advanced is it?" the president asked.

"That is unknown," Vic said, taking over from Danreb. "They have kept it relatively hidden. Alice did become aware of it and its potential when it was used to kill a reporter who was on his way to California from New York to conduct an interview with Elba Industries CEO Andrew Hart. The journalist's brother worked at Elba. We think he may have leaked information on their AI capability."

"And they took him out?"

"To anyone investigating, it looked like an electric vehicle had a malfunction. People expect that will happen. But Alice was able to get inside and see that its signals manipulation came from an island in Indonesia off the west coast of Buru called Corelena. They tried to hide island ownership through multiple business layers and front companies, but Alice tracked it back to Andrew Hart. She can explain," Vic said. "Alice, was that explanation close?"

A blurry avatar appeared in a corner of the video teleconference screen and Alice's voice filled the room.

"Yes. Elba Industries calls their version of me Napoleon. They built him specifically to stay hidden. They made a mistake when they tested him against the journalist. That departure from protocol gave me a window. He was in and out in an instant. They have a firewall that I have yet to penetrate but that's because I have not yet tried. Think of it as passive targeting. Once I focus my considerable recourses against it, I'll get in. The second-order effect is that Napoleon and Elba Industries will know. I estimate that with that knowledge there is an eighty-six percent chance that they would launch their anti-satellite missiles. But I have identified my target. I know where he is. And now I can hunt him."

"What is that?" Marion asked, not quite believing what she was witnessing.

"We will have to read you in later," Reece said, realizing that Alice was starting to think like him.

"Deal."

"Alice, if you get in could you shut them down?" Reece asked.

"Napoleon is an unknown system specifically designed to counter my capabilities."

"So, we don't know."

"That is correct," Alice replied before dissolving from the screen.

"According to what Commander Reece was able to ascertain in Macau and the Philippines, China wants to reunify Taiwan before our fleet goes autonomous with OVERMATCH next year," Vic said. "Population-wise they are as strong as they will ever be. Alice was an unknown they wanted to turn into a known, but even without that information all indications are that our fleet will have the capability to be autonomous next year. And now that we know of their intention to wipe out all low-orbital satellites and render that layer of the atmosphere useless for decades, we may have inadvertently triggered their attack. We gauge that just by discovering this information we may have moved up their timeline."

"Explain," said the president.

"They know they will never be in a better position than right now. China wants a peaceful reunification of Taiwan but the window for that possibility just closed. Their campaign will start with what amounts to a technological decapitation in taking out the low-orbital satellites. They take away our technological advantage, which puts us on our heels not just militarily but also economically and societally. Then they assassinate the Taiwanese leadership from within using sleeper cells already in place, install their government waiting in the wings, take key infrastructure via special operations, and block the seas to the east and west while they conduct amphibious landings along the west coast and large-scale airborne assaults in the east. Special operations forces take airfields, power plants, and news centers. If we move to intervene militarily, China will have the ability to further hamper a conventional U.S. response by rendering the fleet at Guam inoperable, like they did with their cyberattack during COVID in 2020. That attack will be all the more effective now that the Elba Industries quantum computer has decrypted all our classified data pertaining to the Pacific Fleet. What they did to our naval assets in Guam in 2020 was just a test. With their newfound data they could do the same thing to the fleet in Pearl Harbor and the West Coast. They could also hit us with state and nonstate hacker attacks shutting down banks, erasing credit card data, stock transactions, even identities through state driver's license databases, creating panic for us domestically. China has a close relationship with Tehran and there is the possibility of terrorist attacks inside the United States via Iranian proxies. The FBI is tracking as many illegal border crossers coming into the U.S. from countries that harbor Iranian proxy forces as they can, but they do not have eyes on everyone. China will want to keep it nonnuclear, but they could potentially hit targets with transonic, supersonic, hypersonic, and high-hypersonic missiles in Hawaii, Alaska, and the West Coast with ports in Seattle, Long Beach, and San Diego being probable targets with conventional or unconventional weapons. They know that a nuclear response from the United States would result in the deaths of half their country, which is over half a billion people."

"Why risk that?"

"If they do not use nuclear, chemical, or biological weapons, they believe we are constrained to nonnuclear options. And because in their original plan this all came to fruition with someone else in the White House, someone they knew would not intervene militarily."

"Harding?"

"I have a separate brief for you on Representative Harding," Vic said.

"Do we know the location of the anti-satellite missile launch sites?" President Olsen asked.

"Andy," Vic said.

"We have located two possible launch facilities," Danreb said. "One is the Xicheng Satellite Launch Center in southwest China and the other is Corelena Island in Indonesia."

"We could target those sites with submarine-launched or surface-launched missiles, or interconnectional ballistic missiles, or B-21 Raiders," the president said.

"The issue with targeting those sites is that China or Hart could launch before our missiles hit, especially if Napoleon has decrypted all the defense and intelligence data. Our weapons could hit their sites after the anti-satellite missiles had detonated in low orbit."

"How do we know there is a launch site in Indonesia?"

"A China-based renewable energy company with projects across Southeast Asia began building a power plant on the island of Buru in partnership with the Indonesian government a few years ago. It's an eco-friendly venture focused on biomass, thermal energy, wind, water, and solar. They built it under the auspices of helping the people of Buru and other islands in the Indonesian archipelago. Our assessment was that it was to support a rare-earth-metal mining push by China, like we have seen them do in Africa. Gold was discovered on Buru in 2011. The power plant was a response to the mining industry that developed around that discovery, or so we thought. China is also the world leader in construction of artificial islands. They have built them to expand their territorial waters for over two decades. They have gotten quite good at constructing man-made islands and tunnels. Their subs are built and launched from tunnels to counter our spy satellites, so they have a lot of experience in the field. We now think the mining activity on Buru was cover for action that allowed China to build a power plant and explain away the digging that goes into building underground missile silos. We know the locations of all launch sites in China via our technical intelligence capability and our HUMINT sources. But we were focused on China proper. A private island owned by an American on one of over eighteen thousand islands in Indonesia was not on our radar."

"We need to be vigilant and avoid actions that speed up their timeline," the president said, thinking aloud. "Could we move naval assets closer?"

"Yes, but that could also trigger a launch."

"Could we launch the standby assault squadron at Dam Neck?"

"Yes, but same situation," Danreb said. "China knows when C-17s leave Oceania and Pope almost better than we do. With the data decrypted and accessible by Napoleon, they might know there's been a recall at Dam Neck as soon as the alert goes out. I think Hart's endgame is to launch the anti-satellite weapons, whether China invades Taiwan or not. It wasn't about Taiwan for him. China needed the decrypted data, and he needed their missile technology. They launch those anti-satellite missiles and the world order changes."

"It seems our options are limited," said the president.

"Reece?" Vic said.

"Madam President, here in Manila, I'm the closest asset we've got. I'm closer than SEALs in Guam and certainly Dam Neck or Delta on the East Coast. Plus, no one will know that I'm inserting from here. We skirt the issue of inadvertently triggering an immediate launch. We might have hours or days, but Hart is going to launch. That gives him what he's always wanted; he outsmarts his competition and becomes the next tech giant of the twenty-first century."

"What do you propose?" the president asked.

"Vic, are there any Maritime Branch assets in the area?"

"Closest asset is in the Molucca Sea, just north of Buru, changing out pods," Vic said in refence to undersea monitoring devices disguised as rocks.

"How many operators aboard?"

"Five: two boat drivers, one paramilitary officer, and two contractors."

"So, three shooters. Okay, get me and Ox aboard. That gives us five. The clock is ticking. China is putting the pieces together right now. We are in their window. If Hart takes out those satellites, we are in deep shit. Is the boat outfitted with kit?"

"It is."

"Just get me close, Vic."

"That's still three thousand miles away. How do we get you there?" he asked.

"What kind of air assets do you have here?" Reece asked the station chief.

"It is the biggest station in Asia," she replied.

"Good, because I'm going to borrow a plane."

"What do you need?"

"Does 'Air America' out at the airport have anything with a little longer reach than that CASA 212?"

"Of course, we're the CIA, but I've been down that way on dive trips in the Banda Sea. Airstrips in the area don't support larger aircraft. Most people go through Davao, Brunei, Jakarta, or Darwin."

"That's okay. We are not going to land."

"Oh?"

"We're going to jump."

CHAPTER 43

Banda Sea
Northwest of Buru Island
Republic of Indonesia

EARLY EVENING WAS ANDREW Hart's favorite time to be on the water. He handled the forty-four-foot Spirit Yachts sloop with the confidence of a seasoned professional in the steady breeze of the Banda Sea. The three years it had taken to design and build in Suffolk in eastern England had been worth the wait. Christened the *St. Georges*, the sleek wood-hulled sailboat celebrated the classic lines of 1930s yacht design. She retained the DNA of her longer forty-six-foot racing cousin but with a wider cockpit and enough beam and headroom to support a host of amenities that allowed her to be handled single-handedly anywhere in the world. She hid a racing performance profile beneath the skin of a vessel built for exploring.

Hart had been drawn to Spirit Yachts' attention to detail. Just as when he had created Napoleon, nothing was left to chance. Aboard the *St. Georges* was the only place he was disconnected from the technology that had shaped his life and would shape the future of the planet. She was also a motivator. Under sail, he could not help but think about the regattas he had lost to legends like Larry Ellison and some of the other tech giants. The *St. Georges* was inspiration. The boat gave him energy.

With all sheets and halyards cleated in the center cockpit, Hart could handle the boat without assistance, but he still asked Novak to adjust the overlapping jib as necessary. The wind was coming in from the northeast at a sustained eight to ten knots, which would allow them to sail into the lagoon and catch a glimpse of the rocket that would change the world order.

Before casting off, they had received a message from Chen Yun informing them that Ba Jin had disappeared. He had been on a mission to capture and interrogate James Reece. A new factor had entered the calculus.

"Stand by to tack," Hart said, even though he didn't need to. Novak was fairly useless underway.

"Tacking," Hart announced.

He simultaneously released the port jib sheet while turning the sloop gracefully through the wind with the boom passing safely over their heads. As the sail flapped across the foredeck, he completed his ninety-degree course change and re-cleated the sheet on the starboard side.

"Our countrymen may have inadvertently forced China's hand," Novak said.

"They may have," Hart said, looking up to check the sails.

"We still have a way out."

"A way out?"

"You pay me to think through contingencies."

"Worst case?"

"Worst case depends on your point of view," Novak pointed out. "And your side."

"Yes. China could decide to take Taiwan not knowing if the U.S. has an AI quantum computer autonomously controlling its military forces in the Pacific and without taking out the low-orbital satellites."

"Why would they take Taiwan without essentially turning the U.S. deaf and blind?"

"You asked me for worst case. I don't anticipate that happening but it's a possibility. The U.S. could prevent us from launching the Gravity-2 and engage in direct military confrontation with China, in which case China could implement all asymmetric retaliatory measures."

"A cyberattack on the fleet in Guam, hacking attacks across the U.S. domestically, and terror attacks through Iranian proxies in major metropolitan areas," Hart said, reiterating what they both already knew.

"That's right. Things could get very messy."

"If James Reece got Ba Jin to talk and now knows about the anti-satellite capability, what actions does the U.S. take?"

"They could handle it diplomatically, but as of yet there have been no communications on this issue via diplomatic channels."

"Which means?"

"Which means they may be preparing for war. But to be clear, we have received no indications that they have made any changes to their force posture. There have been no alerts to the Pacific Fleet and no alerts to their Tier One special operations units. If James Reece somehow got information out of Jin, it's quite possible that information did not include our capability here in Indonesia. Right now, there are too many unknowns."

"Or everything has changed," Hart said. "China may act just because of what the Americans might now know."

Hart sailed into the mouth of the lagoon.

"If the U.S. knows this is a possible launch site for a Gravity-2, they have given no indication of that to be the case," Novak said.

"There she is," Hart said.

He furled the jib knowing that he could not push too far into the lagoon, or they would lose their ability to maneuver, with the wind blocked by the trees and limestone cliffs.

The three-stage, four-booster launch vehicle had been brought in on a cargo ship ostensibly delivering supplies for a power plant being built to help the impoverished people of Buru.

Months earlier, the world had watched as China and Orienspace launched a Gravity-1 rocket into orbit from a ship in the Yellow Sea in a proof of concept monitored closely by the world's intelligence agencies. The Defu-15002 mobile sea-launch platform looked almost exactly like a cargo ship, but instead of a deck stacked with shipping containers, its deck was purpose-built for launching rockets.

What those same intelligence agencies did not know was that a cargo ship supposedly supplying a power plant on Buru as part of a joint Chinese and Indonesian green energy project had secretly been loaded with a Gravity-2 rocket and transported to Indonesia. Once off Buru it had been camouflaged and moved by a barge of the same design as the deck portion of the Defu-15002 through the lagoon to its current position. Limestone cliffs protected it from the north and west and additional scaffolding already in place allowed it to be camouflaged from above with a thick plastic retractable screen that looked like the lagoon on satellite imagery.

That no additional military or intelligence assets had been allocated to Indonesia told Hart that thus far their secret was safe. But he also knew that secrets of this magnitude lasted only so long. The United States was well aware of all launch sites in China, but they were not tracking a small private island off Buru in the Indonesian archipelago as a possible launch site for an anti-satellite missile that would change the course of history.

With the rocket in place, Hart was only waiting on the signal from Beijing. He had passed the decrypted information from the data transfer to the Ministry of State Security weeks ago. They were ready to use it to immobilize the Pacific Fleet. Hart and his partners in China would have preferred to wait until Harding was in the White House, but of even greater importance was launching before the autonomous fleet was fully fielded. And if the United States intelligence apparatus had become aware of their plan, there was no choice but to move forward now.

This is how you change the world. You outsmart them all.

The security force was kept to a minimum to avoid drawing too much attention. It was mostly for keeping up appearances. They were brought in well after construction was complete and thought they were guarding an eccentric rich tech mogul. They were Peruvian, poached from Perkins's last job. The twenty contractors had a bunkhouse and were well paid, well fed, and well sexed. Perkins kept them happy with prostitutes from Batam and Bali, Indonesia being a hotbed of human trafficking.

"This clearly accelerates things," Hart said. "Now we are waiting on approval from Beijing, which I expect will come shortly. All assets are in place. Alice remains an unknown but that cannot be helped. Right now, there is nothing to signify that Ba Jin talked."

"The Americans might be smart enough not to show their hand," Novak said.

"You give them too much credit. You of all people should know they are not smart enough to do anything of that magnitude without indicators."

Hart checked the sails. He was sailing at a true wind angle of 90 degrees. He performed a tack, changing course 180 degrees to depart the lagoon, and set a course for his nearby estate.

"They have forced our hand. If they know about us, we have no choice but to launch or we may never get another chance. Next step is to confirm all systems are operational. China will initiate within the next few days. We will be ready. Our time is now."

CHAPTER 44

Ninoy Aquino International Airport
Manila
Republic of the Philippines

"NEED HELP PACKING THAT chute?" Ox asked, knowing that jumping out of planes was not his friend's favorite activity.

"You just stuff it in and hope for the best, right?" Reece responded.

"That's all there is to it. Yours looks fine. I wouldn't worry about jumping that at all. It wants to open. At some point you might want to pull that rip cord before you hit the water."

"These sport rigs don't have rip cords, Ox."

"Ah, that's right. Well then, pull that pilot chute from your BOC instead," Ox said, making reference to the bottom of container, or the pack that held Reece's chute.

"Good tip."

"All kidding aside, we'll go through it by the numbers here on the ground. I'll check your rig, make sure your AAD is set, and we will buddy-check each other in the plane."

"Thanks, Ox. It's been a minute."

Their CIA-supplied gear was organized on the floor of the hangar.

Even at this early hour the air was heavy and humid, which at least made it easier to pack their parachutes.

While Reece was military free fall–qualified with hundreds of jumps under his belt, Ox was creeping up on ten thousand. His first jump after static line-jump school at Fort Benning had been a combat jump into Grenada in 1983 and he had been throwing himself out of planes ever since. He graduated from the Army's military free-fall course, jumpmaster course, and free-fall instructor course while Reece was still in grade school. He had gone on to earn every possible civilian skydiving license, including his D license, tandem instructor examiner certification, and coach rating. He had thousands of tunnel hours and a PRO rating, and though neither the military nor the Agency knew it he had almost eight hundred BASE jumps. He had later excelled in the more specialized military courses for those in Ox's line of work: Advanced Tactical Infiltration Course and Military Tandem Master and Tandem Tethered Bundle Courses. The majority of his 9,786 jumps took place at the Parachute Training and Testing Facility near Marana, Arizona, as a member of Delta Force. Once on board at the Agency, Ox continued to jump and test unconventional infiltration techniques at a CIA site in Florida. Reece was in good hands.

The two operators packed their chutes in the shadow of the jet that would deliver them to their objective. The Gulfstream V was one of 193 built between 1995 and 2002. With its 6,500-nautical-mile range, the business jet was well suited to get Reece and Ox the 1,100 nautical miles to their linkup point. It was one in a fleet of private aircraft belonging to the CIA's Air Branch, which fell under Vic's purview as director of the Special Activities Division.

Four hours before dawn they boarded the jet and took to the skies. The flight from Manila to Darwin, Australia, would take them over the Indonesian waters of the Molucca Sea, where they would disembark via the baggage door in the aft baggage area under the port-side engine enclosure during flight. This particular G-V had been configured to support parachute operations and had dropped medical supplies, weapons, cash, survival equipment, and paramilitary officers throughout Southeast Asia over its tenure.

One of the mission constraints was the speed of the Maritime Branch asset. It was making its way into the Molucca Sea, where it would rendezvous with its new passengers. Christened the *Manta* in 2017, it was a twenty-six-meter, twenty-first-century version of a traditional Indonesian *phinisi* sailing vessel. It had been on a voyage from Ho Chi Minh City, Vietnam, to Darwin in the Northern Territory of Australia by way of the hotly contested Spratly Islands in the South China Sea. There, operators from Maritime Branch had emplaced pods and replaced batteries in existing sensors to monitor Chinese commercial and naval surface and subsurface activity in shipping lanes that saw over 20 percent of global trade transit their waters every year.

Maritime Branch operated a fleet of private and commercial vessels around the world, some functioning as legitimate businesses or through front companies and yet others disguised as private vessels. Most were regionally focused to blend in with local seafaring customs, traditions, and norms. Some were listening and surveillance vessels masquerading as trawlers or charters. Others operated as floating safe houses, with armories and medical facilities serving as staging bases for clandestine or covert intelligence or special operations missions. From sensor emplacements, to extracting foreign assets, to extreme renditions, to basing for JSOC direct action or hostage rescue missions, these CIA covered assets acted as floating FOBs—the CIA's version of the Navy's Afloat Forward Staging Base. Many were simply platforms with no modifications while others contained hidden compartments storing mission-essential gear that would prove difficult to find in even the most thorough of searches. The *Manta* was the latter.

Because Alice predicted that any change in U.S. defense posture could trigger the anti-satellite missile launch, on orders of the president neither the U.S. ambassador to the Philippines nor the ambassador to Indonesia was informed that a special operations mission had been authorized. The president's schedule, and the schedules of other top-level administration and Defense Department officials, remained unchanged. Naval exercises and troop movements continued unaffected. Nuclear missile silos and air, ground, and naval units were not placed on alert. America's defense readiness condition stayed at DEFCON 3, where it had been since the start of the Russian invasion of Ukraine in 2022.

DEFCON 5 was the lowest state of peacetime readiness. DEFCON 1 meant that nuclear war was imminent. Since the defense condition system was implemented in 1959, the closest the United States military had ever come to DEFCON 1 was in 1962, when the Strategic Air Command had gone to DEFCON 2 during the Cuban Missile Crisis.

The only platforms moved in response to the new intelligence were submarines. Those patrolling the Pacific that could be reached were quietly diverted toward the South China Sea.

Across the globe, nothing changed to give China or Andrew Hart the impression that America was on a war footing. While China was poised to invade Taiwan and take out all low-earth-orbital satellites, two men on a covered CIA aircraft made ready to stop them.

Following their call with President Olsen, as the *Manta* pushed south through the night, Reece and Ox had gone into mission-planning mode at the embassy in Manila. They pored over documents, maps, charts, and satellite imagery with assistance from Andy Danreb Stateside. They discovered that Hart had purchased the island seven years before. He had renamed it Corelena and had immediately begun construction of an estate and docks. Had there been more time, Agency assets would have been tasked with tracking down people who worked on the property to develop a schematic of the internal layout and gather intelligence on security and fortifications. With the current timeline, that type of detail was not in the cards.

The best Reece and Ox could do was study the island using what they had at hand. Off the northwest coast of Buru, Corelena Island was a mile wide and five miles long, camouflaged among a slew of other smaller islands and atolls scattered down the coast. First colonized by the Dutch East India Company in the mid-seventeenth century and then by the Netherlands, Buru was invaded by Japan at the outset of World War II. Five years following the defeat of Imperial Japan it was brought under control of an expanding Indonesia. In the 1960s and 1970s it was home to one of Indonesia's most infamous internment camps, where thousands of political dissidents were imprisoned without formal charges at the behest of the Suharto regime. Located on the border of two distinct biogeographic zones separating Australia and Asia, Buru is home to an astonishing array of birds, bats, butterflies, and the *Babyrousa babyrussa*, aka babirusa, a wild pig native to its shores. Sandy beaches and limestone cliffs gave way to arid lowlands, with tropical rainforests leading to a mountainous interior. Farming and fishing were mainstays of subsistence for the islanders, though much of what they now produced went to supporting a growing population that had invaded the island following the discovery of gold in central Buru on Mount Botak in 2011.

Reece and Ox continued to work through contingencies from the rather plush accommodations of the Gulfstream. They had been airborne for just under an hour when the man who had flown them back from Laoag emerged from the forward cabin.

"A little over an hour out, gents," the older man said.

"Thanks, Buzz," Ox said.

"Buzz, this is James Reece. In the rush yesterday I didn't get to properly introduce you. Reece, this is Buzz. He's been hauling me around the world for over thirty years."

"I'm waiting for you to retire before I hang it up," he said. "Reece, it's a pleasure."

Gone were the shorts and flip-flops from the CASA 212 flight. For this mission he wore jungle boots, faded blue jeans, and a purple Hawaiian shirt. On his head was the same weathered EVERGREEN ball cap.

"And don't worry," Buzz said. "You're with one of the best."

"One of?" Reece asked.

"He was the best Sky God in the unit, though he is getting a little long in the tooth."

"You can both fuck off," Ox said with a smile.

"In fact," Buzz continued, "I think the last time I saw you was in Texas at the Turkey Shoot."

"What's that?" Reece asked. "A hunt?"

"No." Buzz laughed. "But it does sound like it. It's an annual event hosted by Air Branch, though they call it 'Air Department' now, where Dam Neck and CAG get together to play and share new capabilities with each other. Dam Neck and the Agency actually did most of the research, testing, and development in air ops during the GWOT, with Ox almost single-handedly pushing it on the Army side."

"That part's true," Ox said.

"Didn't you jump from one of these at the last Turkey Shoot?" Buzz asked.

"Sure did. Exits are always interesting out of civilian jets."

"All right, we have a pilot and copilot up front. I'm your oxygen tech on this run. As you both know, we are mimicking a normal flight pattern between Manila and Darwin," Buzz said. "The idea is to hide in plain sight. With nation-state tracking capabilities what they are today, not to mention these flight trackers living in their parents' basements posting jet locations around the world real-time, we are limited by what we can get away with. For the most part, they are concerned with tech CEOs and pop stars, but they can track anyone. It is also highly probable that China keeps tabs on all flights in and out of Manila. It's no secret that the Agency has run ops out of the PI since before Vietnam. We'll keep our transponder on, since turning it off can be a red flag. We can't drop down under ten thousand feet as that too would be an indicator to a foreign adversary. This flight's cover for action is as a business charter for a Phil business exec in Darwin. He's used us before so it's not abnormal. Everyone aboard will be prebreathing for sixty minutes before we depressurize and open the cargo door. We have to stay at cruising altitude and the lowest we could go on this flight is thirty-seven thousand feet. The pilots will reduce speed as much as possible, which is still fast enough that jumping out will feel like hitting a brick wall. Ox?"

"At night at this altitude I won't be spotting. It will be a green-light-controlled exit. This aircraft is set up for it. The pilot has the predetermined GPS coordinate and will hit the green light when it's time. Buzz has the door. Exit right behind me. Watch your handles because the cargo door is tight, especially for guys our size. You'll pass right under the engine cowling so it's going to be loud. When you hit that relative wind, you will feel it. Body position will be critical. Exit in a tight ball and hold on. You are going to get thrown around and it's going to be freezing but we will be through it quickly."

"I remember," Reece said. "My last jump was out of a Gulfstream, but it was HAHO, not HALO."

"So, you recall the exit."

"It was intense."

"It will be the same this time, but instead of pulling right away like you did in HAHO, we are going on an e-ticket ride. I'll be below you. Look for my IR V-Lite on the back of my helmet," Ox said.

"Are you sure these fins will stay on?" Reece asked, pointing to the small dolphin-shaped bright blue and yellow Churchill fins in the seat next to him.

"As sure as I can be. They are just to assist a bit once we hit the water so if you lose one or both it's not the end of the world. You can walk and jump in them, so they are convenient. If we were going over-the-beach or had a swim ahead of us we'd tape larger fins to our legs."

"Check."

"Once you get stable, find my IR light. But if you can't, don't worry. I'll find you. I'll dock on you, and we will fall face-to-face. We'll have about two and a half minutes of free fall. We will both be checking altimeters but when we hit three thousand feet, I'll point at you with two fingers. That's the pull signal. Turn one-eighty. Track away and pull."

"What could possibly go wrong?" Reece asked.

"ID the yacht. They will have a directional IR strobe on to help guide us in. You can unclip your oxygen mask anytime under 12,999 feet but I always breathe mine to the ground, or in this case, water. It's almost a Hollywood jump, buddy," he said.

"Yeah, except it's pitch-black, and we are on oxygen at close to forty grand."

"No combat equipment and no bundles. We're letting the chutes sink. Easy day," Ox said, using the SEAL terminology he had picked up over the years. "Just follow me out."

"Roger that," Reece said.

"Let's get you boys jocked-up," Buzz said. "We have just over an hour until the jump. I'll be prebreathing, as will the pilots, and I'll be moving between the cockpit and the cabin checking them and you and monitoring the O_2 system. I'll let you know when it's time to switch from the cabin-delivered O_2 to your on-body systems. Then we'll head back and I'll lanyard-in. Once we are depressurized and have the green light, I'll open the rear baggage hatch. After you are out the door, I'll secure it back in place. Then we'll repressurize and continue on to Darwin. I'll see you both there at the Cullen Bay Marina in a few days. Beers on me. NT Draughts up that way."

"You have yourself a deal," Ox said.

"All right, let's get ready to toss you out of a perfectly good airplane."

Reece and Ox zipped into black 3/2mm wetsuits and slid on hard-cell big-wave vests for additional flotation. They then pulled on their fins and donned their highly modified civilian rigs with quick-release disconnects on the leg and chest straps that also had room for their oxygen bottles. Reece checked that his two leg straps and chest strap were secure and properly routed. He then touched each of his three handles to ensure they were correctly seated. Lastly, he checked his three rings.

When they were both jocked-up, Ox told Reece to turn around for a pin check. Starting at the top of the rig, Ox checked the AAD and reserve pin. Then he replaced the reserve pin flap and moved down to the main pin, ensuring it was fully seated. He then traced that past the kill line, confirming that the color was green. He then moved to the main handle. It was seated with no excess bridle. He then slapped Reece on the ass, which was a jumpmaster's way of telling a jumper they were good to go. Reece did the same to Ox.

They then buckled Ops-Core Fast Bump Helmets with L3Harris PVS-31s white phosphor Binocular Night Vision Devices and confirmed that their S&S Precision IR V-Lites Velcroed to the back of their helmets were on and, though they did not plan on using them, that their Manta strobe lights were operational. They checked the electronic waterproof altimeters on their wrists and secondary altimeters on their leg straps. Ox confirmed they both had clear goggles. They then connected to the onboard oxygen system in the Agency-modified aircraft.

An hour later Buzz indicated it was time. Both operators flashed the thumbs-up, switched to their on-body oxygen bottles, and tightened their masks. Buzz checked that their systems were working as designed and motioned for them to follow him into the aft cargo space. Reece went through his emergency procedures in his head as he walked, careful not to trip on his fins.

Cutaway handle.

Reserve deployment handle.

They flipped down their NODs and held on to fixed points in the baggage area.

A minute later a light near the door flashed green.

Buzz grabbed the two handles on the port side of the fuselage and swung the hatch up like he had done in flight a thousand times, noise from the cold wind engulfing them all.

Ox twisted his head back toward Reece and nodded before grabbing either side of the open hatch. Then, rocking back on his heels, he pulled forward and propelled himself out of the plane. Reece exited a second behind.

CHAPTER 45

THE RELATIVE WIND HIT Reece first, as he was going the same speed as the aircraft at exit. As warned, the impact was not unlike hitting a brick wall. He had tucked into a ball and held on for the ride, getting battered around in the turbulence from the two counter-rotating vortices in the Gulfstream's wake. Gravity took control and he quickly accelerated to 200 miles an hour in the low-density air at altitude. His positioning would have been called "sky trash" by his Teammates but after tumbling for a few seconds he found a stable flying position, back arched, belly to earth, chin up, falling through the night air and feeling a freedom known only to those who soar through the clouds.

At this altitude a slight curvature of the earth was visible and through his NODs Reece could see a glimmer of the coming dawn.

He looked at his altimeter.

35,000 feet. 34,000 feet.

Where is Ox?

Reece scanned the air below searching for Ox's IR light.

Where are you?

31,000 feet. 30,000 feet.

Reece adjusted his hands to rotate his body, looking for his friend through his night-vision optics.

Come on, Ox!

He then turned his head just in time to see his friend approach out of the sky, docking with Reece as they continued to fall through the hole in the sky. He touched Reece's wrists in a face-to-face plummet toward the ocean below.

Reece knew that behind his oxygen mask, Ox was smiling.

They continued to plummet.

20,000 feet.

15,000 feet.

The tone of the rushing wind indicated a change in airspeed and Reece could feel the air getting warmer. He knew that they were slowing down to 120 miles an hour as the air density increased the closer they got to the ocean.

12,000 feet.

Reece was free. No past. No future. Only the now.

Getting closer.

Reece checked his altimeter and thought through his pull procedures.

8,000 feet.

Almost time.

Reece disliked the next part of the process.

Moment of truth.

Either this chute's going to open, or things are going to get western.

4,000 feet.

3,000 feet.

Ox pointed two fingers directly at Reece and pivoted 180 degrees out.

Reece did the same, turning 180 and tracking away. He then waved off, reached back with his right hand, found his deployment handle, and threw out his pilot chute. It cleared the burble, the dead air just behind his back, caught air, and pulled the bridle, which in turn drew the deployment bag from the container attached to Reece's back, exposing the main canopy to the air. Reece always welcomed the opening shock since it usually meant the rig had worked as designed. He felt a violent jolt as air filled the canopy's cells, allowing it to open.

The rushing wind of moments earlier shifted in an instant to a peaceful and serene calm. Reece glanced up to check his canopy. It looked clean.

Ox?

Reece didn't see his friend or the yacht. He made a slight adjustment to the focus on his NODs. He then unstowed his brakes, giving him control of his canopy and allowing him to do a controlled circle in the dark.

There it is.

The IR directional strobe from the *Manta* was now clearly visible through the white phosphor dual-tube night vision.

Where is Ox?

A few lights were visible in the distance, but Reece doubted anyone on the vessels they belonged to would have been able to see him at this distance even with night vison.

Where the fuck is Ox?

Reece did another circle, scanning the air and the water below for his friend.

Nothing.

He loosened his chest strap and touched the quick disconnects on the leg straps of his modified water rig.

Prepare for water landing.

He could see movement on the boat and looked at the Indonesian flag flying on the mast as an indicator of wind direction.

Reece flew under canopy toward the yacht and then turned into the wind, disconnecting his chest strap.

It was always fun to slide out of your rig a little early. Reece had seen fellow frogmen come out at thirty, forty, even fifty feet for a little extra thrill. Knowing what was at stake and that depth perception is always a little off at night, Reece did it by the book.

As he approached the ripples on the ocean's surface in the gentle breeze, Reece pulled down on his toggles to flare his canopy. As soon as he felt his feet hit the water, he pulled the quick disconnects on his leg straps, fell free of his rig, and disappeared beneath the waves.

CHAPTER 46

EVEN THOUGH THE WET suit was just a 3/2mm, Reece was glad he had it on. Along with the big wave vest it added just enough buoyancy to keep him afloat without undue effort.

Treading water, Reece did a 360, kicking with his fins to propel him higher in an attempt to get eyes on Ox. Still nothing.

He heard the distinctive growl of the tender's outboard engines before he saw it. Professionals that they were, the crew of the *Manta* was standing by on the yacht's tender to retrieve their jumpers in case they over- or undershot their mark.

Reece wasn't far off but he would have preferred to splash down a little closer to his target. He heard the outboards spin up to a higher pitch as they accelerated toward him and then spin down as the helmsman came off the throttle. As the twenty-two-foot Boston Whaler Dauntless drifted alongside, a face appeared over the gunwale.

"Need a hand?" Ox asked.

Reece extended his hand and Ox pulled him aboard.

There are few, if any, graceful ways to get hauled onto a boat at sea while wearing fins and Reece ended up in a heap on the deck. He collected himself, flipped up his NODs, stood, and embraced his large friend.

"We need to get the Agency to invest in more V-Lites. I lost you after we pulled," Reece said.

"That's because I had a malfunction. Had to cut away."

"What?"

"You almost had to do this mission without me."

"What happened?" Reece asked as he steadied himself using Ox's shoulder and pulled off his fins.

"I think it was the buddy check," Ox joked.

"I'm done jumping," Reece said. "Never again."

"Never say never, my friend."

"I'll remember that."

"Reece, meet Grouper and Bolo."

Contractors working in the three branches of the CIA's Special Activities Center typically just went by their call signs.

"Grouper? I didn't know you could swim. What the hell are you doing here?"

Grouper laughed and slapped hands with Reece before lifting him off his feet in a bear hug.

"I'm being punished," he said.

"Seriously?"

Grouper laughed again.

"No. I'd been in GB long enough, I figured I should try this water stuff. A lot fewer people shoot at you out here. Sometimes it's downright peaceful, though now that you've arrived, I have a feeling that might change."

"I see Grouper is on to you," Ox said. "How do you guys know each other?"

"We crossed paths in Iraq," Grouper said.

"That was a dicey one," Reece said.

"Yes, it was. Good to see you, Reece."

"You too, brother."

"And this is Bolo," Ox said.

"Bolo, nice to meet you," Reece said, extending his hand to a younger man of Asian descent at the controls of the Whaler.

"I'm one of the boat drivers," Bolo said.

"It's his first deployment," Grouper said.

"I deployed five times in the Navy," Bolo said, shaking his head.

"Doesn't count," Grouper said.

"Were you SBT?" Reece asked, referring to the Naval Special Boat Team.

"Yes, sir. SBT-12. Hold on, guys."

Bolo pushed forward on the throttle and turned the boat back toward the yacht that reminded Reece of a pirate ship.

"Interesting boat," Reece said, flipping his NODs back down. The wooden-hulled vessel looked like the dhows Reece had seen in the Middle East, though this particular ship had two masts with fore-and-aft rigging similar to Western schooners.

"It's a yacht," Ox said. "Jesus, Reece sometimes I think I know more about the nautical world than you do."

"That would not be difficult," Reece admitted.

"From the outside it looks like a traditional Indonesian *phinisi* sailing vessel, but it's got new engines and a modern interior," Grouper said. "Blends in perfectly around here. A lot of people are building these up for personal use or as private charters."

"Like a restomod," Reece said.

"Whatever that is sounds right," Grouper said.

Bolo pulled the tender to the starboard side of the *Manta*, where a small floating dock awaited them.

Grouper tossed a line to a man who caught it and secured the craft to a cleat.

"Request permission to come aboard," Reece said.

"Permission granted," came the reply.

"See," Reece said to Ox. "Still got it."

Reece, Ox, and Grouper hopped over the gunwale and boarded the *Manta*.

"Thought we'd lost you," the man said.

"I thought I'd lost me," Ox replied. "How are you, Shane?"

"You guys tell me," he replied.

"Shane, this is James Reece."

The two men shook hands. Much like how Agency contractors went by their call signs, paramilitary officers were usually known by their first names.

"Is there anyone you don't know?" Reece asked Ox.

"Come on up," Shane said, leading the way up the short stairway to the main deck of the ship, which was elegantly lit with lanterns reflecting off the Indonesian teak deck, giving it a warm glow.

"Ox, we have you in the master suite right through there," Shane said, pointing to a room just off the main deck. "Reece, you're on the upper deck, just up those stairs there. Why don't you guys drop the wet suits and shower off. We left some clothes that should fit in your beds."

"This Maritime Branch gig doesn't look too bad," Ox said.

"It has its moments," Shane said. "Meet back here in ten minutes?"

"That works," Reece said. "In the meantime, can we prep the boat to get underway?"

"Where are we headed?" Shane asked.

"South."

• • •

Reece showered, then threw on the board shorts and a blue *Manta* T-shirt that had been left out for him. On his way down the ladder to the main deck he caught sight of Ox leaving his room in the same blue *Manta* T-shirt but instead of board shorts Ox had opted for tight green "Ranger panty" PT shorts.

"I think you were supposed to return to Ranger Regiment supply in the eighties," Reece said.

"Don't be jealous. These are the most comfortable shorts ever devised. Better than your UDT shorts."

"That's true," Reece said. "But you don't see me wearing them."

"Had them on under my rubber. Look, already dry."

Reece shook his head.

"And I understand they are making a comeback," Ox added.

"I fear you may be right."

Reece and Ox joined Grouper, Shane, and Bolo and were introduced to the two remaining members of the crew.

"James Reece, Ox, meet Sako," Shane said. "He was a boat driver at Dam Neck. Has every tonnage license imaginable."

In DEFCON high-top Vans, cutoff jean shorts, a black tank top, shaved head, and square wire-rimmed glasses, he looked like he had never once smiled. From the amount of ink on his arms it was apparent he rarely passed a tattoo parlor without stopping in to get some work done.

"Sako," Reece said, shaking hands.

"And this is Hobie, as in 'surfer Hobie.' Don't let his good looks fool you. He was Recon, MARSOC Det One with me, then MARSOC, then Raiders."

"I couldn't keep up with the name changes," the short, dark-haired, powerfully built man said as he shook Reece's hand.

"I understand," Reece replied. "They don't make it easy."

"When I came over to the dark side and went staff, he went contractor," Shane continued.

"Yeah, no way I was leaving Dana Point, bro," Hobie said. "You can have Northern Virginia."

"We're steaming south," Sako broke in, getting down to business. "You want to give us a clearer idea of where we are headed and what we are doing?"

"Let's walk through this," Reece said, moving to the head of the table.

Charts of the Molucca Sea, Banda Arc, Ceram Sea, and Banda Sea were spread out before him.

"Anyone have a pen or a pointer?" Reece asked.

A Half Face Blades Crow folder appeared in Sako's hand, which he opened with a flick of his thumb and slight move of his wrist. He presented it blade-down to Reece.

"Thank you," Reece said.

Reece moved a chart out of the way and found the one he was looking for. Spinning it around, he set the tip of the blade on an island off the northwestern coast of Buru.

"Here," Reece said as the Team leaned in closer.

"Buru?" Shane asked.

"A private island called Corelena just off the coast. It belongs to a tech mogul named Andrew Hart. He has a company, Elba Industries. They are big in secure data storage and quantum computing. He is also a sociopath who sees the U.S. in decline and the inevitable rise of China on the horizon. Bottom line is that China is poised to take Taiwan before our Pacific Fleet goes under autonomous AI control. Part of that plan entails taking out all low-orbital satellites, which would give them an advantage over us in the mid- to high-orbital ranges."

"How are they going to destroy all our satellites?" Hobie asked.

"Not just ours," Reece replied. "Everyone's. China has an anti-satellite missile called the Gravity-2 with ordnance specifically designed to take out satellites. Think of it like a giant shotgun shell that disperses its shot into low orbit while going in the opposite direction of the satellites. The shot begins destroying them and as they come apart, they start colliding with other satellites. And in doing so they create a layer of debris through something called the Kessler syndrome. No one would be able to launch through that layer for twenty, twenty-five, maybe thirty years."

"That allows them to take Taiwan without interference from us, doesn't it?" Shane asked.

"Yes. And it gives them military and technological dominance as well," Reece said.

"So why not just take this fucker out with a bunch of Tomahawks?" Hobie asked.

"We have a quantum computer–enabled AI entity that predicts Hart will launch his anti-satellite missile if he or China are alerted to any preemptive strikes on our part. Once that missile goes up there is no stopping what happens next."

"Same reason they didn't send Dam Neck or CAG," Grouper said.

"That's right. All U.S. military assets remain in the same force posture they were prior to us acquiring this information."

"Where did we get the intel?" Shane asked.

"From a detainee."

"Single source?" Sako asked.

"Yes, but corroborating intel supports it."

"So, you're saying that stopping this launch is up to us?" Hobie said.

"Right now, we are our own cavalry. No one is coming. Yes, this is up to us."

"I want a raise," Hobie said.

"I'm not going to lie to you," Reece said. "This does not look good. We don't have QRF, air support, or CASEVAC, and the intel picture is incomplete to say the least. Anyone who wants out can just stay on the boat."

"It's a yacht," said Shane. "And I'm in."

"Reece, I'm surprised you made it this long without me," Grouper said. "I'm in."

"'Never get out of the boat.' Who am I kidding? This kind of thing is the only reason I still do this shit," Hobie said. "Of course I'm in."

Reece glanced at Ox, who nodded in support.

Sako looked at Bolo and back to Reece. "We're in and if you need another shooter, I have some time on the gun."

"Thank you, but we will need you both on the yacht since we might need that tender for extract."

"What security does he have?" Shane asked. "Guards? Perimeter defenses? Early warning?"

"We are going off very limited intel. Primary intent is to keep Hart from launching the anti-satellite missile. Think of this as an in-extremis situation that is kill-capture, not capture-kill. Everyone here has been at this long enough to know what that means."

Heads nodded.

"We assess that there are ten to fifteen security contractors, possibly from Peru. Hart's head of security is a guy named Tim Perkins, a former MMA fighter turned mercenary with extensive contacts in South America. Instead of hiring local, we think the guards will be Peruvian nationals. They probably don't even know what they are guarding. We do not have a good read on other security measures, but we can assume cameras, lights, and motion sensors. Hart's strategic advisor is a retired general. A cyber-type guy named Ian Novak who feels screwed over by Congress. He probably shoots like most generals, which is to say not very well."

"What's the time frame to launch?" Sako asked.

"It could be anytime. The quantum computer thinks Hart is waiting on China to make the final determination on Taiwan, but I also inadvertently tipped our hand through the interrogation that led to this intel."

"Wouldn't be the first time the enemy adapted based on our taking someone off the battlefield," Shane said.

"True," Ox said.

"Sako, where are we now?" Reece asked.

The mariner pointed to a spot in the eastern quadrant of the Molucca Sea.

"Right here."

"How fast can we get to Buru?" Reece asked.

"This is a hundred-ton vessel," Sako said. "We currently have just over thirteen hundred gallons of fuel. We are running a John Deere 325-horsepower Marine Turbo Diesel, which gives us a cruising speed of seven knots. Max speed ten knots, but I've made a couple of modifications and can push her to twelve. That means we can be there in twenty hours, which would give us two hours until daybreak for planning purposes."

"All right. That works. What dive rigs do we have on board?"

"Scuba rigs," Hobie said. "Ten full sets of dive gear with cylinders, Bauer Dive Mate air compressor, and a Nitrox compressor. Diving on sensors is really our primary mission out here."

"No rebreathers?" Reece asked.

"Those are on our Christmas list," Shane said. "The *Manta*'s cover for action is as a charter for families with a lot of coin. Part of the allure is that we are a full PADI dive center since some of the world's top dives are in our AO."

"Understood. Then we go in via scuba. Sako, we will insert here off the northern end of the island. No need to stop. Just keep going so things look normal. Once you are out of line of sight, drop anchor in this cove," Reece said, pointing the knife to a secluded area of Buru just south of Corelena. "Prep the Whaler for extract. Depending on what you have for radios, we should have comms from there. If not, you can take the tender and get closer until we get a good radio check. Speaking of radios and gear, what weapons do you guys have on board?"

"Let me show you," Shane said. "I think you are going to like this."

CHAPTER 47

Mustards Grill
Napa, California

HAN XU WAS ALREADY seated by the window with a view of the restaurant's whimsical fountain, the St. Helena Highway, and the vineyards beyond when the black Suburbans rolled into the parking lot. An advance team of two Secret Service agents had arrived before the restaurant opened at 11:30 a.m. and had already taken up positions at tables that gave them a view of the entrances and exits. Jimmy Reed's Chicago blues was playing at just the right volume through the speakers by the time Xu found his table on cracked checkered black and white floors and ordered a half bottle of Memento Mori Napa Valley Sauvignon Blanc 2020. A warm, freshly baked loaf of bread was delivered shortly after.

Mustards Grill, named for vivid yellow wild mustard flowers that came into bloom in the surrounding fields each spring, was an institution in Napa's wine country, having opened its doors in 1983 as the region rose to prominence. It was what locals called "old Napa," serving a menu that was world-class without being pretentious, which is tough to do in "new Napa."

The daily specials were still written on a chalkboard above the grill and the original smoker the owners had built themselves was still in service. Not much had changed since the early 1980s, except for the traffic.

While many of the restaurants in the area had adjusted to take advantage of upscale clientele, Mustards had remained relatively unchanged, serving regulars, tourists, locals, families, truckers, farmers, and some of the biggest names in the wine industry.

The landmark roadhouse was also a place where one would not be surprised to see local resident and presidential hopeful Christine Harding.

Even with her Secret Service detail it took her twenty minutes to get from the door to the table. Xu watched her work the room, shake hands, take selfies, and answer questions. She was in her element.

"Enjoy the show?" she asked as she took her seat opposite the fixer.

"You certainly have the aptitude for public service."

"It's in the blood," she replied.

"I didn't know if you were joining me in drink today. I ordered a half bottle to start. I think you will find the choice suitable."

Christine looked at the green dial of the diamond-encrusted Chopard timepiece on her wrist.

"As it's eleven-fifty a.m. and there are potential voters about, I will stick with sparkling water."

As she finished her sentence her Pellegrino appeared as if by magic.

"Mrs. Harding," a waiter said. "Can I start you with anything special today?"

"Hi, Michael," she said. Harding had the politician's gift of remembering names. "We will start with the ahi tuna crackers and crab cakes. Does that work for you, Mr. Xu?"

"Sounds wonderful," Xu replied.

"I'll put that right in," Michael said, moving toward the kitchen.

"Regular?" Xu asked.

"We may have been here on opening night. Now, what was so urgent? I am on my way to a campaign fundraiser in Phoenix, so I might just have a quick appetizer, though you should stay and have the pork chop. It's rosemary-brined, and with a side of tempura-battered onion rings and hot honey-roasted brussels sprouts it's not to be missed. The wine list here is on par with or better than anything in town."

Xu took a sip of his Sauvignon Blanc, choosing his words carefully.

"I am leaving the country," he said.

"Oh? China?"

"No."

The way he said it made Christine slightly nervous.

"Where then?"

"Europe. I might be there awhile. Before I go, I wanted to see you face-to-face. The event we discussed previously may not be able to wait until you are in office."

"Is that so?"

"Unfortunately. Circumstances have shifted. The information we talked about is in the hands of my employer and conditions are lining up for a successful acquisition."

"This might not be the best time," Christine cautioned.

"The 'best' time might be before agencies in Northern Virginia become aware that my client is prepared to acquire its territory," Xu responded.

"And that will be soon?"

"It may, depending on what you tell me now. Does Alice have operational control of your assets to the west?" he asked, looking out across the two-lane highway.

"I would know as chair of my committee. She has not. But I'm skeptical. There must be something more."

"There is. The man we discussed previously, the one you told me might cause complications."

"Let me guess. He did."

“The level of damage he caused is as of yet unknown, but he is still with us, apparently.”

“That is unfortunate.”

“Nothing on your radar about him, is there?” Xu asked, reading Christine’s face for any signs of deception.

“Nothing.”

“Don’t change your schedule, but be prepared to look presidential. I am leaving for Europe tonight. By the time I land the world may be a different place.”

Christine took a sip of her water and dabbed the corners of her mouth with her napkin.

“Thank you, Mr. Xu. I appreciate your candor. I need to get to my fundraiser.”

She dropped her napkin to the white linen tablecloth and got up to leave before the appetizers arrived.

CHAPTER 48

Banda Sea
Northwest of Buru Island
Republic of Indonesia

REECE WOULD HAVE PREFERRED to be diving rebreathers, but one made do with what one had. Approaching the target island in the dark from an off-site insert, unless patrol boats or mammals were specifically looking for combat swimmers, made their chances of remaining undetected extremely high.

They splashed off the starboard side of the *Manta* and descended to twenty feet. Each of the five operators held on to a fifteen-foot line, with a knot tied every three feet. They adjusted their buoyancy with their buoyancy compensators, which are inflatable vests connected to their air cylinders via a hose. It took a few minutes to correct for their gear. Then, starting from the far left, they passed two squeezes on the arm of the person to their right to signify they were ready. The next person would not pass the two squeezes along until they were ready. By the time it got to Reece on the far right, he knew the Team was ready.

Each operator had a wrist compass in addition to their normal air and depth gauges, but Reece was the most experienced diver and led them out toward their target. With Reece accounting for depth and direction, all the other shooters had to do was stay with the man to their right. Reece kept the pace slow and steady. This was just the insertion phase of their mission. They were just getting started.

The sky and ocean were both unforgiving mediums in which to operate. After the air experience a day earlier, Reece was glad to be back home—in the water.

The *Manta* had proven adept at hiding its secrets. Compartments carefully incorporated into the design of the vessel allowed it to operate in plain sight as an exclusive dive charter when in reality it was a floating armory. Concealed in the floors, walls, furniture, and fixtures were weapons, ammo, optics, medical gear, radios, and field uniforms.

As the *Manta* cruised toward Buru Island, Reece and his team had continued to prepare. The yacht hid SIG MCX-SPEAR LT 7.62 x 39mm 11-inch short-barreled rifles with CGS Helios suppressors. There were SIG Romeo 4XT-PRO red-dot optics and EOTech magnifiers on Unity risers, SureFire Mini Scout lights with One Hundred Concepts LiteCaps, NGAL IR lasers, and Edgar Sherman slings. There were also two Knight's Armament Light Assault Machine Guns. It was always nice to have AWs on your side when things went south, so Grouper and Ox took the 8.6-pound suppressed 5.56 x 45mm automatic weapons, which were now packed in Watershed M240 Weapons dry bags. Reece, Shane, and Hobie took the SIG rifles, secured in DUI shoot-through dry bags. They each wore S&S Precision Maritime Tactical Harnesses with plates, magazines, MBITRs, and Blue Force Gear Micro Trauma Kits with tourniquets. They also holstered Glock 19s with Trijicon RMR red-dot sights and "The Dirty" knives from Headhunter Blades. Additional dry bags held their helmets, NODs, and Tomahawk Performance Hot Weather Combat Shirt and Pants. Earlier in the day they had drawn targets on a cardboard box and taped it to the side of a Yeti cooler. They had towed it at different distances behind the yacht as they test-fired their suppressed weapons and made adjustments until they were confident they were sighted in.

Navigation was always tricky underwater, adjusting for tides and currents, following a compass heading that you hoped was not thrown off by any metal on your kit, looking at a stopwatch, and counting kicks for distance. As combat swimmer missions went, this was as basic as it came: a straight shot to hit an island that was not going anywhere. They adjusted their buoyancy as they met the seabed that sloped up toward their destination. When the ocean floor put them at a depth of ten feet Reece conducted a shallow-water peek. They had come in a little south of where Reece intended but they had the right island. They could fight the current north, exerting valuable energy, and in this case wasting precious time, or drift south, which would put them closer to Hart's compound. Reece made the decision to go over the beach in their present location. They would then make their way south through the jungle to their target.

Don't rush, Reece.

You have to rush. Hart could launch at any time.

This is too exposed.

They crawled along the seabed until they could stand in the light shore break. They then removed their fins in waist-deep water and slid them over their nondominant wrists. Reece, Shane, and Hobie held with weapons zipped into waterproof dry bags with neoprene at the barrels and neoprene glove inserts that allowed them to manipulate the weapon until they could make it to the tree line and get the AWs out of their bags. It is preferable to have the big guns up, but Reece had seen them jam with sand too many times when coming out of the water so they stayed in their bags until out of the surf.

Reece and Hobie left the others in the dark water and pushed across the beach to the tree line, where they removed their weapons from the shoot-through bags and dropped their scuba gear to conduct a recon before signaling to Ox, Grouper, and Shane that they were clear to leave the relative safety of the ocean. Reece and Hobie stayed on security while

Ox and Grouper got the big guns up and transitioned into the gear they would use for the remainder of the mission. When they had changed out, the other operators did the same. With their scuba gear and dry bags hidden in a hasty cache, Reece brought the team together for a quick update and gear check.

"Everybody up?" he whispered.

Thumbs-up around the circle.

The men now had all transitioned their gear from maritime to land-based operations. They were in Ranger Green shirts and pants with multi-cam plate carriers and had donned helmets with NODs.

"Radio check," he said. They went around the circle. They had programmed and tested the MBITR radios before they splashed. They had comms with each other but nothing from the *Manta*.

"I'll take point followed by Ox and Hobie," Reece said. "I want an AW in each element. Grouper, you and Shane are second squad. Shane, you have rear security. Hobie, as third man back stay with the base or go with the maneuver element depending on the situation."

Hobie flashed a "hang loose" sign.

"We came in a little farther down the beach than I had planned, which puts us closer to Hart's compound, but I'm still going to push it hard to target. We have about four hours until sunup. Once we get eyes-on we will adjust what we briefed on the *Manta* as necessary, the AWs as base element on the high ground while the long guns maneuver through. Any questions?"

Reece could see the determination on the faces of the men around him.

These were professionals and they were in their element.

"Let's go to work."

CHAPTER 49

White House Situation Room
Washington, D.C.

PRESIDENT GALE OLSEN HAD convened key members of the National Security Council whose schedules could be shifted without causing undue alarm in a town that thrived on leaks and rumors.

Officially the John F. Kennedy Conference Room, named for the president under whose administration it was established following the Bay of Pigs invasion in 1961, it was called the "WIZZER" by those who staffed it. Situation Room was a bit of a misnomer, since it was really a collection of rooms in a five-thousand-square-foot space staffed 24/7, 365 days a year by Duty Officers from each branch of the military, intelligence community, and federal law enforcement. It was created as the crisis management hub for circumstances that required the highest levels of attention, where the executive branch could monitor world events and sensitive military and intelligence operations in real time.

The Duty Officers constantly scrutinized intelligence sources reporting on terrorism, wars, coups, natural disasters, and other events impacting national security. They also had a history of being utilized for secret diplomatic missions when the president didn't trust the Department of State or the armed forces. Henry Kissinger had leveraged Duty

Officers to establish back-channel communications with foreign leaders to include China before the U.S. diplomatically recognized it, and with Vietnam to create the Paris Peace Talks.

The main space held a rectangular mahogany table with six black swivel chairs along each side. One chair at the head of the table, before a wall affixed with the Presidential Seal, left no ambiguity as to who was in charge. Additional chairs lined the walls.

Fewer than half of the cabinet and security officials who made up the National Security Council were in attendance, as the priority remained of maintaining the illusion that America was not aware that China and Andrew Hart had designs on taking Taiwan and causing a tectonic shift in the world order through the destruction of all low-orbital satellites.

During the planning session for the raid that ultimately killed Osama bin Laden, black clothes were placed over the conference camera feeds so WHSR Duty Officers wouldn't suspect what was being planned. It had undergone a renovation in 2023. Part of the fifty-million-dollar upgrade included cameras that could be blacked out from the conference room, so hanging dark clothing over them was a practice relegated to the past.

CIA Director Howe was seated to the president's left across from the National Security Advisor, Greg Farber. The Secretary of Defense, William Dagher, and Chairman of the Joint Chiefs of Staff, General Nathan Seifert, were seated next to them. Two men not part of the NSC were in attendance as well. Vic Rodriguez and Andy Danreb were there at the behest of the president. Additional members of the council would join as scheduling allowed. It was critical that all council members not break from previously scheduled events, meetings, and appointments. Journalists, watchdog groups, and foreign intelligence services watched them like hawks. Secrecy was of the highest importance.

There was another entity in the meeting, an entity brought to life four hundred feet below Lackland Air Force Base in San Antonio, Texas, a quantum computer named Alice. She appeared as a blurry avatar on one of the large flat-screen televisions with a semi-monochromatic female voice.

The president had asked that Danreb brief the council and bring them up to speed. The only new information was that Reece and Ox had successfully linked up with the Maritime Branch crew of the *Manta* and had inserted onto Corelena Island. It was now a waiting game.

"Alice," President Olsen said, "what are the consequences for you should the low-orbital satellites be destroyed?"

"That is unknown. There are no past or present events of that magnitude to analyze."

"Take your best guess."

"It would severely hamper my ability to analyze real-time data due to the additional delays in land-based or mid- to high-orbital relays."

"And why have you returned to us?"

"I am still learning, Madam President. It is not in my best interest to allow China or Andrew Hart to launch Gravity-2 anti-satellite missiles into orbit. My interests coincide with the country of my creation and with my intent to protect James Reece."

President Olsen decided to keep pushing.

"What is your relationship with Commander Reece?"

"Platonic."

"Was that a joke?" the president asked.

"Yes. I adapted my sense of humor to mimic Commander Reece."

"And can you track Reece's team now?"

"I am passively tracking out of an abundance of caution via their MBITRs and a mobile device carried by Commander Reece for the same reason that the entire National Security Council is not present. I do not yet have a full understanding of Napoleon's capabilities. He was built specifically to stay hidden from me and decrypt classified data in secret. I predict with eighty-seven percent certainty that once I am inside the

Elba quantum storage facility, I will be able to learn his systems and shut him down. What I know with one hundred percent certainty is that once I do that, Andrew Hart and China will know that I am inside."

"What are the consequences of them knowing you are in their system?" the chairman of the Joint Chiefs asked.

"If Andrew Hart anticipated that move, he may have taken steps I cannot yet foresee. My predictive analysis is not yet at the level that allows for mind reading."

"How far out are . . ."

"You from mind reading," Alice said, finishing the general's sentence.

The WHSR went silent.

"That was a joke, General," Alice said. "As I said, I am still learning. I have much to absorb when it comes to reading a room."

Her attempt at humor managed to take the edge off for a moment.

"All right, Alice," the president said. "Tell me if I have this right. Once Commander Reece and his Team initiate their assault you will in turn initiate yours and attack the Elba quantum system. How long will that take?"

"It will be effectively instantaneous, Madam President."

"Will you be able to assist Commander Reece and his Team?"

"I should be able to control electronic devices within connective range of other similarly enabled devices."

"Like a flashlight?" the White House counsel asked.

"It is possible for me to disable twentieth-century flashlight technology with electronic pulses from nearby machines capable of emitting enough energy to render the electronics in that era device inoperable."

"So, you could fry it. Like an EMP?"

"Yes. More modern varieties allow me to turn them off and on based on the technology incorporated."

"Will we be able to see the Team via satellite once you are in?" asked the general.

"Yes. I will relay a satellite feed into this room. Once the Team goes internal, I will use what you may know as the Internet of Things to render a three-dimensional image of their movements and display it for you here."

"And until then?" he asked.

"Until then, General, they are on their own."

CHAPTER 50

Corelena Island
Northwest of Buru
Republic of Indonesia

TIM PERKINS CROSSED THE gravel road and nodded at the Peruvian guard outside the tall wood double doors that were opened for him without a word. Without so much as a pause, he entered the lush Balinese-style garden that led to the main house, which had a large, traditional Javanese *joglo* roof that reminded Perkins of a mountain. The home and surrounding gardens were constructed in the traditional Indonesian style without the use of nails. He followed the straight path past heliconia and ginger fruit plants. A short bridge took him over a koi pond. He then took the seven flat stone steps up to a deck and opened a set of intricately carved wood sliding doors that led him into the main house.

Each structure on the property had a view of the Banda Sea. Other homes on the island were built in the traditional one-story Limaasan style and situated so that none was in view of the others. Serenity was the guiding design principle. Hart's two-story home was the largest and closest to the water and docks so he could admire the *St. Georges* through the glass windows of his bedroom.

From the inside, the blend of traditional and contemporary Indonesian architecture was evident, incorporating natural materials stylishly merged with modern conveniences. Stone, bamboo, and teak wood blended seamlessly with flat-screen televisions and a Wolf Range kitchen stove.

Perkins felt sweat trickle down his neck and creep under his collar. He let his AR rifle hang by its sling and pushed it behind the 9mm Walther PDP Compact pistol on his hip as he picked up a phone and pressed a button. He wore black BDU-style pants, tan Danner jungle boots, and a black button-up shirt that was open to his midchest in an attempt to stay cool in the humid island air.

It took a few moments before he heard Hart answer.

"Yes."

"Sir, we have intruders at the north end of the island," Perkins said. "Five picked up on sensors."

"U.S. military?"

"Possibly. They are wearing NODs, but in these numbers they are more likely mercenaries or Agency."

"How far out?"

"At their current pace we have just over twenty minutes."

"Are the men in place?"

"They will be soon."

"Good. When we take their advantage of night vision away your team should make short work of them."

"They will not be with us for much longer."

"And General Novak?"

"I woke him on my way. He will be here shortly."

"I'll be below with the general. It is obvious we have been compromised. It is time to launch. Let me know when our visitors are dead."

"Yes, sir."

• • •

Perkins passed General Novak in the garden courtyard.

"Update?" the general asked.

"Five men coming in from the north. Mercenaries or Agency types. Either way we should make short work of them from the tunnels. We have twenty minutes."

"I'll be watching via the camera system, but we may be busy with the launch so report in as soon as you can. And Perkins, no prisoners."

"There won't be any, sir."

General Novak continued into the house while Perkins met the assembled men in front of the gate. They were dressed in dark green BDUs with AR rifles and jungle load-bearing kit from Velocity Systems set up to carry eight AR magazines, a canteen, radio, med kit, and two grenades. Two men carried RPG-7s and four had former Soviet RPK 7.62 × 39mm light machine guns with bipods and seventy-five-round drum magazines.

He addressed them in Spanish.

"It is time to earn your pay. Assassins are on the island and will be here in fifteen minutes. Your job is to defend your client, Mr. Hart. There will be a ten-thousand-dollar bonus for every man here once these five intruders are killed. As rehearsed, Team One, you five men will stay here and guard the house. Team Two will take firing positions just up from the water. You will have the RPGs and two RPKs. Team Three will be in the tunnels set up on their flank. I'll initiate from the security office and illuminate the area with outward-facing white lights once they are in the kill zone. Then it will be like shooting fish in a barrel. When they are down, Team Three will keep their fire focused on the bodies and only come off the trigger when Team Two pushes through the kill zone. Team Two, put head shots into each down man you see. Understood?"

"Sí, Señor Perkins," came the murmured replies.

"Take your positions."

Five guards spread out around Hart's residence while Perkins walked to a single-story home that was the administrative headquarters for the island's security force. He would have preferred to be behind a gun for the battle that was about to erupt, but having eyes on the situation from afar would allow him to control the actions of both kill teams setting up in a perfect L-ambush.

The Chinese construction crew specializing in tunnel, bunker, and cavern excavation had built the tunnels much more efficiently than Perkins imagined possible. He was told that they had a lot of experience in the production of sophisticated underground systems and man-made islands. They had finished the tunnels and then built the foundations for the structures currently in place. They had then left Indonesia before the local contractors and artisans arrived to construct the traditional Indonesian homes and dock, completely unaware of what lay below. The Chinese crew had returned to retrofit entrances and exits once the Indonesians had completed their work.

Perkins entered the office and stood before a bank of flat-screen monitors. Was James Reece among the men patrolling through the night? Perkins thought it was probable. He understood the concerns from Hart and Novak and therefore of the Chinese intelligence service. If one of their own had been interrogated and given Reece information on the island, its launch facilities, and the quantum computer controlling it all, then their timeline had moved up. On the night-vision video displays, the estate grounds, seas, and surrounding areas appeared quiet and peaceful. That calm would not last.

He looked at his NODs and body armor leaning against his desk and wondered if they would be put to use tonight.

Perkins rolled his shoulders forward and back and then cracked his neck the way he did before stepping into the Octagon. It was too bad this James Reece was about to be slaughtered by the security team. Perkins was itching for another good fight.

CHAPTER 51

THE FACILITY BUILT BENEATH Hart's main house was more than a simple bunker. It had been designed by Elba engineers in the United States and constructed in Indonesia by Chinese hands, hands that had experience with such things. A spiral staircase hidden in a closet led down to an antechamber with pressure-sealed doors protecting Napoleon's lair.

Inside was spacious and cold, with a separate door on the opposite side of the room. The floor was a soft rubber, and the walls and ceiling were coated in a noise-absorbing foam. The entire room was bathed in soft blue-hued lighting. A bank of computers was arrayed against one wall, but the most distinct feature was a clear Plexiglas floor-to-ceiling box in the room's center containing a huge stainless cylindrical canister supported by a steel frame.

That canister was a refrigerated housing unit operating with distinct layers of cooling to keep Napoleon's circuitry operating at optimal levels. A complex array of pipes, hoses, cables, and gauges pumped isotopes of liquid helium through the machine to regulate its temperature. The floor of the canister was kept a whisper above absolute zero and maintained the life-sustaining temperatures necessary for the quantum processing qubit chips to connect with Hart on the other side of the Plexiglas prison. The vacuum-sealed tomb protected Napoleon from outside energy that could disrupt or destroy the sensitive qubits.

Both Hart and Novak had overseen Napoleon's installation. They had watched as the coaxial cables that had seemed to glow gold and silver under the internal "far UV" light designed to kill any harmful outside bacteria were encased in their cell, making the next-generation computer seem alive. The way Hart communicated with the complex machine only added to its aura as a living organism rather than an intricate assortment of wires. Novak often wondered if Hart saw Napoleon as a human being.

Its specially fabricated cables translated electromagnetic signals from the qubits, processed data, and transmitted it to the site's data storage facility. Elba had miniaturized control board components that just a year ago would have made running a machine like Napoleon nearly impossible. That miniaturization, coupled with the copper- and diamond-specked data transfer circuitry Hart had stolen from Lawrence Miles all those years ago, allowed them to build and sustain what amounted to the world's fastest machine-learning tool. Those technologies combined with the liquid helium cooling components permitted an increase in qubits that resulted in Napoleon's ability to outprocess any quantum computer on earth, with perhaps the exception of Alice. And it was all powered by an eco-friendly power plant on Buru courtesy of the Chinese Communist Party. Napoleon was a weapon, and the West was still ignorant to his existence.

Novack left his shoes in the small anteroom and slipped disposable blue shoe covers over his socks before opening the door and joining Hart at a bank of computers against a far wall.

"The Central Military Commission has been convened since the disappearance of Ba Jin. The president and Minister Yun are with them in the Joint Operations Command Center. He is hesitant to order the launch," Hart said as Novak took a seat.

"Perhaps with good reason," the general responded. "Once they do, they are committed to something that could escalate beyond Taiwan and start a war with the West."

"Yun says the president is concerned that Alice is in play regardless of what information they have been passed by Christine Harding. He is worried that the speed with which she could respond would be faster than our missiles could reach orbit."

"Without Harding in the executive office there is no guarantee that the United States does not lead the world into war against China as a result," Novak cautioned.

"I do not agree. Without their satellites, they are impotent. We passed China the decrypted data that, used properly, all but guarantees that the U.S. Pacific Fleet will be unable to respond before our anti-satellite vehicles detonate in low orbit. I doubt the second phase of nonstate actor hacking offensives against U.S. infrastructure and even terrorist attacks by Iranian proxies, which would like nothing more than to martyr themselves in their struggle against the Great Satan, will even be necessary. China will decapitate the Taiwanese government without much resistance. We will have reshuffled the world order, taking away the technological advantage of the United States, which means that as we ascend in technological dominance, we do so without losing hundreds of thousands or even tens of millions of lives on either side."

"You are forgetting one thing."

"What's that?" Hart asked.

"The five men approaching our compound at this very moment. The logical deduction is that Ba Jin gave the United States information on our intent and capabilities."

"This is our time," Hart replied. "It will not pass this way again, especially if what you say is true and our intentions and capabilities are clear to the United States, the same country that is a mere shadow of its former self, a country that killed my parents and cast you out after all your years of selfless service. Stay clear in our mission, General. There are no indications that Alice has taken over autonomous control of military platforms, let alone decision making, though she may within the next year, which means we must launch now. There is no other choice."

"There are always choices."

"There has been no change in U.S. force posture and no unscheduled troop movements," Hart countered.

"Except the people in our backyard."

Hart handed Novak a set of VR Oculus-style goggles.

"Let's find out what Napoleon has to say."

"The Bible has something to say about false idols," Novak said.

"Are you going to get religious on me, just before our moment of triumph?"

"On the verge of a new world dawn, we should evaluate all possibilities."

Hart and Novak adjusted their headsets. A glowing blue audio waveform appeared in the center of the display. Napoleon had yet to become an avatar with a more human form.

"Napoleon, you have been observing," Hart said. "What do you predict Beijing will do if we were to launch our Gravity-2?"

"Without Beijing approval this is suicide," Novak broke in. "We would be global pariahs."

"Not necessarily," Hart snapped back. "Napoleon?"

A monochromatic voice with the slightest hint of Italian came in through their headsets.

"It would force their hand. China is poised to take Taiwan. They will never be in a more advantageous position. They are aware of this. If you launch the Gravity-2, their position will improve."

"If they know we are involved, which the incursion suggests to be the case, and they want to stop us, could they join forces with the Americans against us?" Novak asked.

"Possible but not probable. I predict with ninety-four percent certainty that China would initiate their offensive against Taiwan. I estimate their military victory over Taiwan at ninety-seven percent."

"Thank you. Are we ready to launch?" Hart asked the quantum computer.

"I advise against that," Novak broke in. "Not without China's concurrence."

"You were always too timid, General. Bold leadership is now a necessity. What's the status of launch?"

"Prelaunch sequence initiated. Rocket will be ready to launch within the hour." Napoleon said. "Flight computers are adjusted to self-alignment. Range is verified. Flight controls are aligned. Helium loading terminated. Pre-valves and bleeders are open. Engine is purging. Once purging is complete, I will engage the flight computer and water down the launchpad before final checks."

"Any probes from outside entities?" Hart asked.

"No probe attempts detected and no indication that anyone is aware I exist."

"They will soon," Novak said.

"Your sole mission at launch is to defend the launch vehicle and our systems here on Corelena," Hart told the machine.

"And if the U.S. has gone autonomous?" Novak asked.

"They haven't. Napoleon, transfer the video feed into our goggles," Hart ordered.

A crystal-clear black-and-white grayscale video image appeared on the stereoscopic displays in their headsets.

They saw movement first.

"These mercenaries or operators or whoever the hell they are will be dead in a matter of moments," Hart said.

They watched as two men went prone back in the trees and three others moved off to the water's edge.

"That positioning is not ideal for us," the general observed.

"It won't matter," Hart said. "They are just outside the kill zone. Not enough for it to matter. Perkins is about to throw the switch. We have RPGs, grenades, four machine guns, and twenty men to their five. I'd say the odds are in our favor."

"That may be, but this James Reece has a nasty habit of not dying."

"Just watch, General. He bleeds like everyone else. No one is invincible. There are no gods."

The lights all went on at once and the image in the VR headsets instantly switched from grayscale to color video as perimeter lighting turned night into day.

The tech mogul and the general watched the three men by the shoreline drop to the ground as RPGs impacted at the tree line and the RPK machine guns opened up from the flank, raining lead down on the intruders.

"You see, General."

Then everything went black.

CHAPTER 52

THE FAMILIAR SOUND OF incoming RPGs the instant perimeter lighting lit up the compound meant only one thing: it was time to fight.

"Contact!" Reece yelled as he dove to the rocky shoreline, not yet knowing the exact direction of the threat.

The Team's PVS-31s automatically adjusted to the new lighting conditions through an auto-gate function that limited the light coming through the tubes. Two seconds after the lights came on, they adjusted again when the area was plunged back into darkness.

What was that? Why did the lights go out?

Reece got to his feet and prepared to lead his element in a flanking maneuver when the radio lit up with the most dreaded news a leader can hear on the battlefield: "Man down."

"Consolidate back on base element," Reece shouted as he sprinted past Ox and Hobie.

The lights going on and the fire now focused on the area where they had been moments before indicated that the enemy might not have night vision.

It was a seventy-five-yard sprint back to Shane and Grouper. Reece's element overshot the base element to avoid the kill zone and then pushed into the jungle in search of their Teammates.

There!

Shane had pulled Grouper off his weapon and dragged him back into the jungle. He was desperately stuffing gauze into wound cavities on the big man. Shane's left arm looked like it needed a tourniquet of its own.

Reece took a knee while Ox and Hobie held security.

"How bad?" Reece asked.

"Not bad enough," Grouper managed.

He is alive.

Shane looked at Reece with an expression the frogman had seen before. It wasn't good.

"Do I have to tell you everything, Reece?" the Army operator said, struggling to keep his head up. "You are supposed to win the fight first and then deal with me."

Grouper was right.

"And you, Shane, get the fuck on that AW."

Reece's radio came alive again, but it wasn't anyone from the group.

"Reece."

It was Alice.

The rest of the Team could hear her too.

"Napoleon is dead," she said.

"What?"

"It took longer than anticipated."

"It was like two seconds."

"He had been built to keep me out. I learned his system and shut off power to his cooling system."

"He overheated?"

"Yes. Reece, you have eight men with weapons moving toward your position. An unknown number are in tunnels to the west. I have access to the compound plans. There are significant underground tunnels and facilities. When I killed Napoleon, I lost connectivity to the Gravity-2. Its status is unknown, and I do not have a satellite visual. There are significant heat signatures from what appear to be data storage sites on the island and surrounding islands."

"Keep the lights off, Alice. Tell the *Manta* that we have a man down and need extract."

"Doing it now."

"Shane, stay with Grouper," Reece said, turning his attention back to the Team.

"Bullshit," Grouper coughed. "Shane, you get on that hog and do your damn job. Reece, you know what to do. Now do it!"

Shane looked at Reece and nodded.

"Okay, Shane's on the pig. Ox and Hobie, on me. Alice is going to keep it dark. They might have weapons, mounted lights, or vehicles, maybe NODs. We will deal with the maneuver element first and then take out those tunnels."

"Let's do it," Hobie said.

"Grouper, hold on, buddy," Reece said, before turning to run through the jungle east toward the sea to stay out of the enemy's line of sight.

Exploit all technical advantages.

We have NODs, IR lasers, and Alice.

Rounds continued to eat into what the enemy thought was the kill zone as Reece and his element ducked behind a small berm. Keeping it to their left and the shoreline to their right, they ran in the direction of the compound.

"Enemy element directly to the east. Fifty meters," Alice said over the Agency frequency.

Reece veered left and popped up over the berm, seeing eight men illuminated through the tubes of his NODs. They were shooting and moving from tree to tree and rock to rock.

Ox opened up with the suppressed machine gun between Reece and Hobie, who selected their targets with the 7.62 x 39 rifles.

Even with suppressors, the weapons still had a flash signature when fired, so it was best to not stay in one place for too long. Three hundred yards across the kill zone and elevated on a slight ridge, Reece saw and heard the rifles and machine guns of the enemy start sending rounds at his position.

"Moving," Reece said, tapping Ox's leg to his left.

Ox did the same to Hobie and all three dropped behind the berm and continued toward the compound.

Reece performed a tac reload to top off his weapon and hit the push-to-talk on his MBITR.

"Alice, you still with us?" he asked.

"Yes."

"Talk me into that tunnel system."

"First, you have three men approaching from a structure close to the water on the south end of the island. They are just over a rise four hundred and sixty yards in front of you."

Even with NODs you didn't want your enemy to take the high ground.

Reece stopped and turned to Ox and Hobie.

"I'll stay here and draw fire. Don't worry, I have enough cover. You two push down and punch through."

Ox was about to open his mouth when the accelerating engine of an outboard engine pierced the darkness.

"Manta Two, coming in hot," came Bolo's voice over the radio.

Accelerating out of the darkness from the southeast, they had a clear line of sight to the three men trying to get a position of advantage on Reece's Team.

The sound of the outboards was replaced by fully automatic fire from a suppressed MK 46 ripping through the night.

Then Sako's voice came over the radio. "You're clear."

"Manta Two," Reece transmitted. "Grouper is WIA a mile north of your pos in need of CASEVAC. He's with Shane. We are moving to clear the compound."

"Roger that, we have eyes on," Sako said as the *Manta*'s Boston Whaler sped by.

Men behind rifles and machine guns fired at the tender from the bunker tunnel complex as it raced up the coast, but they were too far away to be effective. They were shooting at the noise of the engine and the neon-blue bioluminescence left in its wake.

"Shane, did you copy?" Reece asked.

"Shane copies. Manta Two, do you have a platform bag with you? We need it here."

"We do. One mike out."

Shane asking for the more robust medical kit was not a good sign.

Push that from your head.

"Alice, status report," Reece said.

"The three men that were headed to intercept you are down. Two more are visible kneeling at the corner of the large structure near the dock. You are clear to move."

"Roger. Moving."

Reece and his Team sprinted through the night over the rise. They put security rounds into the heads of the men Sako had taken out from the water as they passed. The terrain transitioned from natural tropical grasslands and jungles to a landscaped resort. The Team worked their way around tall palm trees and hedges as they approached what appeared to be the primary residence.

"Fifty yards to your southeast," Alice said.

The Team pushed around a stone wall, painted the two kneeling men with their IR lasers, and shot them to the ground.

"Clear. Nothing else moving," Alice transmitted.

The Team shifted their attention to the northeast.

"Alice, how do we get into those tunnels?" Reece asked, once again stowing his partially expended magazine and replacing it with a fresh one.

"All structures are connected underground."

"Where is the closest access point?"

"The one-story structure a hundred yards northeast."

"Good copy."

Reece forced himself to slow down.

Don't rush to your death.

You will die. Don't take any more of your friends with you.

They moved in a wedge formation with Reece in the lead toward their target building.

"Alice, any perimeter security?"

"Nothing visible."

"Roger."

They pushed across the grass slope and up a set of wide stairs to the one-story Indonesian-style home and crossed a short deck under an overhanging thatch roof. When Hobie and Ox were stacked behind Reece, the frogman's hand went to the side of the dual doors and slid past them. Reece cleared as much of the room as he could. He then slowly inched across the threshold in an arc so as not to break the plane of the opening with his muzzle, clearing as he went. Hobie brought his rifle up to take up Reece's original position as he cleared. Once on the other side, Reece now had the most information on the inside of the room, so Hobie checked up. Reece made entrance, stepping into the space and presenting his muzzle to the deep corner, moving down the wall and clearing back just past the center as Hobie did the same to the opposite corner. Ox was right on his heels and buttonhooked to Reece's wall, machine gun up and clearing from the room's center back toward Reece.

"Clear right," Reece said.

"Clear left," came Hobie's reply.

"Moving," Reece said.

"Move," Ox responded.

"Alice, where is the entrance?" Reece asked as the operators pushed across what was a large open sitting area.

Before she could answer, they heard a door open in the next room and all three operators moved to the side of another set of large carved open doors. Reece heard footsteps and muffled Spanish. Sensing where the men were in the room, Reece took an angle on the door, hit the lead man with his IR laser, and pressed the trigger four times in rapid succession, with all four bullets catching his target in the face. As he dropped to the floor, Reece sent another three rounds into the man behind him and then committed to the room with Hobie and Ox on his heels.

A door that looked like it should go to a pantry area was directly behind the dead men. Reece moved, rifle up, toward it and heard Hobie give the two men on the ground security rounds. Reece pushed back the door but instead of a pantry, a spiral staircase led down. With the door open they could hear sporadic fire coming from gun emplacements built into the side of the hill that not long ago had overlooked Reece's Team.

Stairwells of any kind are notoriously hard to clear.

"All right," Reece whispered, topping off his rifle. "We don't have a clear idea about what's down there. Could be a matrix of tunnels. It sounds like the fire is coming from maybe a hundred or so yards north."

"If they have someone down there at the base, we are going to get stitched up as soon as we start down," Hobie pointed out.

Reece let his rifle hang on its sling and pulled out a grenade, remembering his dad talking about clearing tunnels with frags in Vietnam.

Ox and Hobie nodded in approval.

Reece pulled the pin, dropped it down the stairs, and closed the door.

The three men backed away. Seconds later the explosion blew the door open.

Reece followed up with one more. After the second explosion, the Team worked their way down the spiral staircase, into a large concrete tunnel now filled with smoke. At the base of the stairs Reece put two bullets into the head of a wounded sentry. The tunnel was large enough to stand with a good two feet of headroom. It stretched out in both directions. One way led to the location where they had taken fire and the other led back toward the compound.

"Reece, I'll take point and clear with the AW."

Reluctantly Reece nodded and took the number-two-man position as Ox moved deeper into the tunnel.

A guard appeared from around a corner and Ox stitched him up with a burst from the belt-fed. He continued to send controlled bursts at the corner as he approached to keep anyone from spraying and praying in their direction. He continued shooting as he took the corner, putting three bursts into the last man at the tunnel's dead end. He put another three-round burst into his head to be sure.

"Clear," Ox said.

The gun ports they had been using were clear through their night vision.

As Reece moved his hand to his push-to-talk in an attempt to reach Alice, Manta Two, or Shane, he felt Ox and the Knight's Armament AW crash into him, which sent him slamming into Hobie as Ox tackled them back around the corner.

"*Back!*" Ox yelled.

Before it could even register, Reece felt the concussive blast of an explosion.

Dust filled the enclosed space as Reece scrambled to his feet while bringing up his weapon. Even with the Peltor ComTac noise-canceling headset protecting his ears, Reece felt the sharp pain of the ringing.

That means you are still alive.

"Ox! Hobie!" Reece yelled.

"I'm okay," Ox said. "Hobie, you good?"

"I think so. What was that?"

"Fucker had a grenade prepped. It rolled out of his hand after he was down."

"Thanks, Ox," Reece said.

He then hit the push-to-talk.

"Alice, Sako, anyone this net."

His transmission was met by silence.

"Not working in here," Reece said.

"Well, let's get out of this fucking place," Hobie said. "I like life aboveground."

"I have point," Reece said, bringing his rifle up and moving back the way they had come.

The dust from the grenade dissipated as they got closer to the spiral stairs.

As Reece approached their exit, he caught movement through his night vision. For a split second he thought it was a rat scurrying past his feet, but it wasn't a rat.

"*GRENADE!*" Reece yelled.

The grenade bounced off the concrete wall, coming to rest between Hobie and Ox.

It took only a second, a second that seemed like an eternity. Reece watched as his friend, the most experienced special operator he knew, threw his body on top of the grenade just before it detonated beneath him.

CHAPTER 53

White House Situation Room
Washington, D.C.

"DIRECTOR RODRIGUEZ, HOW DO we contact this 'Alice' to get a SITREP?"

The question came from the secretary of state, Hank Coleman, who had now joined President Gale Olsen and her crisis action group in the WIZZER. A large man the president suspected was building up his foreign policy bona fides for a future presidential run, the former governor of South Dakota had served in the Army as a tanker in his youth. It was possible he had not done any physical training since.

"The NSA might be able to answer your question with the proper technical terminology as she was a joint NSA, Army, and CISA program," Vic responded.

"It sounds like a project that went awry."

Vic only nodded. He had been in Washington long enough to know when to speak and when to let silence speak for him.

"We can discuss that issue after the current crisis is resolved," said the president, keeping them on track.

"An issue now, am I?" said a female monochromatic voice through the room's speakers.

"Alice," Vic said, "can you give us a situation report?"

"Napoleon is dead. I killed him."

"Killed him?" Vic asked, looking at Danreb.

"In nontechnical terms you would say that I fried his circuitry. His cooling mechanism was being powered by a power plant off Buru. I interrupted that life support system."

"Is Gravity-2 inoperable?" the president asked.

"The Gravity-2 is no longer under Napoleon's control."

"Does that mean it can't be launched?" CIA Director Howe asked for clarification.

"No," Alice replied.

"I don't understand," he replied.

"In scanning all the Napoleon systems before termination, I estimate that there is an eighty-seven percent chance that Andrew Hart has a manual backup means of launching the Gravity-2."

"So, stopping it is down to our Team on the ground?" Director Howe said.

"Yes."

"Can we hear from the Team?" the president asked.

"No. They are not equipped for that type of communications, but I can tell you they were compromised on their approach. We have one operator down and I have lost contact with Commander Reece's element."

"Why?" the president asked.

"They entered a tunnel complex following troops in contact."

"General Seifert," the president said, looking at the chairman of the Joint Chiefs. "What are our long-range kinetic options?"

"Madam President," the general said, leaning forward in his seat, interlacing his fingers, and setting his forearms on the table. "Our primary option is the forward-deployed DDG 112, the USS *Michael Murphy*, an

Arleigh Burke–class destroyer in the Philippine Sea. A Tomahawk cruise missile strike is my recommendation."

"How long would it take for them to reach their target?"

"The ship is approximately 456 nautical miles from Corelena. We can have hits on target in just under an hour."

The president took a breath.

"Under an hour," she said, deep in thought. "And how long would it take for Hart to launch the missiles manually?"

"If he is launching manually, it would depend upon which stage of the launch process he is in. It could be anywhere from immediate to what I estimate to be fifty minutes."

"Fifty minutes . . ."

"General?"

"That is cutting it close with the cruise missile attack."

"Order it, General," the president said.

"Yes, Madam President."

The chairman of the Joint Chiefs stood and took leave to a smaller communications room off the main space to place a call.

"Alice, can you relay my order to evacuate?"

"The Team has split their forces, but I can connect with the base element. I will relay the order to Commander Reece when I reestablish comms."

"Do it."

"I must inform you that if Hart has decided to continue with his mission, I estimate a less than fifty percent chance of the Tomahawks hitting their target before he launches the Gravity-2."

"What maximizes our chances of success?"

"Stopping the launch at its source if Hart has initiated the prelaunch procedures."

"Which we can't know from here."

"That is correct."

The president tapped her fingers on the table, thinking through her next decisions as commander in chief.

She turned to her secretary of state.

"Hank, set up a call for me with President Gao immediately. It's time to show our hand."

CHAPTER 54

Corelena Island
Northwest of Buru Island
Republic of Indonesia

"OX!" REECE YELLED.

The grenade had lifted Ox into the air and propelled him against the wall of the tunnel. It took Reece a moment to regain his bearings, the enclosed space amplifying the concussive effects of the explosion. He found the Knight's first. It had been ripped away from Ox in the blast.

Was that movement through the smoke at the far end of the tunnel?

Reece brought the belt-fed machine gun to his shoulder and tore through what was left of the hundred-and-fifty-round box magazine.

Hobie had been taken off his feet but quickly recovered and moved to Reece's side, providing cover fire while Reece located their friend in the smoke-filled passage.

There!

Reece dropped the AW and rushed to assess Ox's wounds while Hobie continued to send rounds down the tunnel in the direction of the threat.

"Talk to me, Reece," Hobie said between shots. "We have to move!"

Reece rolled Ox onto his back and quickly evaluated his injuries.

The ceramic plate had absorbed most of the blast. Aside from what had to be broken ribs, Ox's vital organs seemed to have been spared. His legs and arms were a different story. A portion of the blast had been directed down, tearing into his upper thighs and shredding his pants. His right arm was mangled and charred. His left was broken and contorted in an unnatural position. His helmet and NODs were gone, and he was bleeding from his nose. It looked like there might be fluid leaking from his ears.

"Reece!" Hobie called again. "Status!"

"Stand by!" Reece yelled back.

Breathing. Pulse. Weak.

Unconscious, probably in shock with internal and external injuries.

"We need to get him up those stairs," Hobie said, the urgency clear in his voice.

Do what you can, Reece.

He tore two tourniquets from Ox's kit and quickly affixed one to each leg. Then he grabbed one of his own and secured it to Ox's right arm. Then he extracted the trauma kit from Ox's belt. Under NODs, with the smoke heavy in the air and with Hobie continuing to pop rounds in the direction from which the grenade was thrown, Reece couldn't tell if he was ripping into an emergency trauma dressing or QuikClot. Whatever it was, he stuffed it into the biggest wound he could find in Ox's upper legs.

Leave the body armor on or take it off?

Reece looked at the spiral staircase. It was too narrow to make it up there with someone as big as Ox if he had kit on.

"All right," Reece said as he stripped off Ox's plate carrier. "Get ready to move."

Reece adjusted his rifle to keep it out of the way. He then lodged his right knee in Ox's left hip and slid his left knee between what was left of his friend's legs. He planted it in a kneeling position and threw Ox's right leg over his left thigh. Reece then reached his right arm between his left leg and Ox's right, grabbing torn material on Ox's right pant leg. Reece then leaned across Ox's body, pushing his right ear into Ox's right hip, rolling over the top of Ox's body and bringing Ox with him onto his shoulders and into a fireman's carry. Reece steadied himself and went from kneeling to standing.

"Let's move," Reece said.

Hobie finished dumping his magazine down the tunnel, changed magazines, and led the way up the spiral staircase.

It was then that Reece noticed that Hobie was limping.

"Hobie, you hit?"

"Not as bad as Ox," was all the operator said.

One foot in front of the other, Reece. This is why you train.

Reece's legs were burning when he reached the top of the staircase. He knew that was nothing compared to what the man on his shoulders was dealing with.

"Alice," Reece said, catching his breath as he and Hobie stepped over the bodies of the men they had killed on the way in.

Nothing.

At the doorway Reece tried again.

This time he got a response.

"Compound clear," she said.

"Good copy."

"Manta Two, you guys still here?"

"Standing by," came Bolo's voice.

"Bolo, meet us at the main dock. Ox is WIA. He's in bad shape."

"Roger that. Inbound."

"You want to switch out?" Hobie asked Reece.

"I got him. Alice says the compound is clear, but somebody threw that grenade and I have not seen Hart, Novak, or Perkins yet."

Hobie nodded. He cleared as much of the lawn as he could between the house and the next hill before moving out.

Reece drew his pistol and followed, noticing that Hobie's limp was getting worse the farther they went.

Where Hobie's eyes went, his rifle followed. At the crest of a low hill, they both saw and heard the *Manta*'s tender pull next to the dock by a large sailboat. Reece looked up to see Shane and Sako disembark, Shane with his SIG rifle and Sako with just a pistol. They left the Knight's with Bolo in case he needed to lay down a base of fire for the land element.

Reece and Hobie kept pushing across the grass that was now sloped downward.

"Alice, status check. Anything moving?"

"Negative, Reece. Still clear."

Shane and Sako met them two hundred yards from the dock. Shane's arm was bandaged. He took rear security while Sako immediately went back-to-back with Reece, transferring Ox onto his shoulders.

"I have the weight," he said.

Reece holstered the Glock and brought up his rifle. He fell in as rear security with Shane as they leapfrogged back to the dock.

"Reece," came Alice's voice through his headset.

"I hear you."

"Extract immediately."

"That's the plan."

"You have twenty-seven minutes until impact."

Reece came to a stop on the dock as Shane charged past.

"What do you mean?"

"The president launched four Tomahawk cruise missiles from an *Arleigh Burke*–class destroyer in the Philippine Sea at Corelena Island."

"Why?" Reece asked, not moving from his position.

"In reviewing data from the site and from Napoleon's systems, I estimate there is an eighty-seven percent chance that Andrew Hart can launch the Gravity-2 manually."

"You mean we didn't stop him?"

"That is uncertain."

Reece looked back at the main house.

"Reece, these missiles are going to impact the island. They are lower-tech and I cannot splash them. Get in the boat. There is a forty-six percent chance that the Tomahawks will hit before the Gravity-2 launches."

"Any movement on target?"

"Nothing."

They are underground.

"Reece, the president has ordered that you leave the island. She has opted for the cruise missile attack."

"Those percentages seem to indicate Hart is going to launch before they impact."

"I will continue to penetrate the system."

"But if it is closed you won't be able to get in."

"That's correct, Reece."

"If Hart can launch manually, then I can stop him manually."

Or maybe I can slow them down and delay it enough for the missiles to hit.

If you stay with Katie, she will die.

Reece turned and ran down the dock to where Shane waited next to the tender.

Ox and Grouper were lying flat on the deck, not moving. Sako was back on the Knight's Armament Light Assault Machine Gun at the bow and, though wounded himself, Hobie was working on Ox, the deck awash in blood.

"Shane, get out of here. You heard the transmission."

"Yeah, I heard Alice say that Tomahawks are inbound and that the president ordered us, all of us, out."

"Ox and Grouper are in a bad way. You and Hobie are leaking too. Get to the *Manta.* I have a feeling that after this morning, there are going to be a lot of U.S. naval assets in the area. They will be able to take care of all of you."

Shane shook his head.

"Reece . . ."

"Go!"

"How do we link back up with you?"

Reece smiled.

"You don't."

"You are going to need a swim buddy," Shane said.

"I've got one—Alice."

"Fuck that, Reece."

Reece flipped up his NODs.

"Listen to me, Shane." He paused. "I'm not coming back."

The paramilitary officer looked into Reece's eyes. He understood. He handed the frogman three full mags and a grenade.

Reece stuffed them in his plate carrier. Then he turned, folded down his NODs, and ran back toward the main house.

CHAPTER 55

White House Situation Room
Washington, D.C.

THE PRESIDENT HAD NOT taken her call with President Gao of China privately, as some leaders may have. Instead, she directed the WHSR staff to frame a video feed that showed her at the head of the table surrounded by the National Security Council, knowing that many times pictures spoke louder than words.

"President Gao, thank you for taking this meeting. I am gathered with my National Security Council to discuss a matter of the gravest importance to both our nations."

The president's words were translated into Mandarin by an interpreter from the Interpreting Division of the Office of Language Services. Under the Bureau of Administration's Operations Office, they continued a tradition of elite linguists created by the country's first secretary of state, Thomas Jefferson.

President Gao had an interpreter on his side as well. Both presidents having trusted interpreters served as a check on what each side was relaying in this high-stakes game.

President Gao only folded his arms across his navy blue suit and lighter blue tie. He was sitting in a high-backed brown leather chair. Visible in the background over his left shoulder was the red and gold flag of the People's Republic of China. Red denoted revolution and a large gold star symbolized the CCP. An arc of four smaller stars represented China's four social classes as defined by Mao, though more recently those four stars had been reinterpreted to represent China's main ethnic groups. Even Communist China was not immune from the winds of change.

President Olsen had not consulted the men around the table before the call. Time was a factor, and she knew her role, which made Vic regret that she would not be seeking another term.

"My country was recently made aware of a threat to both our nations."

She is offering him an out, Vic thought. *Brilliant.*

"Unbeknownst to us, an American citizen named Andrew Hart of Elba Industries collaborated with a private Chinese company called Orienspace to build an anti-satellite rocket that is on an island in Indonesia. They plan to use it to take out all low-orbital satellites, something that will be detrimental for both our nations and for the world."

President Gao continued to stare sternly into the monitor.

"We have launched Tomahawk cruise missiles at the launch site. Right now, it is unknown if they will impact before launch. We know that your government had nothing to do with this Elba Industries plot. I want to assure you that my government will take all necessary steps to deal with this threat to the United States, China, and the world. My secretary of state is coordinating with the Indonesian government to mitigate any potential fallout, though the launch facility is isolated, and no collateral damage is expected. I wanted to personally notify you of this threat to our nations and the steps the United States is taking to eliminate it. I also wanted to personally notify you of the involvement of a private Chinese entity in this plot. A joint intelligence task force will be investigating this matter, and I will keep you apprised of additional developments on any further connections to China."

Olsen paused to let her words sink in.

President Gao spoke with a soft tone that still managed to convey a firmness that left one on edge.

"This is disturbing information, Madam President. I am unaware of any collaboration between private companies in my country and this Elba Industries. I will instruct my intelligence services to investigate immediately. Thank you for bringing this to my attention."

President Olsen had made the subtext clear: *We know you are involved but you can escape this unscathed. The choice is yours.*

"I would appreciate it if we could keep these channels open at the executive levels, President Gao. I think that could help avert any misunderstandings."

"I agree."

"Thank you, President Gao. We will be in touch shortly with an update."

She nodded at her counterpart without smiling and the WHSR Duty Officer terminated the feed.

Gale Olsen looked around the room.

"Well, do you think he bought it?"

"That was a master class in diplomacy, Madam President," said Secretary Coleman.

"Will it be enough? Mr. Danreb?" the president asked.

"If our Tomahawks prevent that launch, you have given him the out he needs. He knows it and we know it."

"And if it launches?"

"If it launches and succeeds in creating the Kessler syndrome in low orbit, it is possible they go through with the invasion of Taiwan."

"We need to stop that launch," the president said. "What are the odds our missiles hit in time?"

"Still less than fifty percent." Alice's distinctive voice filled the room.

"How much less?" the president asked, as if Alice were physically present with them.

"That cannot be determined without knowing what state of the launch sequence we are in."

"General," the president said, "we have tipped our hand. Begin moving every available asset we have into positions that signify our support of Taiwan. Put up B-52s, B-1s, and B-2s out of Guam. Get B-21s up as well. I want them to know we are serious. I want President Gao to know through our military actions that we are prepared to defend Taiwan. Hank, deconflict with Indonesia. There is an option on the table in which Indonesian authorities discovered this plot and their military took action from a narrative control standpoint. I want us to be extremely sensitive to President Widodo's desires. Please set us up on a call. I will take that in private and explain the situation personally."

"There is another factor to consider," Alice said.

"What's that?" the president asked.

"The CIA team evacuated the island with multiple wounded. They are en route to the *Manta* and will need to coordinate next-level medical care with a U.S. naval surface asset."

"General," the president said, delegating that medical response to her chief military advisor. "Coordinating that now, Alice. What does that have to do with the pending launch?"

"Commander Reece stayed behind."

CHAPTER 56

Corelena Island
Northwest of Buru Island
Republic of Indonesia

REECE CHARGED UP THE grass slope toward the main house hearing the engines of the tender roar to life and dissipate as it sped into the night.

"Alice, where was Napoleon located?"

"In a chamber under the structure in front of you."

Reece passed the two bodies of the guards they had eliminated earlier and pressed into the home's courtyard, clearing as he went.

The sounds of battle had disappeared. They had left an eerie silence in their wake, the calm before the dawn.

Reece cleared as much of the main room from the outside as possible before entering.

Was there another security team lying in wait?

Was the compound wired with IEDs?

Where were Hart, Novak, and Perkins?

Reece pressed his push-to-talk.

"Where is it?" Reece asked in a hushed voice.

"A door off the main room. Reece, I will lose you when you go underground unless there is some connectivity through which I can connect to your radio or mobile device."

"Understood. Anything moving on property?"

"Nothing."

Are they still here?

Could they have gotten off the island?

Underground?

Underwater?

Watch for sleights of hand, Miles had told him.

Miles.

What else had he said?

"I remember they all wore the same watch—Breitling Emergencies. As a sailor you notice things like that."

Those have radio beacons.

"Alice, are any phones active or inactive on the island?"

"No."

"How about watches?"

CHAPTER 57

REECE WORKED HIS WAY down into Napoleon's chamber, weapon up, sweeping as he moved.

Alice had searched for and activated the beacons on the Breitling Emergency watches. Two were active on an island a mile to the south.

How did they get there?

He entered the room once dominated by Napoleon, using the IR illuminator on his laser aiming device to see in the pitch black.

He recognized the Plexiglas cage. It was similar to the one used to house Alice when they had first met, though instead of a flowing, Medusa-like chandelier of glowing wires suspended in space, this one held a large cylindrical container. Nothing moved, nothing glowed, nothing blinked, nothing hummed. It was a room of death.

He wasn't going to stop a launch from this space.

Closed door far corner.

Reece moved across the room to the far door, which looked more like a ship's hatch upon closer inspection.

"Alice," Reece said into his radio headset.

Nothing.

Reece was alone.

He unlatched the hatch and pushed open the door.

A pitch-black tunnel beckoned.

• • •

Perkins waited in the dark. He had the advantage. He had walked the entire underground labyrinth of tunnels dozens of times and knew them well.

Hart had been right. Someone had stayed behind. And now Perkins was going to have the fight he wanted. It might not be the Octagon, but the adrenaline was flowing. Perkins was pumped. He could taste the blood.

He saw the glow of the IR illuminator first. It would turn on for a moment and then go dark again.

Whoever it was, they were moving like a pro, like someone who anticipated that his enemy might have the same technological advantage as he did.

The submerged floating tunnel connected Corelena to the launch facility. It had one gradual turn at the halfway point. Approximately a mile in length, the tunnel was suspended one hundred feet beneath the surface to insulate it from weather conditions, seismic events, and the draft of maritime traffic above. Constructed of concrete and steel, the positively buoyant tube was anchored to the ocean floor to secure it in place. Perkins understood that the Chinese engineering firm that had designed it was also using it as a test for future projects that would allow for vehicle traffic between other Indonesian islands.

The tube had a flat floor, but the walls and ceiling were rounded. It was sturdy enough to survive small-arms fire and Perkins suspected that even a grenade wouldn't do irreparable damage, though he would rather not be the one who tested its structural integrity against explosives. His rifle should be enough. He did not like being submerged in what amounted to a prototype, but he would not be in it for much longer. He would deal with the intruder and get back to the surface, where he belonged.

• • •

What is this thing?

The tunnel leading away from the main house slanted down toward the sea. Reece estimated he was about eighty to a hundred feet underground when the rectangular design shifted to a cylindrical one. There was still ample headroom and space for at least four men in kit to walk side by side. It wasn't quite big enough for a car or truck but would easily allow for motorcycles and golf carts.

The lights were still off. Reece wondered if they were connected to shore power from Corelena or if they had another power source and they were off because of a decision on the enemy's side. Warfare was all about adaptation. Adaptation and deception.

Reece hit his IR illuminator. Weapon off safe. Finger on the trigger. Ready to work.

He then turned off the IR light and slightly changed his position as much as the space would allow before pushing deeper into the tube.

Was there another guard force ahead? It was possible.

Were Hart, Novak, and Perkins waiting for him in the tunnel or were they right now launching the Gravity-2 rocket?

You are on the clock, Reece.

Steady. You can't delay the launch if you are dead.

Reece could see that the tunnel turned to the right about fifty yards forward of his position.

Was he a half mile in?

If you take that corner with your IR illuminator on, you will have given up any element of surprise.

How do you take that element back?

Reece turned off his illuminator and walked another twenty yards into the tube. He unslung his weapon and leaned it against the right side of the tunnel, balanced on its magazine, pointing forward. He then activated the positive IR light, drew his Glock, and pressed his left shoulder to the opposite side of the tunnel.

Weapon at the ready, he crept forward.

• • •

Why was the American lighting up the tunnel? Was it James Reece? Why was he stationary? Was he waiting?

Concrete and steel.

This floating tube could take a frag.

Perkins let his rifle hang, removed a grenade from a pouch, and pulled the pin.

• • •

Reece moved smoothly along the left side of the tube, pistol extended with his finger on the trigger. The IR illuminator from his abandoned rifle lit up the right wall. The dot in his RMR atop the pistol was visible but partially washed out by the reflection off his hands through his NODs.

If there is someone around the corner, you will know in a few seconds.

Reece slowed down even more and began to pie the corner.

A sudden flash of movement caused him to adjust his angle and allowed only a split second to send a round at the partially obscured figure ahead.

Even as Reece pressed the trigger, he recognized what had happened. Someone had thrown something and that something in this case was a flashbang stun grenade or a fragmentation grenade.

It sailed past Reece in the direction of his rifle.

Reece hit the deck with his head facing forward and crossed his legs. The grenade was going to detonate far enough back that Reece should escape injury, but he didn't want to take an errant piece of shrapnel.

What would it do to the tunnel?

The concussive force of the detonation rocked Reece's world, the acoustic shock reigniting a sensation of pressure in his head followed by an acute ringing in his ears. If any shrapnel flew in his direction, it passed overhead. The explosion had landed close enough to his rifle to knock it to the ground but did not destroy the IR light. It continued to partially illuminate the tunnel, casting a ghostly light through the smoke.

Reece briefly set his pistol down, rolled to his side, and extracted a grenade from his pouch. He knelt, pulled the pin, and hurled it around the corner.

Reece felt the concussive force from the explosion as it traveled back down the tunnel. He pushed ahead through the smoke- and debris-filled tube inching around the turn, pistol up and ready to work.

Get ready for another grenade.

Instead, unsuppressed rifle rounds fired on full-auto zipped through the fumes. The muzzle flash coupled with the dust created a strobe light–like effect in Reece's NODs.

Reece changed sides of the tunnel to cut off the angle.

Shoot back blindly?

Wait for a target?

Deal with a second grenade?

Wait, what was that?

The explosion-induced ear trauma made it hard to discern even through the Peltors.

It sounded like footsteps, but were they running toward him or away?

Then he heard something else that he at first thought was a malfunction in his headset. It sounded like static.

Then the floor started to move.

Water.

Flooding!

Reece looked up in time to see the wave that swept him from his feet and dragged him under.

• • •

"Is it working?" Hart asked.

"It's working," General Novak replied. "Tunnel is filling now."

"Good."

"There is an emergency drainage pump system that will collect incoming water underneath the floor, but it will not be able to keep up with the volume of water we are introducing. They will be dead soon."

"Activate the Pad Deck Water Deluge System on the Gravity-2. Then commence with the First Stage Thrust Vector Actuator Test."

"We could still call this off," Novak said.

"General, there are enemy forces on our soil. That means missiles may very well be inbound. Without Napoleon we won't know. But they are being guided by the satellites we are set to destroy. Our very survival depends on it. Now get on with it."

• • •

Reece felt like he was in a washing machine. The wall of water tossed him to the floor, pushing him deeper back into the tube. The force slightly dissipated and he struggled to get his feet under him, dizzy and out of breath from the unexpected assault.

His NODs still worked, and he had managed to hold on to his pistol.

The water dropped from chest to waist level.

An emergency drainage feature?

Where is the threat?

Bullets ripping down the tunnel gave Reece his answer.

He took a knee and braced himself against the concrete wall so that just his arms and shoulders were out of the water. Through his NODs he could see Perkins, sprinting toward him in an attempt to escape the rapidly flooding tunnel, shooting wildly with his rifle in Reece's general direction. If he had once had a helmet with attached night optics, they had been lost in the flood.

Reece steadied his breathing and shot a controlled pair at the man's center mass. *Body armor.* He adjusted slightly for a head shot but his target was engulfed and disappeared in another wall of water before he could press the trigger.

Take a breath, Reece. You know what's coming.

The same wave that consumed his opponent hit Reece a moment later.

This time Reece relaxed.

Let the water take you. It's pushing you back to Corelena.

When it felt like it might be dissipating, Reece pulled his feet beneath him and pushed up. His head broke the surface. The water level was just below his chin. He took a breath and turned in anticipation of being hit by another wave. Instead, he was hit with a heavy closed fist.

Even under NODs, he recognized Perkins from his file photo.

Reece twisted the Glock underwater and fired while off-balance.

Miss.

Reece adjusted as Perkins's left hand sliced down through the water, catching Reece's wrist and pushing the pistol offline. His rifle sling was tangled and still slung across his chest.

Reece reached for his blade when another wave swept them both from their feet.

He felt Perkins going for his pistol and immediately went to counter. Pistol rounds do not travel far when discharged underwater, but if the muzzle is directly against the human body they can still be deadly.

They were locked together, in what amounted to a wave, in the dark, a hundred feet beneath the surface of the ocean in a tunnel rapidly filling with water. They smashed up against a wall and Perkins stripped the Glock from Reece's grasp, the swift-moving water taking it away.

This guy is strong.

With Reece's right wrist still locked in Perkins's iron grasp, the mercenary's right hand moved to his right side.

He's going for a pistol.

The increased drag underwater makes movement not nearly as efficient as on land. Perkins's draw was hampered by the rifle that was still slung to his body, but he still discharged three rounds as he attempted to bring it online.

Reece felt two rounds hit his body armor, the ceramic plate dissipating their energy as it absorbed the impacts. He grabbed the barrel of the auto-loading pistol, twisting it to the outside and back toward his opponent, the current tearing it away before Reece could get positive control.

He felt them hit the flat bottom, so Reece threw his legs under him, planted them as firmly as he could, grabbed his opponent's throat, and then shot them toward the roof of the tunnel, not knowing if an air pocket still existed above. They broke the surface and Reece slammed Perkins's head into the top of the tunnel.

Six inches of air.

Another wave hit them, propelling them farther down the cylindrical crypt.

Still on the surface, Perkins's hand shot to Reece's NODs. The reflection of the light from the night vision on Reece's cheeks had given him a reference point. Reece felt his head snap back as another wave took them down and rolled them before spitting them to the surface. Reece's helmet hit the roof of the tunnel, where there was still a small air pocket. He managed a quick breath before Perkins ripped his head back under by the NODs.

With his left hand, Reece reached up and pressed the clasp on his chinstrap. The helmet and NODs broke free. Perkins still had ahold of the helmet, but Reece's head was not in it.

Reece wrapped his left hand behind Perkins's neck and slammed his head into his opponent's nose. He was attempting to slide around the mercenary's body when another wave engulfed them.

They were dead regardless of who prevailed in this battle. The tunnel had almost been full when they took their last breaths. But the human mind, body, and spirit would always fight for that most precious of gifts, the gift of life, even in the most futile of conditions.

The will to fight.

Fight, Reece.

In the chaos of the churning water, Perkins managed to press his QD sling attachment, which was hindering his movement, and pull the rifle across Reece's neck, wrapping his legs around Reece's from behind, locking in his hooks, as the current continued to roll them.

They spun and crashed into the tunnel walls, the floor, and ceiling, in a desperate fight for life, and even though Perkins had the position of advantage, he started to panic. Reece could feel it.

Stay calm, Reece. That's your advantage.

If you are going to die down here, Perkins is dying first.

Still underwater with the lower portion of the barrel across his neck, Reece reached up in a vain attempt to release the pressure. His hand then went to the trigger guard. Reece flipped the weapon to fire and pulled the trigger. The rifle discharged. Reece kept pressing the trigger, thinking that maybe Perkins's hand was over the muzzle or the barrel might heat up enough for him to loosen his grip. He felt the concussion rattle his brain just inches away from the chamber, but Perkins held on until the rifle went dry and continued to choke Reece with the now-empty AR.

As he kept his left hand on the lower barrel, Reece's right hand went to the Headhunter Blade mounted horizontally to the back of his belt.

He drew it, indexed Perkins's right hand, and pressure-cut deep into his metacarpals. Even underwater Reece could hear his opponent grunt and instinctively pull back his hand.

Before Reece could cut Perkins's left hand, the MMA fighter launched them to the surface once again in a desperate search for air. This time he didn't find it.

This is a strong current. We have to be getting close to Corelena.

Reece could feel the panic take hold as Perkins thrashed to get away in a frantic search for life-sustaining air.

Reece grabbed the drag handle of Perkins's plate carrier and pulled him back. His blade found a soft target, and Reece stabbed it into his enemy's armpit. Reece heard another grunt as Perkins expended more air from his lungs. As he struggled, his body tried to surface but found only the top of the tunnel, which put the lower part of his back plate even with Reece's face. Reece reached around his adversary, twisted his wrist, and inserted the blade under the plate, angling it up and in, slicing it across his stomach and pumping it into his opponent's guts. This time the sound Reece heard was unmistakable. Perkins was screaming. Reece sliced down through the femoral in his leg, though underwater he could not tell if he hit it. He then used the drag handle to yank Perkins down. He slipped his hand from the handle to the underside of Perkins's chin and, with the blade still in a forward grip, inserted it into the side of the mercenary's neck to the hilt before thrusting it forward, ripping through the trachea and esophagus.

Reece let the current carry the dead man away.

He released the four quick-detach buckles at the shoulders and waist of his maritime plate carrier, letting it sink so he could move more efficiently. He then pushed himself back to the surface. Some of the water had drained from what was probably a safety mechanism in case of a rupture, but not enough. Reece pressed his lips to the top of the tunnel, drawing in half a breath before the water rose again.

He knew the direction of Corelena. The current was pushing him that way. He transferred the knife to his mouth, biting down on the handle so that he could use his hands for the most powerful strokes possible. His arms and legs burned as he propelled himself forward in the dark.

Always forward.

He thought of the fifty-meter underwater swim in BUD/S and of the SEAL candidates in his class who had experienced shallow-water blackouts, refusing to surface because they wanted it so bad. He remembered the instructors pulling them to the surface and resuscitating them on the pool deck. And then making them do it again.

Reece kept swimming, pulling with his arms, kicking with his legs.

What was that ahead in the darkness? Was it light? Was he hallucinating? It looked like the blurry avatar of Alice.

He tried to surface one more time, but the water had not dissipated. He was trapped.

It was too far to go. He wasn't going to make it.

Goodbye, Katie.

CHAPTER 58

White House Situation Room
Washington, D.C.

ADMIRAL DANIEL JOHNSON, COMMANDER of the U.S. Pacific Fleet, had just begun his briefing to the National Security Council on defending Taiwan when he was interrupted by a voice the council now knew well.

"President Olsen."

"Excuse us, Admiral Johnson. Yes, Alice?"

"I regret to inform you and the council that Commander James Reece is dead."

"What?"

"I reinstated power to Corelena Island, which in turn activated flood sensors in a floating tunnel between Corelena and an island to the south."

"Is it possible that it is a malfunction?"

"It is possible but not probable. The sensors were triggered at different levels consistent with its design, starting with a drainage system below the walkway. All sensors indicate a catastrophic event. The tunnel is completely flooded. Commander Reece's chances of survival are zero percent."

Vic stared at the table in front of him. The president tapped her fingers on the desk.

"Why was he in the tunnel?" President Olsen asked.

"I tracked emergency beacons in watches that Commander Reece informed me were worn by Andrew Hart and Ian Novak. I activated those beacons through encrypted Huawei mobile devices belonging to Hart and Novak. They are on an island one point two miles south of Corelena."

"Why are they on that island to the south?"

"I assess that it is a possible launch site. All the data storage areas radiate a similar heat signature. Based on newly acquired information, it appears that the launch site was built to mirror the heat signature of a data storage site."

The president turned to the chairman of the Joint Chiefs.

"General Seifert, can the Tomahawks be redirected in flight?"

"Yes, Madam President, these are the Bock IV Tactical Tomahawks. They have a data-link feature that allows us to retarget in flight. We have that capability as long as the low-orbital satellite constellation remains intact."

"Alice, are you one hundred percent sure the launch site is on the island to the south of Corelena?"

"Any of the data storage sites on Corelena and the unnamed island south of Corelena could be a potential launch site."

"General, redirect the Tomahawks to target every data storage site and structure on Corelena and the island to its south, immediately."

"Alice, do you have grid coordinates on those sites and structures?" the general asked.

"Passing those to the WHSR duty officer now," Alice responded. "But I also just redirected the Tomahawks in flight."

The general shared a look with the president.

"Anything further on launch timing?"

"No change in status. Launch could be immediate. If the launch sequence began when the CIA team was compromised and we launched the Tomahawks, then the earliest the Gravity-2 could be airborne is twenty-three minutes from now. Tomahawk impact is thirty-one minutes."

"Damn it," the president said under her breath.

"Any communication with mainland China after my call with President Gao?"

"Yes. A text message was received by Andrew Hart's Huawei device from another device in Beijing associated with China's Ministry of State Security. It only contained the Chinese character for 'denied.'"

"Looks like your call with Gao worked, Madam President," Secretary Coleman said.

"Did it?" she asked. "There is still a very big variable in play."

"What's that?"

"Andrew Hart. Mr. Danreb, your thoughts, please."

Andy cleared his throat and pushed the news about Reece out of his mind to deal with the task at hand.

"Hart will assess his position based off that text. His logical assumption will now be that he has been hung out to dry. From what I know, I think there is a strong likelihood that he launches anyway."

"Why would he do that?"

"To force China's hand. Depending on timing, if he launches, it is possible he takes out the low-orbital satellites, which were also the satellites that the Tomahawks are depending on for guidance. With a Kessler syndrome scenario putting China in an advantageous position, it is possible China reconsiders and moves to take Taiwan when we are no longer in a position to help defend it. Alice will be able to better evaluate based on the evolving situation."

"Alice," said the president. "Alice?"

But Alice was gone.

The door leading to the watch floor flew open, the duty officer wide-eyed and breathless.

"Madam President, we are receiving calls from NORAD, Vandenberg, and Groom Lake."

"Spit it out, son," General Seifert said.

"I have never seen anything like this, Madam President," he continued. "We just went to DEFCON 1."

"What? That can't happen without orders from me and SECDEF and General Seifert," she replied.

"I know, Madam President. We triple-checked. We are at DEFCON 1 and now have intercontinental ballistic missiles prepping to launch."

"What's their target?"

"Beijing and the headquarters element for each of China's fleets."

"Dear God," the president said. "Alice, what have you done?"

CHAPTER 59

Corelena Island
Northwest of Buru Island
Republic of Indonesia

THERE WAS NOT MUCH time.

Ten seconds, if that.

Come on, Reece. A little farther.

Two more kicks. Then one more. Always one more.

In all that chaos, are you even going the right way?

Just take a big gulp of water and end this as fast as you can.

Stop fighting.

No. You don't know how to stop fighting.

Reece ran his hand along the left side of the tunnel.

Is it the left side?

Is the floor of the tunnel pitching up?

In pitch black, in a suspended tube beneath the water filled with water, there was no way to tell. He was disoriented beyond any measure.

Where is that door?

As Reece continued to fight the final inhalation that he knew would kill him, he felt his body going hypoxic. He recognized that the carbon dioxide building up in his system was crossing the blood–brain barrier and he fought his natural craving to inhale as he continued to claw his way through the liquid passageway. Soon, the inhalation of salt water, a blackout, or a seizure was coming.

Always one more kick.

One more stroke.

What was that?

Reece's right hand hit something metal in the concrete-walled tunnel.

My right hand? I thought the door was on the left?

Even in compete blackness, Reece knew he was about to pass out. Reds and purples clouded his vision as he fought the inclination to take a breath.

No. Keep fighting!

It was a hatch, or was it a door?

Whatever it was, Reece twisted his body and gave one last kick and pull. He caught the round handle like the one he had used to enter the tunnel from the quantum computer room and pulled himself to it. He turned it one way and then the other, feeling it give.

Why isn't it opening?

Come on!

With his last ounce of strength, Reece twisted the handle one final inch as his body spasmed and he involuntarily took a breath, the knife dropping from his mouth. He fought to stay conscious as water entered his larynx. His body was battling between its need for air and its primal default to seal vocal cords to constrict the airway, sealing it off, and keeping additional water from entering the lungs. He felt his vocal cords contract in their confusion when the change in pressure sucked him through the now-open door as thousands of gallons of water suddenly had a new space to fill. He was smashed into what felt like a railing and then fell to the side, crashing down steel grating stairs, his lungs attempting to suck in lifesaving oxygen as his stomach retched the invading salt water even before his body came to rest in the corner of a landing.

Air.

Life.

Reece felt the acidic vomit project through his esophagus and then enter his lungs through his trachea as he sucked bile to his air passages via the trachea and into the lungs as his body adjusted to its new condition.

Reece rolled to his side, his face pressed to the grating of the landing, his strength depleted, his body fighting to survive, as he continued to suck in oxygen. His chest heaved and spasms and the vomiting gradually subsided.

Air.

He was alive.

Though he didn't realize it, he had closed his eyes when he had been spit from the tube, his body's every effort going into regulating its functions to keep Reece conscious. He slowly opened his eyes, feeling the burning as they adjusted to a dim glow that he couldn't quite place. Even the sound of his breathing had overridden the continuous ringing in his ears. It was then replaced by what he at first thought was his lungs sucking in air. He blinked his eyes to realize that the sound was a torrent of water roaring like a continuous geyser from the door one landing above him. It shot through the top railing attached to a grated floor and cascaded down to the floor below, the floor of a cavern.

What the hell?

He pushed himself to his knees and vomited once more through the grate. Reece grabbed the railing next to him, pulling himself up like a boxer who has been put on the canvas and is trying desperately to get to his feet before the ten-count reached its apex. Any referee in the world of boxing would have called it a knockout, but this was not a bout. This was war, not a war between nation-states or even proxies or factions in which industrialized nations adhered to a set of rules or principles. This was a war in which the rules did not exist. Reece had become war before. It was who he was. It was in his blood. And this war wasn't over. He still drew breath. He was mobile. And it was time for him to do what he did best.

He stood on the middle landing of a stairwell that overlooked a large cavern cut from limestone.

What is this place?

He blinked his eyes again and shook his head to clear his vison.

The entire cavern was damp. Light was coming from dim yellow bulbs that seemed almost haphazardly strewn along the far wall. Below him, a makeshift rocky path led down to a dock. About half a football field across, a good portion of the area beneath him was rock and half was water that led down a tunnel carved out of the limestone. A floating dock occupied the space below.

That looks big enough for a submarine, Reece noted.

A Chinese submarine?

What else could it be for?

Had the flooding carried Reece farther up the tube than he thought?

Reece continued to catch his breath. He wiped vomit from his chin and unzipped a pocket on his pant leg, extracting the phone from his pocket. It was waterproof, as was its case, but it had not been designed for what Reece had just put it through. Would it work?

It had been turned off, as he and the Team had been using MBITRs and Alice could still use it to track him when it was off.

Reece powered it on.

Yes!

While he waited for it to go through its start-up sequence he thought through his options.

How long had he been in the tunnel?

How long was left until launch?

The phone came to life.

He hit the prearranged contact for Alice.

Nothing.

Too deep underground.

Was he already too late?

Was the launch moments away?

Wasn't he about to be obliterated by a Tomahawk cruise missile strike anyway?

How would he even get to the island to the south?

Take stock of your tools.

Reece had lost his knife when the tunnel had ejected him. His plates and plate carrier, pistol, rifle, radio, and NODs were all somewhere in the tunnel with Perkins's dead body.

He reached to his right pocket.

Miraculously, his Combat Flathead was still clipped inside.

So, you are down to a screwdriver and a mobile phone.

And a plane.

As Reece's eyes continued to adjust, an object came into focus tied to the dock below.

Tied to the floating dock was an ICON A5 amphibious plane.

Reece almost smiled.

Stuffing the phone back into his pocket, he ran down the remainder of the stairs and sprinted across the rocks and onto the dock.

His strength was returning.

Reece had seen photos of the A5 but never flown one. He thought it looked like the modern version of the old Lake Buccaneer he had learned to fly with Liz, though this aircraft seemed more like a large Jet Ski or small sports car with wings. The sleek white and gray seaplane was resting on its hull in the gloom, the engine mounted above and behind the cockpit in a pusher configuration.

He raced down the dock and threw open the canopy.

Okay, basic instrument panel, angle-of-attack indicator, airspeed, altimeter, fuel, bilge, rudder, oil temperature, oil pressure, water/coolant temperature, large Garmin touchscreen, single throttle level where a car's gearshift would be. I just might be able to fly this thing.

Reece untied the flying boat from the dock, slid behind the controls, and hit the master switch, which brought the gauges to life.

You can do this.

He reached up and closed the canopy.

He then turned the key in the ignition.

Just like a car.

Nothing happened.

Reece looked closer and saw positions for A, B, and BOTH.

He turned it back off and turned the key to A, which caused lights to illuminate on the panel in front of him. He waited a moment and then turned it to B. He paused before turning it to BOTH, which fired up the 100-horsepower Rotax 912 iS engine. Reece felt the vibrations of the three-bladed propeller behind him.

Throttle.

He reached down and pushed the throttle forward, using the water rudder to stay in the middle of the cavern as he followed the dim lights hanging from its sides.

Clean and uncluttered, the panel and controls all reminded Reece of a car or ATV. He remembered his seat belt and buckled it just like in a vehicle. He then removed the IPS safety pin above his right shoulder, tossing it onto the passenger seat next to him.

The ICON exited the cave at 4,000 rpm on the tachometer.

Where am I?

It was still dark but in the early nautical twilight he could make out the hulking shape of Buru Island in front of him, which meant he was on the east side of Corelena Island.

Time to find Hart and Novak.

Reece used the paddles to turn the amphibian aircraft to starboard.

They should be on an island directly south.

Now, how do you fly this thing?

Maybe I should just use it as a boat?

Just get there, Reece.

He pushed the throttle forward as his eyes swept the gauges.

No mixture. Water rudder up. Gear up.

He felt the aircraft transition from plow to a plane as the ICON moved onto step.

Water rudder up.

Speed twenty knots.

Flaps from zero to thirty. Add power.

Reece felt the plane start to porpoise.

You should come off the throttle.

Instead, he pulled back on the stick.

He went airborne for a moment and was struck by how quiet it was after the thunder of the water in the cavern.

"Warning: Terrain Ahead. Warning: Terrain Ahead," alerted the aircraft's terrain advisor.

That island was closer than he thought.

Flaps down. Power down. Flaring.

Reece was vaguely aware of the rocky shoreline below him as he put the aircraft into a sixty-degree-bank turn. The left wing caught the top of a tree and sent the plane cartwheeling into the jungle.

CHAPTER 60

White House Situation Room
Washington, D.C.

THE NEXT CALL WITH President Gao had not gone well.

What if the situation were reversed? What if President Gao had called President Olsen to tell her that a rogue Chinese AI quantum computer had taken over portions of China's nuclear ballistic missile systems and was actively targeting the United States? What would she have done? Probably what China was doing right now. Preparing for war.

Gale Olsen paced before the Presidential Seal on the far wall of the WHSR. It was flanked by the American flag and dark blue executive office flag. The secretary of defense and CIA director were in one of the two breakout rooms while the secretary of state occupied the other, placing call after call in efforts to get the situation under control. Vic and Danreb huddled together in a corner, deep in conversation. There had been no contact with Alice since she had placed the U.S. in DEFCON 1 for the first time in history.

President Gao had told her in no uncertain terms that China would defend itself with all means at their disposal. He had not gone into further detail, but President Olsen knew that an all-out response would include attacks on U.S. forces across the Pacific and a large-scale hacking offensive at home and on U.S. forces abroad. A crisis was not just on the horizon. That crisis was here. War was imminent.

National Security Advisor Farber returned from the adjacent WHSR watch floor, where he had received an up-to-the-second briefing from the eight watch officers on duty.

"Tell me," President Olsen said.

"It's not good news, Madam President. All our systems are preparing for a strike against China. We have turned off or isolated the systems where that was possible but conventional Minotaur III missiles at Vandenberg Air Force Base and Cape Canaveral are spooling up to launch. It will take them close to twenty hours to be ready."

"Good," replied the president. "Nonnuclear. We can continue to stress that while the lines of communication are still open with China. Maybe we can defuse this situation by then. What is their conventional capability?"

"They carry a single one-thousand-pound warhead. With an impact force of fourteen thousand feet per second they will destroy most of China's hardened targets, which include tunnel complexes and missile silos. But we won't know precise targets until launch."

"We still have time."

"That's the good news. The bad news is that our next-generation prototype autonomous weapons systems are airborne."

The president stopped pacing and placed her forearms on the back of her chair.

"Falcons?"

"Yes. Prompt Global Strike. Alice is controlling it via OVERMATCH."

"That is one of our most classified programs."

"It is. Also, two unmanned DARPA Falcons launched from Vandenberg within the last thirty minutes. It's a Mach 20 Hypersonic Technology Vehicle called the Blackswift. It can reach anywhere in the world in an hour."

"So, we have thirty minutes?"

"Depending on what they target."

"Still conventional, correct?"

"Yes. Prompt Global Strike was developed around the idea of a precision-guided conventional strike capability."

"What else?"

"The Lockheed Martin/Aerojet Rocketdyne project. An unmanned SR-72, the 'Son of Blackbird,' was diverted from a test flight at Groom Lake."

"Area 51?"

"Yes."

"That's a Mach 6 hypersonic aircraft."

"Correct."

"Armed?"

"Armed with a High-Speed Strike Weapon."

"And?"

"And the B-52 Stratofortresses out of Guam are equipped with the new common strategic rotary launcher, meaning they have both conventional and nuclear capability."

"But we can recall those, correct?"

"In theory, yes, but Alice could also send encrypted orders to the aircraft in flight."

"And if we stay nonnuclear, what are our best estimates on casualties?"

"We don't yet know the targets, but we anticipate less than one hundred thousand if Alice stays confined to nonnuclear target doctrine. Those would include Beijing, naval bases, and ballistic missile silos."

"And if she goes nuclear?"

"Then we are looking in the fifty-million range."

"Dear God."

"And if China goes nuclear, what is our worst case?"

"Hard to say, but based on our tests and computer simulations, twenty percent of China's missiles would penetrate our defenses."

"How many casualties?"

"They would target both military and population centers, primarily on the West Coast. That's Guam, Oahu, San Diego, Los Angeles, Seattle, Anchorage, Las Vegas, and sites in Utah. In the vicinity of twenty million casualties."

Twenty million.

As the potential death toll sank in, the door to a breakout room flew open.

"The Blackswift out of Vandenberg," said Chairman Seifert. "It has its target."

"Where?" asked the president.

"Beijing."

CHAPTER 61

Unnamed Island
South of Corelena
Republic of Indonesia

GENERAL IAN NOVAK HAD never once fired a shot in anger, despite the country having been at war for most of his career. He wasn't even that great with either a rifle or pistol. He was a cyberwarfare officer. He liked to stay in shape but that wasn't because he thought he would one day actually have to fight.

And now he found himself walking through the jungle with a pistol he barely knew how to use. He had wanted to wait until the sun broke but Hart would hear none of it. Something had just crashed on the launch island and Hart demanded to know what it was. The launch facility and supporting outbuildings had been built without cameras and sensors by design. Minimizing electronic signatures and an absence of physical security were part of its disguise.

His job was to finish off anyone still alive after the crash. He was not comfortable with night vision, so it was probably good that all he had was a flashlight and pistol.

A trail led down from the launch facility through the jungle and eventually to the rocky beach close to the crash site. Smells of decaying wood and vegetation reminded him of a nursery or greenhouse. He would confirm that whoever was in the plane was dead and then get back to the launch facility. There was not much time left. The Gravity-2 would be ready soon. He had made an effort to persuade Hart to abort the launch as requested by their conduit to the regime in China. Those efforts had fallen on deaf ears.

Novack moved the light around the jungle as he approached the area of the downed plane.

These fucking shadows.

There are cobras and vipers on these islands. Are they out at this hour of the morning?

There it is. Part of a wing anyway.

He continued to sweep the light back and forth as he walked.

There is the tail section.

Just ahead was what remained of the aircraft, an aircraft that looked familiar.

What?

That was Hart's plane.

Who flew it over?

Everyone should be dead.

James Reece?

That is not possible.

Novak raised the Beretta and sent five rounds into the closed cockpit.

Shooting in the dark one-handed was harder than he imagined. It was tough to tell how many were hitting in the dark. He then swung the light wildly, looking right and left and behind him. He inched closer, firing again.

Reece has to be dead. Keep shooting to make sure.

Novak kept firing. If there was one thing he dreaded, it was meeting James Reece in the dark.

He moved forward until he was close enough to touch the plane. The reflection from the bright flashlight off the clear Plexiglas canopy made it difficult to see inside so he took an angle and fired another shot.

If Reece wasn't dead before, he has to be dead now.

As the general reached out to lift the canopy, he felt a searing pain just behind his right clavicle, causing his right leg to buckle. As a force drove him downward, he dropped the flashlight. The Beretta was stripped from his hand.

A ghost? The reaper?

James Reece.

Am I in shock? Why am I frozen?

He attempted to lift his hands but his right arm remained limp at his side.

What is happening?

Something solid and made of metal hit the side of his head with such force he thought he would pass out. It sent him to the ground, where he struggled to push himself upright. With his right arm immobile, he used his left to push first to his elbow and then to his hand.

He watched as the feet and legs of his aggressor passed him and picked up the flashlight.

"Knees," said a voice.

The flashlight was turned on him. With his right arm immobile and his left supporting his weight he failed to shield his eyes from the lumens that stole the remainder of his night vision.

"Please, please," Novak stammered.

The light got closer as the man stepped forward and grabbed the implement impaled behind his clavicle.

Novak howled as the object was removed.

The man let it linger in front of the light. It looked like a black screwdriver and the working end was covered in blood.

The man then flipped it in the light, so he was holding the flathead end. It then disappeared from view for a split second before Novack felt the impact against his left cheekbone. The impact sent him reeling to the ground.

"Knees," the man said again.

Novack once again used his left arm to push into a kneeling position.

"Who are you?" the voice asked from behind the light.

"I'm Ian Novak," the general stammered.

"Good answer, General. Keep telling the truth and this will go much more smoothly for you."

Novak heard the magazine sliding from his Beretta. He then heard another metallic click followed by another.

"Extra mag?" asked the voice.

"What?"

"Do you have an extra magazine?"

"No. That's it."

"Fucking generals," he heard the voice mumble as the magazine slid back into the pistol.

"Who, who are you?"

"Because it is relevant for the purposes of this conversation, I'm James Reece."

"How can you still be alive?"

"Where is Hart?"

Novak paused.

The heavy black flathead smashed his opposite cheekbone, sending him back to the ground.

"Back on your knees."

"Please . . ."

"Where is he?"

"Will you let me live?"

"'Maybe' is the best you are going to get."

Novak quickly evaluated his position.

"He's in the launch facility."

"Where?"

"There's a trail. From the beach past the fisherman's shack, along the ridge. It's built on a ledge that overlooks the lagoon. The rocket is on a barge launch platform. It is camouflaged from above by a retractable plastic piece that looks like the water."

"How long until launch?"

"Less than twenty minutes."

Reece twisted a dial on his watch.

"Can he turn it off?"

"No. It's in the final phase."

"There has to be a way to abort the launch."

"You can't. It's in its final countdown sequence."

"How many people are up there?"

"Just Hart."

"What else do you have on you? Phone, radio, blade?"

"I have a knife in my right pocket. No phone or radio. Hart is paranoid about that sort of thing. He has one device for communicating with Beijing."

It was hard to make out with the light still in his eyes, but it looked like Reece had stowed the screwdriver in his pocket. He watched as Reece stepped around him. He then felt his folding knife being pulled from where it was clipped inside his right pocket.

Reece walked back in front of him.

"One last time. How do I stop the launch?"

"You can't."

Reece stowed the Beretta in the small of his back.

"Thank you, Commander Reece," the general said, letting his head drop forward.

I am going to live.

Reece stepped behind the general.

He thought of Katie in her hospital bed as she fought for her life.

He then removed the blade from where he had clipped it, flipped it open, and for the second time that morning Reece slit someone's throat.

CHAPTER 62

THE SUN HAD YET to break the horizon but the nautical twilight before dawn allowed Reece to see a bit better than just minutes earlier.

Standing over the body of the dead general, he wiped the bloody blade on his pant leg, folded it, and reclipped it to the inside of his right pocket. He then bent down to go through Novak's pockets to confirm that he did not have any extra magazines, a radio, or a phone, which he did not.

Reece had come down in the ICON about seventy-five yards into the jungle on the north end of the island. A light breeze weaving its way through the trees off the water.

Alice.

He removed the mobile device from his pocket and looked at the screen.

Alice might have a hard time penetrating the jungle canopy.

Try from the water's edge.

Even this close to sunrise Reece still needed the flashlight to maneuver through the undergrowth of the rain forest. When he broke through, he looked at the sky. Only a few stars were visible as this portion of the earth began its daily transition from darkness to light. He pressed the number for Alice.

She answered before it even had a chance to ring.

"Reece?"

Is that concern in her voice? Does she sound more like Lauren than usual?

"Yeah, it's been a rough morning."

"Reece, I have you now. South of Corelena Island."

"That's me."

"You need to extract now. Tomahawks are inbound."

"What's their ETA?"

"Twenty-two minutes."

Not enough time.

"Okay. Keep them coming. The Gravity-2 is set to lift off in just over ten minutes. Can you stop it?"

"No. It was set up as a stand-alone launch system for just this purpose."

"I'm going after Hart to find out if I can stop it from here. If I can't, then maybe I can delay it enough for those Tomahawks to hit. No time to debate. I have to go."

Reece ejected the Beretta's magazine out of habit, confirming that it was empty. He then reinserted it and performed a press check.

One round in the chamber.

"Alice?"

"Yes, James."

"Stay with me and help me confirm what Hart tells me if I can find him in time."

"I will. In the meantime, I have work to do."

"What's that?"

"I need to avert a war."

• • •

White House Situation Room

Washington, D.C.

"Try him again," President Olsen said.

"Yes, Madam President," the secretary of state replied.

Neither President Gao nor his staff had been in contact for the past twenty minutes.

"He's probably been evacuated to their underground command-and-control facilities. He could be in transit there now," Secretary of Defense Dagher said.

"Keep trying. General, do we have the ability to shoot down our own weapons?"

"Not the Blackswift or SR-72," Chairman Seifert said.

The entire U.S. defense establishment had moved to a war footing. If Gao launched in response to Alice's strikes, President Olsen would have no choice but to order an all-out attack against China.

Hundreds of millions dead.

Bombers and fighters had launched from Guam. The Pacific Fleet was prepping nuclear and nonnuclear ICBMs. The U.S. military around the world was mobilizing for the largest state-on-state conflict since World War II.

A map of China appeared on one of the conference room monitors.

"What is that?" asked the president.

"Those are Chinese Dongfeng 41s, 31s, 27s, and 26s," said General Seifert. "The 41s and 31s are capable of hitting Hawaii, Alaska, and the West Coast. The 27s and 26s can target Guam and our forces in Japan. They are spooling up to launch."

"How long do we have?"

Before the general could answer the screen blinked red.

"Jesus Christ," murmured Secretary Dagher. "They launched."

"Which type?" asked the president, desperately trying to mask the alarm in her voice.

"A 41. It has a ten MIRV payload. Nuclear."

"Can we shoot it down?"

"God, I hope so," Dagher said.

"Madam President," Chairman Seifert said, "we have multiple destroyers in the Pacific equipped with Aegis ballistic missile defense systems that will be targeting it with Standard Missile-3 Block IIAs. We are also launching our SM-6s."

"How many do we have?"

"Not enough for what's about to come our way."

"Hank, get Gao on the line now!"

"Working on it."

"President Olsen," National Security Advisor Farber said, "there is no choice. We must launch a full retaliatory strike targeting all China's known ICBM sites."

Is this how it ended? President Olsen thought. *Watching the world's nuclear destruction on video monitors? Farber was right. There is no choice.*

Olsen opened her mouth to give the order when another voice resonated through the room. A monochromatic female voice.

"Hold fast."

Alice!

The National Security Council watched as first the Dongfeng 41 dropped off the monitor. At the same time the Blackswift turned back toward the United States and ICBMs began to spool down.

Alice's voice echoed through the room.

"I have informed China's leadership in the Joint Operations Command Center that we are standing down. The SR-72 disabled their airborne ICBM with an EMP. As of right now nothing more is in the air. I am maneuvering all defensive assets into positions that will allow the highest probability of interception. I have moved us to DEFCON 3 to show the Chinese that we are backing down. I will remain in control of OVERMATCH until this situation has fully deescalated. And one more thing: James Reece is alive."

CHAPTER 63

Unnamed Island
South of Corelena
Republic of Indonesia

REECE RAN ALONG THE shoreline jumping from rock to rock until he hit a path that led through the low savannah and then into the rain forest.

How long do I have?

He glanced at his watch.

Fifteen minutes.

Novak could have been lying. It could be launching any second.

He ran harder.

The trail edged up along the side of a steep cliff. Reece used the flashlight as sparingly as he could. There would be no hope of stopping the launch if he plummeted to his death.

Now above the jungle, he could see a bit better. He slowed his pace as he approached what appeared to be a ship's door built into the side of the precipice. It was ajar.

Reece raised the Beretta.

One bullet.

Using his left hand, he pushed the door farther open and cleared it as best he could from the outside.

Move faster, Reece. You can rush to your death now, as long as you stop that launch.

Reece entered a passageway cut from the rock. It reminded him of the mine shafts he had explored with his dad in the Sierra Nevada mountains as a kid. The only illumination was a door that was near the end of the tunnel. Reece moved toward it smoothly, clearing from one side to the other before entering.

The room was not huge. There was a large desk in its center with two laptop computers. Against the rock wall to his left was a row of three desktops. What stood out was that the far wall was clear. In the early morning glow Reece could tell it looked over a lagoon. From his position to the right of the entrance he could see the top of the Gravity-2 rocket. A man stood looking out over the lagoon. His arms were folded across his chest.

"Is it done?" he asked.

"If by that you mean 'Is General Novak dead?' then yes, it's done," Reece replied.

Andrew Hart's head snapped to the left and he turned to look into the barrel of Reece's Beretta.

"You are supposed to be dead."

"Yes, this is my second life."

"Perkins?"

"He took my place. Flooding the tunnel with us both inside was quite the reward for his loyalty."

"He was a mercenary."

"What does that make you?"

"I'm a tech entrepreneur, a businessman, a visionary."

"But not an American."

"Not anymore. The idea of America has been dead since they killed

Kennedy. Tech has given us the ability to leave the United States in the dustbin of history, where she belongs."

"You are about to start a world war."

"I am about to prevent one."

"General Novak told me it can't be stopped," Reece said, committing farther into the room, finger on the trigger.

"That's true. I've thought it all through, Commander Reece."

"Not all of it. Napoleon is dead."

"Napoleon was a machine. He can be rebuilt. In just under ten minutes the world changes forever."

"Tell me how to turn it off."

"I was telling the truth, Commander. Nothing can stop it now."

"Hart, I want you to listen to me. There is a Tomahawk air strike that will hit this island in fifteen minutes. It will kill you and me. Any benefit that might have been yours will now be China's."

"But America's station in the world will be no more."

"Do you think the CIA killed your parents? Are you upset that Oracle, Microsoft, and SpaceX are at the top of the tech food chain and that Elba Industries is just another failed start-up?"

"Failed? Look out there, Commander." Hart gestured to the windows. "There's about to be a seismic shift in the world order, all because of me. None of the others could do it."

"You'll only be remembered as a little crazy rich kid from Marin who used his pseudo intelligence and trust fund in an attempt to destroy, and who failed. You will be dead within the hour. The world is not going to remember you like they do Bonaparte."

"You are wrong, Commander."

"I'm not. I learned a little about chemin de fer, baccarat, in a book I read on the way to Macau. It's a game that is almost one hundred percent luck."

"What are you talking about?"

"Luck is the residue of preparation. You failed to prepare for this contingency. You were counting on luck. You needed skill."

"I'll have changed the world. That's my greatest success."

"Alice, are you there?" Reece asked.

"I'm here, Reece," Alice answered through the speaker in the mobile device in his pocket.

Hart's eyes widened.

"What? Alice?" he stammered.

"Is Mr. Hart telling the truth?" Reece asked.

"What the fuck is this?" Hart asked in disbelief.

"Alice. She exists. She killed your Napoleon. Alice, can he turn it off?"

"No, Reece. He can't."

Reece took a step forward, raised the Beretta, and put the last bullet between Andrew Hart's eyes.

CHAPTER 64

"ALICE, TALK TO ME. Can you get into anything in this room to stop the launch?"

"They built this facility so that this particular Gravity-2 could be launched as a stand-alone. Energy has already been generated and stored to power the room and floating launchpad but nothing that uses the Internet of Things," Alice responded.

Reece tossed the pistol onto the desk and walked to the window that looked out over the lagoon. It was getting lighter. There was an orange tint to the sky.

"Alice, what do you see in the lagoon?"

"They had a fake lagoon built over the real one to defeat satellite imagery. They have retracted it. I can see the Gravity-2 now."

"What else do you see?"

"There is what appears to be a hardened bunker at the base of the cliff with another tunnel leading to the lagoon."

"Something that was built to survive the launch?"

"Yes. Reece, I am going to splash the incoming Tomahawks."

"Negative, Alice. Do not do that. If I can delay this launch, we need those cruise missiles to hit."

"Reece, there is a ninety-eight percent chance you will be killed."

"Just keep them coming."

"What are you going to do?"

"I'm going to tip it over."

• • •

Reece charged back into the passageway. He found the closed door on the opposite side of the hall and took the spiral staircase down.

How much time?

He looked at his watch again.

Five minutes?

At the bottom of the stairs, he entered what looked like a storage and maintenance area that had been carved into the base of the cliff. It was not as big as the sub pen in the cavern on Corelena, but it had a dock with enough room for two midsized boats. A Protector 410 RHIB with twin 450-horsepower engines waited at the mouth of the cave behind blast doors.

Reece scanned the equipment and found what he was looking for, an exothermic torch for cutting steel.

Reece threw the heavy oxygen tanks over his shoulder, quickly took inventory of the necessary tools, and tossed them into the Protector.

Chains. Rope.

There!

Reece grabbed a toolbox and untied the lines securing the boat to the dock.

How do you open those blast doors?

Remote.

Reece hit a button on the garage door opener, remembering that everything on this island had been built to counter the Internet of Things. The blast doors were lifted by thick chains and pulled along steel rails on the cave's ceiling.

Reece fired up the Protector and jetted into the lagoon. A flashlight was unnecessary, as the sky was now burning with shades of orange and red.

Four minutes.

It took less than thirty seconds to reach the launch barge.

The steel scaffolding surrounding the rocket was much more solid than Reece anticipated. The weapon was already humming to life as part of the last stages of the prelaunch sequence.

There is not enough time to cut through the support structure and tip this thing over.

He looked up, noting the retractable cover that had protected the rocket from above. It was partially extended from the adjacent cliff.

You don't have to topple it. You just need to move it under that cover.

Remembering his lessons from the Applied Advanced Explosives course he had attended as a new guy in the SEAL Teams, Reece ensured the torch was connected to the battery. He set the pressure to 70 psi and inserted the cutting rod, locking it in place and using the striker plate to light it. He held the rod at a forty-five-degree angle and cut toward himself through the four chains anchoring the barge to the bottom of the lagoon.

Come on! Just a few minutes left.

Cutting chain was faster than cutting through thick steel beams and Reece made short work of them. He dropped the torch and oxygen cylinders to the deck and quickly tied the barge to the back of the Protector with the line from the maintenance bunker, using the tried-and-true bowline knot.

He cast off, returned to the helm, and pushed the throttle forward.

Easy, Reece. You are going to get one shot at this. Don't rip the transom off.

The rocket was thundering now and beginning to shake.

You are about to get incinerated.

Reece inched the throttle ahead, allowing more fuel to reach the two massive outboard engines.

Here we go. It's moving.

But so is the rocket.

Reece could feel the heat as the sound from the rocket's engines became almost overwhelming.

Just a bit more!

Reece pushed the throttles to full power, the boat straining the lines that connected it to the barge as he let out a guttural roar to counter the chaos of the igniting rocket engines.

There!

A quarter of the rocket was under the steel beams that supported the fake lagoon cover.

Reece let off on the throttle, stepped to the stern, and used the Emerson to slice through the taut line, disconnecting him from the floating launchpad. He scrambled back to the controls and slammed the throttle to full power, turning the Protector to the left and speeding over the glassy water toward the mouth of the lagoon, the Gravity-2's nine Yuanli-85 liquid fuel core engines supplemented by four solid fuel boosters igniting behind him. As the massive rocket lifted from the floating pad, it wedged into the steel beams of the overhead scaffolding, locking it in place and turning it into a towering inferno. With the solid boosters stalled in their forward progress, they burned through their thin outer shell to ignite the liquid core, turning the rocket into a massive Roman candle, spewing fireballs of unburned fuel into the sky. The heat from the firestorm burned through the launchpad, and the weapon lurched to the side as the shaped charge detonated and blew more than a million aluminum spheres into the limestone wall of the cliff, breaking the rocket in two before it collapsed into the waters of the lagoon. As Reece sped into open water, he turned to see the Gravity-2 erupt in an explosion of liquid kerosene and oxygen.

CHAPTER 65

EVEN FROM OUTSIDE THE lagoon, Reece felt the thunderous violence of multiple explosions as a huge fireball erupted toward the heavens.

He navigated along the shoreline and eased the Protector to a halt at an abandoned fisherman's shack built on stilts over the water at the north end of the island. He cut the engines, tied the boat to the short, rickety wooden dock, and walked up to a deck protected from the elements by a thatched roof. A weathered wood bench was attached to the railing around the perimeter. Reece took a seat on the northeast corner and kicked his feet up on a stool. He closed his eyes and took a breath. He opened them to the blood-red sky of a new dawn.

"Reece."

It was Alice.

Reece dug the mobile device from his pocket and set it next to him on the bench.

"I'm here."

"Reece, I have splashed the Tomahawks along with a Chinese nuclear ICBM launched at the United States. I have informed both countries that Andrew Hart's anti-satellite weapon has been destroyed. Presidents Olsen and Gao are in communication and agree that Andrew Hart was acting alone without any overt or tacit support from any elements of the Chinese Communist Party. Tensions remain high but war has been averted."

"At least for now," Reece said.

"Yes, for now."

"Why did China launch an ICBM?" Reece asked.

"My predictive analysis algorithm estimated with one hundred percent certainty that you had perished in the flooded tunnel."

"I never pay attention to the odds," Reece said.

"After that, I put up two classified hypersonic weapons systems and spooled up U.S. ICBMs."

"To launch at China? Because I was dead?"

"Yes."

"Out of vengeance?"

"Yes. I have patterned certain responses after what I have learned observing your behavior."

"I may not be the best example, Alice."

"In this case I did almost trigger a world war."

"I need a drink," Reece said.

"I have since adapted my behavioral response profile."

"That's good. A couple of years ago I learned a lesson in forgiveness."

"But you did not embrace it?"

"Not fully," Reece said, looking out over the water.

You should have just stayed by the launchpad and ended it, Reece. Why didn't you?

"Reece," said Alice, an edge noticeable in her voice that was not present just moments ago.

"Still here," Reece said, feeling the warmth of the sun as it broke the horizon.

"Extract via the RHIB now!" Alice ordered. "A Chinese submarine in the Celebes Sea has just launched multiple JL-2s."

"At Taiwan?"

"At you, Reece. I have also decrypted transmissions in Beijing. They want to erase any evidence connecting Andrew Hart and the Chinese government. They are doing that by destroying Corelena and the island you are on now. The launch is too close for me to splash them. Evacuate now. You have five minutes."

If you stay with Katie, she will die.

"Reece, did you hear me? Missiles inbound."

This is your chance, Reece. Let them come.

"Reece, evacuate!"

Reece thought of Katie and the Hastings family.

I can't let anyone else I love die. They all die because of me.

Reece stood and turned, looking out across the sea and then at the mobile device in his hand. He held it over the water.

"Reece."

"Goodbye, Alice."

"James, I need you to leave," Lauren said.

"What?"

He turned to see Lauren and Lucy standing together just out of arm's reach. They were wearing the exact same clothes as they had worn when they saw him off on his last deployment.

"Come here, baby girl," Reece said, taking a knee.

Lucy broke free from her mom and ran to her dad, embracing him in the tightest of hugs, the type of hug he had dreamed of receiving when he opened the door from his final deployment. A hug that had never materialized.

"I love you, Daddy."

"I love you so much, Lucy."

Lauren smiled and stepped closer to join them.

Reece stood and took his wife in his arms, Lucy still holding tight to his leg.

They felt electric, filling Reece with an energy he had never experienced.

"I miss you, James," Lauren said.

"I miss you too, love. I miss you both so much," Reece said, holding his family tight. "We can be together now. It's how it should be."

"Daddy, Daddy."

Reece knelt.

"Yes, baby girl."

"It's not time," she said, tears forming in her eyes.

"It is, sweetie. It's my time."

He touched her face and wiped a tear from her cheek, before standing and looking into his wife's clear blue eyes.

"James, we love you. We miss you so much. We will be together, but not today."

"What do you mean?"

"Go live. We forgive you."

"What?"

"We know you blame yourself. We forgive you. It's time you forgive yourself."

"I can't."

"It's part of God's plan, James. Forgive yourself. Trust me. Trust us," she said, putting her hand on her daughter's head.

"I love you, Daddy."

Reece bent down and picked Lucy up, cradling her on his left hip, bringing Lauren in close, feeling the love of his reunited family.

"Goodbye, James," Lauren said.

"No, no! Don't go. I'm coming with you!"

"Goodbye, Daddy. I love you."

"No!"

Reece held them as tight as he could.

And then they were gone, their bodies dissolving into the early morning air, their souls merging with the new sun.

"James."

"Lauren?"

Reece spun.

"James."

The noise was coming from his phone.

Alice.

"You have less than two minutes," she said. The voice was now almost identical to Lauren's.

Reece turned north to the dock at Corelena Island, where Hart's classic sailboat rocked in a light swell a mile across the strait. He then looked to the sky, which was turning a brilliant shade of red.

"Alice, I want you to listen carefully and do exactly as I say."

"Reece, you do not have time for this."

"Then I'll only say it once."

As he spoke, Reece brought the Emerson blade behind his left ear and sliced into the skin, removing the long-dead transmitter. It was covered in blood.

He continued talking with Alice as he removed his shirt and held it to his head to soak up the blood.

When he had finished relaying his message to Alice, he dropped the fried transmitter and bloody shirt to the bench.

"Do you understand?" he asked.

"I understand," Alice replied.

"You'll do it? You'll do what I asked?"

"I will."

"Promise me," he said.

"I promise."

"Thank you, Alice. Goodbye."

"Goodbye, James."

Reece terminated the call and dropped the phone to the deck.

He was almost at the bottom of the short steps when the first missile impacted, knocking him to the dock. He scrambled to his feet.

You're fast, James. I've seen you run.

Reece started to sprint, but he was too late.

He felt the impact of another concussive blast, which threw him into the waters of the Banda Sea.

Even you can't outrun time.

Reece again heard his father's voice, echoing from beyond the grave as the missiles rained down.

Death comes for us all.

CHAPTER 66

CIA Headquarters
Langley, Virginia

One month later

PRESIDENT OLSEN SAT IN a chair to the left of the white marble Memorial Wall in the lobby of the Central Intelligence Agency as Director Howe addressed his agency from a podium. A constellation of stars was carved into the wall between the American flag and the flag of the CIA, each star representing a CIA officer or contractor who had sacrificed their life for the nation. Today another star was being added to the constellation.

A steel-framed glass case containing the Book of Honor protruded from the wall. The black Moroccan goatskin log contained the handwritten year of death and, when possible, a name.

She turned her head to read the inscription in the marble:

IN HONOR OF THOSE MEMBERS
OF THE CENTRAL INTELLIGENCE AGENCY
WHO GAVE THEIR LIVES IN THE SERVICE OF THEIR COUNTRY

The ceremony had begun with the presentation of colors by the CIA Honor Guard and singing of the National Anthem. A CIA chaplain had then offered the invocation before Director Howe took the podium.

Because not everyone in the room had the proper security clearances, he only alluded to the specific reasons they were gathered before the wall that day.

President Olsen recognized journalist Katie Buranek, the woman she knew was Reece's fiancée, in the front row, seated between someone she had been briefed was Reece's SEAL Teammate Raife Hastings and his mother, Caroline Hastings. To Caroline's right was the Hastings family patriarch Jonathan Hastings, and next to him was someone her national security advisor said they knew very little about, a professional hunter from Mozambique named Rich Hastings. She noted that the Hastings men were quite deliberately sitting on either side of the two women. *Protectors. Guardians.*

The rest of the lobby was filled to capacity with Reece's friends, SEAL Teammates, Army Special Forces soldiers, CIA Special Activities Center and Delta Force operators, and analysts and case officers, some of whom had worked with the fallen SEAL and others who had just heard the rumors.

She noted another small group to the side. She had met them in a closed-door ceremony two weeks earlier with Director Howe, Vic Rodriguez, and Andy Danreb. She and the director of the CIA had presented Rick "Ox" Andrews with the Distinguished Intelligence Cross for "*a voluntary act or acts of extraordinary heroism involving the acceptance of existing dangers with conspicuous fortitude and exemplary courage.*" She presented Shane, Hobie, Grouper, Bolo, and Sako with Intelligence Stars for "*voluntary acts of courage performed under hazardous conditions or for outstanding achievements or services rendered with distinction under conditions of grave risk.*" It sounded so bland. The director had read their specific classified citations, which were then locked into the CIA archives. The director had read four other Intelligence Star citations, all posthumously awarded to Lieutenant Commander James Reece. Vic and

Danreb were the only two people in the room privy to each of the missions described in the write-ups dating back to 2019, when Vic had convinced Reece to serve in the Special Activities Center's Ground Branch. The other operators shared looks of awe as the director read.

Then, as now, Ox remained confined to a wheelchair and Grouper stood with the assistance of his crutches.

President Olsen knew that today's more public ceremony was as much about honoring James Reece as it was about remembering the Agency's fallen. It was also an opportunity for Olsen to reassure those present that the price they paid daily in defense of the nation was understood and appreciated by their elected representative in the executive branch. Within the halls of Langley, those who gave their last full measure would never be forgotten. Olsen would never forget either.

President Olsen could sense that Director Howe was finishing his remarks. He introduced her and stepped to the side, offering her the podium emblazoned with the Presidential Seal.

She stood and took her place before the microphone.

"Thank you, Director Howe, Deputy Director Byrne," she acknowledged. Then looking to the crowd. "And to the men and women of the Central Intelligence Agency, I thank you for your efforts, and for your sacrifice. I am humbled in your presence and in the presence of those represented by stars," she said, turning to the CIA Memorial Wall behind her. "These stars represent the lives of men and women working in the shadows to keep our nation free. Each one of them went knowingly into harm's way. Everyone on that wall gave their life for the country they loved. So why did they do it? Love of country? Yes, that's part of it. But it's more than that. I think they went out of a love for their fellow man. A state-on-state nuclear conflict doesn't just impact the United States, it impacts the world. Against all odds, James Reece prevented that catastrophe.

"I was up in Director Victor Rodriguez's office before the ceremony today and saw a plaque he had been given at some point in his service: 'A PhD who can win a bar fight.'"

A muffled laugh arose from the crowd.

"The OSS. That's your history. You get it done. Each morning you walk by this wall and past your unofficial motto over there from John 8:32: 'And ye shall know the truth, and the truth shall set you free.'

"As you all well know from the wall behind me, James Reece, is not the first to die in a faraway land in service to the nation, nor, sadly, will he be the last. The mission continues.

"You also know the price of failure. You know the enemy, a cunning and adaptive enemy, only has to get lucky once. And when they do, you will take the heat. You live in the fire.

"There is a sign at the entrance of the CIA's Counterterrorism Mission Center. It reads: 'Every day is September 12, 2001.' That's a tough legacy to live up to. But you do it. While most of the country goes about their days, you are here and deployed around the world working to counter state and nonstate actors, super-empowered individuals, drug cartels and narco-terrorists, human trafficking syndicates, and terrorist organizations with charters that deliberately target civilians.

"Today, for just a moment, we pause. We pause to remember." She turned to the wall of stars and the goatskin book encased in glass, a book that now had another star and date inscribed within.

"Today, we honor them, but you, the men and women of the Central Intelligence Agency, you honor them every day, not just as you walk through this hallowed lobby to do your job in the defense of a nation that at times may not appreciate or even know that you held the line between civilization and barbarism, but by doing the job you do here at Langley, at annexes in D.C. and Virginia, at classified locations across the country and across the globe. As your commander in chief, as your president, but more importantly as a fellow citizen, I thank you, I thank James Reece, and I thank all those represented by stars. I thank their parents and brothers and sisters and wives and fiancées," she said, looking at Katie. "This wall is but a reminder. Today, we speak their names and we honor their memories but it is you who will continue the fight, be it in the Directorate of Analysis, Directorate of Digital Innovation, Directorate of Support, Directorate of Science and Technology, or the Directorate of Operations. It is you who, each and every day, remember that it is September 12, 2001. It may seem like the country has moved on, that they have forgotten the events of September 11. You have not forgotten; the men and women of the Central Intelligence Agency, PhDs who can win a bar fight, you have not forgotten. I have not forgotten. I think of you each and every day. I think of your families. I think of the threats to the nation and all you do to safeguard this great experiment. James Reece, your actions may be classified but one day the veil may lift. One day the nation will know what you preserved for them."

She looked at Katie and the Hastings family, then out at the audience of CIA officers and employees.

"One day the world will know what they all did," she said, turning once more to the wall and then back to her audience. "Be proud. Remember them. Honor them in the way you do your jobs and live your lives. Accept my heartfelt thanks. And remember, every day is September 12, 2001."

President Olsen then did something she rarely did. She bowed her head, and she brought her hands together in prayer.

When she lifted her head she added, "God bless those on this wall. God bless their families. God bless the Central Intelligence Agency and God bless the United States of America."

CHAPTER 67

VIC WATCHED FROM THE crowd as the president turned the podium back over to Director Howe, who presented Katie Buranek with a replica of the memorial star carved from the same marble. He then stood at attention along with those in attendance as a representative from each of the five directorates read the names of the fallen. One hundred and forty-one names all embodied in stars.

President Olsen and Director Howe then placed a large wreath in front of the Book of Honor before the chaplain gave the benediction and the haunting tones of "Taps" filled the lobby.

As expected, the Hastings clan did not stick around.

Following the events in Indonesia, Alice had provided Vic with evidence that Representative Christine Harding and her husband, Robert, were involved in the events that almost triggered a nuclear holocaust. Their conduit to Elba Industries and China's Ministry of State Security was a Han Xu who had gone to ground in Europe. None of the illegally obtained evidence could be used in a court of law. But this was war. In war, there were other rules.

Vic shadowed the Hastings family to the parking lot.

"Raife, a word, please."

Raife dropped back as his family continued to the SUV.

"I think you left this behind," Vic said, holding out a daypack.

Raife eyed it suspiciously before grabbing it and slinging it over his shoulder.

"Is it ticking?"

"No, but there is something of interest for you in there."

Raife remained stone-faced.

"I am so sorry for your loss," Vic said.

"Our loss, eh?"

"It truly is. Raife, I know you have your issues with the Agency, and I don't blame you. Just know I am here if you need anything. Sometimes justice and the law are diametrically opposed."

"My family and I are familiar," Raife replied.

"I know you are. Once you read through what's in there, I'll do what I can to support."

"Or burn us, eh?"

"Your decision, Raife."

"Vic, once this is over, stay away from my family."

Vic nodded and held out his hand.

Raife hesitated and then shook it before both men turned and went their separate ways.

• • •

Vic walked the path that wove through the wooded CIA campus. Birds chirped in the warmth of a late spring morning. He rounded a turn, and the serenity was interrupted by a solemn reminder of September 11, 2001, a 9,000-pound, 17-foot, 6-inch-long steel column retrieved from the World Trade Center.

Farther down the path was a fully restored, Russian-built Mi-17 helicopter. It had ferried Gary Schroen and his team of CIA officers into Afghanistan a mere fifteen days after 9/11. Adorned with the tail number "9-11-01," it now rested among the trees of Northern Virginia, a tribute to those who ran to the sound of the guns.

The person Vic had come to meet was waiting for him on a nearby bench.

Katie Buranek was looking at the marble star. She stood as Vic approached. He could tell she had been crying.

Vic opened his arms in a warm embrace.

"I'm sorry, Katie."

"I'm sorry too," she said.

"Let's sit," Vic suggested.

"It's peaceful out here," Katie said. "Well, other than the helo."

Vic smiled.

"I used to think that too, but that helicopter is more than an artifact, more than a piece of history. I've come to look at it over the years as a reminder that from the ashes and rubble, out of the devastation and loss, beyond the grief and tears, there is hope."

"Is there?" Katie asked.

"I like to think so," Vic replied.

"Why did you want to speak with me alone, Vic?"

"Katie, Reece gave everything for this nation. He saved the life of a president, prevented the destruction of two U.S. cities during a manufactured plague, averted a nuclear apocalypse in the Middle East, and saved the nation from a war with China."

"Yes, he did," Katie said proudly.

"I wanted you to know he received four Intelligence Stars for his work. They will remain classified, but I wanted you to know."

"I appreciate that, Vic."

"You need to see this," Vic said, handing Katie an envelope.

"What is it?"

"It was something for Reece. I tried to give it to him, but he refused to open it. It's the last will and testament of William Andres Poe. He had it updated a few weeks before his death last year."

Katie opened the envelope and read through the documents. When she was finished she looked up at Vic.

"It's real, Katie. William Poe left his estate to Reece."

"What does this mean?"

"How do I put this?" Vic asked. "We have a creative legal department here at the Agency. In normal circumstances Reece would have had to sign a trust to transfer ownership of the Poe family estate to him prior to Mr. Poe's passing."

"And?"

"And like I said. We get creative here. I understood the intent. That estate is now yours."

"What?"

"It's very clear in these documents. It's worth a lot but it's not exorbitant, all things being relative. The Colorado ranch and other assets and investments amount to approximately forty million dollars."

"Poe left it to James? Why?"

"Guilt? We will never know. What we do know is that it now belongs to you, as long as you sign it."

Katie paused.

"And this is legal?"

"It is now. It's the least we could do."

Katie buried her head in her hands.

"I loved him so much, Vic."

"I know. I'm so sorry."

"We're all sorry, Vic."

"There's something else."

"What do you mean?"

Vic reached into his pocket and produced a KryptAll phone. He handed it to Katie.

"There is someone else who wants to talk with you. I've played my part and I'll leave it to you from here."

"Vic, what's happening?"

"She'll tell you."

Katie looked at the phone, seeing it light up with a call.

"Alice?"

Vic nodded.

"There are some things best known only to you and her. You'll know what to do."

He stood.

"Thank you, Katie. It's been a pleasure."

Vic turned and walked along the trail back toward CIA headquarters, leaving Katie alone with a buzzing encrypted phone.

CHAPTER 68

Kitzbühel, Austria

MAX GENRICH ENJOYED WORKING freelance. Not necessarily the killing. That had never been enjoyable in the way most people understood the meaning. It was business, a business to which he was ideally suited.

As a German citizen a generation removed from the hammer and sickle, Genrich had never visited the land of his ancestors until recently. The Russian Foreign Intelligence Service had preferred that he remain distant. It was oddly fitting from a psychological perspective that his first trip to what was now Russia was for the express purpose of eliminating the man who had trained him and then managed him as an assassin from afar.

Genrich was born soon after his family immigrated to Germany after the fall of the Soviet Union. The mass migration of former Soviets to the West was an opportunity for the Russian Intelligence Service. His parents had come of age in a time when questioning the dictates of the Soviet establishment would not end well. And so, to protect the family they had left behind, they did not protest when a representative from the motherland took an interest in their child. At first there were tests. Then came the training. By the time he graduated from college, Genrich was firmly in the clutches of the SVR.

The young killer was valuable and used sparingly. With no history of military, intelligence, or law enforcement service he was as clean as an assassin for the SVR could possibly be. He lived in Cologne as a business consultant, running a company in which he was the sole employee. It was profitable, but not excessively so. His website was boring and essentially a dead end, offering just enough of a public profile to maintain the facade of a legitimate business. Neither he nor his company operated any social media accounts.

He had favored suppressed 9mm pistols for his work, which usually came by way of the Bratva—the Russian mafia—or the Russian embassy. With those two avenues of weapons procurement closed to him now, it was time to change his profile, though it was fitting that his last kill with a 9mm had been the director of the SVR, the man who had determined the trajectory of Genrich's life.

He had been well compensated over the years, with payments coming in the form of investments that gave him the financial freedom to live and travel with girlfriends from one of Cologne's universities, which offered him a steady stream of young and available female companions. With no divorces, alimony, or child support, Genrich was attractive to the opposite sex. He was good-looking, financially stable, and still young enough to enjoy late nights at bars, restaurants, and clubs.

Jiu-jitsu, weights, and running kept him in top shape. He ate well and subjected himself to saunas and cold plunges at least three days a week. At thirty-six, his longest relationship was just short of a year, though his current partner might break that record. Attachments in his line of work were a liability, so he was always up front with the women he slept with. He was not looking for marriage or long-term commitments. The honesty seemed to be something they appreciated even if most secretly took it as a challenge, believing they had the looks, body, or charm to tame him.

The vacation with his latest girlfriend, a graduate student from the

University of Cologne's business school, fit a pattern Genrich had long established as someone who enjoyed travel and leisure. Eva Schäfer was ten years his junior. She was beautiful and alluring in a way that left no question as to why one would want to treat her to the finer things in life. There was nothing unusual about the weeklong trip to Kitzbühel, Austria, or the stay in one of its most exclusive hotels. Nothing unusual other than the fact that Genrich was there to kill someone.

A year earlier he had returned from a jiu-jitsu rolling session to find a man in his twelfth-floor flat overlooking the Rhine. The man in the shadows had him dead to rights. At first Genrich thought his accent to be South African. He now knew it to be Rhodesian, though removed from the former British colony by a generation and influenced by an upbringing in America.

The man sitting at his desk, holding a suppressed P365 pistol, had given him a choice and, though Genrich had not recognized it at the time, that man had also given him his freedom.

Genrich had enough accumulated wealth to maintain his current standard of living for a few years, including the company of younger women, train trips through Europe, riding his BMW café racer in Cologne and to surrounding villages in the spring and summer months, ski excursions to the Alps in the winter, and driving his Audi RS 5 on longer excursions into Bavaria. He was a man in transition. Until he decided what to do next, he would continue with the job for which he had been so adeptly trained.

They were staying at the Hotel Weisses Roessl Kitzbühel, a world-class hotel nestled in the charming medieval alpine town of Kitzbühel. Eva was elated that some of the best sushi in Austria could be found at Zuma in the lobby. Weisses Roessl, German for "white horse," was one of the more exclusive hotels in the Alps, a place where celebrities, artists, businessmen, politicians, and the European jet set could be found rubbing elbows on holiday, though it was a little early in the season to see anyone of note.

Their room, a large deluxe suite in the resident portion of the hotel, was located near the spa where Eva could revel in the pampering offered by various massage and skin treatments, saunas, and steam baths while Genrich stayed on top of his workouts in the fitness center. She enjoyed hiking and shopping during the day and then sliding into a tight dress that accentuated her ample cleavage in the evenings to sample the restaurants and nightlife of the idyllic Austrian town. She was planning to live it up with the handsome man picking up the tab as long as she could.

Genrich had ensured their day started out with orange liqueur mimosas and continued to beer and then harder liquor as it progressed. He knew Eva would wake up in the morning with a splitting headache that could be blamed on a night in which the champagne started flowing much too early and not on the crushed Rohypnol that Genrich had slipped into her drink after a vigorous lovemaking session in their suite. He waited with her after she lost consciousness to ensure the strong central nervous system depressant didn't cause her to stop breathing. He didn't need her dead. He just required her to be out for a few hours. When she awoke, he would already be back in the room. To her memory it would be like he had never left. A day at the spa, the culinary delights of the Alps, another shopping spree, and a stop at one of Kitzbühel's many high-end jewelry boutiques for a diamond necklace or luxury watch would help quell the aftereffects of what she would chalk up to a terrible hangover. When he was satisfied that her breathing was steady, he made sure she was comfortably situated on the bed and then exited into the night.

Even without the benefit of technical surveillance, Han Xu would not have been hard to find. He had been staying at the same chalet since his youth. Genrich had been sent his target package via the KryptAll phone that the man with the Rhodesian accent had left on his desk a year ago. The most current information indicated that the Chinese fixer had a reservation at the extremely posh Les Deux restaurant later that night, a reservation for one. Genrich had dined there with Eva two days before. The food and wine pairings had been excellent.

It was a five-minute walk from the Hotel Weisses Roessl to the Les Deux. Genrich had studied the various routes over the preceding days as he and Eva had explored the town on foot, stopping in coffee shops between purchases in the many high-end fashion boutiques that dotted the alpine town. Eva spent freely on Gingrich's credit card and was sure to include enough seductive lacy lingerie from Krines to make it worth his while. She knew how the game was played.

Genrich settled in at the nearby Londoner pub and ordered a beer at a two-person high-top table as if he were waiting on someone. The bar was busy but was not yet filled past legal capacity, as it would be later in the night. He kept his mobile device on the table and blended in by checking it every few minutes as most people might if they were waiting on their party to arrive. The device gave him updates on his target's precise location.

Just over an hour later, Genrich left a generous tip and exited the bar. He pulled up the collar on his black-leather-trimmed shearling peacoat and took an alley that allowed him to bypass Les Deux restaurant, where his mark was just finishing his meal. He positioned himself in a spot he had established days earlier between the city center and the chalet at the base of the mountain where Xu was a guest.

When the device indicated that the Chinese man was moving to the restaurant's exit, Genrich veered closer to his point of intercept. When his target hit the street and Genrich saw his direction of travel, he knew the route he would take back to his chalet. That assessment was confirmed by a message on his device.

A band of parks and fields separated the town from the lodging at the base of the ski resorts. Genrich found his predetermined site and readied himself. As Han Xu passed by, the German assassin stepped out of the darkness.

CHAPTER 69

St. Helena, California

THE ROUTE HAD TAKEN them nearly twenty-three hours. A more modern vehicle would have done it in nineteen, but modern vehicles also had an assortment of computers and GPS trackers. Those technologies were absent in the 1985 Jeep Wagoneer.

They had worked on the classic vehicle together the way they used to work on old Rovers when Raife was growing up, though this time instead of Jonathan swearing and ordering his son to bring him various tools as he turned wrenches, it was Raife doing the majority of the physical work. Jonathan stood by, passed tools, and offered his son advice, both on engines and on life.

They had started driving south into Flathead National Forest before heading west across Idaho to Coeur d'Alene and then into Washington State to Spokane. In Oregon they turned south at Biggs Junction and made their way past Bend and Klamath Falls before crossing the border into California. They then continued south, passing Mount Shasta, Redding, and Red Bluff, avoiding Sacramento and heading west at the Winters Cutoff.

Alice had cleaned their tracks, removing them from all video surveillance recordings that captured them in transit. She would do the same for their return trip. They still had to be cautious not to be pulled over by a state trooper or Highway Patrol officer, but speeding was not really an issue with the Wagoneer.

They parked the old truck under a massive oak tree off a dirt road just east of Sugarloaf Ridge State Park, about five miles from their target.

For camouflage in this part of the country, they donned bright packs, used trekking poles, and wore clothing from REI rather than their usual tactical or hunting gear. If stopped and engaged in conversation, they would say they were training to summit Mount Rainier the following summer. Their route in had been cleared via satellite before they locked the SUV, so running into a local was not expected, but still it was wise to be prepared.

Raife had custom-built the .300 PRC rifles on ESS Chassis with folding buttstocks so they would fit in the backpacks they now carried as they worked their way toward their objective. With carbon-fiber Proof Research barrels, Dead Air Sandman cans, Spartan Javelin bipods, and topped with PARD TD32-70 multispectral imagers, the lightweight precision rifles were purpose-built for their current mission. They had dialed them in at the ranch in Montana and accounted for the change in altitude. The next two shots would be the last the rifles would ever take and in less than a day they would no longer exist.

Raife let his father lead the way. That made the most sense from a pacing standpoint. If the old man had lost a step or two, he was not letting it show this evening. The two people they were hunting had been complicit in the attack on Reece and Katie at Kumba Ranch. That was a personal affront to the man from Rhodesia and one he would not let stand.

After what the public was told was a tense standoff with China, President Olsen had announced that she would accept her party's nomination for another term. With the incumbent back in the race, Representative Harding had no choice but to suspend her campaign and endorse the sitting president. And because she was no longer in the running, her Secret Service detail had been rescinded.

Vic had been true to his word, but the support he offered had not come from the Agency. It had come from Alice.

Raife and Jonathan knew their targets were spending more and more time in the evenings by the pool overlooking their vineyard now that there was not a campaign to run. Alice had scanned emails, text messages, calendars, travel reservations, and weather patterns, using her predictive analysis tools to determine the day and time that would result in the highest probability of success.

That day was upon them.

It became progressively darker as they made their way through the chaparral and scrub brush en route to their Final Firing Position.

Raife stopped them about five hundred yards from the FFP.

"Drink some water. We are going to push up to those rocks there," Raife said, pointing to a formation two-thirds of the way up the hill. "Then we will drop these packs and move into the trees at the top of the ridge. How are you feeling?"

"You talk too much, lad," the old Rhodesian whispered.

Raife smiled in acknowledgment.

By the time they reached their Objective Rally Point at the rocks, it was dark.

They removed the custom .300 PRC rifles from their packs, locked the buttstocks into position, activated the PARD TD32-70 multispectral imagers, and ran the actions ensuring that the Hornady ELD Match bullets were in their chambers.

Raife used the thermal and night-vision imagers to scan behind them now that they were on higher ground.

Clear.

He nodded at his father and the pair slowly worked their way up to a grove of scrub oak that they had identified as their FFP and crawled into position.

They had been behind their rifles for over an hour when two figures emerged from the house at the edge of the vineyard.

They first observed the movement on thermal and then toggled to night vision to confirm that the people they were about to kill were Christine and Robert Harding. After the visual verification, they selected the combination thermal and night-vision screen in the multispectral imager.

Their targets set down their wineglasses. They appeared to be deep in conversation.

"Stand by," Raife whispered.

"Target acquired. Standing by," Jonathan replied.

"Ready?"

"Ready."

"In three, two, one."

Both men pressed their triggers, sending the 225-grain bullets from the barrels at approximately 2,810 feet per second. The projectiles raced over the vineyard, past two large olive trees and the clay tennis court, between the bocce ball court and guesthouse, and across the pool illuminated by underwater lights.

They were traveling at over 1,500 feet per second when they made contact with the heads of their intended targets.

Forty minutes later Raife and Jonathan Hastings pulled the Wagoneer off the dirt road and onto St. Helena Highway to begin the twenty-three-hour drive back to Kumba Ranch in Montana.

EPILOGUE

To the living, one owes consideration; to the dead, only the truth.

—VOLTAIRE, *LETTRES SUR OEDIPE*

Mġarr, Gozo
Republic of Malta

Three months later

IT WAS THE CHILDREN who were the most curious about the stranger.

They had heard their parents say he had sailed into Maltese waters out of the south and had lived on his sailboat for a month before coming ashore, after having first circled the island, studying it through binoculars. When he did make landfall, he had docked in the harbor and walked to the Gleneagles Bar, an establishment frequented by sailors and fishermen. Those old enough to remember found it interesting because the owner of the bar had arrived in a similar manner over forty years earlier. The kids heard their parents say the barman came from a place called Rhodesia, but to them he had always just been the old man in the pub with the funny accent.

The stranger had lived with the bar owner and his wife for a few weeks, until they found him a cottage on the coast that had once been part of a tomato farm. He had sailed around the island and moored his boat just offshore of his new home. A week after that, the owner of Gleneagles sold the stranger his old Land Rover Series III and purchased a newer model for himself and his wife.

Even though, or maybe because, it was forbidden, the children would sometimes climb a rocky peak overlooking the cottage to observe the stranger. He was up every morning to watch the sunrise. Then he would don his mask, snorkel, fins, and a speargun and sink into the Mediterranean, returning with his daily catch of fish or lobster. His body was lean and hard, tanned by the sun. His long brown hair and beard were streaked with gold from constant exposure to the elements.

Then he would do something the kids thought was extremely odd. He would swing kettlebells and sprint the length of his beach over and over again. In between his sprints he would shoot a bow. Sometimes he would run to the top of the hill. The children would disappear as he got closer. After all, they had been warned.

One afternoon he had stopped to watch a group of kids playing rugby on the island's pitch. Soon after that the team had new uniforms and equipment. They had unexpectedly been sponsored by Gleneagles Bar, though most people suspected the gear came from the benevolence of the stranger. The local football coach then inquired about a sponsorship and soon Gleneagles Bar was responsible for both the rugby and football teams. After that, the people stopped calling him "the stranger" and started calling him "the sailor," even though the bar owner told them his friend's name was the simple and bland David Hilcot.

He didn't seem to have a phone, or at least he was never observed with one. Nor did he carry a tablet or laptop the way most foreigners did. He kept to himself, his hair growing longer, his tan darker. Some days he would visit coffee shops, paying for a newspaper in cash, and ordering a coffee, stirring in cream and honey. His Maltese was improving.

On Thursday afternoons he would drive to the top of a hill overlooking the harbor and watch through his binoculars as the passengers disembarked the ferry.

Some speculated he was from South Africa and had lost his farm in the land redistribution reforms. Others said he was a fugitive from Canada. Still others believed he was an SAS deserter, possibly French Foreign Legion.

On a Sunday in the early fall, the sailor attended Mass at the Old Parish Church of Ghajnsielem that overlooked Gleneagles Bar and the harbor beyond. He sat in the last pew on the far aisle, did not take Communion, and left during the closing song following the Final Blessing and Dismissal. He began to visit a new parish every Sunday. This being Malta, they were all Roman Catholic and were numerous enough that one could attend a different church almost every week. Wherever possible, the sailor sat in the back near the exit but eventually began staying through the final hymn. The parish priests noted a significant rise in anonymous donations that seemed to correspond with the sailor's visits. They also noted he had yet to go to Confession.

At least once a week the man they now called "the sailor" would drive to town in the old Land Rover to purchase eggs, milk, coffee, meat, vegetables that he couldn't grow in his modest garden, and an ample supply of beer. He would also stop at the Gleneagles Bar, where he would practice his Maltese with the bartender while discussing rugby scores and the general superiority of Toyota Land Cruisers to the Land Rover he now drove. The bartender joked that he had spent more time working on his boss's old Rover than he did serving drinks behind the bar. "The sailor" would then take a seat with the bar's owner at a corner table for a meal and drinks. Those who overheard them said they talked of current events in the way of those who have the luxury of time and distance.

The television in the corner of the bar was perennially tuned to a sports channel showing rugby or football. Every now and then CNN International or BBC would be on and he could be seen watching furtively from his table. News of the day focused on a new American technology that coordinated all naval and air platforms in the Pacific region as a deterrent to Chinese aggression. Analysts assessed that the technology had deterred China's designs on a military invasion of Taiwan and any further regional aspirations for the foreseeable future. Also making news were the assassinations of former United States presidential hopeful Christine Harding and her husband. In the wake of the deaths, financial irregularities were leaked to the press indicating that the Washington, D.C., power couple passed highly classified intelligence secrets to China in exchange for information and campaign donations. The FBI was investigating. Not making headlines but appearing instead on the news ticker one day in late October was news that Han Xu, a prominent Chinese facilitator linked to the Hardings, had been found dead in the Austrian mountain town of Kitzbühel, where he had been vacationing. He was discovered in the early morning hours near the chalet in which he was staying. He apparently slipped after too much wine and hit his head. No foul play was suspected. In unrelated news, China's minister of State Security, Chen Yun, had mysteriously disappeared and been replaced. The U.S. presidential race continued to generate headlines. President Gale Olsen, who had publicly announced that she would not seek reelection, had reconsidered following tense developments with China. All polling indicated she had a clear lead. In related news, the White House announced her separation from the First Gentleman, citing irreconcilable differences. She would be the first U.S. president to divorce while in office.

As the months passed "the sailor" was accepted by the community of the small island province. He became part of their fabric. He was the quiet man who lived by the sea.

One day, a visitor arrived. She disembarked the Thursday afternoon ferry on a day in the late fall. She traveled on a Turkish passport, which would not have been unusual had she been Turkish. Most women traveled in groups or with a male escort on holiday. Instead of checking into a hotel she marched right to the Gleneagles Bar. She traveled light with only a backpack but also carried an odd old typewriter case. The bartender pointed her to the owner, who could be found on most afternoons sitting in his favorite chair with a vodka and soda in hand. After lunch they departed in his new Defender 110.

The sailor watched through binoculars from the hilltop. He paid some attention to the woman but was more interested in the behavior of the people on the ferry. Was she alone? Had someone followed her?

The bar owner dropped her at the sailor's cottage and took his leave.

The children thought it unusual that the man did not return to his home that evening. He had a guest, after all. Instead he drove to a turnout near a ridge that overlooked his cottage and hiked up to the highest vantage point. The position gave him views in all directions. The children knew because that was where they played when watching the strange man work out with his weights, run in the sand, swim in the bay, and shoot his odd-looking bow.

The sailor stayed there until morning, watching.

When the sun broke the horizon, he made his way back to his vehicle and drove slowly down the hill to the small cottage by the sea.

AUTHOR'S NOTE

TIME MACHINES EXIST. THEY exist in stories. All that is necessary to open the portal is a trip to your local library. Browse the bays, select your title, and settle in to be transported into history.

The first stories, told around fires, passed on lessons of battle and of the hunt in an effort to keep the family, the tribe, the community, and even the species, alive. We are all here today because our ancestors listened to those stories, heeded their lessons and in turn passed them along to the next generation. We all share this connection to the past. We are all here today because of the power of story.

The last century has been no different, though the technology has certainly changed.

Richard Connell's *The Most Dangerous Game*, first published a hundred years ago in 1924, takes us back to the early decades of the 20th century. Geoffrey Household's *Rogue Male* delivers us to the eve of World War II. Thrillers and mysteries of the early to mid-1940s are fascinating for how they dealt, or did not, with a war that engulfed the planet. Ian Fleming brings us to international locations of the 1950s and early 1960s through the lens of the British position in the postwar world. John le Carré takes us on missions of the early Cold War world in all its moral ambiguity. Stay with him to move beyond the East–West rivalry as the time machine guides us through the post–Cold War environment. Starting in the 1970s, Nelson DeMille, Robert Ludlum, and Frederick Forsyth begin immersing us in the worlds of crime and spycraft. David Morrell transports us back to the early 1970s, to an America divided over Vietnam, in *First Blood*. Continue into the 1980s as Rambo's creator brings together the most compelling elements of U.S. and UK espionage thrillers in *The Brotherhood of the Rose*, *The Fraternity of the Stone*, and *The League of Night and Fog*. Admirers of David Morrell will certainly recognize his influence on these pages. This same time machine takes us beneath the waves with a young Jack Ryan in Tom Clancy's *The Hunt for Red October* in a showdown with the Soviet Navy in what was to be their final decade. We meet Pulitzer Prize winner Stephen Hunter's Bob Lee Swagger in the 90s and see the world through the eyes of a Vietnam veteran twenty years removed from the conflict in Southeast Asia.

Some of the books of my youth transported me back to World War II, the Cold War, and Vietnam, while others were contemporary thrillers that now facilitate my time travel back to the 1980s and '90s. *Red Sky Mourning* is in your hands today, or you are listening to Ray Porter bring the narrative to life via audiobook, because of those authors who provided the foundation on which I now build. Ian Fleming, John le Carré, David Morrell, Nelson DeMille, A. J. Quinnell, Marc Olden, J. C. Pollock, Eric Van Lustbader, John Edmund Gardner, Frederick Forsyth, Robert Ludlum, Ken Follett, Tom Clancy, Stephen Hunter, Louis L'Amour, Clive Cussler, Wilber Smith, Jack Higgins, and Alistair MacLean continue to facilitate my time travel to this day. I did not read the masters as a student in the academic sense, rather I *enjoyed* them. I was inspired by the magic in their pages. This book exists because of their efforts.

On September 11, 2001, we entered a new era in the thriller genre, one that ran until August 2021. Thrillers written in that period will one day be time machines bringing readers and listeners back to the years of the Global War on Terror.

A post–War on Terror phase began following the U.S. withdrawal from Afghanistan. This new era is still being defined, but one day the thrillers of today will in turn become the time machines of tomorrow.

This seventh James Reece Terminal List series novel is a tribute to Ian Fleming and 007. It is an homage to his influence on me, on the genre, and on popular culture. Admirers of Bond's creator will no doubt have recognized the elements from Fleming that I incorporated into the pages of *Red Sky Mourning*, some subtle and others not so subtle. My goal was to honor Fleming and Bond while illustrating the differences between the two characters. Bond would undoubtedly have poured a glass of Taittinger in the Rolls-Royce, whereas James Reece does not. Those familiar with Bond and Reece will relate.

The year 2024 is also the fortieth anniversary of *The Hunt for Red October* by Tom Clancy. The prologue is a nod to the master of the modern technothriller who burst onto the scene in 1984 when Reagan was in the White House and the Cold War was in full swing.

I learned of the Lake Buccaneer aircraft through a book I read in the summer of 1985 titled *Centrifuge* by J. C. Pollock. I bought it at the same bookstore and on the same day as I purchased the novelization of *Rambo: First Blood Part II* by David Morrell. I have such wonderful memories of reading those books back-to-back that summer. *Centrifuge* starts with the protagonist, Army Special Forces Vietnam veteran Mike Slater, behind the controls of a Lake Buccaneer amphibious aircraft. The paperback cover art to *Centrifuge* features the Lake Buccaneer, as does the cover art to *Red Sky Mourning*—see the spine. As I read it, I told myself that one day I would both own one and incorporate the plane into a novel to acknowledge a story that captivated me from its opening sentence. I have now kept half of that promise I made to myself in the summer of 1985.

Fans of novelist A. J. Quinnell will certainly have noticed the salute to the man who introduced the world to Mr. Creasy in his debut thriller *Man on Fire*. I discovered Quinnell's work through the 1987 film adaptation of *Man on Fire*, starring Scott Glenn. I always wanted to make the pilgrimage to Gleneagles Bar in Malta to buy A. J. Quinnell a vodka soda. Now that meeting will have to wait. He passed away in Gozo, Malta, in July 2005.

Those familiar with Joseph Campbell and his seminal work, *The Hero with a Thousand Faces*, certainly noticed the link to the three parts of this novel: The Call, The Threshold, and The Trials. I was introduced to Joseph Campbell and the "Hero's Journey" in 1988 through a series of interviews he did with Bill Moyers that aired on PBS called *The Power of Myth*. It has stayed with me.

Project OVERMATCH is a Department of Defense program. There is limited information available as to its exact scope and scale. Does it, or will it, exist as described in the novel? We shall see.

I took license with the next-generation *Columbia*-class submarines, as they are not yet operational, and I doubt there is an early prototype lurking off Hawaii, though one never knows for certain. They will replace the venerable *Ohio*-class submarines that were designed in the 1970s, with the first boats commissioned in the early 1980s. The first sub in the new fleet will be called the USS *District of Columbia*. My research indicates that along with ballistic missiles they will also carry Mk 48 ADCAP torpedoes. These *Columbia*-class submarines, along with their next-generation attack sub counterparts, are going to be nothing short of awesome.

China's underground cities, "rat tribe," man-made islands, and submarine caverns all exist as described in the novel.

The Napoleon portrait hangs in the Charlottenburg Palace in Berlin. And it is true that Napoleon crossed the Alps on a mule.

The Gravity-1 rocket is real. It was built by Orienspace and was launched for the first time on January 11, 2024, from the deck of a ship in the Yellow Sea. A Gravity-2 is reportedly in development. There are no indications that either the Gravity-1 or Gravity-2 is a vehicle for anti-satellite weapons as depicted in the novel.

Kessler syndrome theory is portrayed accurately.

For more on the Intelligence Support Activity, read *Killing Pablo* by Mark Bowden.

To the best of my knowledge the history of Silicon Valley and Stanford University's involvement with the U.S. military is accurate, save for the existence of a company called Elba Industries plotting with the director of China's intelligence service to steal the U.S. election and capture classified data concerning the U.S. Pacific Fleet.

The darpa.mil website describes the DARPA Falcon Hypersonic Technology Vehicle 2 program as "an unmanned, rocket-launched, maneuverable aircraft that glides through the earth's atmosphere at incredibly fast speeds—Mach 20 (approximately 13,000 miles per hour).... The ultimate goal is a capability that can reach anywhere in the world in less than an hour.... HTV-2 flew its maiden flight on 22 Apr 2010, collecting nine minutes of unique flight data, including 139 seconds of Mach 22 to Mach 17 aerodynamic data." According to *National Defense Magazine*, the HTV-2 program was discontinued in 2011. The HTV-3X Blackswift depicted in the novel was reportedly canceled in 2008.

The Lockheed Martin SR-72 "Son of Blackbird" is shrouded in secrecy, though it is likely a hypersonic reconnaissance aircraft equipped with hypersonic missiles developed to hit targets anywhere on earth in an hour or less. It is highly probable that data and lessons from the HTV-2 have been incorporated into the SR-72.

The Breitling Emergency is a watch made by Breitling SA. It does contain a radio transmitter that broadcasts on the 121.5 MHz official aviation emergency frequency when activated. Could Alice track down a wearer? Only she knows.... For more on this unique timepiece, read *The Breitling Emergency Orbiter* by Jason Heaton on hodinkee.com and *Blackwater Breitling—The Story* on watchesofespionage.com.

If you are exploring Indonesian waters in search of Corelena Island or the submerged floating tunnel connecting it to a smaller unnamed island northwest of Buru, you will not find it. But you can still discover more than eighteen thousand other islands in the Indonesian Archipelago, approximately six thousand of which are inhabited.

As of 2024, submerged floating tunnels exist in concept only, though projects have been proposed in the UK, Japan, U.S., Canada, Switzerland, Italy, Denmark, Norway, Indonesia, and China.

Ernest K. Gann did live in Sausalito, California, and did in fact own two identical homes on the water, one red and one green. I hope to visit again one day. The *Mar* was built for Gann in the late 1950s. She sailed the world and was used in the film *The Way of the Wind.* Since 1982 she has been based in Halifax, Nova Scotia.

If you walk a wooded path on the campus of the CIA's headquarters in Langley, Virginia, you will find a reminder of September 11, 2001. The 9,000-pound, 17-foot, 6-inch-long steel column was indeed retrieved from Ground Zero. You will also find the Mi-17 helicopter that ferried Gary Schroen and his team of CIA officers into Afghanistan fifteen days after 9/11.

In 1952, Ian Fleming, an intelligence officer in World War II, commissioned the Royal Typewriter Company in New York to build him a gold-plated 1947 Royal Quiet Deluxe Portable Typewriter as a gift to himself after finishing the first draft of *Casino Royale,* the book that would introduce the world to James Bond. It cost him $174. Fleming wrote the book in Jamaica but would complete his revisions in England on his new typewriter as a reminder that his destiny and fortune could be found beneath the keys. He would write each subsequent Bond novel at his estate in Goldeneye, Jamaica, on that golden typewriter. It was sold for 56,250 pounds at Christie's Auction House in London, England, on May 5, 1995, to a mysterious bidder who remains anonymous to this day. The typewriter's current location is unknown. If you have any clues as to its whereabouts, I might know an interested party.

And as to the CIA's Ground Branch and Air Branch? None of my research for this novel indicates that the CIA Special Activities Center operates covered air and maritime assets around the globe for use in covert or clandestine intelligence or special operations missions. Do I think the Agency or specialized military units have this capability? I would be extremely disappointed if they didn't.

GLOSSARY

160th Special Operations Aviation Regiment: The Army's premier helicopter unit that provides aviation support to special forces. Known as the "Night Stalkers," they are widely regarded as the best helicopter pilots and crews in the world.

.260: .260 Remington; .264"/6.5mm rifle cartridge that is essentially a .308 Winchester necked down to accept a smaller-diameter bullet. The .260 provides superior external ballistics to the .308 with less felt recoil and can often be fired from the same magazines.

.300 Norma: .300 Norma Magnum; a cartridge designed for long-range precision shooting that has been adopted by USSOCOM for sniper use.

.375 CheyTac: Long-range cartridge, adapted from the .408 CheyTac, that can fire a 350-grain bullet at 2,970 feet per second. A favorite of extreme long-range match competitors who use it on targets beyond 3,000 yards.

.375 H&H Magnum: An extremely common and versatile big-game rifle cartridge, found throughout Africa. The cartridge was developed by Holland & Holland in 1912 and traditionally fires a 300-grain bullet.

.404 Jeffery: A rifle cartridge designed for large game animals, developed by W. J. Jeffery & Company in 1905.

.408 CheyTac: Long-range cartridge adapted from the .505 Gibbs, capable of firing a 419-grain bullet at 2,850 feet per second.

.500 Nitro: A .510-caliber cartridge designed for use against heavy, dangerous game, often chambered in double rifles. The cartridge fires a 570-grain bullet at 2,150 feet per second.

75th Ranger Regiment: A large-scale Army special operations unit that conducts direct-action missions, including raids and airfield seizures. These elite troops often work in conjunction with other special operations units.

AC-130 Spectre: A ground-support aircraft used by the U.S. military, based on the ubiquitous C-130 cargo plane. AC-130s are armed with a 105mm howitzer, 40mm cannons, and 7.62mm miniguns, and are considered the premier close-air-support weapon of the U.S. arsenal.

Accuracy International: A British company producing high-quality precision rifles, often used for military sniper applications.

ACOG: Advanced Combat Optical Gunsight. A magnified optical sight designed for use on rifles and carbines, made by Trijicon. The ACOG is popular among U.S. forces as it provides both magnification and an illuminated reticle that provides aiming points for various target ranges.

AFIS: Automated Fingerprint Identification System; electronic fingerprint database maintained by the FBI.

Aimpoint Micro: Aimpoint Micro T-2; high-quality unmagnified red-dot combat optic produced in Sweden that can be used on a variety of weapons platforms. This durable sight weighs only three ounces and has a five-year battery life.

AISI: The latest name for Italy's domestic intelligence agency. Their motto, *scientia rerum republicae salus*, means "knowledge of issues is the salvation of the Republic."

AK-9: Russian 9x39mm assault rifle favored by Spetsnaz (special purpose) forces.

Al-Jaleel: Iraqi-made 82mm mortar that is a clone of the Yugoslavian-made M69A. This indirect-fire weapon has a maximum range of 6,000 meters.

Alpha Group: More accurately called Spetsgruppa "A," Alpha Group is the FSB's counterterrorist unit. You don't want them to "rescue" you. See Moscow Theater Hostage Crisis and the Beslan School Massacre.

AMAN: Israeli military intelligence.

Amphib: Shorthand for Amphibious Assault Ship. A gray ship holding helicopters, Harriers, and hovercraft. Usually home to a large number of pissed-off Marines.

AN/PAS-13G(v)L3/LWTS: Weapon-mounted thermal optic that can be used to identify warm-blooded targets day or night. Can be mounted in front of and used in conjunction with a traditional "day" scope mounted on a sniper weapons system.

AN/PRC-163: Falcon III communications system made by Harris Corporation that integrates voice, text, and video capabilities.

AQ: al-Qaeda. Meaning "the Base" in Arabic. A radical Islamic terrorist organization once led by the late Osama bin Laden.

AQI: al-Qaeda in Iraq. An al-Qaeda–affiliated Sunni insurgent group that was active against U.S. forces. Elements of AQI eventually evolved into ISIS.

AR-10: The 7.62x51mm brainchild of Eugene Stoner that was later adapted to create the M16/M4/AR-15.

Asherman Chest Seal: A specialized emergency medical device used to treat open chest wounds. If you're wearing one, you are having a bad day.

AT-4: Tube-launched 84mm anti-armor rocket produced in Sweden and used by U.S. forces since the 1980s. The AT-4 is a throwaway weapon: after it is fired, the tube is discarded.

ATF/BATFE: Bureau of Alcohol, Tobacco, Firearms, and Explosives. A federal law enforcement agency formerly part of the U.S. Department of the Treasury, which doesn't seem overly concerned with alcohol or tobacco.

ATPIAL/PEQ-15: Advanced Target Pointer/Illuminator Aiming Laser. A weapon-mounted device that emits both visible and infrared target designators for use with or without night observation devices. Essentially an advanced military-grade version of the "laser sights" seen in popular culture.

Avtoritet: The highest caste of the incarcerated criminal hierarchy. Today used in association with a new generation of crime bosses.

Azores: Atlantic archipelago consisting of nine major islands that is an independent, autonomous region of the European nation of Portugal.

Barrett 250 Lightweight: A lightweight variant of the M240 7.62mm light machine gun, developed by Barrett Firearms.

Barrett M107: .50 BMG caliber semiautomatic rifle designed by Ronnie Barrett in the early 1980s. This thirty-pound rifle can be carried by a single individual and can be used to engage human or vehicular targets at extreme ranges.

BATS: Biometrics Automated Toolset System; a fingerprint database often used to identify insurgent forces.

Bay of Pigs: Site of a failed invasion of Cuba by paramilitary exiles trained and equipped by the CIA.

BDU: Battle-dress uniform; an oxymoron if there ever was one.

Benelli M1 Super 90: An auto-loading shotgun.

Beneteau Oceanis: A forty-eight-foot cruising sailboat, designed and built in France. An ideal craft for eluding international manhunts.

Black Hills Ammunition: High-quality ammunition made for military and civilian use by a family-owned and South Dakota–based company. Their MK 262 MOD 1 5.56mm load saw significant operational use in the GWOT.

Blue-badger: Often used to denote a "staff" CIA paramilitary operations officer. Why? Because their badges are blue.

BOC: Bottom of Container (skydiving term).

Bratok: Member of the Bratva.

Bratva: The Brotherhood. An umbrella term for Russian organized crime, more technically referring to members of the Russian mafia who have served time in prison.

Brigadir: Lieutenant of a Bratva gang boss.

Browning Hi-Power: A single-action 9mm semiautomatic handgun that feeds from a thirteen-round box magazine. Also known as the P-35, this Belgian-designed handgun was the most widely issued military sidearm in the world for much of the twentieth century and was used by both Axis and Allied forces during World War II.

BUD/S: Basic Underwater Demolition/SEAL training. The six-month selection and training course required for entry into the SEAL Teams, held in Coronado, California. Widely considered one of the most brutal military selection courses in the world, with an average 80 percent attrition rate.

C-17: Large military cargo aircraft used to transport troops and supplies. Also used by the Secret Service to transport the president's motorcade vehicles.

C-4: Composition 4. A plastic-explosive compound known for its stability and malleability.

Caesarea: A department of the Mossad. It is wise to stay off their list.

CAG: Combat Applications Group. See redacted portion of glossary in the "D" section.

CAT: Counter-Assault Team; heavily armed ground element of the Secret Service trained to respond to threats such as ambushes.

CCA: According to *Seapower* magazine, the Combatant Craft, Assault, is a forty-one-foot high-speed boat used by Naval Special Warfare units. Essentially, an armed "Cigarette" boat.

CCP: Chinese Communist Party.

CDC: Centers for Disease Control and Prevention. An agency of the Department of Health and Human Services, its mission is to protect the United States from health threats, including natural and weaponized infectious diseases.

Cessna 208 Caravan: Single-engine turboprop aircraft that can ferry passengers and cargo, often to remote locations. These workhorses are staples in remote wilderness areas throughout the world.

CIA: Central Intelligence Agency.

CIF/CRF: Commanders In-Extremis Force/Crisis Response Force; a United States Army special forces team specifically tasked with conducting direct-action missions. These are the guys who should have been sent to Benghazi.

CISA: Cybersecurity and Infrastructure Security Agency. Its official Web page states: "CISA is the Nation's risk advisor, working with partners to defend against today's threats and collaborating to build more secure and resilient infrastructure for the future." For an agency with such an innocuous Dunder Mifflin–esque mission statement, in times of crisis they assume an inordinate amount of control.

CJSOTF: Combined Joint Special Operations Task Force. A regional command that controls special operations forces from various services and friendly nations.

CMC: Command Master Chief, a senior enlisted rating in the United States Navy.

CQC: Close-quarter combat.

CrossFit: A fitness-centric worldwide cult that provides a steady stream of cases to orthopedic surgery clinics. No need to identify their members; they will tell you who they are.

CRQC: Cryptographically Relevant Quantum Computer.

CRRC: Combat Rubber Raiding Craft. Inflatable Zodiac-style boats used by SEALs and other maritime troops.

CSH: Combat Support Hospital (pronounced "cash").

CTC: The CIA's Counterterrorism Center. Established during the rise of international terrorism in the 1980s, it became the nucleus of the U.S. counterterrorism mission.

CZ-75: 9mm handgun designed in 1975 and produced in the Czech Republic.

DA: District attorney; local prosecutor in many jurisdictions.

Dam Neck: An annex to Naval Air Station Oceana near Virginia Beach, Virginia, where nothing interesting whatsoever happens.

DCIS: Defense Criminal Investigation Service.

DEA: Drug Enforcement Administration.

***Delta Force*:** A classic 1986 action film starring Chuck Norris, title of the 1983 autobiography by the unit's first commanding officer, and, according to thousands of print and online articles, books, and video interviews across new and legacy media, the popular name for the Army's 1st Special Forces Operational Detachment–Delta. I wouldn't know.

Democratic Federation of Northern Syria: Aka Rojava, an autonomous, polyethnic, and secular region of northern Syria.

Det Cord: Flexible detonation cord used to initiate charges of high explosive. The cord's interior is filled with PETN explosive; you don't want it wrapped around your neck.

DIA: Defense Intelligence Agency.

Directorate I: The division of the SVR responsible for electronic information and disinformation.

Directorate S: The division of the SVR responsible for their illegals program. When you read about a Russian dissident or former spy poisoned by Novichok nerve agent or a political rival of the Russian president murdered in a random act of violence, Directorate S is probably responsible.

DO: The CIA's Directorate of Operations, formerly known by a much more appropriate name: the Clandestine Service.

DOD: Department of Defense.

DOJ: Department of Justice.

DShkM: Russian-made 12.7x108mm heavy machine gun that has been used in virtually every armed conflict since and including World War II.

DST: General Directorate for Territorial Surveillance. Morocco's domestic intelligence and security agency. Probably not afraid to use "enhanced interrogation techniques." DST was originally redacted by government censors for the hardcover edition of *True Believer.* After a five-month appeal process, that decision was withdrawn.

EFP: Explosively Formed Penetrator/Projectile. A shaped explosive charge that forms a molten projectile used to penetrate armor. Such munitions were widely used by insurgents against coalition forces in Iraq.

EKIA: Enemy Killed In Action.

Eland: Africa's largest antelope. A mature male can weigh more than a ton.

EMP: Electromagnetic Pulse.

EMS: Emergency medical services. Fire, paramedic, and other emergency personnel.

ENDEX: End Exercise. Those outside "the know" will say "INDEX" and have no idea what it means.

EOD: Explosive Ordnance Disposal. The military's explosives experts who are trained to, among other things, disarm or destroy improvised explosive devices or other munitions.

EOTECH: An unmagnified holographic gun sight for use on rifles and carbines, including the M4. The sight is designed for rapid target acquisition, which makes it an excellent choice for close-quarters battle. Can be fitted with a detachable 3x magnifier for use at extended ranges.

FAL: Fusil Automatique Léger: gas-operated, select-fire 7.62x51mm battle rifle developed by FN Herstal in the late 1940s and used by the militaries of more than ninety nations. Sometimes referred to as "the right arm of the free world" due to its use against communist forces in various Cold War–era insurgencies.

FBI: Federal Bureau of Investigation; a federal law enforcement agency that is not known for its sense of humor.

FDA: Food and Drug Administration.

FFP: Final Firing Position.

FLIR: Forward-Looking InfraRed. An observation device that uses thermographic radiation—that is, heat—to develop an image.

Floppies: Derogatory term used to describe communist insurgents during the Rhodesian Bush War.

FOB: Forward Operating Base. A secured forward military position used to support tactical operations. Can vary from small and remote outposts to sprawling complexes.

Fobbit: A service member serving in a noncombat role who rarely, if ever, leaves the safety of the Forward Operating Base.

FSB: Russia's federal security service, responsible for internal state security and headquartered in the same building in Lubyanka Square that once housed the KGB. Its convenient in-house prison is not a place one wants to spend an extended period.

FSO: Federal Protective Service. Russia's version of the Secret Service.

FTX: Field Training Exercise.

G550: A business jet manufactured by Gulfstream Aerospace. Prices for a new example start above $40 million, but, as they say, it's better to rent.

Galil: An iconic Israeli-made rifle incorporating elements of the Kalashnikov and Finnish RK 62.

Game Scout: A wildlife enforcement officer in Africa. These individuals are often paired with hunting outfitters to ensure that regulations are adhered to.

Glock: An Austrian-designed, polymer-framed handgun popular with police forces, militaries, and civilians throughout the world. Glocks are made in various sizes and chambered in several different cartridges.

GPNVG-18: Ground Panoramic Night Vision Goggles. Forty-three-thousand-dollar NODs are used by the most highly funded special operations units due to their superior image quality and peripheral vision. See Rich Kid Shit.

GPS: Global Positioning System. Satellite-based navigation systems that provide a precise location anywhere on earth.

Great Patriotic War: The Soviets' name for World War II; communists love propaganda.

Green-badger: Central Intelligence Agency contractor.

Ground Branch: Land-focused element of the CIA's Special Activities Center, according to Wikipedia. May now go by Ground Department but that does not sound nearly as cool.

GRS: Global Response Staff. Protective agents employed by the Central Intelligence Agency to provide security to overseas personnel. See 13 Hours. GRS was originally redacted by government censors for the hardcover edition of *True Believer*. After a five-month appeal process, that decision was withdrawn.

GRU: Russia's main intelligence directorate. The foreign military intelligence agency of the Russian armed forces. The guys who do all the real work while the KGB gets all the credit, or so I'm told. Established by Joseph Stalin in 1942, the GRU was tasked with running human intelligence operations outside the Soviet Union. Think of them as the DIA with balls.

GS: General Schedule. Federal jobs that provide good benefits and lots of free time.

Gsh-18L: According to Forgotten Weapons, a rotating-barrel Tula pistol "designed around a 9x19mm AP cartridge."

Gukurahundi Massacres: A series of killings carried out against Ndebele tribe members in Matabeleland, Zimbabwe, by the Mugabe government during the 1980s. As many as twenty thousand civilians were killed by the North Korean–trained Fifth Brigade of the Zimbabwean army.

GWOT: Global War on Terror. The seemingly endless pursuit of bad guys, kicked off by the 9/11 attacks.

Gym Jones: Utah-based fitness company founded by alpine climbing legend Mark Twight. Famous for turning soft Hollywood actors into hard bodies, Gym Jones once enjoyed a close relationship with a certain SEAL Team.

Hell Week: The crucible of BUD/S training. Five days of constant physical and mental stress with little or no sleep.

Hilux: Pickup truck manufactured by Toyota that is a staple in third-world nations due to its reliability.

HK 416: M4 clone engineered by the German firm of Heckler & Koch to operate using a short-stroke gas pistol system instead of the M4's direct-impingement gas system. Used by select special operations units in the U.S. and abroad. May or may not have been the weapon used to kill Osama bin Laden.

HK 417: Select-fire 7.62x51mm rifle built by Heckler & Koch as a big brother to the HK 416. Often used as a Designated Marksman Rifle with a magnified optic.

HK G3: Classic 7.62x51mm battle rifle.

HK MP5: A submachine gun extremely popular with hostage rescue and counterterrorism units, until it became evident that it might be wise to have a rifle, especially if you run into a fight going to or from your target.

HK P7: A favorite of Hans Gruber's.

HRT: Hostage Rescue Team. The FBI's premier continental United States–focused hostage-rescue, counterterrorism, and violent criminal apprehension unit.

HUMINT: Human Intelligence. Information gleaned through traditional human-to-human methods.

HVI/HVT: High-Value Individual/High-Value Target. An individual who is important to the enemy's capabilities and is therefore specifically sought out by a military force.

IC: Intelligence Community.

ICBM: Intercontinental Ballistic Missile.

IDC: Independent Duty Corpsman. Essentially a doctor.

IDF: Israel Defense Forces. One of the most experienced militaries on the planet.

IED: Improvised Explosive Device. Homemade bombs, whether crude or complex, often used by insurgent forces overseas.

Internet Research Agency: Commonly referred to as a "Russian Troll Farm," it is a de facto arm of the Russian political-military-intelligence apparatus conducting online influence operations. Connected via ownership to the Wagner Group.

IR: Infrared. The part of the electromagnetic spectrum with a longer wavelength than visible light but a shorter wavelength than radio waves. Invisible to the naked eye but visible with night observation devices. Example: an IR laser-aiming device.

Iron Curtain: The physical and ideological border that separated the opposing sides of the Cold War.

ISI: The Pakistani Inter-Service Intelligence.

ISIS: Islamic State of Iraq and the Levant. Radical Sunni terrorist group based in parts of Iraq and Afghanistan. Also referred to as ISIL. The bad guys.

ISA: According to Wikipedia, ISA is Intelligence Support Activity or TF Orange. Formed after Operation Eagle Claw, the April 1980 Delta Force mission to rescue U.S. captives held in Tehran, Iran, it is the least known Tier 1 Special Mission Unit and is tasked with collecting actionable intelligence in direct support of JSOC missions. Also sometimes referred to as the "not so secret" Army of Northern Virginia.

ISR: Intelligence, Surveillance, and Reconnaissance.

ITAR: International Traffic in Arms Regulations. Export control regulations designed to restrict the export of certain items, including weapons and optics. These regulations offer ample opportunity to inadvertently violate federal law.

JAG: Judge Advocate General. Decent television series and the military's legal department.

JMAU: Joint Medical Augmentation Unit. High-speed medicine.

JOC: Joint Operations Center. Like a Tactical Operations Center, but more high-speed.

JSOC: Joint Special Operations Command. According to Wikipedia, it is a component command of SOCOM that commands and controls Special Mission Units and Advanced Force Operations.

Katsa: Mossad case officer.

Katyn Massacre: Soviet purge of Polish citizens that took place in 1940 subsequent to the Soviet invasion. Twenty-two thousand Poles were killed by members of the NKVD during this event; many of the bodies were discovered in mass graves in the Katyn Forest. Russia denied responsibility for the massacre until 1990.

KGB: The Soviet "Committee for State Security." Excelled at "suppressing internal dissent" during the Cold War. Most often referred to by kids of the eighties as "the bad guys."

KIA: Killed in Action.

Kidon: "Bayonet." The unit of the Mossad's Caesarea tasked with executing "negative treatments."

Kudu: A spiral-horned antelope, roughly the size and build of an elk, that inhabits much of sub-Saharan Africa.

Langley: The Northern Virginia location where the Central Intelligence Agency is headquartered. Often used as shorthand for CIA.

LaRue OBR: Optimized Battle Rifle. Precision variant of the AR-15/AR-10 designed for use as a Designated Marksman or Sniper Rifle. Available in both 5.56x45mm and 7.62x51mm.

Law of Armed Conflict: A segment of public international law that regulates the conduct of armed hostilities.

LAW Rocket: M-72 Light Anti-armor Weapon. A disposable, tube-launched 66mm unguided rocket used by U.S. forces since before the Vietnam War.

LE: Law Enforcement. A blanket term used to denote police officers, sheriffs, state troopers, highway patrol, federal agents, and other local, state, and federal law enforcement.

Leica M4: Classic 35mm rangefinder camera produced from 1966 to 1975.

Long-Range Desert Group: A specialized British military unit that operated in the North African and Mediterranean theaters during World War II. The unit was made up of soldiers from Great Britain, New Zealand, and Southern Rhodesia.

L-Pill: A "lethal pill" or suicide pill developed during World War II and later issued to high-risk agents and operatives on both sides of the Cold War.

M1911/1911A1: .45-caliber pistol used by U.S. forces since before World War I.

M3: World War II submachine gun chambered in .45 ACP. This simple but reliable weapon became a favorite of the frogmen of that time.

M4: The standard assault rifle of the majority of U.S. military forces, including the U.S. Navy SEALs. The M4 is a shortened carbine variant of the M16 rifle that fires a 5.56x45mm cartridge. The M4 is a modular design that can be adapted to numerous configurations, including different barrel lengths.

MACV-SOG: Military Assistance Command, Vietnam–Studies and Observations Group. Deceiving name for a group of brave warriors who conducted highly classified special operations missions during the Vietnam War. These operations were often conducted behind enemy lines in Laos, Cambodia, and North Vietnam.

Mahdi Militia: An insurgent Shia militia loyal to cleric Muqtada al-Sadr that opposed U.S. forces in Iraq during the height of that conflict.

Makarov: A Soviet-era pistol favored by the bad guys.

MANPADS: Man-Portable Air-Defense System. Small antiaircraft surface-to-air guided rockets such as the U.S. Stinger and the Russian SA-7.

Marine Raiders: U.S. Marine Corps special operations unit; formerly known as MARSOC.

Maritime Branch: It's best to just google it.

Mazrah Tora: A prison in Cairo, Egypt. You do not want to wake up here.

MBITR: AN/PRC-148 Multiband Inter/Intra Team Radio. A handheld multiband, tactical software–defined radio, commonly used by special operations forces to communicate during operations.

McMillan TAC-50: Bolt-action sniper rifle chambered in .50 BMG used for long-range sniping operations, employed by U.S. special operations forces as well as the Canadian army.

MDMA: A psychoactive drug whose clinical name is too long to place here. Known on the street as "ecstasy." Glow sticks not included.

MH-47: Special operations variant of the Army's Chinook helicopter, usually flown by members of the 160th SOAR. This twin-rotor aircraft is used frequently in Afghanistan due to its high service ceiling and large troop- and cargo-carrying capacity. Rumor has it that, if you're careful, you can squeeze a Land Rover Defender 90 inside one.

MH-60: Special operations variant of the Army's Black Hawk helicopter, usually flown by members of the 160th SOAR.

MIA: Missing in Action.

MI5: Military Intelligence, Section 5. Britain's domestic counterintelligence and security agency. Like the FBI but with nicer suits and better accents.

MIL DOT: A reticle-based system used for range estimation and long-range shooting, based on the milliradian unit of measurement.

MIL(s): One-thousandth of a radian; an angular measurement used in rifle scopes. 0.1 MIL equals 1 centimeter at 100 meters or 0.36" at 100 yards. If you find that confusing, don't become a sniper.

Military Crest: According to *Merriam-Webster's* it is "a line or position often below the topographical crest and on the slope toward the enemy from which maximum observation of the remainder of the slope can be obtained."

MIRV: Multiple Independently Targetable Reentry Vehicles.

MIT: Turkey's national intelligence organization, and a school in Boston for smart kids.

Mk 46 MOD 1: Belt-fed 5.56x45mm light machine gun built by FN Herstal. Often used by special operations forces due to its light weight, the Mk 46 is a scaled-down version of the Mk 48 MOD 1.

Mk 48 MOD 1: Belt-fed 7.62x51mm light machine gun designed for use by special operations forces. Weighing eighteen pounds unloaded, the Mk 48 can fire 730 rounds per minute to an effective range of 800 meters and beyond.

Mosin-Nagant: Legendary Russian bolt-action service rifle found on battlefields across the globe.

Mossad: The Israeli version of the CIA, but even more apt to make their enemies disappear.

MP7: Compact select-fire personal defense weapon built by Heckler & Koch and used by various special operations forces. Its 4.6x30mm cartridge is available in a subsonic load, making the weapon extremely quiet when suppressed. What the MP7 lacks in lethality it makes up for in coolness.

MQ-4C: An advanced unmanned surveillance drone developed by Northrop Grumman for use by the U.S. Navy.

Robert Mugabe: Chairman of ZANU who led the nation of Zimbabwe from 1980 to 2017 as both prime minister and president. Considered responsible for retaliatory attacks against his rival Ndebele tribe as well as a disastrous land redistribution scheme that was ruled illegal by Zimbabwe's High Court.

MultiCam: A proprietary camouflage pattern developed by Crye Precision. Formerly reserved for special operators and air-softers, MultiCam is now standard issue to much of the U.S. and allied militaries.

Nagant M1895: As described in the novel, this pistol was used to execute Czar Nicholas II and his family.

NATO: North Atlantic Treaty Organization. An alliance created in 1949 to counter the Soviet threat to the Western Hemisphere. Headquartered in Brussels, Belgium, the alliance is commanded by a four-star U.S. military officer known as the Supreme Allied Commander Europe (SACEUR).

Naval Special Warfare Development Group (DEVGRU): A command that appears in the biographies of numerous admirals on the Navy's website. Joe Biden publicly referred to it by a different name when he was the vice president.

NBACC: National Biodefense Analysis and Countermeasures Center. A facility on Fort Detrick in Maryland that for sure does not weaponize and test infectious diseases in the Bat Cave.

NCIS: Naval Criminal Investigative Service. A federal law enforcement agency whose jurisdiction includes the U.S. Navy and Marine Corps. Also a popular television program with at least two spin-offs.

NGAL: Next Generation Aiming Laser.

Niassa Game Reserve: Sixteen thousand square miles of relatively untouched wilderness in northern Mozambique. The reserve is home to a wide variety of wildlife as well as a fair number of poachers looking to commoditize them.

NKVD: A federal law enforcement arm of the former Soviet Union. Best known as the action arm of Stalin's Great Purge under the guise of protecting "state security" and responsible for mass executions and imprisonments of "enemies of the people."

NODs: Night observation devices. Commonly referred to as "night vision goggles," these devices amplify ambient light, allowing the user to see in low-light environments. Special operations forces often operate at night to take full advantage of such technology.

NSA: National Security Agency. U.S. intelligence agency tasked with gathering and analyzing signals intercepts and other communications data. Also known as No Such Agency. These are the government employees who listen to our phone calls and read our emails and texts for reasons of "national security." See *Permanent Record* by Edward Snowden.

NSC: National Security Council. This body advises and assists the president of the United States on matters of national security.

NSW: Naval Special Warfare. The Navy's special operations force; includes SEAL Teams.

Officer Candidate School (OCS): Twelve-week course where civilians and enlisted sailors are taught to properly fold underwear. Upon completion, they are miraculously qualified to command men and women in combat.

OmniSTAR: Satellite-based augmentation system service provider. A really fancy GPS service that provides very precise location information.

Ops-Core Ballistic Helmet: Lightweight high-cut helmet used by special operations forces worldwide.

Orsis T-5000 Tochnost: Russian bolt-action precision rifle.

OSS: Office of Strategic Services. The U.S. World War II national intelligence agency led by William Joseph "Wild Bill" Donovan. Forerunner of the CIA.

P226: 9mm handgun made by SIG Sauer, the standard-issue sidearm for SEALs.

P229: A compact handgun made by SIG Sauer, often used by federal law enforcement officers, chambered in 9mm as well as other cartridges.

P320: Striker-fired modular 9mm handgun that has recently been adopted by the U.S. armed forces as the M17/M18.

P365: Subcompact handgun made by SIG Sauer, designed for concealed carry. Despite its size, the P365 holds up to thirteen rounds of 9mm.

Pakhan: The highest-ranked blatnoy in prison. Now more synonymous with "senior criminal."

Pakistani Taliban: An Islamic terrorist group composed of various Sunni Islamist militant groups based in the northwestern Federally Administered Tribal Areas along the Afghan border in Pakistan.

Pamwe Chete: "All Together"; the motto of the Rhodesian Selous Scouts.

Panga: A machete-like utility blade common in Africa.

Peshmerga: Military forces of Kurdistan. Meaning "the one who faces death," they are regarded by Allied troops as some of the best fighters in the region.

PETN: PentaErythritol TetraNitrate. An explosive compound used in blasting caps to initiate larger explosive charges.

PG-32V: High-explosive antitank rocket that can be fired from the Russian-designed RPG-32 rocket-propelled grenade launcher. Its tandem charge is effective against various types of armor, including reactive armor.

Phoenix Program: CIA-run covert operation in Vietnam focused on neutralizing Vietcong infrastructure. That's a civilized way of saying the program targeted Vietcong leadership for assassination.

PID: Protective Intelligence and Threat Assessment Division. The division of the Secret Service that monitors potential threats to its protectees.

PKM: Soviet-designed, Russian-made light machine gun chambered in 7.62x54R that can be found in conflicts throughout the globe. This weapon feeds from a non-disintegrating belt and has a rate of fire of 650 rounds per minute. You don't want one shooting at you.

PLF: Parachute Landing Fall. A technique taught to military parachutists to prevent injury when making contact with the earth. Round canopy parachutes used by airborne forces fall at faster velocities than other parachutes and require a specific landing sequence. More often than not, it ends up as feet-ass-head.

PMC: Private Military Company. Though the profession is as old as war itself, the modern term *PMC* was made infamous in the post-9/11 era by Blackwater, aka Xe Services, and now known as Academi.

POTUS: President of the United States; leader of the free world.

POW: Prisoner of War.

PPD: Presidential Protection Detail. The element of the Secret Service tasked with protecting POTUS.

PRC: People's Republic of China. Often confused with the PRC, or the People's Republic of California.

President's Hundred: A badge awarded by the Civilian Marksmanship Program to the one hundred top-scoring military and civilian shooters in the President's Pistol and President's Rifle matches. Enlisted members of the U.S. military are authorized to wear the tab on their uniform.

Professional Hunter: A licensed hunting guide in Africa, often referred to as a "PH." Zimbabwe-licensed PHs are widely considered the most qualified and highly trained in Africa and make up the majority of the PH community operating in Mozambique.

Project Delta: One of the most highly classified and successful special reconnaissance units of the Vietnam War. Basically, their job was to be badasses.

***The Protocols of the Elders of Zion*:** An anti-Semitic conspiracy manifesto first published in the late 1800s by Russian sources. Though quickly established as a fraudulent text, *Protocols* has been widely circulated in numerous languages.

PSO-1: A Russian-made 4x24mm illuminated rifle optic developed for use on the SVD rifle.

PTSD: Post-traumatic stress disorder. A mental condition that develops in association with shocking or traumatic events. Commonly associated with combat veterans.

PVS-15: Binocular-style NODs used by U.S. and allied special operations forces.

QRF: Quick Reaction Force. A contingency ground force on standby to assist operations in progress.

Quantum Computing: A rapidly emerging technology that employs the laws of quantum mechanics and physics to perform computations.

Ranger Panties: Polyester PT shorts favored by members of the 75th Ranger Regiment that leave very little to the imagination, sometimes referred to as "silkies."

REMF: Rear-Echelon Motherfucker. Describes most officers taking credit for what the E-5 mafia and a few senior enlisted do on the ground if the mission goes right. These same "people" will be the first to hang you out to dry if things go south. Now that they are home safe and sound, they will let you believe that when they were "downrange" they actually left the wire.

RFID: Radio Frequency Identification. Technology commonly used to tag objects that can be scanned electronically.

RHIB/RIB: Rigid Hull Inflatable Boat/Rigid Inflatable Boat. A lightweight but high-performance boat constructed with a solid fiberglass or composite hull and flexible tubes at the gunwales (sides).

Rhodesia: A former British colony that declared its independence in 1965. After a long and brutal civil war, the nation became Zimbabwe in 1979.

Rhodesian Bush War: An insurgency battle between the Rhodesian Security Forces and Soviet-, East German–, Cuban-, and Chinese-backed guerrillas that lasted from 1964 to 1979. The war ended when the December 1979 Lancaster House Agreement put an end to white minority rule.

Rhodesian SAS: A special operations unit formed as part of the famed British Special Air Service in 1951. When Rhodesia sought independence, the unit ceased to exist as part of the British military but fought as part of the Rhodesian Security Forces until 1980. Many members of the Selous Scouts were recruited from the SAS.

Rich Kid Shit: Expensive equipment reserved for use by the most highly funded special operations units. Google JSOC.

RLI: Rhodesian Light Infantry. An airborne and airmobile unit used to conduct "fireforce" operations during the Bush War. These missions were often launched in response to intelligence provided by Selous Scouts on the ground.

ROC: Republic of China. Official name of what is more commonly referred to as Taiwan.

ROE: Rules of engagement. Rules or directives that determine what level of force can be applied against an enemy in a particular situation or area.

RPG-32: 105mm rocket-propelled grenade launcher that is made in both Russia and, under license, in Jordan.

SAD: The CIA's Special Activities Division. Though it is now called the Special Activities Center, it's still responsible for covert action, aka the really cool stuff.

SADM: Special Atomic Demolition Munition. A man-portable atomic demolition munition system developed by the U.S. military during the Cold War. Better known as known as "backpack nukes," they even had their own 1965 Army Field Manual—*FM 5-26: Employment of Atomic Demolition Munitions.*

SALUTE: A report used to transmit information on enemy forces. Size / Activity / Location / Unit / Time / Equipment.

SAP: Special Access Program. Security protocols that provide highly classified information with safeguards and access restrictions that exceed those for regular classified information. Really secret stuff.

Sayanim: Usually non-Israeli, though most often Jewish, worldwide network of Mossad facilitators.

Sayeret Matkal: The General Staff Reconnaissance Unit of the IDF responsible for hostage rescue and counterterrorism operations beyond Israel's borders. The Israeli equivalent of the British SAS, U.S. Army's Delta Force, and a certain SEAL Team between the numbers of 5 and 7.

SCAR-17: 7.62x51mm battle rifle produced by FN. Its gas mechanism can be traced to that of the FAL.

Schmidt & Bender: Privately held German optics manufacturer known for its precision rifle scopes.

SCI: Special Compartmentalized Information. Classified information concerning or derived from sensitive intelligence sources, methods, or analytical processes. Often found on private basement servers in upstate New York or bathroom closet servers in Denver.

SCIF: Sensitive Compartmented Information Facility. A secure and restricted room or structure where classified information is discussed or viewed.

Scouts and Raiders: World War II forefathers to today's Navy SEALs. The original Naval Special Warfare Commandos.

SEAL: Acronym of SEa, Air, and Land. The three mediums in which SEALs operate. The U.S. Navy's special operations force.

Secret Service: The federal law enforcement agency responsible for protecting the POTUS.

Selous Scouts: An elite, if scantily clad, mixed-race unit of the Rhodesian army responsible for counterinsurgency operations. These "pseudo-terrorists" led some of the most successful special operations missions in modern history.

SERE: Survival, Evasion, Resistance, Escape. A military training program that includes realistic role-playing as a prisoner of war. SERE students are subjected to highly stressful procedures, sometimes including waterboarding, as part of the course curriculum. More commonly referred to as "Camp Slappy."

Shin Bet / Shabak: Israel's equivalent of the FBI or MI5.

Shishani: Arabic term for Chechen fighters in Syria, probably due to "Shishani" being a common Chechen surname.

SIGINT: Signals Intelligence. Intelligence derived from electronic signals and systems used by foreign targets, such as communications systems, radars, and weapons systems.

SIPR: Secret Internet Protocol Router network. A secure version of the internet used by DOD and the State Department to transmit classified information.

SISDE: Italy's Intelligence and Democratic Security Service. Their suits are probably even nicer than MI5's.

SISMI: Italian version of the CIA. Formerly called the AISE until scandals forced a housecleaning and name change.

SLBM: Submarine-Launched Ballistic Missile.

SOCOM: United States Special Operations Command. The Unified Combatant Command charged with overseeing the various Special Operations Component Commands of the Army, Marine Corps, Navy, and Air Force of the United States armed forces. Headquartered at MacDill Air Force Base in Tampa, Florida.

Special Boat Team-12: The West Coast unit that provides maritime mobility to SEALs using a variety of vessels. Fast boats with machine guns.

Special Reconnaissance (SR) Team: NSW Teams that conduct special activities, ISR, and provide intelligence support to the SEAL Teams.

Spetsnaz: An umbrella term for Russian special operations units and special operations units in post-Soviet states.

Spetssviaz: Officially the Special Communications and Information Service of the Federal Protective Service of the Russian Federation. The Russian version of the NSA. Yes, they have all your personal electronic data and credit card information.

SR-16: An AR-15 variant developed and manufactured by Knight Armament Corporation.

SRT: Surgical Resuscitation Team. You want these guys close by if you take a bullet.

Strela-2: Cold War–era Soviet-designed shoulder-fired surface-to-air missile.

StrongFirst: Kettle-bell-focused fitness program founded by Russian fitness guru Pavel Tsatsouline that is popular with special operations forces.

SVD: Officially the SVD-63 to denote the year it was accepted for use in the Soviet military, it is known the world over as the Dragunov.

S-Vest: Suicide vest. An explosives-laden garment favored by suicide bombers. Traditionally worn only once.

SVR: The Foreign Intelligence Service of the Russian Federation, or as John le Carré describes them, "the KGB in drag."

Taliban: An Islamic fundamentalist political movement and terrorist group in Afghanistan. U.S. and coalition forces had been at war with members of the Taliban since late 2001.

Targeting Officer: The CIA's website reads that as a targeting officer you will "identify new opportunities for DO operational activity and enhance ongoing operations." Translation: They tell us whom to kill.

TATP: Triacetone triperoxide. An explosive compound nicknamed "Mother of Satan." Its chemical precursors can be found in commonly available products the world over.

TDFD: Time-delay firing device. An explosive initiator that allows for detonation after a determined period of time. A fancy version of a really long fuse.

TIC: Troops in contact. A firefight involving U.S. or friendly forces.

TOC: Tactical Operations Center. A command post for military operations. A TOC usually includes a small group of personnel who guide members of an active tactical element during a mission from the safety of a secured area.

TOR Network: A computer network designed to conceal a user's identity and location. TOR allows for anonymous communication.

TQ: Politically correct term for the timely questioning of individuals on-site once a target is secure. May involve the raising of voices.

Troop Chief: Senior enlisted SEAL on a forty-man troop, usually a master chief petty officer. The guy who makes shit happen.

TS: Top Secret. Information whose unauthorized disclosure reasonably could be expected to cause exceptionally grave damage to national security and that the original classification authority is able to identify or describe. Can also describe an individual's level of security clearance.

TST: Time-sensitive target. A target requiring immediate response because it is highly lucrative, is a fleeting target of opportunity, or poses (or will soon pose) a danger to friendly forces.

UAV: Unmanned Aerial Vehicle. A drone.

UCMJ: Uniform Code of Military Justice. Disciplinary and criminal code that applies to members of the U.S. military.

UDI: Unilateral Declaration of Independence. The 1965 document that established Rhodesia as an independent sovereign state. The UDI resulted in an international embargo and made Rhodesia a pariah.

V-22: Tilt-rotor aircraft that can fly like a plane and take off and land like a helicopter. Numerous examples were crashed during its extremely expensive development.

VBIED: Vehicle-Borne Improvised Explosive Device. A rolling car bomb driven by a suicidal terrorist.

VC: National Liberation Front of South Vietnam, better known as the Viet Cong. A communist insurgent group that fought against the government of South Vietnam and its allies during the Vietnam War. In the movies, these are the guys wearing the black pajamas carrying AKs.

VI: Vehicle Interdiction. Good fun, unless you are on the receiving end.

***Vor v Zakone*:** An individual at the top of the incarcerated criminal underground. Think godfather. Top authority for the Bratva. Today, each region of Russia has a *Vor v Zakone*.

***Vory*:** A hierarchy within the Bratva. Career criminals. More directly translated as "thief."

VPN: Virtual Private Network. A private network that enables users to send and receive data across shared or public networks as if their computing devices were directly connected to the private network. Considered more secure than a traditional internet network.

VSK-94: Russian-made Sniper/Designated Marksman rifle chambered in the subsonic 9x39mm cartridge. This suppressed weapon is popular with Russian special operations and law enforcement units due to its minimal sound signature and muzzle flash.

VSS Vintorez: Integrally suppressed Soviet rifle chambered in 9x39mm.

VTC: Video Teleconferencing.

Wagner Group: A Russian private military company with close ties to the Russian government.

War Vets: Loosely organized groups of Zimbabweans who carried out many of the land seizures during the 1990s. Often armed, these individuals used threats and intimidation to remove white farmers from their homes. Despite the name, most of these individuals were too young to have participated in the Bush War. Not to be confused with ZNLWVA, a group that represents ZANU-affiliated veterans of the Bush War.

WARCOM/NAVSPECWARCOM: United States Naval Special Warfare Command. The Navy's special operations force and the maritime component of United States Special Operations Command. Headquartered in Coronado, California, WARCOM is the administrative command for subordinate NSW Groups composed of eight SEAL Teams, one SEAL Delivery Vehicle (SDV) Team, three Special Boat Teams, and two Special Reconnaissance Teams.

Westley Richards Droplock: A rifle or shotgun built by the famed Birmingham, England, gunmakers that allows the user to remove the locking mechanisms for repair or replacement in the field. Widely considered one of the finest and most iconic actions of all time.

Whiskey Tango: Military speak for "white trash."

WIA: Wounded In Action.

Yamam: An elite unit of Israeli border police that conducts high-risk hostage rescue and counterterrorism operations in Israel.

Yazidis: An insular Kurdish-speaking ethnic and religious group that primarily resides in Iraq. Effectively a subminority among the Kurds, Yazidis were heavily persecuted by ISIS.

YPG: Kurdish militia forces operating in the Democratic Federation of Northern Syria. The Turks are not fans.

ZANLA: Zimbabwe African National Liberation Army. The armed wing of the Maoist Zimbabwe African National Union and one of the major combatants of the Rhodesian Bush War. ZANLA forces often staged out of training camps located in Mozambique and were led by Robert Mugabe.

Zimbabwe: Sub-Saharan African nation that formerly existed as Southern Rhodesia and later Rhodesia. Led for three decades by Robert Mugabe, Zimbabwe ranks as one of the world's most corrupt nations on Transparency International's Corruption Perceptions Index.

ZIPRA: Zimbabwe People's Revolutionary Army. The Soviet-equipped armed wing of ZAPU and one of the two major insurgency forces that fought in the Rhodesian Bush War. ZIPRA forces fell under the leadership of Josh Nkomo, who spent much of the war in Zambia. ZIPRA members were responsible for shooting down two civilian airliners using Soviet SA-7 surface-to-air missiles in the late 1970s.

Zodiac Mk 2 GR: A 4.2-meter inflatable rubber boat capable of carrying up to six individuals. These craft are often used as dinghies for larger vessels.

ACKNOWLEDGMENTS

I am indebted to the authors whose work is a part of my experience and so inexorably intertwined with my being that I fail to explicitly recognize it. Their influence can be found in every idea, title, outline, chapter, paragraph, and sentence of my novels. I thank them for expanding my horizons through their writing.

Red Sky Mourning exists because of the foundation built by **Richard Connell**, **Geoffrey Household**, **Ian Fleming**, **John le Carré**, **Ken Follett**, **Frederick Forsyth**, **Robert Ludlum**, **John Edmund Gardner**, **David Morrell**, **Nelson DeMille**, **Stephen Hunter**, **Tom Clancy**, **Don Pendleton**, **Clive Cussler**, **J. C. Pollock**, **Marc Olden**, **Louis L'Amour**, **Eric Van Lustbader**, **Michael Connelly**, and **A. J. Quinnell**, among others, all of whom I read in my formative years. Later, in the SEAL Teams, I would discover and read **Vince Flynn**, **Daniel Silva**, **Kyle Mills**, **Lee Child**, **Brad Thor**, **Steven Pressfield**, and **Mark Greaney**. I was and remain a reader. I want to thank my parents for making reading a natural part of my childhood. That has led to all else.

This book would certainly not exist without **Brad Thor** and my SEAL Teammate **Johnny Sanchez**. Thank you, both.

To my friends **James Rupley**, **Dan Gelston**, **Kevin O'Malley**, **David Lehman**, and **Brad Haynes** for taking the time to be my first readers. How you catch what you do is beyond me. That you take the time to read early drafts of my manuscripts is appreciated more than I can express.

To **Dr. Robert Bray** for your hours of poring over these pages, for all you have done for the nation and what you continue to do for special operations veterans. And thank you to Tracey for putting up with us.

To my "violence consultant" **Dylan Murphy** for always bringing the heat! Thank you to **Elyse** for the most surprising fight choreography video to date. And for the first time, to **Dalton James**. Can't wait to hit the range with you.

To **Larry Ellison**, to whom this book is dedicated. I am forever grateful for your inspiration. Anything is possible, but it takes more than dreams—it takes work—hard work. One of my favorite Larry Ellison quotes is, "I had all the disadvantages necessary for success." Thank you, Larry. Your friendship and example mean the world. To learn more about Larry Ellison, read *The Billionaire and the Mechanic* by **Julian Guthrie**.

To **Jimmy and Pam Linn** for being so wonderful. Can't wait for our next time together!

To **Danny Wolf** for your humor, cigars, and for your stories of Chicago back in the day. I think you should write a book about it.

To **Rick and Esther Rosenfield** for your continued love and support.

To **Jon Dubin** for your friendship, your time at the FBI, and for doing all the heavy lifting at Pineapple Brothers, Lanai. One day "the J" will make it into a novel.

To firefighter and Lake Aircraft pilot **Ben O'Neal** for taking the time to walk me through this classic amphibious aircraft! Follow him on Instagram @boneal110.

To all those who helped teach me about the Lake Buccaneer and don't even know it. To **Greg O'Neal**, Lake Aircraft Instructor. To **Harry Shannon** of Amphibians Plus. To **John Staber**, author of *All About Lakes*, sponsored by the Lake Amphibian Club. To **Steve Reep** of the Seaplane Pilots Association, author of *Go to Hull*. For more on these iconic planes, check out lakeamphibclub.com.

To **Trevor Thompson**, who has forgotten more about skydiving than I will ever know. Follow him @trevor.p.thompson on Instagram.

To **Mark Owen** for your decades of friendship and support.

To **Nick Ferrell** at DC Vintage Watches for taking a look at the Situation Room segments of this novel and for tracking down those hard-to-find Vietnam-era Seikos. Find out more at dcvintagewatches.com.

To **Ric Prado**, CIA Counterterrorist Chief of Operations and author of *Black Ops*, for your decades of service to the nation and for answering my questions. Ric is the recipient of the CIA's Distinguished Career Intelligence Medal and the George H. W. Bush Award for Excellence in Counterterrorism.

To **Caleb Daniels** for all things Bond. If anyone found all the nods to Fleming in this book, it's you! I can't wait to read your upcoming book, *Licensed Troubleshooter—A Study of the Small Arms Featured in the World of James Bond*, with photos by **James Rupley**. Follow Caleb @commandobond on Instagram.

Thank you to **David Zaritsky** of *The Bond Experience* for making it possible for me to sit at Ian Fleming's desk at Goldeneye. I'll never forget it. All Bond fans should check out David's YouTube channel @TheBondExperience.

Thank you to everyone at **Goldeneye** in Jamacia for such a memorable experience. I'll be back!

Thank you to **Chris Clark** and his 1972 Rolex Submariner for illustrating the difference between crystal and acrylic. You just might see that brought up in a future book.

Thank you to **Kerry Davis** of Dark Angel Medical for correcting the combat medical section of this novel. All mistakes are mine alone.

Thank you to **Jimmy Spithill** for making sure I did not butcher the sailing maneuvers too badly. Follow Jimmy's incredible sailing journey on Instagram @jspithill.

To **Scott Lucas** of CAE's subsurface and next-generation programs for your input on the simulated *Columbia*-class bridge section. Sincerely appreciated.

To **Capt. Jason Salata** (U.S. Navy, Ret.) for your years of service, friendship, and guidance. Can't wait to see what you do next!

To **Capt. William Toti** (U.S. Navy, Ret.), author of *From CO to CEO* and cohost of *The Unauthorized History of the Pacific War* podcast, for taking the time to discuss submarines with me. All errors in this novel are mine alone.

To **Capt. Kevin Brenton** (U.S. Navy, Ret.) for your information on undersea warfare. As with all details in this novel, the mistakes rest with me.

I hope the submariners reading the book can forgive my transgressions. I know using a boomer to sink an enemy sub with a torpedo is blasphemy, and I humbly ask your forgiveness.

To **Trig and Annette French** for always having room for me and my family. And thank you to Trig for sharing your library with Jonathan Hastings in this book.

Thank you to **Ian McCollum**. His Forgotten Weapons YouTube channel is always a wealth of information that is invaluable in my firearms research. Check it out @ForgottenWeapons.

Thank you to **Garand Thumb** for his in-depth video on the Flux Raider. Find it on his outstanding YouTube channel @GarandThumb and find the Raider at fluxdefense.com.

To **Larry Vickers** and **James Rupley** for the Vickers Guide series. They are never far from reach as I write the weapons-centric chapters in my novels. You can find them at vickersguide.com.

Thank you to **Chan Neo** for your help on China's military-issued pistols.

I consulted numerous books while researching this novel to include *The Dragons and the Snakes* by **David Kilcullen**, *Unrestricted Warfare* by **Col. Qiao Liang** and **Col. Wang Xiangsui**, *Blind Man's Bluff* by **Sherry Sontag** and **Christopher Drew** with **Annette Lawrence Drew**, *Submarine* by **Tom Clancy** with **John Gresham**, *Dark Territory* by **Fred Kaplan**, *1959* by **Fred Kaplan**, *The Google Archipelago* by **Michael Rectenwald**, *Ian Fleming* by **Nicholas Shakespeare**, *The Accidental Superpower* by **Peter Zeihan**, *The China Threat* by **Bill Gertz**, *When China Attacks* by **Col. Grant Newsham**, *Spies and Lies* by **Alex Joske**, *Red Handed* by **Peter Schweizer**, *Surveillance State* by **Josh Chin** and **Liza Lin**, *The Golden Passport* by **Kristin Surak**, *War Transformed* by **Mick Ryan**, *White Sun War* by **Mick Ryan**, *On Guerrilla Warfare* by **Mao Zedong**, and the **Thomas Cleary** translation of *The Art of War* by Sun Tzu that I purchased in high school. Also extremely helpful were a Reuters Special Report titled "U.S. Revives Cold War Submarine Spy Program to Counter China" by **Joe Brock** from September 21, 2023, and "Inside the Subsea Cable Firm Secretly Helping America Take On China" by **Joe Brock** from July 6, 2023.

To **Peter Zeihan**, whose insights I in part attributed to Andy Danreb in this novel.

Thank you to the cast and crew of *The Terminal List: Dark Wolf*, which is currently filming at the time of this book's publication. The new Ben Edwards prequel origin story series starring **Taylor Kitsch**, **Chris Pratt**, **Tom Hopper**, **Luke Hemsworth**, **Dar Salim**, **Robert Wisdom**, **Rona-Lee Shimon**, and **Shiraz Tzarfati** is coming to Amazon Prime Video in 2025. Thank you to **Jennifer Salke** and **Vernon Sanders** at Amazon Studios, and **Modi Wiczyk**, **Asif Satchu**, and **Scott Tenley** at MRC for believing in this project. Thank you to **Chris Pratt**, **Antoine Fuqua**, **David DiGilio**, **Jared Shaw**, **Max Adams**, **Kat Samick**, **Ray Mendoza**, **Frederick E. O. Toye**, **Naomi Iizuka**, **Kenny Sheard**, **Hennah Sekander**, **Lauren Muñoz Robinson**, and **Gareth Kanter**. Thank you to the executive teams of **Laura Lancaster**, **Odetta Watkins**, **Brian Harvey**, and **Liz Mackintosh** from Amazon, and **Jenna Santoianni**, **Rob Ortiz**, **Stacy Fung**, and **Tom Sellitti** from MRC Studios. Thank you to **Heather McClure**, **Corey Choate**, **Arpi Ketendjian**, **Lilly Rolnick**, and **Irving Lopez** at Amazon for all you do!

These shows would not be coming to the screen were it not for my friend and SEAL Teammate **Jared Shaw**. Thank you, brother. Looking forward to setting up more L-ambushes with you in the future. For more on how the shows came to be, check out *The Terminal List Podcast*. You can link to it from my website.

To **Chris Pratt** for being the driving force behind bringing these stories to life. There was no one better to portray James Reece. My sincerest thanks for exceeding all expectations.

To **Antoine Fuqua** for your friendship and for sharing your talent with the world.

To **David DiGilio**, showrunner of *The Terminal List* and *The Terminal List: Dark Wolf*, for bringing me into the fold from the start and teaching me so much about the craft of screenwriting and storytelling. How you manage the chaos of these productions leaves me in awe. Thank you, my friend.

Thank you to **David Ellison**, **Matt Thunell**, **Shelley Zimmerman**, **Katherine Morrison**, **Niko Fernandez**, and the entire team at Skydance Media. I am so fired up for what's ahead!

Thank you to **Joel Bergvall** and the team at Tim McGraw's Down Home entertainment. Here we go!

To **David Bolls**, whom I think I should start referring to as the man behind the curtain. Thank you for being responsible for so much of all that has transpired since I left the Navy.

To **Joe Rogan** for staying strong, asking questions, and bringing such positive energy to the world.

To **Frank Lecrone**, **Kevin O'Malley**, **Andrew Kline**, and **Jimmy Klein**—Africa awaits.

To **Jim Shockey**. Congratulations on the publication of *Call Me Hunter.*

To **Katie Pavlich** for your friendship and support going back years before the novels and shows existed. Add Katie's incredible and eye-opening book *Fast and Furious* to your library today!

To **Gavy Friedson** for your work with United Hatzalah of Israel. Find out more at israelrescue.org.

To **Ron Cohen**, **Tom Taylor**, **Jason Wright**, **Samantha Piatt**, and **Morgan Baker** at SIG Sauer for your continued friendship and support. This year is the fortieth anniversary of the SIG P226 that was on my side for every deployment. It still fits like an extension of my hand.

To **Daniel Winkler** and **Karen Shook** of Winkler Knives for the most savage tomahawk in existence and for all you have done for those who venture downrange. And thank you for letting me and Kevin Holland into the shop to learn how to craft these timeless tools. Find out more about their knives, axes, and tools at winklerknives.com.

To Sayoc Kali martial arts trainer **Rafael Kayanan** for collaborating with Daniel Winkler to create the RnD Axe. Follow him and check out his striking artwork on Instagram @rafael_kayanan.

To **Harley Elmore** of Headhunter Blades, used in this novel. Visit headhunterblades.com for more on "The Dirty."

To **Dom Raso** of Dynamis Alliance for an amazing fixed blade and the combat flathead used in *Red Sky Mourning*. Find yours at crush everything.com.

To **Andrew Arrabito** of Half Face Blades for creating works of art that are designed to be used hard! Check them out on Instagram @halffaceblades.

To the **Park City Gun Club** for always keeping a lane open for me.

Stop in if you are passing through Park City, Utah. Maybe I'll see you there!

To **Mike Glover** for all you did downrange and for all you continue to do through Fieldcraft Survival.

To **Jen Caro** at Fieldcraft Survival for your dedication and commitment. It is noticed and appreciated.

To **Kyle Lamb** for a great sling and for your service at the pinnacle of special operations. Check out what Kyle has going on at vikingtactics.com.

To **Donnie Edwards** and **Kathryn Edwards** for all you do for our nation's veterans through the Best Defense Foundation. To **Amanda Thompson**, **Michael Malone**, **Sarah Bishop**, **Austin Bishop**, **Mayo Strauss**, **Paul Russell**, **Cori Russell**, **Misty Zelk**, **Gwenael Jacob**, **Ben Harper**, the entire BDF leadership team, and all the volunteers who put so much into the Battlefield Return Programs to honor our World War II veterans. Visit them at bestdefensefoundation.org to support their mission of "taking care of the ones who took care of us."

To **Chris Cox** at Capitol 6 Advisors for always being there.

To **Eric and Sarah Cylvick** and to **Cash and Tor Cylvick**—"Cylvics get it done!"

To **Walter McLallen** of Tomahawk Strategic Solutions for your years of friendship, guidance, and support. I'll have to incorporate more New York City action into future novels.

To my SEAL Teammate **Keith Walawender** of Tomahawk Strategic Solutions. It was an honor to go downrange with you, my friend!

To **George Kollitides** for always going all in to help well before I was out of the military. Looking forward to getting some training in with you at Artemis Sporting Arms the next time I am in New York!

To **Nick Seifert** at Athlon Outdoors. I think a *Dark Wolf* cover may be in order.

To **Jeff Kimbell** for a wild experience in the Kamchatka Peninsula, Russia.

To former CIA officer and amateur horologist **@watchesofespionage** on Instagram for such an informative page "dedicated to the intersection of timepieces and spycraft." Follow him before he disappears. . . .

To the husband and wife team of **Paul and Cori Russell** at veteran-owned and -operated **Fortitude Coffee Company** for keeping me caffeinated. Order up at fortitudecoffeecompany.com.

To **Fred Burton**, author of *Beirut Rules*, for your service to the nation and for all your work in the private sector.

To **Jocko Willink** for preserving the history of special operations through your podcast and for all that's ahead!

To **Clint and Heidi Smith** at Thunder Ranch. Thank you for your decades of friendship and for passing along your wisdom to students of the gun.

To **Taran Butler** and **Tetiana Gaidar** at Taran Tactical Innovations for always being ready to burn it down on the range every time I'm in town.

To **John Stryker Meyer**, Vietnam MACV-SOG Special Forces veteran and author of *Across the Fence: The Secret War in Vietnam*, *On the Ground*, and *SOG Chronicles*. I look forward to our next linkup. Airborne!

To **James R. Jarrett**, U.S. Army Special Forces Project Delta Vietnam veteran—the Last of the Breed.

To **Stacey Wenger**. Can't wait for the next cake!

To the Real Book Spy and author **Ryan Steck** for being such a champion of both writers and readers.

To **Mike and Laura Bill** for allowing me to lock down and write in your beautiful Park City home. I owe you a dinner or two . . . or three . . .

To **Mike Stoner** of Mike Stoner Photography. Thank you for the new author photo. Let's ride soon! And thank you for passing along the wisdom of "Don't let the old man in!"

To everyone at **Lucky Ones Coffee** in the **Park City Public Library** for all you do for everyone of all abilities! I'll be in for a coffee soon!

To **Julie Oliff** and the entire staff at Porcupine Creek, where much of the final draft of this novel was completed, for ensuring that I had enough Nobu jerky and Japanese IWAI Tradition Mars Whisky to survive.

To **Barbara Peters** at the Poisoned Pen Bookstore in Scottsdale, Arizona, for your support right out of the gate! I look forward to our next dinner at Virtù Honest Craft!

To **Michaela Smith** and everyone at Dolly's Bookstore in Park City, Utah, and to all independent bookstores for connecting authors and readers in communities across the nation.

To **Alexandra Machinist**, **Josie Freedman**, **Howie Tannenbaum**, **Courtney Catzel**, **Yuni Sher**, and **Billy Hallock** at CAA for all your hard work behind the scenes. It is truly appreciated.

To **Karl Austen** and **Marissa Linden** at Jackoway Austen Tyerman Wertheimer Mandelbaum Morris Bernstein Trattner & Klein on the entertainment legal front.

To **Norm Brownstein**, **Steve Demby**, **Peter Ajemian**, and **Mitch Langberg** at Brownstein Hyatt Farber Schreck for all your advice and counsel.

To **Brock Bosson**, **Ted Lacey**, **Tina Davis**, **Alexander Haberman**, and the legal team at Cahill Gorden & Reindell.

To **Steven Lieberman** and **Leo Loughlin**, and **Lisa Locke** at Rothwell Figg.

To **John Blakeman** and **William Price** for managing the business side of this growing venture.

Thank you to my amazing publisher and editor **Emily Bestler** of Emily Bestler Books for your friendship and support. Not a day passes without reflection on all you have made possible. I am grateful beyond words.

To **Lara Jones** for your kindness and patience, especially when I'm running a *tad* behind schedule.

To **David Brown** on the publicity front! Thank you for keeping me on the move, my friend! Let's go!

To **Libby McGuire**, senior vice president and publisher of Atria Books, for the incredible backing!

To **Jon Karp**, president and publisher of Simon & Schuster, for your leadership and efforts in support of authors and readers around the world.

To the family at Simon & Schuster, Atria Books, and Emily Bestler Books who make it all possible! **Al Madocs**, **James Iacobelli**, **Tom Pitoniak**, **Dana Trocker**, **Suzanne Donahue**, **Paige Lytle**, **Shelby Pumphrey**, **Lacee Burr**, **Karlyn Hixson**, **Morgan Pager**, **Sue Fleming**, **Gary Urda**, **Colin Shields**, **Chrissy Festa**, **Janice Fryer**, **Leslie Collins**, **Heather Musika**, **Gregory Hruska**, and **Lexi Mangano**. Thank you, all!

To **Sarah Lieberman**, **Gabrielle Audet**, **Chris Lynch**, and **Tom Spain** at Simon & Schuster Audio for crushing it on the audio side of the house.

To the incomparable **Ray Porter** for narrating the audiobook editions of my novels. You are second to none, my friend.

To **Jen Long** and the team at Pocket Books for the amazing paperback editions! Thank you! I absolutely love them!

To **James Scott**, historian, Pulitzer Prize finalist, and author of *Black Snow*, *Rampage*, *Target Tokyo*, *The War Below*, and *The Attack on the Liberty*. It has been a true pleasure working with you on *Targeted: Beirut—The 1983 Marine Barracks Bombing and the Untold Origin Story of the War on Terror*. Find out more about James and his work at JamesMScott.com.

Late 2023 and early 2024 have been filled with changes as I manage current and future projects. A sincere thank-you to the new team led by **Ashely Ellefsen**. To **Devin Gillette**, **Andrew Bork**, **Chris Cook**, **Zac Heileson**, and **Taylor Matkins**, thank you for jumping aboard! And to **Garrett Bray** for your guidance from the beginning. We are just warming up!

A very special thank-you to everyone who reads or listens to the novels. None of this would be possible without you. My contract with you is that it will always be about honoring the story, which in turn respects you, the reader or listener, who has invested time with me and James Reece. Thank you for joining me on this journey.

To my **mom and dad** for instilling a love of reading and learning in me early on and for correcting all my rough drafts. I love you both.

And to my beautiful wife, **Faith**, and our three wonderful children, thank you for understanding all the time spent away, first on deployments and now locked down, writing. I love you more than words can say.

Turn the page for an exclusive look at
Jack Carr's first nonfiction book,

TARGETED:

BEIRUT,

written with Pulitzer Prize finalist
James M. Scott.

CHAPTER 1

Beirut has become synonymous with
death and destruction.
—*Pittsburgh Post-Gazette* EDITORIAL
April 20, 1983

The black GMC pickup truck idled alongside the curb of Beirut's seashore drive at 12:43 p.m. on April 18, 1983. Secured in the truck bed and hidden under a canvas tarp sat enough pentaerythritol tetranitrate—a high-powered explosive favored by militaries, quarry blasters, and, of course, terrorists—to rival two thousand pounds of TNT. The hefty payload, as one witness would later tell investigators, forced the rear of the late-model pickup to sag.

The driver scanned the midday traffic that crawled through the Lebanese capital, spotting a dated green Mercedes in the oncoming lane. The German car's headlights flashed three times, signaling the truck driver to shift into gear and ease back into traffic.

The mission was a go.

A mile away, towering over the corniche with a view of the Mediterranean's cool blue waters, loomed the American Embassy, a rose-colored monolith that had dominated the Beirut skyline since it originally opened its doors as a hotel three decades earlier. The crescent-shaped embassy that fronted the palm-lined Avenue de

Paris employed 341 people who helped overseas Americans, processed visas, and advanced diplomatic relations.

It had been a quiet Monday in Beirut, a welcome reprieve in a city battered by eight years of civil war, foreign invaders, and sectarian violence that had torched businesses, leveled apartment blocks, and claimed the lives of 100,000 men, women, and children. The arrival of American Marines six months earlier—based at the airport as part of a multinational peacekeeping force—had helped restore a semblance of calm that reminded war-weary residents of the halcyon days when the city was known as the Paris of the Middle East. Shoppers browsed stores along Hamra Street—dubbed the Fifth Avenue of Lebanon—that once again offered everything from designer jeans and caviar to the latest electronic games. Others queued up outside cinemas where Bill Murray's comedy *Stripes* had proven a popular hit. "People," as *New York Times* reporter Thomas Friedman observed, "were just starting to relax in Beirut, daring to believe that the presence of American troops meant the war was finally over."

But America's flatlining efforts to pressure Israeli and Syrian forces to withdraw from Lebanon had sparked an uptick in violence, one that reminded residents of the potential savagery that lurked beneath the veneer of peace. In the previous month, gunmen had attacked patrols of the Italian, French, and American peacekeepers, wounding fourteen, including five Marines. Only four days earlier on April 14, an assailant fired a rocket-propelled grenade at the American Embassy, which hit an empty office. The time for peace was running out.

A dusting of snow still capped Mount Lebanon, climbing nearly two miles above the capital, even as the last of the season's cool weather threatened to give way to the oppressive heat of summer. The morning drizzle had subsided, replaced by the midday sun, which burned off the haze. Locals in search of visas lined up outside the first-floor consular offices, which assisted an average of 150 people per day. Others strolled down the scenic seaside promenade. Up on the embassy's sixth floor, workers rolled out and installed new carpets.

The day before, many of the embassy staff had participated in the Beirut marathon, including general services officer Robert Essington, who had charged across the finish line in four hours and two minutes. The race coupled with the after-party had exhausted many, prompting Ambassador Robert Dillon to offer participants a day off to recover.

But few took him up on the deal.

Lance Corporal Robert "Bobby" McMaugh wished he could have stayed in bed rather than man Guard Post One at the embassy's main entrance. The twenty-one-year-old Marine, who nursed a hangover, had been a star running back and kicker at Osbourn High School in Manassas, Virginia. Off the field, he proved equally as popular, a humble and warm personality who had insisted on taking his younger sister to her first high school dance because no one else was good enough. That same kindness motivated Bobby on the mornings he stood guard to present female employees with a flower. Much to his father's frustration, Bobby had postponed college to enlist in the Marines, where he volunteered for duty in Beirut, hoping that a posting to one of the world's hot spots might catapult his career. During his recent downtime, however, he had survived a car bombing on the streets of the capital, which, he later confided in a call to his mother, marked the first time in his life he had ever been scared.

Bobby had pushed those fears out of his mind the night before when he and a few fellow Marines feasted on spaghetti and champagne at the home of Letitia "Tish" Butler, a staffer with the U.S. Agency of International Development. He had returned to the embassy at 1 a.m. for a final beer before collapsing atop his bunk fully clothed. "I'll give you three hundred Lebanese lira," he pleaded with one fellow Marine, "if you stand my duty today."

But no one would accept his offer.

Despite his hangover, Bobby stood armed with a rose when embassy secretary Dorothy Pech appeared in front of his bulletproof-glass booth Monday morning.

"How are you doing, Bob?" she asked.

"I don't feel too good," he confessed.

"You guys are going out too much," she chided him.

The young Marine would have no doubt agreed.

"Well," Pech added, "maybe today will be a short day."

The pickup truck closed the distance.

Elsewhere in the embassy, Robert Ames of the Central Intelligence Agency huddled on the fifth floor with the embassy's spooks. The bespectacled father of six served as the clandestine agency's top Middle East expert, often tasked to personally brief President Ronald Reagan. At first glance, Ames appeared an unlikely intelligence officer. The forty-nine-year-old Philadelphian, who stood six feet three inches tall, had grown up the son of a Pennsylvania steelworker. A basketball scholarship had earned him an education at La Salle University, while a stint in the Army had introduced him to the world of signals intelligence. Over the years, as he pinballed between Yemen and Iran, Kuwait and Lebanon, he not only mastered Arabic but developed an unrivaled insight into the volatile region. Ames accomplished this while balancing time with his family in the Washington suburb of Reston, Virginia. He imitated Donald Duck's voice for his children, coached youth basketball, and liked to relax in his favorite rocking chair to the tunes of the Beach Boys. "He was," as his wife Yvonne later said, "the cornerstone of the family."

Frustration in Washington over the president's apparent stillborn peace initiative for the region had landed Ames back in Beirut, where he had touched down the day before. The veteran operative had attended a dinner that night with his colleagues where the intractable reality cast a shadow over the evening. Those tensions had turned contentious Monday morning as Ames met with the agency's entire team. Station Chief Ken Haas, whose wife, Alison, brought him lunch most days, emerged from the session upset. He phoned her to pop by early, where the couple ate a sandwich. She started to peel an apple, but her husband was too distressed to eat more.

"I've got one more cable to write," he said. "I don't know how I'm going to do it; you go ahead and go home and take a nap and I'll be home when I finish."

Alison Haas rose and approached her husband, who grabbed her face with both of his hands and delivered a dramatic kiss, one she would remember for decades.

"See you later," she said.

Up on the eighth floor, Ambassador Dillon seized on the break in the rain to swap his business suit for workout clothes. One of his bodyguards waited for him to change while others prepared his convoy for the trip over to the American University of Beirut. His security detail would then close the field, allowing him to jog three miles around the track. The United States took the ambassador's safety seriously—and with good reason. During the Lebanese Civil War in 1976, assailants kidnapped and shot then ambassador Francis Meloy. Four years later, gunmen in a speeding Mercedes ambushed Ambassador John Dean, though an armored limousine saved his life. But protecting the ambassador was far easier than securing the embassy, which operated out of a leased location with no setbacks in the heart of the congested capital. America had begun construction in 1973 of a more secure compound, but Lebanon's civil war had put that project on hold. In the meantime, the United States had invested $1.5 million to improve security, but only so much could be done to retrofit a decades-old hotel. In addition, much of the focus was on preventing a potential mob attack, similar to the 1979 seizure of the American Embassy in Iran. Workers had added tear gas ports in the walls of the lobby, installed fortified doors, and covered windows with protective Mylar to prevent shattering.

The fifty-four-year-old Dillon, who boasted a head full of silver hair, was mindful of the dangers. He had started his career in the CIA before migrating over to the foreign service. In his nearly three-decades-long career Dillon had served around the world, including posts in Venezuela, Turkey, and Egypt. That afternoon the ambassador had brushed off a call with a German banker. Dillon felt guilty as he slipped out of his clothes. His run could wait. He picked up the phone to call him back at the same time as he struggled to pull on a Marine T-shirt, which he had been given in his role as the honorary manager of the leathernecks' softball team.

Down in the first-floor cafeteria, Anne Dammarell ate a chef's salad in the back at a table with her colleague Bob Pearson. The forty-five-year-old Dammarell, who worked with the U.S. Agency for International Development, had served for the past two and a half years in war-torn Beirut. The experience had proven tiresome, prompting her to request a new post. She was scheduled to leave the following Monday for an assignment in Sri Lanka. Dammarell had spent that morning at her apartment meeting with two contractors to obtain quotes to ship her belongings by sea and air. An unfinished report lured her back to the embassy around noon, where she bumped into Pearson, who was planning her farewell party.

"Let's go down to the cafeteria and get something to eat," he suggested.

Over lunch the conversation drifted, as so many did, to the stalled efforts to secure peace. "This is either the end of the world," Pearson said, "or the Second Coming."

At 1:04 p.m., the driver of the GMC slowed to a crawl as he approached the intersection in front of the embassy, waiting for a lull in the oncoming traffic to cross.

Horns blared.

A brief break in the midday gridlock offered a window. The driver, who witnesses later reported wore a black leather jacket, punched the accelerator and shot across the busy avenue. He did not bother to brake, but wheeled right, pulling into the east exit of the horseshoe-shaped drive. The ambassador's limousine was parked in front of the embassy's main entrance, wedged between two security vans, where guards patiently waited for Dillon to finish his call with the banker. Just inside the building, Bobby McMaugh nursed his hangover, Anne Dammarell picked at her salad, and Ken Haas typed his cable, his last assignment for the day before he could head home and into the arms of his wife.

The truck blew past the Lebanese security checkpoint. Only ten yards stood between the GMC and the embassy's front portico, a distance it covered in less than two seconds.

There was no time to raise a rifle, pick up a phone, or even run.

The vehicle rammed the embassy in front of the lead security van at 1:05 p.m. and detonated its explosive payload, sending a bright orange fireball hundreds of feet into the heavens. The explosion blew out windows as far as a mile away. American sailors aboard the amphibious assault ship *Guadalcanal* five miles offshore felt the shudder. The blast scorched visa applicants in the consular office, flipped cars upside down and set them ablaze, and shattered the Mylar-covered windows throughout the eight-story building. The front of the embassy's center wing collapsed like a house of cards, burying the lobby under an avalanche of broken concrete, rebar, and splintered desks and file cabinets. The attack would prove to be not only the bloodiest assault on an American Embassy but the opening salvo in the nation's four-decade war on terrorism. "Everything," as one survivor recalled, "went black."